Dear Reader,

Writing is a rather lonely business so it was a delight when, after a few years of being published, I began to receive letters from fans all over the world. Most liked my books, but a few did not. There is a vast audience out there, and it is hard to please them all—some wanted more sex in the books and some thought there was way too much. Several penitentiary inmates asked me to write their personal stories, and a few requested my picture. I debated sending one of me and my grandchildren but in the end decided not to correspond with any of them. One lady at a California booksigning was excited to know that I lived just ten miles from "where she was conceived." Another reader wanted me to talk to her teenage son about how to treat a lady. I wouldn't have missed any of these experiences for the world.

A theme in the fan mail has been interest in my early, out-of-print books; so, my publisher has been bringing them back in anthologies, including *Promisegivers*. Seeing my older novels get a new life is as gratifying as giving readers a few hours of escape from everyday life. If a housewife is able to forget the dishes in the sink and lose herself in one of my stories or if a lonely convict shares a dream of love, I feel real satisfaction.

As you can tell, I love hearing from my readers. Please write to me via my Web site or care of my publisher.

Sincerely,

Dorothy Garlock

www.dorothygarlock.com

DOROTHY GARLOCK

Promisegivers

GCP

GRAND CENTRAL
PUBLISHING

NEW YORK   BOSTON

Copyright © 2008 by Dorothy Garlock
Amber-Eyed Man copyright © 1982 by Johanna Phillips
The Planting Season copyright © 1984 by Dorothy Garlock
All rights reserved. Except as permitted under the U.S. Copyright Act of 1976, no part of this publication may be reproduced, distributed, or transmitted in any form or by any means, or stored in a database or retrieval system, without the prior written permission of the publisher.

Cover design by Diane Luger
Cover illustration by Aleta Rafton

Grand Central Publishing
Hachette Book Group USA
237 Park Avenue
New York, NY 10017
Visit our Web site at www.HachetteBookGroupUSA.com

Grand Central Publishing is a division of Hachette Book Group USA, Inc. The Grand Central Publishing name and logo is a trademark of Hachette Book Group USA, Inc.

Printed in the United States of America

First Mass Market Paperback Printing: February 2008

10 9 8 7 6 5 4 3 2 1

Table of Contents

Promisegivers

BOOK ONE

THE PLANTING SEASON

CHAPTER ONE

"OH, FOR CRYIN' out loud! Damn that man! He's out there again."

"He is? Let me see! Ohhhh . . ." The high-pitched squeal of the teenager caused the shaggy brown dog to lift his jowls off the floor, cock his head, point his ears, and let out a husky sound between a bark and a growl.

"Lay right there and bark, you worthless hound. You wouldn't get up and bite anyone if he was carrying off everything in this house." The tall blond woman's hair swept straight back from her forehead and hung down her back in a single thick braid.

"Where, Iris? What's he doing? Ah . . . Oooh . . . look at that red hair!"

"Get away from the window, Brenda," Iris said sharply. You'll get nail polish on the drapes," she finished lamely.

"That ain't it, and you know it. You just don't want him to see us looking."

"Don't say ain't." Iris stomped across the room and flung herself down in a chair. The stuffing was beginning

to show on the padded arm, and she carefully straightened the crocheted doily she had pinned there to cover it.
"That . . . bastard has gone to the zoning commission,
sure as hell!"

"Don't swear! You won't let me."

"You're fourteen and I'm thirty. That should give me a
license to swear if I want to," she said crossly.

"You're thirty-two, Iris. I can count. And I'm almost
fifteen." Brenda sat down cross-legged on the floor beside the dog and shook the bottle of nail enamel.

"You're just what I need today, snippy little sister. You
spill that polish on the carpet and you'll wish this *old*
woman were in East Siberia."

"You don't have to be an old maid. You could have
married Stanley."

"Oh, for heaven's sake! There's no such thing as an old
maid in this day and age. And don't start on Stanley. I've
got enough on my mind without your bringing up that
creep." Iris stretched her denim-clad legs out in front of
her and crossed her booted ankles. She reached behind
her and pulled the long, thick braid over her shoulder before she rested her head against the back of the chair and
folded her arms over her chest. "And please be quiet. I've
got to think."

"You've been thinking for a couple of months," Brenda
grumbled. "A few more minutes' of thinking won't change
a thing."

"I was depending on that wishy-washy zoning commission to keep that trailer out of my grove."

"It's not a trailer, it's a mobile home. And it isn't your
grove." Brenda blew on the blood-red polish she had applied to her nails.

"Enjoy those claws while you can, my girl. It's almost planting season, and you're bound to lose those nails when your pretty little hands are glued to the steering wheel of the tractor every minute you're out of school."

"What's *he* going to do? I thought he was coming out here to learn to be a farmer. How is he going to learn anything if I do all the work?" Brenda capped the polish bottle, and rolled over onto her stomach so she could get a better look at her scowling sister.

Iris had always looked younger than her age until recently. Now the signs of her years of struggle to farm the land and supply a stable, comfortable home for her sister were beginning to show. Faint lines of strain had appeared lately between her brows and at the corners of her eyes and mouth. Her sun-tanned face often had a pensive look, with shadows of worry beneath her eyes.

Iris's wide mouth, its lower lip fuller and softer than the upper one, turned down at the corners, reflecting her less-than-happy mood. Her blond hair was her most startling feature, but her eyes ran a close second. They were wide and blue-gray, deep-set, and tilted at the outer corners, under well-defined brows only a shade darker than her hair. They glared now at the young girl who was more like a daughter than a sister.

"You know I don't like for you to bring that dog into the living room," she said irritably. "He gets hair and mud and Lord knows what else all over the carpet."

"Just cause you're mad and can't do anything about *him*, you're taking your spite out on Arthur." Brenda rolled onto her back and scratched the dog's shaggy head. "Ain't that right, Arthur?"

"Don't say ain't."

Brenda sighed heavily. "I *haven't* been able to see him up close. Do you think he'll come to the house?"

"I sure as hell hope not!"

"Don't swear." With the quickness of youth, Brenda flipped up onto her knees so she could rest her chin on Iris's slim thigh. "It isn't so bad, Iris. He could have moved into the house, you know."

"Over my dead body!"

Brenda looked up with a sympathetic smile. "Couldn't you vamp him?"

"Vamp him? You've lost your marbles!" Iris got to her feet and stood with her hands on her hips, looking down at the younger girl. Brenda was long-limbed and slightly gawky, due to her height. Her nose, lightly dusted with freckles, turned up pertly, giving her face a pixieish look. Her hair was several shades darker than her sister's, and parted in the back, with bunches tied with ribbon hanging over each shoulder.

"Dad should have had his head examined for taking old Mrs. Lang on as a partner," Iris said. "I tried to get him to go to the bank, but he was bound and determined to sell half the farm to her. He must have thought she would die before he did and would leave it to him in her will." Iris began to walk up and down the room, paused to move the curtain aside so she could peek out toward the grove, snorted, and let the curtain fall back in place. "That fool is out there stepping off the place where he's going to put that rolling shoe box!"

"I don't think anyone knew old Mrs. Lang had a grandson in the Navy. She used to talk about Junior. It was Junior this and Junior that. I thought she was just making it up."

"Well, she wasn't. John D. Lang, Jr. is living proof."

"I thought only really old men retired, Iris. Does he have to work?"

"I don't know about that. The lawyer told me that he went into the Navy when he was eighteen and retired after twenty years of service," Iris said drily.

"Then he's not young! Oh, shoot! He's old. Thirty-eight . . . *wow!*"

Iris raised her eyes to the ceiling. "Yeah. He's practically got one foot in the grave."

"That's for sure! And he's too old to learn to farm. Maybe he likes you, Iris. He wouldn't be too old for *you.*"

"Thanks a lot." Iris turned her head away, hiding her face, suddenly contorted with the pain of remembering her forty-five-year-old father bringing home a bride less than half his age. A year later, the year she graduated from high school, Brenda was born. A year after that the young bride took off for parts unknown, disillusioned with being married to an *old* man who didn't have the money she thought he had. During Iris's college years her father hired a woman to care for Brenda, but since then it had been she alone who'd raised her halfsister.

"Arrr-woof!" Arthur got lazily to his feet and started for the kitchen door.

"You may be a pussycat, Arthur, but you've got super ears." Brenda shot a guarded look at her sister. "He's coming to the house. What are you gonna do?"

"Meet him outside." Iris stomped through the dining room to the kitchen, grabbed a worn denim jacket hanging on a straight-backed chair, and jerked it on over her hooded sweatshirt. She stood on the back steps, digging the hood out from under the back of her jacket, and watched the source of her irritation come toward her.

He was a bear of a man. His height topped her five-foot ten-inch frame by half a foot. Broad in the shoulders and chest, yet solid and lean through the waist and hips, he had long, well-muscled legs and walked with a rolling gait. His easy stride brought him quickly across the graveled drive, past the black iron water pump set on a concrete slab, and through the swinging gate.

Iris stood stock-still, head tilted back, arms folded. She stared in mixed exasperation and desperation, her smoky eyes analytical as they moved over his strong neck, not exactly handsome face, and the shock of brick-red hair. She remembered his face as being harsher when she'd voiced her disapproval after he'd calmly announced his intention to participate actively in the operation of the farm. They had been sitting in the lawyer's office, and Iris had declared in no uncertain terms she thought it stupid— no, downright asinine—for him to assume he could be any practical help on the farm.

The only other time they had met was when she stood on the steps, as she was doing now, and told him she was not going to permit him to move "a long, skinny boxcar of a thing" onto her homestead, and if the prefabricated dwelling had any place at all in the scheme of things it was in a trailer park in town, and not out here.

Iris was slightly breathless with anger as she shifted her gaze from his face to the figure of the zoning commissioner, who was getting into his car, and then back to his face. Smile lines bracketed his wide mouth; his thick red hair looked as if he'd been in a windstorm, and it glistened in the sun; his brilliant, pure blue eyes glinted as he assessed her stance. He was pleased with himself, Iris realized, and she was filled with even more resentment.

"The commissioner says there's nothing in the county ordinance to prevent me from putting the mobile home right out there." John waved his hand toward the grove of pine and spruce trees that had been planted by her grandfather as a windbreak when he'd built the house eighty years before.

Iris stiffened visibly but didn't speak. His heavy, brown brows lowered in a frown as he noticed her reaction. Before he could speak again the screen door opened behind Iris and nudged her aside so Brenda and Arthur could come out.

"Hi."

"Hi. You must be Brenda Ouverson."

"In living color. You must be Junior. Come here, Arthur. That's rude!" She grabbed the dog's collar and pulled him back. "He has to check out everything and everybody that comes on this place," she said with an apologetic grin. "He'll get used to you, but I doubt if Iris will."

"Knock it off, Brenda," Iris said sharply.

"I'm afraid Miss Ouverson will have to get used to me or else sell me her part of the farm." He spoke to Brenda, but his narrowed gaze was on Iris.

"Call her Iris, Junior. Kids at school call her Miss Ouverson when she subs, but nobody else does."

"My name's John." He bent down to rub the dog behind the ears with long, strong fingers. "The plumber will be out tomorrow to run the gas and water lines. It will be simpler if they tie onto your meters and we share the expense."

A quick, nervous spate of words broke from Iris's tight lips. "Why are you so determined to bring that thing out here? This homestead is eighty years old. My father made every effort to preserve its character, and so will I. The barns are old, but they've been maintained beautifully through the years, with an eye to keeping the original design of the buildings. This homestead is graced with an air of dignity and a sense of permanence. You roll that pencil box in here and you'll not only ruin that grove, but you'll create an eyesore the whole county will be talking about."

"You know the alternative," he said softly.

"You know damn well it's unthinkable for you to move into the house with us."

"Everything is thinkable," he corrected with a rueful grin. "But I expect it *would* give the conservative Iowans in town something interesting to gossip about."

"You mean they'd think you were sleeping with Iris? Ha! Fat chance! She won't even kiss Stanley." Brenda nonchalantly swung her leg over Arthur to hold him between her knees while she looked critically at her polished nails.

Iris was almost giddy with embarrassment. Her eyes glittered with both anger and despair, and she turned the full force of them on her sister. "That's enough out of you, Brenda. You've got chores."

"Okay, okay," Brenda said with a lift of her shoulders. "Just don't get your motor all revved up over nothing."

John reached out a big hand and clapped it over the top of her head and gave it a friendly shake. Brenda was not as tall as her sister, but she was equally as thin and willowy. Her legs seemed endless in the tight jeans; beneath the heavy turtleneck sweater she wore there was a hint of small, nicely rounded breasts and a wispy waist.

"See ya." Blue eyes in a pert face darted a look at him. "It's get-rid-of-Brenda time. My sister probably wants to swear at you, and she thinks I've never heard a swear word before. C'mon, Arthur. Let's head for the barn and Dullsville."

John watched her lope away, the dog at her heels. He turned back to the grim-faced woman on the steps. "How old is she?"

"Fourteen, and out of bounds for you," Iris snapped.

"Oh, for the Lord's sake!" He stifled an oath, then spun on his heel to walk away, but turned back with an angry scowl on his face. He pointed his finger at her. "Listen. I could have forced you to sell out to me, as long as I offered to buy your part of this farm and you couldn't raise the money to buy me out. Partnerships work that way, in case you didn't know or have forgotten. I realize this farm has been in your family since its existence, and therefore I'm willing to share it with you—at least until your sister is out of school and on her own. That assumes, of course, we can last that long without killing each other. Now, it can be a pleasant business arrangement or it can be a battle every step of the way." He snapped his teeth together, straightened to his full height and rocked back on his heels. "I didn't spend twenty years in the Navy for nothing. I don't give up easily. I fight for what I want, and I want to live here on this homestead and farm the land my grandmother bought for me."

The stress lines between Iris's brows deepened, and her mouth tensed. "In other words take you and your *cracker box* or sell out to you, at your price, and move on. Is that it?"

"Exactly."

Iris pushed her hands into her pockets and hunched her shoulders. "You've played all the right cards. Or rather your grandmother played them for you."

He shrugged. "Either way, I'm here and I'm staying. I'll be out in the morning with the plumbers. A few days after that I'll bring in the house."

Iris pressed her lips together tightly and half turned, so he couldn't see the tears that glistened on her thick lashes. The tension that had been building in her for days had mounted to produce a splitting headache; all she wanted to do at this moment was slip inside that screened door, hide in the house, and cry. But damned if she would! She wouldn't retreat with her tail between her legs. She'd brazen it out, even if it killed her!

"Iris!" Brenda called from the barn door. "Where's that plastic bucket I use to feed the calf?"

"In the machine shed, where you left it." Iris lifted the heavy braid of hair off her chest and flung it over her shoulder. She looked directly at John D. Lang, Jr. for a full ten seconds before she spoke. "You win, Mr. Lang. But I don't have to like it." She forced herself to concentrate on keeping her poise, her tears at bay, her fists from flying out to hit him, while fantasizing about his disappearing beneath the manure spreader.

John backed off a few steps, hesitated, then said, "The mobile home won't stick out like a sore thumb regardless of what you think. After I finish with it, it'll blend into the surroundings. I plan to add a screened porch across the front to break the straight line and have the whole thing painted to match the trim of this house."

"Oh, great! That should be just dandy. A white house, a green house, a red barn. Christmas all year long," Iris said with a stoical calmness she didn't feel at all. She was pleased to see the flicker of annoyance on John's face.

He half turned so he could look toward the grove. "I'll have the house set in the long way, then the front will face the drive. When I add the porch and the carport, I may have to take out one small tree."

"Noooooo! You're not cutting down my trees!" A pounding began in Iris's head that threatened to make her eyes go out of focus. Since her father's death, five years ago, she had been in charge here, and had guarded every tree as if it were the last one on earth. *No, sir! This sailor wasn't going to cut down a single one of her trees!*

"The grove needs to be thinned. For now I'll only take out the tree with the NO HUNTING sign on it."

"You'll do no such thing! What in the hell did you learn in the Navy that makes you so all-fired smart about thinning a grove?" Chin up, body taut, Iris was mindful of the thudding in her chest, the pounding in her head. Mustering the fragments of her self-possession, she locked her gaze to his and refused to look away.

His eyes were cobalt-blue and fenced with thick brown lashes, topped by reddish-brown brows, which were now drawn together with displeasure. As she watched, his features formed a deeper frown, the muscle in one lean cheek jumping in response to his clenched teeth. His gaze fell from her eyes to the soft and vulnerable curve of her lips, lingered long enough to send an unwelcome tremor through her, and then passed down to the arms folded tightly across her chest. He made no attempt to conceal his impatience with her. The pounding in Iris's head expanded into her stomach and echoed through that empty chamber.

He spread his long, denim-clad legs and hooked his hands in his hip pockets. The movement spread his jacket and revealed an open-neck knit shirt with a small monogrammed symbol on the chest. Iris's eyes flicked to his feet and the blue-and-gray sneakers. A stray thought passed quickly through her mind. Nikes! Good heavens, Who would have guessed they made them that big?

"So this is the way it's going to be, huh?" John said thoughtfully. "You're going to drag your feet every step of the way."

"If necessary." Iris wanted to scream. More than that, she wanted to hit something—preferably *him*.

"I've had young kids come into the Navy with chips on their shoulders. Some thought they knew it all. You can bet they were whipped into line before they shipped out." His brows lifted in a silent message.

"I'm no kid, Mr. Lang, and this isn't the Navy. You're in my territory. We'll see who is whipped into line." Her voice was low, with the force of her anger held in check.

"I-r-is! Where's the pine tar? Candy's got a cut on her fetlock."

"On the shelf in the tack house," she called, grateful for the interruption. Casually, with an outward calm belying both the ache behind her forehead and the dancing devils in her stomach, she began to walk toward the barn. Leaving the *sailor* standing on the walk, she thought that surely he'd have the good manners to leave. Not true. He appeared beside her, matching his stride to hers.

"Who's Candy?"

"Sugar's colt."

"There aren't any horses listed in the farm inventory."

She stopped and turned on him like a spitting cat. "Sugar and the colt belong to Brenda. She bought the mare with money she earned, and she paid the stud fee. There are two more horses on this farm that have never been listed. They belong to me."

"I see," he said—to her back, because she had walked away.

Iris pulled back the bottom half of the barn door, latched it to the top shelf, stepped over the thick doorsill, and into the barn. A single light burned at the end of the row of stalls. For once Brenda hadn't turned on every light in the barn. They had been trying to lower their huge electric bills.

Attempting to ignore John D. Lang, Jr., who was trailing close behind her—and her throbbing head—Iris kicked at the clean straw with her booted feet as she went down the narrow passage. A devilish hope that he'd step in some manure and soil his spotless Nikes briefly crossed her mind.

Brenda was waiting beside a tan-and-white-spotted colt, holding the rope halter and rubbing the soft nose that nuzzled her arm. "I didn't notice it until she followed Sugar in and I saw the blood," she wailed. "There must be some barbed wire down somewhere."

Iris knelt down beside the colt, rubbing her hand up and down the slender leg, keeping well back in case the sharp little hoof lashed out. "Did you get the pine tar?"

"I didn't want to turn her loose. Is it bad? It bled a lot."

"I'll get the tar. Where is it?" The masculine voice came from far above Iris's head.

She stood and gave him a disgusted look. "You wouldn't know pine tar from . . . apple butter," she said, and stomped off down the aisle.

"I don't think she likes you, Junior." Brenda's blue eyes had to look up a long way to reach his face.

"I think you're right."

"She's gettin' one of her headaches. It's been coming on all day. By night she'll be throwing up her socks."

"She suffers from migraines?"

"Yeah. I think that's what she calls them. You're enough to give even me a headache, Junior."

"My name's John."

"Then why was ol' Mrs. Lang always callin' you Junior?"

"Reasonable question." He reached out and fondled the colt's ears. The animal tossed her head.

"Horses don't like to have their ears touched," Brenda said quickly.

"Oh? Sorry. Back to why my grandmother called me Junior. I don't think she realized I had grown up. I was away at sea most of the time, and my trips home were few and far between. Granny sometimes thought I was my dad. How old is the colt?"

"A month. Do you like horses?"

"I like 'em, but I don't know much about 'em."

"I could teach you that. Sugar was my 4-H project a few years ago. She got a blue ribbon at the fair. Hey, we're looking for a new leader. Want to be one?"

"What in the heck would he know about being a 4-H leader?" Iris walked into the stall with a can and paddle in one hand and a roll of paper towels in the other. She knelt down, pried off the lid, and dipped the clean wooden paddle into the thick black tar. "Whoa, girl. Easy, now. This will make it feel better, and keep the flies off, too." Talking to the colt in a calm, smooth voice all the while she dabbed the medicine on the cut, Iris concluded, "That should do it." She wiped the stick clean on the paper towel and replaced the lid on the can. "Put her back in the stall so Sugar can see what we've done to her baby," she said as she stepped up onto the bottom board of the stall to reach the nose of the brown-and-black-spotted mare. She gave her a gentle pat: then the horse's pointed ears stood at attention when Iris brought a handful of molasses-soaked grain and pellets out of her pocket and held it to the soft lips; which quickly began to nibble. "You like that, don't you, girl?" she crooned softly to the horse, and placed a kiss on her nose.

When Iris stepped down too quickly from the rail, a jarring pain coursed through her head; it was followed by a quick succession of pains so sharp that she almost swayed. "Finish up here, will you, Brenda? Feed Buck and Boots for me tonight. I'm going to the house."

"Will you be too sick to take me to town later?" Brenda called as she reached the door.

"Of course not!" she said as confidently as she could manage.

"Do you have migranes often?" John asked while she was closing the bottom half of the barn door.

"No! You're the only big headache I've had in a long time." Iris gritted her teeth.

He ignored her sarcasm. "What do you take for it?"

"Aspirin, aspirin, and aspirin. You caused it," she

blurted. "When you leave it'll probably go with you." Ignoring him now, she concentrated only on breathing deeply to keep her stomach from heaving, and on placing one foot in front of the other so she could get to the house. She reached the screen door and flung it open. "Goodbye, so long, happy sailing," she muttered, and stumbled into the house.

She dropped her jacket on the kitchen floor, jerked her boots off with the bootjack, and reeled to the newel post at the foot of the stairs. She leaned on the rounded top, hoping the demons pounding in her head would let up long enough for her to make it up the steps. Her stomach convulsed, and she groaned.

"Iris, let me help you."

Him again! It was too much. She closed her eyes tightly and held onto the post, knowing that any minute she was going to further humiliate herself with a crying jag. Everything hurt so damn bad!

"What have I done to deserve you?" she croaked feebly. This was the enemy, but strangely, she couldn't fight any longer. An arm slid across her back, and she was pulled against a broad chest. Too sick to reject this gesture of help, Iris leaned into the arms that steadied her and the long, warm body that absorbed the tremors that shook her. Reeling and desperately afraid she would throw up, she let him help her up the stairs.

"The bathroom . . ." She staggered away from him and through the open door, not even bothering to close it, and sank down on the edge of the tub. Holding the blond braid in her hand, she leaned over the stool as the bathroom door closed, allowing her to lose the contents of her stomach in private.

Her migraine had reached gigantic proportions by the time she wet a cloth and grabbed a bottle of aspirin from the medicine cabinet. John was waiting outside the door. His identity was no longer important to Iris. He was help. She headed down the hall to her bedroom with his hand beneath her arm to steady her. Somehow they both made it through the narrow door and to the soft bed. She buried her face in the pillow to shut out the light. Her senses were so numbed by pain that she was only vaguely aware that she was between the cool sheets and the covers were being pulled up around her neck.

At that moment Iris didn't care if it was John D. Lang, Jr. or Adolph Hitler in her bedroom pulling the window shades. She welcomed the darkness. Her mind was a jungle; her stomach an ocean in which nausea kept coming and going in waves. Somewhere along the way she had dropped the wet cloth, but the aspirin bottle was still clutched in her hand. Warm, strong fingers pried hers loose from the bottle. She let go. Nothing mattered but to be left alone.

It wasn't to be. He was back.

"Take this aspirin, Iris." He put tablets in her mouth. She tried to push him away. His arm lifted and turned her, and he held a glass to her lips. Wincing, she swallowed the tablets and a sip of water. He eased her back down on the bed and covered her again.

Later, somewhere in the sea of agony that held her, she felt a warm hand on her forehead, strong fingers gently stroking her temples, soothing away the pain, and at last she fell into a deep dreamless sleep.

CHAPTER TWO

GROGGY, IRIS PUSHED up onto a bent elbow, blinked, and swept the hair back from her eyes so she could see the digital clock. The red numbers swam before her eyes, and she squinted to hold them in place. Nine-thirty? She had slept for five hours? Moving slowly, she threw back the covers and sat up on the side of the bed. The ghost of the headache was still there, but she felt vastly improved. Shaking off the fogginess, she flipped on the bedside lamp, and the room was flooded with a soft glow.

A glass of water and the aspirin bottle sat on the nightstand—along with a new, dark plastic bottle with a prescription label. Iris reached for it, a quizzical frown on her face. Her doctor's name was typed neatly above hers on the label and beneath were the directions for taking the capsules. The prescription had been filled at Casey Rexal Drug, her pharmacy. A misty memory came to mind of being lifted, of something being put into her mouth, of a masculine voice telling her to swallow. Glory! Was she so freaked out from the headache that she took just any medication, like a slave on command?

Iris got to her feet, went to the bathroom, and washed her face. Thank God the nausea was gone. She felt decidedly better. She had to see what Brenda was up to. Longtime habits of concern were hard to forget.

Halfway down the stairs the aroma of freshly brewed coffee caused her bare feet to pause for an instant before they continued on down the steps. Iris swung around the newel post at the same time that her eyes swung about the room. One small lamp burned. The television screen was dark. Strange. Brenda thought the house would cave in if the set wasn't turned on. A stab of uneasiness struck her, and she hurried to the lighted kitchen. Surprise brought her to a halt in the doorway.

John Lang sat at her kitchen table, a cup of coffee at hand. Scattered over the table were books, papers, and magazines. His head was bent, and he was busily scribbling in a notebook. Beneath the pull-down lamp his hair was the color of glazed clay pottery. His back was a broad expanse of blue knit, and as she watched, he put his hand to the back of his neck and squeezed and massaged his neck muscles. Watching him while he was utterly unaware that he was not alone, he suddenly seemed to be truly human.

Iris emerged from the doorway. "What are you doing here, and where's Brenda?" She walked over to the table and grasped the knobs of a high-backed kitchen chair.

He closed the book with a snap and looked intently into her face. "How do you feel?"

"Where's Brenda?" she repeated.

"At play practice. I took her in. I told Miss Hanley I'd be back to pick her up at ten o'clock."

"You did wh-what? It wouldn't have hurt her to miss

one practice." The floor was cold. Iris stood on one bare foot and rested the other on top of it.

He quirked a brow at her grumpiness. "There was no need for her to miss rehearsal. I was going in to get the prescription filled anyway. Do you feel better?"

"Yes," she said, and slumped down in the kitchen chair. She wasn't going to let him rile her. Nothing was worth risking the return of that headache.

"Why haven't you asked the doctor for something for those tension headaches? There's no need for you to suffer like that."

"I don't have them very often—only when something comes along that ties me in knots." Her direct gaze held his.

"I get the message. How about a cup of coffee?"

"I'll get it," she said testily.

"I'll get it." For a big man he moved fast. "Cream? Sugar?"

"Straight from the pot." She had to get him out of here. He was the cause of the headache, and she didn't want another. "Did you charge the prescription to me?"

"Of course not." He passed over the mugs, choosing instead the good cups and saucers. Then he brought the coffeepot to the table and poured some for her and himself. "It was just a couple of dollars. As long as I caused the headache, I can at least pay for getting it fixed." She looked up into blue eyes that flicked over her quickly.

Iris started back, being careful to keep her features deceptively calm, masking her swirling thoughts. He sat down on the other side of the table and put the books and magazines he was using in a neat stack. A quick glance told Iris they were farming periodicals. It was on the tip of her tongue to say something sarcastic, but instead she stared hard at the rangy form lounging in her kitchen chair. It galled her to think of him being here in the house with her asleep upstairs.

He stared back. Iris felt her cheeks grow warm. She became suddenly and uncomfortably aware of the faded old sweatshirt she wore and the strings of hair that hung around her face. The lack of makeup didn't bother her, as she seldom used it. Unconsciously she smoothed the hair back from her forehead and hooked loose strands over her ears.

"You don't have to stay. I'll pick up Brenda."

"You need something to eat. How about a piece of toast?"

She looked at him as if he were warped. "Thanks, but no thanks. I can manage. I've been taking care of myself for a long time," she snapped.

"Thirty-two years, according to Brenda."

"Well . . . glory be!" Iris's laugh held a wealth of bitterness. "Lesson number one. Never leave the enemy alone with little sister. He's very clever at picking her brain."

"I'm not the enemy, Iris."

"If you're not, I hope never to have one." She raised the cup to her mouth and took a big gulp, almost scalding her tongue.

"Careful. You may get another headache."

He sipped his coffee slowly. She watched his hands. They dwarfed the thin cup but handled it easily. His fingers were long, his nails cut close, and he had a sprinkling of reddish-brown hair on the backs of his hands that trailed down to his knuckles. Strong, smooth hands, soft palms. How would they look after a day of shoveling corn, loading manure, moving hog houses, or fixing fence?

The clock on the shelf struck the quarter hour. The sound wafted into the small eternity of silence. Iris jumped up and carried her cup and saucer to the sink.

"You'll have to leave. I've got to get Brenda."

"I told you I was going to do it." He unfolded his long length out of the chair. "It takes fifteen minutes to get to the school, and kids are never out on time."

"How do you know? I don't want her waiting around in the dark outside an empty school."

"Miss Hanley said the practice would more than likely run until ten-fifteen. I've got plenty of time." His calm and easy take-over manner was wildly irritating to her. He came up behind her, reached around, and set his cup and saucer on the counter. He was so big he loomed over her, reminding her of the football player she'd dated in college who had a huge, perfectly proportioned body and an infinitesimal brain.

"As usual, you've covered all the bases." She moved sideways down the counter and picked up a towel to dry the cups, something she usually would not have bothered to do.

He leaned his slim hips against the counter and crossed his long legs at the ankles, drawing her attention to his Nikes and to her own ice-cold bare feet.

"You're beginning to annoy me, Iris," he stated coolly. "I've tried to take into consideration how hard it is for you to let go of a part of the farm operation, especially because you've handled things so well since your father died. From all accounts you're an even better farm manager than he was."

The statement about her father hurt; she tried to shrug it away. "You've had your share of the profits," she said defensively.

"I've no fault with that. But I want to participate in the management of the farm, and I've a perfect legal right to do so. Besides, if you and I can work together, there'll be no need to hire so much extra help. It'll cut expenses."

"Ahhh . . . now we're getting down to the nitty-gritty." She slapped the towel over the rack and turned on him. Her bare feet were planted far apart, and her clenched fists rested on her hips. Headache be damned! "How much help do you think you'll be around here? You don't know the first thing about attaching a loader to the tractor, or filling the silo, or catching and holding hogs so they can be castrated. Brenda will be more help at farrowing time than you'll be." At this point, driven by some unknown force, Iris was goaded into delivering one last taunt. "You can sit in that *cracker box* with your pencil and work on farm accounts. That's as much help as I expect out of you." The slightest flicker of anger appeared in John's eyes, then vanished with a return of his slightly annoyed expression.

"You know, Iris, you might be kind of pretty if you didn't scowl so much. You look as if you're constantly eating a sour pickle." Her mouth opened, closed. He tilted his head in a cocky manner. "I just can't help but wonder if there's a soft woman beneath all that bluster." He took a step, and his hands came down firmly on her shoulders, holding her still when she might have moved away from him. "Maybe I should find out," he said, as if to himself.

"I've got one minute at least before I have to leave to pick up Brenda." The gleam in his eye spoke of the pleasure he received from her surprise . . . and her sudden expression of vulnerability.

He caught her lips quickly, as though afraid she'd fight him. But astonishment had taken temporary advantage of her reason, and her brain refused to tell her muscles to move. The scent of his face and his breath pervaded her being; his mouth was firm, yet soft, his cheeks smooth, yet prickly with a shadow of the day's growth. His arms and shoulders seemed to swallow her, and she fought to stay above the tide of sensuousness his kiss was inspiring, but its force overpowered her, and she yielded, allowing her lips to become soft and to part. He lifted his head, and grinned down into smoky-blue eyes that flew open.

"It's true! There is a woman under there."

Weak from capitulation but strong in the face of his taunt, Iris stepped back and lifted her shoulders in a careless gesture. "Why not? I like sex as well as the next person." It was the only thing she could think of to say, and almost immediately she was ashamed of having said it— so much so that she didn't look back into his eyes, but concentrated on the alligator sewn on the breast of his shirt.

"I'll keep that in mind." He squeezed her arm. His mouth twitched, but he managed not to smile and kept his voice bland as he continued. "Next time we'll take it a step further."

"We'll do no damn such thing!" she hissed. *The toad! The wart!*

"No?" He tipped his head in skepticism. "Wouldn't you like to take step number two and see what happens?"

She gazed into his eyes, so astonishingly blue and lu-minous, and drew a quivering breath.

He was good-naturedly amused by her momentary speechlessness. "Time's up. I'll go for Brenda. You get some shoes on. I don't know if I can handle you with a headache and a cold."

After he left, Iris stood in the kitchen with her fists pressed to her temples. Several crude words slipped through her lips, a luxury she didn't allow herself unless she was alone and exasperated almost beyond endurance. She breathed deeply and tried to stem the tears of rage that were stinging her eyelids.

"You fool!" she muttered. She didn't know to whom she should direct her anger—John or herself. Maybe she could just blame the circumstances that brought him here.

She grasped the back of the kitchen chair. But to sub-mit to his kiss that way. Worse, to respond. Sexual desire for John? Sheer lunacy! It was only a kiss, for heaven's sake, she chided herself. But it wasn't the kiss that both-ered her; it was those feelings she'd had while she was kissing him back. For one short moment she'd been lost in the sweet, warm world of his embrace, and her body had responded like a love-starved spinster's. And the awful part was . . . he knew!

She moved down to the end of the table and looked at the stack of books he'd been using. They were all farm-related. *Land Use*, *Grain Farming*, *Farmer's Weekly*, and several pamphlets from Iowa State University. She restacked them, wishing she had the nerve to toss them out the door.

Did the Navy ever recall retired officers? She asked herself the question while drawing a bath. He had to be an officer. She couldn't imagine that big frame poured into a pair of bell-bottomed pants. If there were a war, he'd be recalled, she mused, sinking down into the warm suds. Well, she couldn't pray for a war in order to get rid of him. The next best thing to hope for was that he'd have hay fever, or a bad back so he couldn't lift bales. Maybe the sight of a calf being born would make him sick. She lay back and fantasized about the harm that could befall a city man on the farm. Like tumbling into the septic tank! She chuckled, but only briefly.

Quickly then she got out of the tub, dried herself, and wiped the steam off the bathroom mirror. The face that looked back at her was scowling. The mouth was pressed tight and turned down at the corners. The brows above the squinted eyes were drawn almost together. Oh, for land's sake! She'd let that . . . that redheaded woodpecker do this to her! Cripes!

Standing nude before the bathroom mirror, Iris took the rubber band from the end of her braid and loosened her hair, all the while trying to relax her facial muscles. She tried parting her lips and lifting the corners. She raised her eyebrows as if questioning and brought her lower jaw out to stretch the skin beneath her chin. None of these seemed to help.

There is a soft woman under there. Why should his stupid words stick in her mind? Taking a deep breath, she puffed out her chest and grabbed the hairbrush. Starting straight back from her forehead she brushed with long, vigorous strokes. Iris was proud of her hair. She thought back to her high-school years, when she stood head and shoulders above any boy in her class, and how she had held onto the compliments she received because of her beautiful, thick, startling blond hair that proclaimed her Swedish ancestry. It had darkened very little since that time. She wore a big floppy hat in the summer to keep the sun from drying it out, and also to shade her face. Iris didn't work at getting a tan; it came naturally. Every morning during the months she worked outside she applied a layer of sun screen to her face and neck to protect her skin from the wind, the dust, and the sun's hot rays. She used very few cosmetics other than eye makeup and lipstick, and weeks went by when she didn't use either of those.

Forcibly restraining herself from spraying her body with her favorite fragrance, as a concession to her bruised ego, she slipped into her nightgown and her terry-cloth robe and went back to her bedroom to find some slippers. She was going to have a talk with Brenda and find out just what she'd told *Mr. Woodpecker*.

Downstairs she turned off all the lights except the one over the back door and the one over the kitchen sink. He wouldn't have the nerve to come in if the house was dark, or almost dark, she reasoned.

Iris sat in a kitchen chair and looked out the window toward the grove. The outside floodlights illuminated about a hundred feet of the yard all around the house. For eighty years there only had been trees and land to see out this window. In a few days there would be lights in the grove and a mobile home implanted there—complete with porch and a carport. Electric and telephone lines would hang over the drive for the first time. Oh, cripes! Had she really grown so old she couldn't bear to see things change? She should have sold out as soon as her father died. Old Mrs. Lang was alive then. She would have bought out her interest for Junior. If that had happened, Iris and Brenda would be well used to living in town by now, and she'd be used to teaching, putting up with the kids who took an art course simply because they thought it was an easy way to make a credit.

Headlights coming down the road brought her thoughts back from the "might have beens" and to the present. With interest rates so high, it was impossible to buy back Jack Lang's interest in the farm, so what to do now? The best you can, old girl, she told herself with just a twinge of self-pity. Stay here and suffer it out. Even if she did sell out to him now, there wasn't a teaching job to be had within a hundred miles, and to move Brenda away from her school and her horses would break her younger sister's heart.

The station wagon bounced up the long drive that curved behind the house and out to the road again in a wide U. The car pulled around and stopped opposite the back door. Iris sat where she was until she heard two doors slam and Brenda's excited voice talking a mile a minute.

"Come on in, John. It's T.G.I.F. night. No school tomorrow. There's an old Vincent Price movie on. Did you see *The Raven*? Yuk! He sends thrills down my spine. Tonight it's *The House of Usher*. I've only seen it twice."

"The house is dark. Your sister may be in bed." The deep masculine voice sounded slightly critical to Iris.

"Oh, no. That's a trick of hers so you won't come in."

The screen door slammed, and Iris fervently wished Brenda's head had been caught in it. Drat that kid! Would she ever pass out of this brainless stage?

"Oh, I see. Well, in that case I'll stay and watch the

movie. The set in the motel room has terrible color, and I can only get one station."

"Super. Do you like popcorn?"

"Love it." They passed through the small narrow room she and Brenda called the mud room, and came into the kitchen. John took off his jacket and hung it on the back of the chair. "I'll even make the popcorn if you point me toward a heavy pan and let me have a little light."

Iris stood in the shadow and seethed. He had seen her. How could he not have seen her in that white terry robe? Damn him again! Brenda flipped on the switch beside the door, and flooded the kitchen and the dining room with light.

"Oh, hi. John's going to stay and watch the movie with me." Brenda took the jar of popcorn out of the cabinet. "How's your head?"

"Better." Iris's eyes raked the big man, who was taking a bottle of oil from the shelf. "But it could get worse!"

"Take one of the capsules I brought from the drugstore," he said calmly. He took the heavy pan Brenda offered him, poured in the oil, and glanced at Iris. His face broke into a smile; friendly, as seen through Brenda's eyes, but smug, as seen through Iris's. "What do you know! Lady Godiva, as I live and breathe."

"Who's that?" Brenda jumped up onto the counter, banged her heels against the cabinet door, then pushed off first one sneaker and then the other, sending them flying across the room, the laces still neatly tied.

I've done something wrong. I know I have! Iris groaned silently as she watched her sister.

"Lady Godiva was the wife of an earl. She rode her horse naked through the streets of Coventry with only her long blond hair to cover her." John poured the corn into the pan and slapped on the lid.

"Why'd she do that?"

"To save the people from paying a tax."

"Who was naked, the horse or the woman?"

Iris grimaced. On leaden feet she went into the living room, sank down in a chair, and picked up a thick paperback novel. Lady Godiva be damned! She jerked open the drawer in the side table next to the chair, took out a rubber band, and secured her hair at the nape of her neck. She was too angry to sit still and read, so she stared at the pages, trying to tune out the pleasant chatter of the two in the kitchen.

Brenda flounced into the room. John trailing her. She flopped on the floor in front of the set, dug into her bowl of popcorn, and complained to Iris about not having turned on the television. John plunked a bowl down in Iris's lap, then sprawled out on the couch with his own, after taking off his shoes in the same way Brenda had done.

"What are you reading?" he asked without looking at her.

"Tiger's Woman."

"She reads historical romances," Brenda said between mouthfuls. "She won't let me read some of 'em."

"Who wrote it? Michener? Jakes?" His long legs reached halfway across the room.

"De Blasis."

"Never heard of him."

"It isn't a him, it's a her," Iris snapped. "There are jobs women can do every bit as well as men, and writing is one of them."

"Okay, I agree with that."

His sudden capitulation surprised her, and she bent her head to read the same paragraph for the fourth time. She wondered if he was here because he was lonely. He was a handsome man, charming when he chose to be. There was an air of experienced masculinity about him that any husband-hungry woman would adore, Iris thought, betting that even at this moment Louise Hanley was sharpening her hunting tools. This community was a nice place to raise a family, but a lousy place to find an eligible man, and Iris thought wryly that she was going to have plenty of female company soon.

She turned pages in her book at regular intervals, looked up several times to find John's eyes on her, and was so unnerved she hadn't the slightest idea what she was reading or what was on the screen in front of her.

It was one of the most uncomfortable evenings of her life, and as it dragged on, Iris decided she hated Vincent Price for making the darn movie in the first place.

There was a loud thump on the back door, then another.

"What the hell was that?" John asked.

"Arthur. He runs and then jumps on the door when he wants our attention."

Brenda rolled over onto her back and kicked her heels on the floor, imitating a child having a temper tantrum. "Darn, darn, darn! I forgot to put Arthur in the barn . . . and this is the good part."

"I'll do it." John began to put on his shoes."

"Arthur is Brenda's responsibility," Iris snapped.

"As long as I'm leaving, I'll put him in the barn and she'll owe me a favor."

"Okay!" Brenda rolled back over onto her stomach. "I'll give you a friendship pin to wear on your shoe."

"You mean a safety pin with a bead on it? I wondered what that was all about."

"Some kids have fifty pins, all from different friends."

"Yours might be the only one I ever get," he said, glancing down at Iris.

"Don't forget your books." She got up to follow him back through the dining room.

"You didn't eat your popcorn."

"I'll give it to Arthur in the morning."

"You should eat something before you go to bed." He put on his jacket.

"'Bye, John. See ya tomorrow," Brenda called.

"Thanks for taking her and bringing her home." Iris said the words begrudgingly.

"Sure. Good night."

Iris, waiting beside the door to switch off the lights, heard John swear. His curse was swiftly followed by a booming "I-r-is! What the hell has this dog been into?"

She looked out the window, and there was Arthur frolicking around John, smeared from one end to the other with . . . A slow smile started in her eyes as realization dawned, and spread to her lips. She had to use every bit of her willpower to keep from laughing.

She opened the door a crack. "What do you mean?" she asked innocently.

"What's this stuff all over him?" John was moving back and forth, trying to keep away from Arthur, who was sure John had come out to play with him.

"Oh, that? That's fresh cow manure. He rolls in it several times each spring. I've never figured out the attraction. Just take hold of his collar and he'll go along with you to the barn. Brenda will give him a bath tomorrow."

"There's no place on his collar where I can . . . He's covered with the stuff! Phew!"

"Sure there is. Just take him to the barn, and tomorrow you'll get a friendship pin to go on your shoe."

Iris shut the door and leaned back against it, with her hand over her mouth to stifle the giggles. When she peeked out the window again John had the dog by the collar. He was almost bent double in an effort to keep Arthur from rubbing against his long legs, while half leading, half dragging him to the barn. She laughed until tears blurred her vision and she had to mop them away with the front of her robe so she could see him standing beneath the yard light wiping his hands on a handkerchief.

The movie had ended when she returned to the living room. She flicked off the set, still giggling, and couldn't seem to stop.

"Why did you do that?" Brenda sat up, cross-legged. "And what's the matter with you?"

"Which question do you want answered first?"

"I don't care."

"The movie was over, and you're not particularly interested in the news." Iris couldn't stop grinning.

"What's so funny about that?"

"It's Arthur and the . . . woodpecker." Iris went into a fit of laughter. Brenda sat with her mouth twisted to one side, waiting. "He was . . ." Another spasm of laughter. "It was so funny. Serves him right, too."

"What happened?"

Iris wiped her eyes on the robe. "Arthur has rolled in

fresh manure again . . ." Giggles followed every word. "You'll have to give him a bath in the morning."

"Oh, no! That lousy dog! That worthless hunk of hair and bone!"

"You know how it gets caked up around his . . . neck?" More giggles interrupted her. "John couldn't find a place to hold onto him so he could get him to . . . the . . . barn." Iris clasped her hands over her stomach. "*Justice*. Justice comes to those who wait," she said smugly, still smiling.

"Poor John. I think you're mean to laugh."

"Poor John, my foot! He needs our sympathy like a hole in the head."

"I think he's cute. Or he would be if he wasn't so . . . so *old*! Miss Hanley's beady eyes lit up like a Christmas tree when she saw him. 'Certainly, Mr. Lang. Yes, Mr. Lang. I wouldn't dream of letting Brenda leave the building until I'm sure you're here, Mr. Lang.' Bossy old toad! She couldn't wait to find out all about him." Brenda gave her sister a sly smile. "I filled the old biddy's ear full. I said he was going to be living here at the farm with us and that you and John were almost—"

"Almost what?" Iris sank onto a chair.

"That you were good friends and almost in love."

"Brenda Ouverson! I could shake you. Why in the world did you say such a thing? It'll be all over the school tomorrow."

"So what? At least I put the kibosh to her plans."

"Oh, mercy! Nothing but marriage puts the kibosh to Louise's plans when she goes after a man. What did you tell him about me besides how old I am?"

"Not much. We went to the Hamburger Hut before he

took me to school. He asked about your headaches and a few things like that."

"After this keep your lip buttoned. Don't discuss me with him, Brenda. The whole situation is difficult enough without your giving him extra ammunition to use against me."

Later Iris lay in bed and listened to her sister move about in her room. Had she been too hard on her? Brenda passed the door on her way to the bathroom. "Iris," came the wail in a few moments.

"What's the matter?" Iris asked, pushing herself up on an elbow.

"I dropped my toothbrush in the toilet."

Iris sank back down on the bed. "Your problem," she called.

"But . . . my teeth will be all hairy by morning!"

"It's either that or fish it out and use it."

"Yuk!"

Iris listened to Brenda's grumblings. She was responsible for shaping that young life, and at times she questioned how good a job she was doing. Suddenly her mind was crowded with memories of lips warm and gentle, of arms strong and unrelenting. The next time we'll take it a step further, he'd said. She flopped over on her stomach and buried her face in the pillow, but she couldn't block the image of smiling eyes and dull red hair from her mind.

CHAPTER THREE

WEDNESDAY.

The mobile home arrived, and changed the look of the homestead forever. Iris watched through the kitchen window, tears rolling down her cheeks.

Begrudgingly, she admitted that John had been careful to see that the least possible damage was done to the yard when the truck pulling the seventy-foot house backed it into the grove. Boards were placed so the huge wheels didn't make deep ruts in the sod, and the men were careful not to scrape the bark from the trees, whose lower branches had been trimmed when the utility pole was set.

Iris turned from the window and wiped her eyes and her nose on the tissue she had balled in her hand. Life as she had known it here on the homestead of her ancestors was over. What she hated about the house, she told herself, was that it was so damned *new!* She had tried to banish thoughts of its owner from her mind, but his image turned up at the oddest times—when she was feeding the horses, drawing water for the sows, washing the dishes. She was disgusted with herself for responding to his kiss like a love-starved spinster; the memory made her feel sick and empty.

During the next week, Iris worked harder than she had ever worked in her life, while doing her best to ignore the activity going on in *her* grove. While she was moving A-frame hog houses out in last year's alfalfa field with the tractor and loader and preparing them to house the pregnant sows, workers were building a foundation under the cracker box, as she thought of it, adding a long screened porch, and attaching a carport with redwood slabs on the side facing the county road. Coarse gravel was hauled in to make a drive, and a new mailbox went up alongside hers.

Every day Brenda leaped from the school bus to see what progress had been made. She was thrilled with the idea of a neighbor in the grove, and completely enthralled with John D. Lang, Jr. Iris tried hard to make allowances for her sister's youthful enthusiasm and not feel deserted.

"You should see it, Iris. It's got a ceiling fan, a microwave oven, and . . . everything."

The days were getting longer as spring approached, and it was still light when they ate dinner now. Iris no longer sat at the end of the table, where she could look out at the grove.

"That's nice," she said absently. "Do you have play practice? If you do, let's get the dishes done. I have things to do while you're gone."

"Yeah, darn it. John was going to build a fire in his fireplace tonight."

"I think you and I should have a little talk right now." Iris's voice held a no-nonsense tone.

"What about?" Brenda said tiredly. "What have I done wrong now?"

"Nothing. You haven't done anything wrong. I've never had to worry about your doing . . . anything *wrong*, after I've explained things to you. You're a very sensible girl for your age."

"Okay. You've built me up. What don't you want me to do?" Brenda looked bored with the conversation, but her fingers were nervously pulling a slice of bread into small pieces.

"Honey, I don't want you spending so much time over there." Iris jerked her head toward the grove. "He's a single man living alone and you're a fourteen-year-old girl."

"Well, so what? I like him, even if you don't!"

"It isn't a matter of liking him or not liking him, Brenda. I don't want you spending a lot of time there. People . . . will talk."

"What about?"

"Well, they don't know him, and they might think—"

"You mean they'll think I'm sleeping with him?"

"Oh, heavens!" Iris looked at the ceiling and then back at her sister's sullen face. "Yes, they might. You know how narrow-minded some people are."

"Yeah." Brenda's face was still rebellious. "It would be just like Stanley's mother to spread around something like that, but it'd be about you, not me."

"I don't want her spreading anything about either of us."

"Can I tell John I won't be over to see him break in the fireplace?"

"When he sees us leave he'll remember about play practice."

It was almost dark when Iris backed the pickup out of the garage. Lights shone from the house to the grove. It was painted a dark green now, although the pressed wood siding had come from the factory a light tan. Iris reluctantly admitted it didn't look as out of place as she'd thought it would, but still she didn't like having it there.

After parking the pickup beside several others, Iris went into the school with Brenda. They walked down the silent hall to the gym-cum-auditorium, which had a stage across one end and pull-down metal bleachers on the sides. The drama teacher sat at a desk near the door.

"Hello, Iris. Are you going to watch dress rehearsal? Brenda's doing splendidly."

"I don't think so, Louise. I have a few errands to do. What time will you finish?"

"About nine. We'll have one more short practice on Wednesday. Brenda said Mr. Lang is planning to come to the play."

"Is that right? I hadn't heard anything about it." Iris tried to wipe the annoyance off her face.

"She seemed quite sure. Also, I've been intending to visit and ask you to help me choose colors for a needlework wall hanging I want to start."

I just bet you have, Iris thought, but aloud she said, "Do that, Louise. I'll be glad to help you."

At the supermarket Iris dug a list out of her pocket and went up and down the aisles filling her grocery cart. She shopped carefully, resisting impulse buying, which ballooned her budget out of control. When she finished she eased her cart up to the check-out counter.

"Hello, Iris. How ya doin'?"

"Fine, Linda. You?"

"Fine. I hear your partner's moved a mobile home out to the farm. I haven't seen him yet, but I hear he's quite a guy. Having a man around should take a load off you, huh, Iris?"

Iris smiled and agreed for appearance's sake. Then she greeted Denny, the boy bagging the groceries.

He grinned shyly. "Is Brenda at play practice?"

"Dress rehearsal. I've got to pick her up as soon as I get the groceries home."

Pushing her cart, the boy followed Iris to the truck. She opened the door of the cab and stepped aside. "I'd like to stop by sometime and see Brenda's horse. That is, if it's okay with you."

"Of course, Denny. But you'd better check with Brenda to be sure she's home."

"I'll do that. Thanks."

As Iris waited at the stoplight on the highway, her thoughts were disconnected. A boy wanted to visit Brenda . . . everyone was talking about John Lang . . . some of the sows had to be rebred and some sold because they were past three years old . . .

The light turned green, and she followed the two-lane highway to the blacktop and turned north, and a mile later, west on the gravel. She knew every foot of the road; she had driven it a thousand times.

It was strange to come down the road and see lights twinkling in the grove. Iris turned into the drive and glanced at the sleek station wagon parked in the carport. I wonder how long he'll last out here in the boonies, she mused. He's seen most of the exotic places in the world—he won't be content to stay here. When he goes I hope he takes that . . . trailer with him. Her thoughts were still running rampant as she picked up an armload of groceries.

"Let me help you." The voice came suddenly, from behind her.

"Oh, good heavens! You scared me to death!" All the

color drained from her face, and her smoky eyes were suddenly large.

"I'm sorry." John took the bag out of her arms. "I didn't
mean to frighten you. I thought you saw me coming across
the drive."

"I'm not used to having people sneak up on me," she
said crossly, her heart thumping up a storm.

"Hand me the other sack. I can take both of them."

Iris put it in his arm and picked up a smaller one. She
walked ahead of him into the house and flipped on the light
switch. John set the sacks beside hers on the kitchen
counter. The close contact with his tall frame made Iris step
back quickly.

"You *are* jumpy, aren't you? You've been working too
hard. You don't have to work yourself to death in order to
avoid me, you know." He began taking the groceries from
the sacks and putting them on the counter.

"I'd have to be out of my mind if I didn't try to avoid a
headache, wouldn't I?"

"Am I still such a thorn in your side?" he asked, on his
way to the refrigerator with a carton of milk.

"More like a pain in the ass," she said bluntly, without
thinking.

He laughed as he moved to reach over her shoulder
and pick up another carton of milk. "That's what I like
about you. I don't have to wonder for a minute what
you're thinking."

Iris skirted him to get to the freezer to put away the
frozen mini-pizzas that were Brenda's favorite snack. She
watched him warily as he crossed the room, stopping at the
window to look out toward the grove. Palms out, his hands
slid into the back pockets of his faded jeans. His forearms

were bare, the cuffs of his shirt casually rolled to just below his elbows. Iris noticed how the muscles of his shoulders and back stirred the cloth of his denim shirt. If his size hadn't been enough to distinguish him, certainly his bearing and that head of dark red hair would have been.

"I see you've pulled the curtains," he said, fingering the thin white cotton panels that had formerly been tied back.

"I usually do in the summer."

"Liar. It isn't summer yet." He turned and leveled his gaze on her.

"That's what I like about *you*. I don't have to wonder what *you're* thinking." She turned his words on him.

"I'm glad there's something about me you like." He raked her with his gaze; starting at the top of her head, he took in every feature of her face, her throat, her breasts. His eyes lingered there for a long moment before moving back up to her face again. "You have magnificent hair. I like it done up like that on the top of your head. You look very stately, very controlled."

"Oh, sure!" She shifted, uncomfortable under his intent perusal. "You'll have to excuse me. I've got to pick up Brenda."

Iris went out onto the narrow enclosed back porch, where the chore clothes were hung and smelly barnyard boots were left on a rubber mat. She waited for him to pass so she could turn out the light and lock the door. He walked purposefully toward her, then stopped.

"You're a fraud, Iris Ouverson," he whispered, and brazenly winked at her. "You're not as crusty as you pretend to be." Ten seconds dragged by while Iris drew a shallow breath, followed by a deeper one. She could see his eyes were full of laughter. "I may have to kiss you again."

She cleared her throat and swallowed hard, then said bravely, "Stop horsing around and get out of here. I don't want—"

"Brenda waiting around outside an empty school." He finished the sentence for her. His hands slid along her upper arms. Slowly he drew her closer to him, until she was pressed against his long length. He lowered his head and nuzzled the hair above her ear. His fingers found their way under her jacket to stroke her back. "I'm glad you're tall. I don't have to bend so far to kiss you." He settled his lips against her mouth and breathed. "I like the way you taste, too. Like a nice, cool, vanilla ice cream cone."

Iris came to her senses and struggled against him, but he refused to loosen his hold. His strength won out, and she ceased her efforts to escape. Soon she was incapable of moving, of protesting. The warmth of his body held her like a magnet, and it was easy to lean against his large masculine frame and surrender to the delicious floating feeling.

The lips that touched hers were warm and sweet as they tingled across her mouth with fleeting, feathery kisses. The arms holding her gradually tightened. His feet moved apart, making his stance wider, and she felt herself being drawn against, then between, hard, muscular thighs that held hers. A longing to love and be loved washed over her. The kiss became more possessive, deepened, her lips parted, his tongue touched hers, and his hand slid over her breast.

She wondered if he could feel the pounding of her heart beneath his hand. His hand? On her breast? Oh! For crissake! She didn't behave this way! She stiffened. He sensed it immediately and loosened his hold, but he didn't release her.

Iris was breathless when he pulled his mouth from hers

and raised his head only a fraction to look down into her face.

"Your eyes are the color of the sea around Palau Island in the Pacific." His whisper was deep and husky. "They change like the sea, too. Sometimes calm, sometimes stormy. I've yet to see them happy and sparkling." He placed a gentle kiss on her forehead. "Try not to resent me so much." His breath was ragged as he gently moved her away from him. "Come on. Let's go get little sister."

The past few minutes had robbed Iris of all logical thought. She stood stupefied for several seconds before she realized he was waiting for her to go out the door. He followed close behind her, turned out the light, and tested the doorknob to make sure it was locked before he shut the door.

Iris automatically went to the driver's side of the pickup but was gently nudged out from under the wheel by John's solid bulk. "I'll drive," he said quietly, and she mindlessly moved over. He fumbled for the lever so he could move the seat back to accommodate his long legs, then started the truck and turned on the headlights. She knew he was looking at her, but she stared stoically out the window, and was relieved when he put the truck in motion.

Iris was thankful for the darkness. Her face burned with embarrassment. She was so disgusted with herself she could have screamed. She was mad! She was a fool! What had possessed her to participate in that . . . little display? She stifled a groan as her mind began summoning back, in feverish detail, the feel of his lips, his arms, and how she had melted into them. Even now the scent of peppery male cologne assaulting her nostrils was doing crazy things to her hormones.

The truck left the gravel road and pulled out onto the blacktopped highway, headed toward the school. The silence was heavy. Not a word had passed between them since they'd left the farm. What the heck do I care what he thinks? she wondered bitterly. I don't even like him!

"Who is Stanley?" His words boomed into the silence.

"What did you say?" She knew, but she had to get her head together.

"Who is Stanley?" he repeated in a quieter tone.

"He's a fellow who lives up the road. We just passed his place. He helps out sometimes when I get in a crunch."

"Do you pay him?"

She met his glance with a pretense of calm. "Sometimes. Other times we trade work. It's a tradition around here to pitch in and help a neighbor if you can."

"What do you do for him?"

"I may spend half a day plowing, spraying, or cultivating for him." His questions were beginning to irritate her.

"I can relieve you of that. Do you date him?"

"Who? Stanley?" She hesitated, then said, "Sometimes." He needn't know that she despised Stanley, who had a hint of a pot belly, though a very well-developed dirty mind.

"The football coach at the high school has been coming out to see you, too, hasn't he?"

"Will you kindly stop pumping my sister?"

He laughed. "You don't have to pump Brenda. Once her mouth gets in gear there's no stopping it. She said the coach had just recently separated from his wife."

There was nothing Iris could add to that. A car swept down the road toward them, the headlights flashing over John's face. His bottom lip was drawn between his teeth, and his brows were beetled into a frown.

There was another long, tense silence. Iris stared at the ribbon of highway and was thankful when the school came into view. John slowed the truck and turned into the parking lot. There were more cars and trucks there than when Iris had brought Brenda, so she knew the rehearsal wasn't over yet. John realized that, too. He turned off the headlights and turned in the seat to look at her. Damn! Why had he parked directly beneath a streetlight?

"Am I going to have to make an appointment with you to discuss my work schedule?"

"Work schedule? There's no schedule on a farm. You do what has to be done no matter how long it takes. If there's any schedule it's from daylight till dark." She hunched down in the seat and looked away from him.

After a brief silence he said flatly, "Are you going to tell me what I can do to help you, or are you going to leave me to skid my wheels?"

"What can you do, for heaven's sake? I spelled it out on the report. This year we're putting in corn, beans, and alfalfa. We have forty sows that produce almost three hundred and fifty pigs a year, and after planting we'll get about fifty feeder calves. You can sure as hell clean out the hog houses, if you want, and—"

"Why do you use the A-frames? Why not put all your sows in the farrowing building?"

The question angered her. "Farrowing building? We don't have such a thing. What we have is a converted chicken house. I put the older sows there and the younger ones out in the A-frames. If I'm careful I farrow them five times a year and have hogs ready for market every couple of months. It's quick money even if the market isn't what it should be."

"I've seen what you use for a farrowing building. Could we add on to it?"

"We could do a lot of things if we had the money," she snapped.

"Would you like me to take charge of the hog operation?"

This question stunned her. "Mercy! What does a sailor know about hogs, except that they make bacon and ham?"

"You'd be surprised." He grinned wickedly. "And here's another little bit of information for you to file away and chew on later. I can attach a loader to a tractor, and what's more, I can fix the engine if something goes wrong."

"You're kidding! Well, glory be! A mechanically inclined sailor!" She made it sound like something that just crawled out from under a rock. John's grin faded.

"Knock off the sarcasm, Iris. You may find out that I know a little something beyond coiling rope and climbing rigging."

"I didn't think they did that anymore," she said lamely. "And I'm sorry. I was surprised, that's all."

"It's okay. I didn't expect you to jump with joy. What's on the bill for tomorrow?"

"A stock buyer will be here in the morning to pick up our marketable hogs. We have about sixty that weigh between two hundred twenty and two hundred forty pounds. After that we spread manure on the forty acres to the south and commercial fertilizer on the rest of the plowed ground. I don't believe in 'land bank.' I use every foot of our four hundred acres."

"I gathered that from your annual report. You don't use many insecticides and herbicides, either. I agree with that." A large hand reached out, and firm fingers turned her face toward him. "It's been a long, hard row for you to hoe, working the farm alone. I don't want to take anything away from you. I want to help you, if you'll let me. I'm as green as spring grass when it comes to farming. All I know is what I've read in books. I'd appreciate it if you'd be patient and teach me. In return I'll bring my mechanical skill and I guarantee you our farm machinery will be kept in tip-top condition."

"That'll be a help. The tractor men charge an arm and a leg every time they come out to fix something." She felt breathless, and foolish, and . . . small. She moved her chin out of his hand when she heard a car door slam. "I haven't been very nice, have I? I'm not usually so bitchy."

"You've been carrying quite a load. Are there other lady farmers around here?"

"A couple of widows who hire people to do the work. Kids are coming out now, John. Brenda will see the truck."

Several cars peeled out of the school parking lot, and Iris gritted her teeth to think that Brenda was reaching the age of the kids driving those cars. Brenda ran to the truck and flung open the door.

"Can we give Jerry a ride home? Purple pot roast!" she blurted when she saw that Iris wasn't alone. "Hi, John. Why didn't ya come in? You'd've made ol' lady Hanley's day!"

"We can give you a ride home, Jerry," Iris said to the boy standing behind her sister.

"Thanks. I'll ride back here." He dropped a canvas bag in the truck bed.

"Sit up here, Jerry. It's too cold back there," Brenda protested, and nudged Iris over toward John. "We sit four lots of times, don't we, Iris?"

Iris didn't answer. John shifted his weight, and she

moved close to him. Her hip was tight against his, her thigh lay along his, and her shoulder was tucked behind him.

"A little more; Jerry can't close the door." Brenda turned, and Iris pressed closer to John. The door slammed.

"Are we all in?" John asked, and Iris heard him mutter, "Humm . . . nice."

"Brenda could sit on my lap," Jerry said after a small hesitation.

"I'd smash your legs. This is much better. Now, if only o' lady Hanley'd come out and see Iris sitting close to John, it'd pay her back for being a grouch."

Iris sucked in a breath, and John laughed. "Oh, to be so young and so uninhibited. Were you like that when you were her age, Iris?" He turned his eyes from the road, and for a few seconds she felt his breath on her face.

"I was so shy that I hardly opened my mouth for fear someone would look at me. I've always encouraged Brenda to speak out, though, to realize that she is entitled to express an opinion. Now I think I might have done better to have taught her a little tact. too."

John's soft chuckle made his rib cage vibrate against her. "Tell me which way to go, Jerry."

Iris's shoulder was pressed firmly behind John's, her chin practically resting on his shoulder. She had only to move her eyes to see his profile. He was smiling. She wondered if it was because he could feel her heart pounding through the breast that was crushed against him.

"It's right on your way—that is, if you're going home, sir."

"You can call him John. He won't mind," Brenda said smugly. "He lives with us out—"

"Brenda," Iris interrupted quickly. She couldn't sit by

and witness the demolition of her reputation. "Let me explain, please. The three of us own the farm jointly, Jerry. The purchase was made for John while he was serving in the Navy. Now that he's out of the service he's going to live on the farm for a while in a tenant house. He does *not* live with us."

"I know all that, Miss Ouverson. I knew how it was. I live at the next place, Mr. Lang. Just pull up there by the mailbox and let me out. Thanks a lot for the ride. I'll be sure and set everyone straight 'bout that, Miss Ouverson. 'Bye, Brenda."

When the door closed, Iris shifted to the middle of the seat and groaned. No one had to set anyone straight about anything, dammit. There was nothing to set straight!

"Do you really let it bother you that people might talk about my living out at the farm?" John asked as soon as they were on the road again.

"This is small town, USA. Of course I don't want to be gossiped about."

"Maybe we should get married," he teased, a broad smile splitting his face.

"Yeah!" Brenda let out a whoop.

"Shut up, you two, and be serious!"

"We'll leave lights on in both houses all night long to throw the gossip spies off the trail," John said. He lowered his voice to a sinister whisper. "And if I come over I'll wait until after dark and wear a black raincoat and slouch hat. Then I'll case the joint before I ring the doorbell."

"We can put one of those bell things across the drive that rings when a car goes over it," Brenda said between giggles. "If it rings while you're in our house you can hide in the basement."

"I could wear a skirt and a shawl and be your old-maid aunt." His laugh rang out, joined by Brenda's, and Iris couldn't hold hers back any longer.

"A six-foot-four Amazon aunt?"

"I'll walk on my knees. See how far I'm willing to go to preserve your reputation?"

By the time they reached the farm they were all laughing together as if they were playing some gigantic joke on the entire county. John let the sisters out and pulled the pickup into the garage. Brenda went into the house, and Iris waited beside the back door. John came toward her swinging the car keys on his finger.

"Come on over and take a look at the *tenant* house," he said, smiling down at her. "We can begin the secret maneuvers tomorrow."

"I was hoping you'd ask us." Brenda squeezed out the back door, almost knocking Iris off the step. "Wait till I put Arthur in the barn. I don't want him rolling in any more cow pies!"

Iris glanced up at the tall man watching her. The yard light was bright enough so she could see the sparkle in his eyes. His face was creased with a smile, and he was breathtakingly handsome. Her eyes couldn't seem to leave his face, and she was unaware that she, too, was smiling.

"Finally." He bent closer, and she could feel his warm breath. "Finally, I see the happy sea. Gentle waves shining in the sun," Her lips parted, but no words came. "Speechless? Good. I like you that way once in a while, too."

CHAPTER FOUR

IRIS STOOD JUST inside the door, not believing that she was really here in the hated house with the *woodpecker*, and that she'd come willingly. She shoved her hands down into the pockets of her jacket, hunched her shoulders, and looked around. The small entry was tiled and surrounded by plush sculptured carpet. She and Brenda slipped out of their boots, a habit acquired by people who work with the soil.

John moved about the living room turning on lights. It was a step lower than the rest of the house, with a prefabricated fireplace on one side and a large picture window on the other. There was a leather couch and chair with a large matching ottoman, end tables and lamps, bookcases, and a television/stereo combination beneath the window.

"Very nice," Iris murmured. "It's larger than it looks from the outside."

"Come see the rest." John led the way into the dining-kitchen area, which was divided from the living room by an ornamental iron railing.

"I've seen it, so I'll turn on the TV." Brenda suited action to words and plunked down on the floor not three feet from the screen. It was on the tip of Iris's tongue to tell her to move back, but she doubted her sister would even hear because the volume was so loud.

The kitchen was well planned, with floor-to-ceiling cabinets, spacious wood-topped counters, and the latest model appliances, including a microwave oven. Iris smiled her approval and followed John down the narrow hallway. He stopped at the first doorway.

"I've put my desk and a lot of my books in this room." He switched on the light and stepped aside so she could see. Her shoulder brushed his chest as she angled her body to squeeze through the doorway, which he practically blocked.

One large hand came out and cupped the back of her head and gently stroked her hair upward toward the swirl on the top. She moved quickly away from him, trying to quell the stirrings in her love-starved body.

"Very nice," she murmured, although at the moment she wasn't seeing anything.

"The bathroom has a garden tub as well as a shower stall," John explained when they reached it. "I'll never use the tub, but I wouldn't have known what to do with the space if they'd taken it out."

The tub was gigantic, set in a corner, and enclosed by peach curtains. Iris couldn't suppress a small laugh.

"Awful, isn't it?" John's eyes twinkled as he watched her. "You have to take the bad with the good. I did get the lavatory cabinet built high enough so I won't break my back every time I wash my face."

"I've often wondered if the people who put in bath fixtures think everyone who uses them is four foot one." She stared into warm blue eyes and suddenly felt much smaller than her five ten.

"We wouldn't have to worry about that, would we?" He was grinning now. Iris moved back. He was too close!

"About what?" She could smell the freshness of his breath. Irrational anxiety bubbled up inside her.

"About having four-foot-one offspring."

Iris didn't realize she was holding her breath, until the air came rushing out in one long puff. "Humph!" was all she could say. His shoulders, the broad chest, smiling face framed with dark red hair not only filled her eyes, but her thoughts, her mind, the center of her self.

She tried for lightness in her voice. "Is this all I get on the fifty-cent tour?"

"You have to pay the guide now." His voice lowered to a raspy tone. "I'm going to kiss you, Iris Ouverson. What'er ya gonna do about it?"

Iris felt the blood rush around her body. She looked at him through thick, curled lashes and knew she wasn't going to do anything. She wanted him to hold her, kiss her, make a thousand little memories for her to tuck away and bring out in the dark of the night when she lay in her lonely bed. She turned her eyes away. He was too astute at reading her thoughts.

John reached out and cupped the nape of her neck with long, warm fingers and pulled her toward him. The smile had left his face, and his eyes held an indescribable expression. Was it tenderness? Iris felt her strength drain out through her toes, leaving her swaying against his tower of strength.

"Ah . . . huh . . . Brenda . . ." she said feebly.

"God bless CBS or NBC or whatever."

"But . . . I don't want you to kiss me."

"Sure, you do."

"Nooo . . ." She shook her head, and her lips moved across his.

"Do that again. I like it." The arm about her waist held her snugly against him, and his hand moved caressingly over the softness of her bottom, then pried into the hip pocket of her jeans. "I've kissed you three times. Each time I liked it better than the time before."

"Two times," she whispered.

"Three. One time you were asleep. Now, hush, and let me get on with it."

"You . . . had no right . . ."

"Your lips are pressed together again. You're being stubborn." He clicked his tongue censoriously. "I'll have to kiss you until they soften. If we're in here much longer, Brenda will come in."

"You're a toad!"

"Turn me into a prince." He kissed her with slow deliberateness, his lips playing, coaxing. Her breath caught painfully in her throat, and then, with a deep sigh, she parted her lips against his and slowly traced the curve of his bottom lip with the warm, moist stroking of her tongue. He opened his mouth and caught the tip gently between his teeth. A flood of pleasure washed over her, sending excitement coursing through her veins. It was strange, because she'd never before wanted to kiss anyone like this.

He raised his head after several hard, quick kisses. His eyes, half closed, looked down his nose into her eyes. His hands were everywhere; on her back, the sides of her breasts, on her rounded bottom. "Have you noticed how well we fit together?" The words came on the fragment of a breath.

"No!" The hands on his chest began to push. She wanted

to jerk away, but she was held fast. Make it light, she told herself, treat this situation as if it's no big deal.

He had hold of her hand now and was leading her past a washer and dryer set in an alcove with sliding doors to hide them from view.

The bedroom was the width of the house. A closet with mirrored doors ran along one side; a queen-sized bed with a headboard for books and a reading light occupied the opposite wall. The end of the room was solid, with small windows. Six stacks of drawers were built in beneath them, covered with a wide ledge. Several framed pictures, a shell inlaid box, and a small bronze statue resided there.

"What in the world will you put in so many drawers?" Iris thought it a reasonable question, considering . . .

John laughed and squeezed her hand. "I never had enough space aboard ship. Maybe I did go a little wild. They're only half full." He turned her toward the full-length mirror on the closet doors, put his hands on her shoulders, and pulled her back against him. She stared at the smiling face above her right shoulder. He lowered his head and pressed his cheek to hers. "Don't you think we make a handsome couple?"

She looked at her slenderness in the jeans and shirt. Her waist was small, her breasts soft and rounded, but her makeup free face—blaa! She was so ordinary! What was there about her that could possibly attract a man like John D. Lang, Jr.?

"We've got to go. School tomorrow, and the hog buyer will be here bright and early." It wasn't hard to put a chill in her voice when she spoke. She pulled away from him and walked quickly back to the living room. "Let's go, Brenda."

"Ohhhh . . . This is about over. Just ten more minutes, Iris. Pl-eee-ze!"

"Well, turn it down. Heavens! You'll be deaf by the time you're twenty." She stood beside her boots and the jacket that lay on the floor next to them.

"Are you going to stand up for ten minutes, or sit down and have a cup of coffee?" John leaned casually against the refrigerator. "It's leftover, but I can warm it up in the microwave."

"Well, all right. Ten minutes, and then Brenda's got to go home and get to bed." She sat down at the table and tried not to stare at him as he poured coffee into two mugs. She had to be out of her mind. Worse than Louise Hanley. A cold shiver raced through her body. She couldn't let him get to her! She didn't want to like him too much! He would go . . . and then what?

John sat down across from her. "How long have you been taking care of your sister?"

"Almost all her life. She was born during my first year at college. Her mother left before she was a year old, and Dad had a woman come out from town to care for her. I finished college in three years and came home to look after both of them. My plans were to find a teaching job when Brenda started school. I did, but driving forty miles every morning in Iowa winter weather got pretty tough." Why was she rattling on like this?

"Does Brenda's mother come to see her?"

"She came once, just before Daddy died. It was the longest week of my life. Daddy was given custody of Brenda when he and her mother divorced. When he died, custody was transferred to me. I'm her guardian until she reaches legal age."

"Is it possible Brenda's mother might want her one day?"

"She can't have her!" Iris said heatedly, and felt a flush rise in her cheeks. The beast! Why did he have to bring up her old fear? "I've taken care of Brenda practically all her life. I'm all she has; she's all I have. I've done my best to teach her to be a decent human being, to respect herself and others. When she's able to take care of herself, I'll cut her loose from my apron strings, but not until!" Her lips quivered when she finished, and a bleakness came into her eyes. She'd recently begun to wonder what in the world she would do when Brenda grew up and left her.

"Bringing up a child alone isn't easy, is it?" John's hand reached across and covered hers.

"You two got to the hand-holding stage already? Wow!" Brenda bounded up the step to the kitchen like a lively colt.

"Don't sit down," Iris cautioned. "We're going."

"Oh, shoot! Dumb old school. Just six more weeks and it'll all be over."

Iris tried to pull her hand free, but John's fingers curled around her wrist, and he turned her hand palm up. He rubbed his thumb across the long, slender fingers, with their neatly clipped, unpolished nails, while his eyes held hers captive.

"It's hard to believe these hands have done all this work."

"Believe it, buster! Farming is more than planting in the spring, harvesting in the fall, and watching the sky in between. Yours won't be so soft six weeks from now." Iris gave her hand a yank, almost upsetting her coffee. She got up quickly, jerking on her jacket and shoving her feet into her boots. She didn't know why his remark about her hand had made her so angry. "Thanks for the tour and the coffee.

C'mon, Brenda." She looked up to see her sister standing with her palms raised, her shoulders hunched, and a quizzical look on her face, while she stared up at John.

"Brenda!" The order shot out sharply as hurt pierced her heart. The action represented a conspiracy between them . . . against her. For the first time in her life she felt her sister's loyalty slipping away from her.

"Iris! Guess what? We've got baby rabbits!" Brenda stood in the mud room stripping off her chore clothes.

Iris glanced at the clock; it was just six-thirty in the morning. "You've finished your chores already?"

"Sure have. John helped me. He took care of the lambs and the hogs. I'm glad. Phew, they stink."

"The lambs are your project, Brenda. You wanted them. Besides, he doesn't know anything about what we've been feeding our animals."

"I told him how much oats and lamb finisher. He wrote it down on a card and put it in his pocket. The same with the cows, horses, and those darned old smelly pigs. I fed the rabbits." Brenda went to the sink and washed her hands. "Elizabeth had eight babies. Boy, are they cute. John said maybe we could get a goat."

"A goat? What the heck for?" Iris dumped a can of tomatoes into the crock pot.

"For fun. He said the sheep could be in the orchard if he put up an electric fence. Would you care if we got a donkey?" Brenda sat down at the table and began to butter toast.

While the electric can opener worked on the top of another can of tomatoes, Iris took a plate of bacon and eggs out of the warming oven and set them on the table in front of her sister. "You and John were so busy talking I'm surprised you had time for the morning chores."

"He's fun. I'm sure glad he came here. Aren't you?" Brenda went to the refrigerator for milk. "Iris? You aren't still mad at him, are you?" She touched Iris's arm.

"Of course I'm not mad at him, you silly girl. Why be unhappy about something you can't do anything about? Let's just say it's hard for me to get used to someone else making decisions around here, but the willow bends as the wind blows, or however that saying goes."

Brenda looked forlorn. "I don't think the saying goes like that."

Iris laughed. "You nut! Got any ideas about dessert for those hungry men who are having lunch here today?"

"How about that pound cake in the freezer? Thaw it and put some peaches and ice cream on it."

"Good thinking. Then I won't have to come in early to stick a frozen pie in the oven."

"I hate pound cake," Brenda admitted with a grin. "Let old Stanley eat it up and get rid of it."

Iris stooped and hugged her on her way to the freezer.

Though her heart was pounding in her breast, Iris tried not to act startled when she opened the door to the farrowing house and saw John hosing it down. He grinned at her and wrinkled his nose against the smell. The legs of his jeans were tucked into the tops of rubber boots. He was wearing a faded denim jacket, and on his head was a green-billed cap that advertised seed corn. She smiled as she watched him check the feeders while the hose ran fresh water into the trough. When she was sure she was in no danger of being sprayed with the hose, she went into the building and looked carefully at each of the big sows that lay dozing in the stalls.

"This one will be the first to farrow," she said when John came to lean on the rail beside her.

"Do you keep a chart on each of them?"

"I don't have that many. Dad was a grain farmer. I started this operation so we'd have a hog to butcher for quick money when we needed it. But the market has gone down. The money we get from the hogs today will go toward buying seed corn."

Iris was well aware, while they stood talking and watching the sow, that John's arm lay casually across her shoulders. She became so aware of it that she moved away. He seemed not to notice, and she was thankful.

The stockman, pulling a long hauling trailer behind his pickup, drove into the barnyard and backed up to the loading chute. Minutes later Stanley came driving in, slowly, as usual. Stanley never did anything in a hurry. He was a thick-set man in his middle forties who for years had nurtured the hope of winning Iris . . . and the farm. Iris had already introduced John to the stock buyer when Stanley came ambling up to the three of them.

"Mornin', Iris."

"'Lo, Stanley. You know Mr. Waterfield. This is John Lang. Stanley Kratz lives down the road," she said, as if apologizing for his presence.

John held out his hand, and Stanley took it after a small hesitation. His eyes roamed suspiciously between Iris and John. "I heard you'd moved in here."

"You heard right," John said firmly, not in the least intimidated.

Alvin Hudson, whose farm bordered Iris's on the east, arrived. Iris had known Alvin and his wife, Ruth, all her life. They had been lifelong friends of her father's and had known her own mother briefly. If she needed a neighbor's help, she went to the Hudsons.

With two groups working, the hogs were rounded up and loaded, with the receipt in Iris's jacket pocket, in less than two hours. John and Alvin worked together, leaving Iris teamed with Stanley. After the trailer of squealing pigs left the barnyard, Alvin and John disappeared into the machine shed.

Iris drew off her work gloves and laid them on the top of a post, then adjusted the red bandanna she had tied gypsy-style over her hair. She knew Stanley wouldn't leave until he had a chance to talk to her alone. Might as well get it over with, she thought, and wondered why she'd ever been so stupid as to go out with him. Lonely and bored had been her excuse then. Now it seemed a puny reason.

"Y'know people are talkin' about *him* moving in here." Stanley was as tactless as usual, Iris thought in disgust. As always when he was nervous, he had a toothpick stuck in the corner of his mouth, and it bobbed up and down as he talked.

"Has someone said something to you?"

"No. But they have to Ma. Why'd'ya let him do it?" Small, dark eyes glittered, and Iris could tell he was seething.

"I don't think that's any of your business, Stanley."

"None of my business?" he asked aggressively. "Y' know I planned on you'n me . . . gettin' together. I ain't gonna stand by and let that sonofabitch come in here and take over."

"Stanley! Calm down. You're making a fool of yourself. I've told you a thousand times there's absolutely no chance of you and me getting together . . . ever! I appreciate your friendship. You've been a good neighbor, but that's all!"

"Ain't good enough, is that it? Wal, I was plenty good enough when you needed help shelling corn and cuttin' pigs. I suppose you forgot that I planted beans for two whole days a couple years ago when you was stuck in the house with that sick kid. You've had the last bit of work out of me, Miss Uppity-up. Ya think you've got a stud bull here, but he won't stay, and you'll come crawling back for help. Wal, you won't get it from me." His anger caused his voice to tremble, and his jaw was rigid.

"You've always had a dirty mind," Iris said calmly. "That's only one of the things I despise about you. I wouldn't ask for your help again if I was drowning. Goodbye." She picked up her gloves and headed for the machine shed.

Stanley stood still for a moment, then stalked to his truck. Iris smiled when she heard the tires screech, throwing gravel. He'll run home and cry on his mama's shoulder. Yuk!

Alvin and John came out of the machine shed as she approached. Iris avoided John's eyes and smiled warmly at Alvin. His blue eyes twinkled, and his leathery face creased in a grin.

"What happened to Stanley? Is there a fire somewhere?"

"Could be."

"I didn't think even a fire'd move Stanley that fast.

What'd' ya do—tie a can to his tail?" Alvin was chuckling and scratching his gray head.

"Nothing as dramatic as that. How about some early lunch? I think it'll be dry enough to get in the field this afternoon."

"You don't have to feed me, gal,"

"Sure, I do. Ruth expected you to stay, didn't she? Just because we finished early is no reason for you not to."

"Wal, Mama did say something about going to town."

"Give me a few minutes and it'll be ready." Iris met John's eyes. There was no way she could keep from including him. "John . . .?"

"You may be setting a precedent, you know."

Why was she so happy? she wondered as she hung her smelly chore coveralls on the porch hook. Usually a confrontation like the one with Stanley would leave her shaking like a leaf.

She washed her face and hands, smoothed her hair, and picked up lipstick to add a little color to her lips, but put it down again. Watch it, my girl. Put that on and you might as well mail him a letter telling him . . . What? She looked at herself closely in the mirror. Iris Ouverson, are you so naive as to let a few kisses from a handsome man rattle you? In the sophisticated world he comes from everyone kisses everyone else, she reasoned, then almost giggled. Well . . . maybe not in the Navy, and maybe not in the same way he kissed her.

Okay, farm gal, be cool, as Brenda would say, and don't get all revved up over a flirtation. But . . .

John! Nearly everywhere her thoughts wandered, he was there.

CHAPTER FIVE

JOHN SLIPPED EASILY into country life. He worked tirelessly, putting in several more hours each day after Iris had driven the big green tractor to the shed to help Brenda with evening chores. That first night she had sent Brenda with a large bowl of stew to leave in his kitchen. He'd had the same stew for lunch, but Iris had reasoned he would be too tired to care about eating the same meal twice in one day. After that it had seemed natural to send over a part of a roast she had prepared in the crock pot during the day, or a portion of a casserole. Usually she could hear the putt-putt-putt of the tractor coming back a little before dark. He was up at dawn, refueling the tractors and tending to the sheep and hogs before Iris came out of the house.

Friday, the night of the play, Iris stayed in the field until a little over an hour before they had to leave.

"We're going to be late," Brenda wailed.

"No, we're not." Iris left her work clothes on the porch and ran barefoot up to the bathroom.

"I'm so nervous I could chew my fingers off up to my

elbows. What if I fall down on the stage? What if I forget my lines? Oh, why did I let you talk me into trying out for the darn play in the first place?"

"Don't blame me," Iris called over the sound of the running bath water. "You had a crush on Tim Pruitt at the time. That's why you tried out."

"I don't have a crush on him now. His breath stinks!"

Iris laughed and stepped into the tub. "Give him a breath mint."

"He's so dumb he wouldn't get the hint. Can I come in?" Brenda didn't wait for an answer, but pushed the door open. "Stacy Watts is having a slumber party for the girls in the cast. I don't know whether I want to go or not."

"Why not? Stacy's your best friend."

"If I fall on my face tonight, I won't go!" Brenda plunked herself down on the stool, her elbows on her knees and her chin in her palms.

"What's gotten into you, Brenda Ouverson? There's not a doubt in my mind that you'll be the best actress on that stage. Why, every play you've been in, every Christmas program, you've been just great. Even at Confirmation you were the best speaker. Reverend Peterson was amazed at how well you spoke, and I was congratulated by ever so many people. Humph! You may have butterflies in your stomach now, but the minute you get on your stage makeup, you'll be cool and collected, eager to perform, in fact."

"Do you really think so? I feel like I've got to throw up."

"Of course I think so. There won't be a mother or sister or anyone there any more proud than I'll be. You haven't let me or yourself down in fourteen years, you useless nuisance, and you won't this time."

"I love you, Iris." Thin young arms went about Iris's shoulders and a quick kiss was planted on her cheek.

"And I love you, squirt. Now, get out of here. I need to get dressed or I'll disgrace *you*."

Iris brushed her hair until it crackled and then pulled it straight back from her forehead without a part and coiled it into a bun on the back of her head. Carefully she applied her makeup and put on gold loop earrings. After spraying herself generously with scent she put on her hose and slender-heeled pumps. Her wardrobe was limited, but the one thing that she knew looked good on her was her teal-blue suit, with its pencil-slim skirt, and the burnt-rose blouse with the soft bow at the neck.

When she was completely dressed she surveyed herself in the full-length mirror attached to the inside of her closet door. Not one to realize she had the classic beauty of her Swedish ancestors, she looked at herself critically and saw a slender, quiet woman whose hair was blond and smooth, whose skin was flawless, and whose blue eyes looked bluer with the faint brushing of eye shadow and liner. She was delighted that her skirt was just the right length and she had no runs in her hose, not even a snag!

"Are you ready, Brenda? We'll buy a sandwich at the drive-in, if you like."

"I ate three mini-pizzas when I came home from school. Iris, what if I get on stage and throw up?"

"If you do, wait till Tim Pruitt tells you he's engaged to another woman. Everyone will think it's part of the script and will marvel at what a good actress you are."

"Oh, you're silly, Iris, just silly," Brenda said with a snort, but she smiled. "Is John coming?"

"I don't know. He hasn't said anything about it to me, and he's still in the field. What's the overnight case for?"

"I may stay at Stacy's. It's okay, isn't it?"

"Well, I guess so. But I'll have to talk to Jane first."

"Why d'ya have to talk to Stacy's mom? I'm almost fifteen." Brenda went down the steps two at a time. Iris followed slowly, trying to get accustomed to walking in the heels she seldom wore.

"You'll be fourteen for eight more months, my crazy little sister who wants to grow up so fast."

Iris backed the eight-year-old Chrysler out of the garage. The car was rarely used, had low mileage, and was in excellent condition. Brenda had gone through a stage when she nagged Iris to sell it and get something newer. Then one day a group of high-school boys had gathered around and admired it as it sat in the school parking lot. Now Brenda thought their "antique" was cool, and washed it down occasionally without grumbling too much.

The auditorium was almost full, and it was just a few minutes until curtain time, when Iris saw John come in the side door. As he gave his ticket to a student and collected a program, his eyes scanned the audience. Then he moved to stand along the wall with others waiting for more chairs to be brought in so they could be seated.

Watching John from her place between Alvin's wife and Stacy's mother, Iris knew that hers were not the only eyes on him. The fact that he was a stranger in this community where almost everyone knew everyone else would be enough to attract notice, but added to that, he stood head and shoulders above most of the other men waiting in line. He was wearing a dark brown suit, a tan shirt, and a tie. Iris smiled. His hair had already begun to rebel against the hairbrush that had tried to smooth it, and was curling over onto his forehead. A warm, happy feeling started in the pit of her stomach and spread. He had promised Brenda that he would come, and he was here.

The houselights dimmed, and Iris nervously clutched at her purse. Let Brenda do well, she prayed silently. Let her be pleased with her performance. She sat rigid for the first few minutes Brenda was on stage, then relaxed and enjoyed the play. Her little sister went through her lines without missing a beat, and, as she had the curtain speech, Iris was sure the roar of applause that followed was all for Brenda.

Numerous curtain calls followed, and a bouquet of flowers was presented to Louise Hanley, the drama coach. When the audience began to file out, Iris and Jane Watts went backstage to congratulate their girls.

Brenda clutched a huge bunch of flowers. "Iris!" Her voice squeaked with excitement. "Look what John sent me! They're even bigger than old lady—" She broke off when Iris, laughing, put her fingers over Brenda's mouth. "He was here, wasn't he? I know I saw him . . . way in back." She leaned forward to whisper in her sister's ear. "I did good, didn't I?"

"You did great! You were the very best, just as I knew you'd be. Now, what are you going to do about the slumber party?"

"I'm going! Will you take my flowers home for me?" Without waiting for an answer, she shoved them at Iris.

"Jane said she'll bring you home in the morning. I'll

be in the field, but you know your usual Saturday chores, and you'd better ride Sugar a little and get that colt used to the lead rope."

"I will. Oh, I will. Iris, I'm so happy. Do you think I could be a movie star?"

"Sure." Iris's eyes were filled with love and pride. "You're pretty enough and you're a good actress. 'Bye, now. Have a good time."

When Iris reached the end of the long hall she looked back in time to see Stanley coming down it. Beyond him Louise Hanley and Brenda stood talking to John. Iris saw him reach out and lay an arm over Brenda's shoulders in a gesture of affection. Then she noticed Stanley bearing down on her. She walked quickly through the door and out into the darkness, hoping she would be lucky enough to reach her car and drive away before he could catch her.

Out on the highway, Iris glanced at the flowers lying on the seat beside her. Did John know how much his thoughtful gesture had meant to a young girl who had depended solely on an older sister for love, guidance, and encouragement? There had never been a strong masculine figure in Brenda's life. It was no wonder she was impressed by him. Her own father had ignored her most of the time, seeing in her the lasting evidence of his own folly in marrying a girl he'd known for only a few weeks.

The growl in Iris's stomach reminded her she'd had nothing to eat since a peanut-butter sandwich at noon. She slowed the Chrysler as she approached a fast-food place, but drove on after looking at the crowded parking lot. When she turned off the highway and onto the graveled county road she noticed a car behind her. Would John be coming home so early?

Iris drove into the garage, turned off the lights, and picked up Brenda's flowers. With her bag over her shoulder, she got out of the car and pulled down the garage door just as car lights came up the drive. She groaned when she recognized Stanley's car. He stopped between her and the back door, so she was forced to stand and wait for him to roll down the window.

"How about going for a bite to eat?"

"No, thank you, Stanley." She added no excuses, and wasn't very civil at that.

"The kid's at the party at the Wattses', so what's keepin' you from comin'?" He turned off the motor.

"The fact that I don't want to go with you." She gave him a hard stare. "Excuse me."

Stanley turned off the headlights and got out of the car before she could reach the back door. She turned to face him.

"Are you still mad about what I said the other day?"

"No. I knew you had a narrow and dirty mind. You merely substantiated it. I don't care what you think, Stanley. Or what your mother thinks, for that matter. If you'll excuse me, I have more important things to do."

"Like what?"

"That's none of your damned business," she hissed. "Now, go!"

Stanley crossed his arms over his chest and rocked back on his heels. "You think you'll get rid of me before *he* comes. Then the two of you will have it nice and cozy without the kid, is that it?"

"Stanley, I've said it once and I'll say it again: you're disgusting."

"He ain't comin'." He waited to see her reaction to his

words, and when she failed to act surprised he added, "He's out with Louise Hanley."

Iris merely shrugged.

"Louise is a hot little piece. Everybody knows it," he said slowly, enjoying every shocking word.

"You're crude! You're a crude man with your mind in the gutter. I wonder how I *ever* thought I could be friends with you. Now, if you don't mind, get out of here!"

"I mind. I know what's got into you. You think I'm not good enough now that there's bigger fish to fry. Wal, I'm not having no woman throw me over for some city dude who thinks he's a *gentleman* farmer. You're stupid, Iris. Just plain stupid! He ain't goin' to stay here for long. I've seen his kind before. He's just like his father. Old lady Lang never knew where he'd land next. He'll play 'round with you, but—"

"That's enough! Keep your opinions to yourself and get the hell out of here." Iris flung open the screen door and fumbled to put the key in the lock.

"Bull! Who do you think you're talking to?" When Stanley grabbed her arm he knocked the flowers out of her hand. They fell to the ground. He lifted them with the toe of his shoe and sent them flying into the bushes beside the back porch.

"You . . . you bastard!" Iris was furious. She faced him like a spitting cat. "That does it! Get off my property, Stanley, and don't ever come back. Neighbor or no neighbor, stay the hell off my place!"

Stanley's face darkened, and his eyes turned hard and cruel. "You always thought you was just a mite better than other folks." His hand tightened on her arm and jerked her toward him.

"Let go of me, you buzzard bait, or—"

"Or you'll what? Seems to me like I got comin' a little bit of what you've been giving away. I ain't as much as had a kiss outta you, so I figure I'll collect now."

Iris was afraid. Stanley was stupid, unreasonable, and crude, but she'd never known him to be physically cruel. From the look on his face she knew he was capable of it now. When he lowered his head to kiss her, she brought the sharp heel of her shoe down on his instep.

"Yeow!" The sound of pain came from deep in his throat. "You bitch!"

Iris was mad and scared. She was also strong. She balled her fist and swung. The blow landed on the side of his face, but he didn't let go of her arm.

"Turn me loose, you . . . you overstuffed toad, or I'll scratch your eyes out!" She tried to stomp on his foot again, but he held her away from him. She lifted her foot to kick him but was hampered by the high-heeled shoes and lost her balance. He hauled her up close to him and tried to find her lips with his. Iris screamed as desperation took control of her. She struggled with every ounce of her strength to avoid the mouth seeking hers.

Neither of them heard the car drive into the carport in the grove, but both heard the angry shout just before John reached them.

"You sonofabitch!"

His fist connected with Stanley's jaw the instant he released his hold on Iris. Stanley stumbled back against the car, regained his balance, lowered his head, and charged. John stepped aside and hit him again. Stanley stumbled back, turned, and draped himself over the hood of the car, breathing hard. John swore viciously.

"Get the hell out of here or I'll beat you to a pulp!"

John stood waiting. Stanley took a handkerchief from his pocket and held it to his nose before he turned away.

"You haven't heard the last of this," he growled. He stumbled around the car and jerked open the door. The dome light shone briefly on his bloody face.

"Neither have you," John said angrily. "You bother her again and I'll do more than bloody your nose. I'll break both your damned legs!"

"You can have her, but you ain't gettin' much!" Stanley shouted, and shot off down the drive without turning on his headlights.

Iris held onto the screen door. She didn't know if she could move. During the struggle she had turned her ankle, and pain was shooting up her leg to her knee. She blinked back tears of pain and humiliation. Her purse lay on the drive, and the flowers were nowhere in sight.

"Did he hurt you?"

"N-no, but I've lost the key." She stood on one foot and made no move to look for it.

"He *did* hurt you! The bastard!"

"I turned my ankle. I don't think I can bend over. The key's down there somewhere." She nodded toward the grass beside the step. Her voice was calm, but her insides were in a turmoil.

John squatted down and ran his hand along the ground. "I'll have to get a flashlight. Will you be okay? Do you want to sit down?"

"I'll be all right." Iris was trembling, but she made an effort to keep her voice steady.

While he was gone she eased off the high-heeled shoe and tried to put her weight on her injured foot. The pain ran up her leg like a sharp knife. "Ohhh . . . damn you, Stanley," she muttered. She couldn't afford to be laid up even for a day at this time of year!

John was back with the light and easily found the keys. "Can you move just a little, so I can open the door?"

"I . . . can hop if you'll help me take off this other darn shoe. This wouldn't have happened if I hadn't been wearing such high heels."

"That bad, huh?" John slid an arm beneath her knees and lifted her easily. Her arm went about his neck. "Open the door." His face was close, his voice low in her ear. Iris obeyed, her heart galloping like a racehorse. He angled their bodies through the door, and the screen slammed behind them. He carried her into the kitchen and stopped inside the door. "Can you find the light switch?" When she turned on the light, she looked directly into eyes just inches from hers. They were smiling. So was his mouth. " 'I'm sorry you've hurt your ankle, but I'm glad I had an excuse to hold you." The smile faded. "Is this the first time he's pulled a stunt like this?"

She nodded. "He's angry because I told him off the other day." She wanted to wrap both arms about his neck and lay her head on his shoulder. She couldn't remember ever being held like this.

"About my being here?"

"Partly. He's had his eye on me . . . and the farm for a while." It was embarrassing to talk about it. She shivered. "We went out to dinner a couple of times. He wasn't quite so repulsive then, and . . . I thought we could be friends."

John chuckled and rubbed his nose against her cheek. Iris felt giddy. "You foolish woman! No single red-

blooded man is going to want to be *friends* with you!" He
set her down on a chair. "I'll take a look at that foot."

"John? . . ." Her voice sounded loud and breathless.
"My purse is out there in the yard, and he . . . he kicked
Brenda's flowers over in the bushes beside the house."

He swore. "My Lord! He got off easy!" John took the
flashlight out of his hip pocket and went out through the
door. When he returned he placed the flowers and her
purse on the table beside her.

"Thank you. And thank you for sending Brenda the
flowers. She was terribly excited. No one has ever given
her flowers before."

"She told me. She did great, didn't she?" He stood
beaming proudly down at her. "The little devil put on a
good show!"

"She was pleased you were there."

Smiling blue eyes looked down into hers, and he
squatted down beside her. "I looked for you."

She wanted to tell him that she had looked for him too,
but she said nothing, feeling a sudden, overwhelming
self-consciousness. She had to change the subject, and
ran her hand down over her ankle, which was noticeably
swollen. "Of all the damned luck! This couldn't have
come at a worse time. We should start planting in a day
or two."

"Don't worry. We will. Take off your stocking and I'll
look at it. I have some elastic wrap over at the house we
can use if there are no broken bones. If there are, it's the
hospital for you."

"No! Nothing is broken. It's just a sprain."

"We'll soon see. Are you going to take off that stock-

ing, or am I going to have to do it?" That endearing grin
appeared again, and Iris had to look away from it.

"I'll do it, but you'll have to leave."

"Panty hose, huh? Think you can manage? I'll run
over and get the wrap. Hey, is that your stomach growl-
ing or mine?" He straightened, looking awfully tall loom-
ing over the chair in which she sat.

"Mine has the bad habit of doing that, but I think this
time it's yours. Didn't you have dinner either?"

"Didn't have time. After you're attended to, I'll scare
up a bite to eat for us. I'll be back in a minute, so if you
want privacy you'd better move fast."

As soon as he was gone, she stood on one foot and
wiggled the panty hose down over her hips to her knees,
sank down on the chair, and drew them off. Her ankle was
rapidly changing color. She shrugged out of her suit
jacket and hung it over the back of the chair. She was de-
bating with herself about trying to hop to the sink to put
the flowers in water, when John came back. He had
changed into jeans, a soft plaid shirt, and sneakers.

He pulled up a chair, lifted her leg, and laid it across
his lap. His obviously experienced fingers moved gently
over the swollen ankle. He probed. Then, with his hand
cupped beneath her foot, he moved the joint carefully. Iris
winced and damped her lower lip between her teeth.

"No broken bones. It's a bad sprain. I'll wrap it, and
you'll have to stay off it for a few days."

"Oh, but—"

"No buts. I've taken care of dozens of sprains during
my hitch in the service. I'm a certified paramedic,
ma'am. You're in good hands."

"Was that your line of work in the Navy?"

"No. I was a commander on a gun boat."

"Did you like it?"

"It was okay at the time. I like farming better."

She stared intently at him as he wrapped her ankle. His profile was sharply defined, his nose straight, his lips firm. What was he thinking? Had there been many women in his life? Had he been married? It would be wonderful to have a man like him to lean on. The thought sent a queer little shock through her body.

"What have you decided?" he asked.

His question caught her off guard.

"Never mind," he said quickly, his voice kind, but his expression stern. He lifted her leg off his lap and eased her foot down until her heel rested on the floor. "Your feet are cold. Where are your slippers? Better yet, I'll go ahead and turn on some lights, then carry you upstairs, and you can put on something more comfortable." He was gone before she could protest. When he returned he scooped her up in his arms.

"John! No! I'm too heavy."

"Put your arms around my neck and you'll be light as a feather."

"I doubt that!" She felt protected and young. Almost cherished. An absolutely new and infinitely wonderful feeling to her.

"Hang on, or I'll drop you," he threatened. Her arms tightened, and it brought her face nearer his. The scent of his skin was dearly familiar.

"Let me walk, John. You can't carry me up those steps."

"Want to bet? What do you weigh? I'd say about one-twenty. Right?" She nodded. "Then, be still." He was breathing hard when they reached her room and he set her down on the edge of the bed. "Nicest workout I've had in a long time. Now, don't put your weight on that foot. Is there anything you can't reach with a few hops?"

"No. I can manage, thank you." The tightness in her chest increased with alarming intensity.

He leaned against the end of the heavy oak bed. "I never knew there were women like you, Iris." He said it as if she were something incredible. His eyes circled the utterly feminine room, with its deep-ruffled crisscross curtains, pale blue carpet, and frilly lampshades, coming back to look hard at her. "You were badly frightened by Stanley. I heard your scream. How come you didn't have hysterics afterwards?" His straightforward stare did more than Stanley's attack to unnerve her.

"I . . . don't know. I guess I'm not the hysterical type." She avoided his eyes, and lifted her hands to tuck stray strands of hair into the bun.

He walked around to stand by the edge of the bed in front of her, and she had to look up a long way to see his face. "You and Brenda have lived here alone for five years?" She nodded, and he said, "Amazing!" He moved about the room, touched a picture of her and Brenda taken when she first came home from college, lifted a brush on the bureau, glanced at a stack of books on the table beside the bed. He turned and gave her a meaningful look. "Do you like grilled-cheese sandwiches?"

Iris let the air out of her lungs with one big puff and chuckled. "Love 'em."

"Good." She hadn't realized quite how serious his expression had been, until he smiled. It made all the difference. "I make the best grilled-cheese sandwich in the

West," he bragged. "Do what you have to do, then yell. I'll come get you," At the door his eyes caught hers and held them. "I have got a bottle of wine I've been saving for a special occasion. I think this is it." The twinkle in his eyes matched the grin on his lips. "By the way, why does Arthur have to stay in the barn at night?"

"You know one of the reasons." Her eyes twinkled back at him.

He cocked his head to one side and studied her. "Oh, yes. I intend to have a talk with you about that." He winked, turned, and moved out of sight with swift grace.

She sat for a long time, fervently wishing for many impossibilities, all involving John D. Lang, Jr.

CHAPTER SIX

IRIS STOOD AT the head of the stairs, her leg trembling from the effort it took to hop down the hall. She knew she could make it down the steps by taking them one at a time and leaning on the smooth oak rail, but first she needed rest. She had slipped into the new caftan she'd made during the winter; one of the soft feminine types of things she liked to wear after supper. The blue material, with a Victorian print, was soft cotton; the fabric had caught her eye at a warehouse sale where prices were slashed drastically. She could never have afforded it otherwise. Usually in the evening she let her hair hang loose, but tonight, recalling John's remark about Lady Godiva, she coiled the braid and pinned it to the back of her head.

She took the steps slowly. The seldom-used ceiling light in the dining room was on. Just like Brenda, she mused. Doesn't know the meaning of the word "economize." At the bottom of the stairs she wrapped her arms around the newel post to steady herself and to give her pounding heart time to slow down.

"What the devil are you doing down here? You stubborn

little jackass!" John's long strides brought him quickly to her, and he scooped her up in his arms. He lifted her high, and her arms automatically went around his neck. "What are you trying to do to me? Don't you want me to have any fun?" He started for the kitchen and stopped. He lowered his head and nuzzled the soft skin of her neck. "I like this." His voice was slightly husky, his face inches from hers. "You're the damndest woman I've ever known. You can go from a tomboy chasing hogs, to looking chic like you did tonight at the school, to soft and womanly like now." His eyes looked into hers for a long, delicious moment, and tides of overwhelming warmth washed over her. "I like this Iris the best." The words came out on a soft breath.

"I'm a complete package," she whispered. Before she could think of something flip to say, he bent his head and kissed her softly.

"Sure, you are. Ready for the party?" He carried her into the kitchen and stood her beside the table, his arm supporting her. "Sit here, ma'am. Dinner will be served in a minute."

The table held two place settings, catsup, and steak sauce. "I thought we were having grilled-cheese sand-wiches."

"A minor problem developed."

"What was that?"

"No cheese." He stirred frozen hash-browns, poked at two small steaks in another pan. "I'll bring you a glass of wine in a minute."

"I don't like sitting here doing nothing."

"You're entitled to be pampered once in a while, so

relax and enjoy it. Besides, you have the perfect excuse tonight—you're an invalid, remember?"

She nodded, smiling happily. After a glass of wine and then some hot food, she decided being pampered was definitely nice!

"Mmmm . . . that was good," she said when she finished her steak. "Where did you learn to cook?"

"Not aboard ship. I knew how to cook when I went into the Navy. I more or less shifted for myself during my school years, and it was cook or live on cold cereal." He filled her wineglass. "We may as well kill the bottle." She thought his eyes were the most beautiful eyes she'd ever seen. "I can just see the wheels turning in your mind. You're thinking that I'm plying you with drink so I can seduce you."

"Are you?"

"Yeah. Just in case the mating salt I sprinkled on the potatoes doesn't work." He gave her one of his wide, winning grins.

She couldn't hold back her own smile in spite of the warmth from embarrassment that flooded her face. "C'mon, be serious. What kind of childhood did you have?"

"My parents were divorced. My mother worked, and I was on my own a lot. But it was okay. How about yours?"

"Mine was okay, too. After my mother died I had my grandma, than an aunt, and my dad. I always had a horse and a dog. It was a good childhood."

"I saw you on your horse one time when I was here visiting my grandmother. You had long blond pigtails hanging down your back. You were maybe fifteen or sixteen. My granny told me to stay away from you, that you were a pure, sweet girl." The look on his face made her breathless. "Granny was right."

Iris sipped her wine and tried not to look at him. Her face began to feel warm again. The intensity of his gaze made her uncomfortable. She picked up the soiled plates and stacked them.

"Brenda will wash the dishes in the morning. One of her Saturday chores," she explained with a short laugh.

John took the dishes out of her hands. "Is this your way of telling me the party is over?" His grin spread that horrible charm over his face. "I was taught that it was rude to eat and run." He cleared the table and rinsed the dishes, stacking them neatly in the sink. He turned to face her, grinning still. "How will you get up the stairs without me?"

"I'll walk. I've been putting a little pressure on my ankle while sitting here, and discovered it isn't that bad." She limped to the counter and back to the table to demonstrate.

John flipped off the overhead light, making the room rosy with only the dim light from over the stove. She turned away. "Do you want me to go?" He was close behind her, his voice almost a whisper, when he repeated the question. "Do you want me to go, Iris?"

She nodded. "I think you should." It was hard for her to say anything.

"You think I want to make love to you. Is that it?"

"No . . . I just think—"

"You're wrong. I want to make love to you very much. I've wanted to since the first time I saw you. Since the very first," he whispered once more, his face near hers, his hands on her shoulders drawing her to his chest.

When she lurched away from him, his hands fell from her shoulders. She went slowly into the dining room, scarcely noticing the pain in her ankle. Her hand found the switch beside the door and clicked off the overhead light. In the gloom the familiar room seemed strange. The feelings stirring inside her were even stranger, and she was frightened by them. She wrapped her arms about the post at the foot of the stairs and rested her chin on the smooth, rounded top. She fought to overcome her inhibitions while the need to be held and caressed blazed fiercely through her.

"Iris?" John's gentle hands pulled her around to face him. Every bone in her body seemed to have turned to jelly. She made not a whimper of protest when his arms closed about her, merely lifting her parted lips for his kiss. His mouth was warm and gentle and gave her room to move away if she wanted to. She found herself clinging to him weakly. His hands moved seductively across her hips and back, tucking her closer to the granite strength of his body. Her mind felt like it was floating. Primitive desire grew inside her, and she became helpless to stop it. These wanton feelings were new and strange to her, and instead of making an effort to control them, she allowed them to take over, to build into sexual intoxication.

It was John who drew back and held her away from him.

"I don't sleep around," she gasped. Oh, dear Lord! That surely was an understatement. Would he be amused to know she'd never been with a man before? Her arms fell from around him.

"I know that." He lifted first one of her arms and then the other and placed them about his neck. He pressed a

sweet kiss to her moist parted lips before his mouth trailed
to her ear. "I'm going to take the pins out of your hair."
Warm fingers smoothed back the strands from her temples
on their way to the back of her head. "I've been wanting
to see it again since that first night. Why were you angry
when I called you Lady Godiva?" Her forehead was
pressed to his shoulder and his whispered words floated
around her. "In some parts of the world a man cherishes
his woman's hair." He unlaced the braid, and his hands caressed the glossy strands that hung past her waist. "You're
a treasure, a rare flower, my Iris." He continued to stroke
her from the crown of her head to her hips.

Mindless, unconscious of time or place, Iris leaned on
him. "I've cut it only one time." It seemed an inconse-
quential thing to say with her lips against his neck.

The hands on her shoulders moved her back, and he
tilted her face with fingers beneath her chin. Her arms fell
to her sides. She felt scared . . . and shy. But his face was
soft with charm and his eyes moved over her warmly. He
took two handfuls of hair and brought the silky strands
forward over her shoulders and smoothed them down
over her breasts. "It would be a crime to cut it," he said,
almost to himself. "I've always had a yearning to see an
old-fashioned girl with long golden hair."

He drew her gently to him, and his lips settled on her
mouth with infinite passion and tenderness. His tongue
made small forays between her lips before it entered her
mouth and searched for sweetness. His hands traversed
her body. Her mouth blossomed under his. Instinctively
she responded by welcoming the invasion of his tongue
and moved her own to gently stroke his inner lips. Her fin-

gers moved to the hair at the back of his neck, spread, and boldly combed and caressed.

His hands gripped the soft flesh of her hips, pressing her soft mound against his arousal. Abruptly his lips were at her ear and he was taking deep breaths.

"Tell me to stop . . . to go home, or it'll be too late." The words seemed wrenched from him. "I . . . ache for you. . . ."

She wanted to speak, to tell him she was still a girl in a woman's body, that she was afraid of the hurt that would follow this giving of herself. She opened her mouth to whisper her fears, but it was too late. He covered her parted lips, his tongue darting hotly in and out of her mouth, exploring every curve of the sweetness that trembled beneath his demanding kiss. Her arms tightened while he ravaged the sweetness of her until she was moaning gently and panting for breath. She kissed him back feverishly, as though swept away by some wild force totally beyond her control.

In a small part of her mind she realized this was what she wanted, had wanted since the first time he kissed her. It was as though it was his right, and she had waited for him. Now, she would know exactly what it was that she had been waiting for. She would learn the mysteries about which she had read and imagined but never truly believed were accompanied by such overwhelmingly forceful feelings. He was almost a stranger to her, his background as different from hers as night from day, she thought frantically. And yet she felt as though she'd known him all her life, wanted him, needed him, loved him. . . .

"Let's go upstairs," he whispered urgently.

Iris shuddered, feeling as though her legs were too

weak to hold her without his supporting arms. She knew she should have been shocked by his suggestion, but she wasn't, for his husky whisper aroused her on some instinctive level long suppressed that was rushing to take control of her virgin body. "Turn out all the lights down here." It was a mere fragment of a whisper from her aching throat.

"Can you make it up the steps alone?"

Even now, his concern was for her, and she cherished it. She nodded, and the cheek pressed tightly against his felt the pull of a day's growth of beard.

Reluctantly, it seemed, his arms fell away from her. His hands at her waist assisted her up the first step and then he left her.

I do love him! she thought wildly. I wouldn't be going to bed with him if I didn't! Oh, dear heaven! It's unreal that I'm doing this.

The light from the yard dimly lit the room. Iris stood at the foot of the bed she had slept in for most of her life. Her face burned, and her stomach muscles clenched and relaxed. Her breathing and heartbeat were all mixed up, as if a motor had been attached to them and their normal rhythm had gone awry. It seemed to her that she stood there for an eternity.

Then he was behind her. He hadn't touched her, but she knew. She leaned back against him. She needed his strength, his assurance. His large, warm hands came around her, circled her rib cage, and pulled her back against his chest. His mouth found the curve of her neck, lips nibbling, his breath tantalizing her skin. She turned in his arms. He had removed his shirt, and she wrapped her arms about his naked torso. Her ragged breath was trapped inside her mouth by his plundering lips, and the floor seemed to fall away at her feet.

"I shouldn't!" she whispered urgently when his lips left hers to gulp air. Ingrained teaching of moral standards surfaced to plague her even now.

"Yes!" he whispered hoarsely. "You're a woman made to be loved and . . . cherished." His hungry mouth searched, found hers, and held it with fierce possession. His hands moved urgently over her. "How do I get you out of this thing?"

"Zipper . . . in back."

Whoosh! She felt the air on her bare skin as the caftan fell in a soft pool around her feet. She backed away from him and sat down on the bed. In one swift flick she rid herself of her slippers, then she slid swiftly between the sheets. Her eyes were riveted on John's tall and shadowy figure, motionless before her. When his hands went to the belt of his jeans, she closed her eyes, and sweet warmth washed over her.

The bed sagged. She could feel his body just beyond her hip. He sat on the edge of the bed for what seemed only an instant before the covers lifted and she felt long, hair-roughened legs against her and arms that seemed to be yards long scooping under and around her. She was gathered tenderly to a warm naked chest thickly matted with soft hair.

He pinned the length of her against him and cradled her head in the crook of his arm. She couldn't move, didn't want to move, and felt as if her heart would gallop right out of her breast.

"Are you shy with me?" he whispered between kisses around her ear. "Don't be. You're beautiful. Your body is strong and neat. It's like velvet, soft, and yet firm and tight. And this wonderful hair . . ." His fingers fumbled with the hooks on her bra, then swept it from her breasts. For the first time, her nipples were pressed against a man's chest. His hand pushed at the panties, and she lifted her hips to help him.

Her palms slid over muscle and tight flesh as if wanting to know every inch of him. So this was what it was like to make love, she thought dreamily, and threaded her legs between his. His sex was large and firm, and throbbed against her flat stomach. She gloried in the feel of him, knowing that soon he would fill that aching emptiness. Her hands moved caressingly up and down his side and over his hips to the small of his back.

His breath came in quick gasps, and he turned her on her back so he could hover over her. He lowered his head and kissed her breast. His tongue flicked the bud, then grasped it gently with his teeth. He nuzzled the soft mound like a baby seeking life-giving substance. His hand moved over her body, prowling ever closer to the ultimate goal, and suddenly it was there at the mysterious moistness. Her legs opened for him.

Tremors shot through her in earth-shaking waves as exploring fingers moved, titillating the pulsing flower of womanhood, until her hips arched frantically against the hand between her legs and she instinctively reached for the male hardness to fill her. She was in a mindless void where there were only John's hands, John's lips, John's body. Her hand circled him and pulled, her knees flexed. She could feel him tremble violently as he slid between her thighs and held himself poised above her. He sought the warm cavern and entered.

Iris gave a small strangled cry. He stopped and lay motionless atop her. The two hands that cupped her hips squeezed, released, and squeezed again.

"Oh, baby! Why didn't you tell me?" He groaned hoarsely against the side of her face.

She turned her head, frantically seeking his lips. "Don't stop!" It was a quavering whimper.

"I can't . . . stop! But, sweetheart . . . darling . . . Oh, God!"

He raised himself. She thought he was going to leave her, and grabbed frantically at his lean hips. He paused, then pierced her savagely with a single, jarring thrust. A stab of white-hot pain forced a choked cry from her lips. A low moan came from his. He supported himself on his forearms, tangled his hands in her hair, and rained feverish kisses on her face.

For a while he remained motionless, allowing her to become accustomed to the feel of him inside her, while his lips searched out every line in her face and sipped at the tears that rolled from the corners of her eyes. Then, slowly, he started to move within her, thrusting carefully. Her arms wound tightly around his back, feeling his muscles strain and stir beneath her palms when he plunged faster and faster. The naked hunger that caught her was both sweet and violent. Every part of him that touched her carried a fiery message to the depth of her femininity, and her hips moved with the surging rhythm of his. He was quivering with the effort to love her tenderly. His heart thundered against her breast. It surprised her that she could feel it over the hammering of her own.

When she thought she would explode, when the pain-pleasure became so intense, she drew his tongue into her mouth. Then she did explode within. The first fantastic sensation was closely followed by another and then another. As she emerged from a long, unbelievable release she was aware of nothing but a wonderful floating feeling and the broad naked shoulders she clung to until the world stopped tilting.

Almost simultaneously, John thrust into her for the last time, his whole body tense with emotion for wild exhilarating seconds. He gripped her fiercely, and the air exploded from his lungs. Then he was still.

Iris lay weak and limp beneath him; her body seemed lifeless even though her heart still beat too quickly in her breast and her blood raced through her veins.

Seemingly awed into silence by the experience they'd shared, John slid to her side and gathered her gently to him.

"Sweetheart . . ." He smoothed her hair back from her damp face and spread it out on the pillow behind her head. "Oh, love!" He placed soft kisses on her forehead, her eyes. "I never imagined that you were . . . were a virgin. I didn't want to be rough, to hurt you, but I was so hungry for you I couldn't help myself." His hand moved down her side to her bottom and then to her thigh and pulled it up so it rested across his. His hand returned to caress the soft rounded flesh of her hips.

"I'm sorry." She said it so low he could scarcely hear, but he did, and he moved his face back so he could see her. Her eyes were closed. He felt a tear drop on his shoulder.

A low growl of protest came from his throat. "Why are you crying? Are you sorry you didn't save yourself for the man you love?"

"No. I wanted it to be you. I'm sorry if you were disappointed."

"Disappointed?" he muttered thickly. "Sweetheart, didn't you know that it's a treasured moment in a man's life when he presses against that barrier? He knows that no man has been there before him and for the rest of her life a woman will remember him." He kissed away the tears. "How can you possibly think I was disappointed? I shall cherish the memory of this night always." His hand moved soothingly over her back in a gentle rhythm. He whispered words of comfort and kissed away the moisture on her face.

Relaxed and dreamy, she listened to the steady beat of his heart beneath her cheek and marveled that his hard muscles and angled frame could provide such a comfortable resting place.

"I suppose you've known many women," she said, not really wanting to know about the women in his life.

"A few. But none the way I know you."

"You mean I'm the only thirty-two-year-old virgin you've slept with?" The words were out of her mouth even while she was thinking them.

The hand on her back came up to cover her cheek and press her face to his chest. "Don't talk about it like that. You're the first real, complete woman I've been with." His voice was deeply sincere.

Her palm slid up his chest to his face and stroked it lovingly. "Your lovemaking is better than anything I've read in a book," she confessed shyly.

He laughed and rolled with her in his arms, her hair covering them. She giggled and clutched at him to keep from falling off the bed.

"This is only the beginning, my beautiful innocent," he said, and wrapped her hair around his shoulders.

"You're the teacher," she said saucily, and boldly nipped him on the chin, then sweetly kissed the spot.

"Will you sign up for the full course?"

"What's the tuition? How many credits? And what are the job opportunities when I graduate?"

He roared with laughter and rolled with her again. They both almost toppled to the floor, only his foot braced against the carpet saving them. On top of him, Iris grabbed at the headboard to keep from falling.

"Stop that!" She laughed, her belly pressed tightly to his. "We're too big for this bed."

He was suddenly still, his foot on the floor, his other leg wrapped over hers. Her hair covered their upper bodies.

"I could feel your laugh," he whispered. "It's truly youthful and innocent. How did you manage to escape the perniciousness of our generation?" She lifted her head to look at him, but he lifted his and caught her lips. Her head followed his down, and they shared a deep, hungry kiss.

It was an exhilarating experience to be in control. Iris felt his heartbeat soar. She angled her nose alongside his and caressed his lips with her own, nibbling, stroking with her tongue, deepening the kiss and withdrawing. She felt and tasted the moistness of his skin. All the adoration she had saved was given to him now. She murmured his name as her lips glided over straight brows, short, thick eyelashes, cheeks rough with stubble, and to his waiting mouth. It was glorious to feel this freedom to love and caress him. Awed by the wonder of it, she paused and pressed her cheek to his.

"Ah, love! Don't stop!" His voice came huskily, tickling her ear. His hands kneaded her rounded bottom and pressed her tightly to the aroused length of him, captured between their bellies. "I've been in a bad way since I've been here; all those nights of wanting you . . ." His leg glided from over hers, and his hand moved to spread her thighs. He lifted her with strong thumbs pressed to her hipbones. When he settled her on him, she gasped with surprise. "Just be still, sweetheart. I won't hurt you." His hands glided over her hips and back and up to the sides of her breasts, which were flattened against his chest. He grasped her head and turned it so his lips could reach her mouth. "We fit perfectly, love," he said, breathing deeply. "We're perfect together." His voice was a shivering whisper that touched her soul.

Much later, as she lay quietly beside him, he turned and buried his face in the curve of her neck like a child seeking comfort. Time and again he had told her how he liked to feel her hair around his shoulders. She covered him with it and stroked his own back from his forehead, loving him, wanting him to love her in return but realizing how improbable it was. She tried to dismiss the feeling of impending heartache. In torment she tightened her arms around him and pressed her mouth to his forehead. Finally she fell asleep, wishing the night wouldn't pass so quickly.

It seemed she had scarcely closed her eyes when a loud noise awakened her. Someone was banging on the door. Shouts followed.

"Fire! Fire!"

CHAPTER SEVEN

FIRE! THE WORD caused an icy ball of fear to knot in the pit of Iris's stomach.

John untangled his limbs from hers and jumped out of bed. He slid into his jeans without benefit of underwear and was pulling them up around his hips as he vaulted out of the bedroom door. The shouts from the yard below and the hammering on the door were persistent.

Iris, forgetting her sprained ankle, cried out when she slammed it against the table as she hurried to slide a robe over her head. She grabbed her shoes and limped at a run after John.

"Barn's on fire!" The shout came through the opened door.

"Iris, call the fire department!" John shouted, and raced back up the steps. He returned with his shoes in his hand as she dialed the number.

Iris carried the phone to the window. Flames were shooting from the roof of the barn. She forced herself to be calm and give directions to the radio operator, who would notify the volunteer firemen.

"Please hurry," she pleaded before she slammed down the phone.

The horror of it really struck her when she limped out the door. Angry flames leaped from the top of the barn, lighting the sky.

"Oh, my God! The animals!"

As if watching a movie, she saw John racing toward the barn. He opened the door and Arthur shot out. She ran in after John.

"Get out of here!" he shouted.

"The horses—"

"I'll get 'em!"

Iris could hear the whinnies of the frightened animals. Disregarding John's order, she ran down the aisle to Sugar's stall. flung it open, and stepped aside as the horse plunged past her, the colt at her heels. Smoke choked her. Burning embers fell into the corridor. The roaring fire was consuming the hay in the loft.

She knew John had reached the west stalls when a frightened horse charged down the aisle. She flattened herself against the railing so she wouldn't be trampled.

One more. She could hear Buck's piercing shrieks of terror and John's bellows as he tried to turn the crazed animal. She ran to the end of the barn. The smoke was thicker here. John didn't see her. He had pushed open the gate thinking the horse would follow him out.

Buck was rearing in his stall, striking futilely at the bars. The gate had swung in instead of out, and the animal was confused,

"Buck! Buck!" Somehow the horse heard her through his terror and over the roar of the fire. She flung the gate open wide, and he plunged through.

She pulled the collar of her robe over her nose so she could breathe, and felt her way along the stalls to the door. John grabbed her and hauled her outside. Gasping for breath, she barely heard him cursing her.

"Damn you! You scared the hell out of me!" He glared down at her. Light from the flames flickered over his naked chest. "Get that hair under your robe! A spark could land on it!"

There was mass confusion. The horses, hogs, and sheep, all frightened, darted around. Arthur ran and barked at the sows, whose heavy bellies made them flounder as they tried to get away from him. The wind was sending burning embers into the yard, adding to the terror of the animals and people there.

"Are the animals out?" a man called.

Iris blinked, barely able to recognize the speaker as Mr. Downs, whose farm was just down the road. His clothes were muddy from the hog pen, and he'd lost his hat. She couldn't remember ever seeing him without that hat.

"All the animals are out!" John called back, his voice hoarse. "The machinery! Help me get it out of the shed. In this wind everything could go!" He took off at a run. "Get the cars, Iris," he shouted over his shoulder.

Iris ran to the house for the keys. Her ankle throbbed with every step. She backed the pickup out toward the grove and then returned for the Chrysler. The robe flopped around her legs and the naked body beneath it shivered, but not from cold . . . from fear.

All the lights on the farm went out. The flames had reached the fuse box. The area was illuminated now by the fire, and the heat scorched her face. Only then did the enormity of what was happening hit her. The barn! The eighty-year-old barn her grandfather had built and the other buildings, too, were burning!

In all her life, Iris had never felt so helpless. The wind seemed to take vengeance, sending the hungry flames higher, fanning them toward the oak tree that spanned the drive. She paused and stared in numbed disbelief, scarcely noticing the car careening into the yard.

"What can we do?" Young Jerry, a friend of Brenda's, grabbed her arm.

"The tack house!" she gasped. "Brenda's saddle is in the tack house!" Two other boys darted past her. "Be careful," she called. "Jerry, help me get things out of the garage—"

The yard was full of neighbors before the shrill sound of the fire-truck whistle announced its arrival. They were too late! Too late! The thought pounded at Iris as she watched the fire spread to the tack house, the garage, and finally the machine shed, where people were helping John put as many small pieces as they could into the loader on the tractor.

The red light on top of the fire truck spun round and round, giving the area an even more eerie appearance. Most of the people standing on the lawn had coats over nightgowns and pajamas. News of a fire spread fast in this small community, where most people had fire and police radios.

The volunteer firemen attached the hose to the water wagon and turned it on the oak tree. The oak tree! The top was blazing and dropping burning branches onto the roof of the house. Oh, God! No! Iris froze. Then John was shaking her arm.

"Go shut the windows. They'll have to wet down the roof." She stood there. "Iris! Go! The flashlight is on the kitchen counter. And . . . put on some clothes." He pushed her toward the door.

Later Iris was to wonder how she managed to get through the early morning hours. Mr. Downs had spotted the fire at 3:00 A.M. on his way home from Des Moines. Before daylight every building on the farm had burned to the ground, with the exception of the house, and it had suffered roof damage. Iris stood among the lilac bushes that lined the lower drive. Tears streamed down her face. In all her life she'd never known such crushing defeat. Not only was her farm in shambles, but so was her reputation. Unaware that Iris was standing in the shadows, her neighbors gossiped about her. The crowd that gathered to watch the fire was buzzing with the news that Mr. Downs had tried to rouse John Lang, because the lights were on in the trailer house. When that failed he pounded on Iris's door and John came out of the house pulling on his pants. Crude laughter followed the telling of the story.

"Not a very good example to set for Brenda . . . He didn't waste any time. . . . But why should he, when she was here and available? . . . I'm surprised at Iris; I never thought of her as being *that* kind of woman. . . . You can't tell about the cool, silent types. . . . Look at her old man, he took that young girl . . . got her pregnant . . . He married her, though; that's more than this guy'll do. . . . I know his type . . . get it while you can!" Snickers followed the remarks. Iris moved away, blinded by tears, her heart as heavy as lead. Being ridiculed by the people she had known all her life cut her to the quick.

Jane Watts brought Brenda home just as dawn was lighting the eastern sky. "We just heard . . . Jerry called."

Brenda looked with horror at what had happened to her

home. She burst into tears and threw herself into her sister's arms. Iris tried to comfort her, but the sobs issuing from her own throat only made Brenda cry harder. At last, Iris was able to get a grip on her emotions. "Sugar and the colt are fine," she said. "You'll have to round them up today. We just turned them loose. The boys got your saddle out of the tack house, and the spare bridles, too. They even carried out that green wooden chest of yours with the old Civil War stirrup in it." Iris's tears mingled with those of her sister. They clung together. Things they had known and lived with all their lives were gone.

"The rabbits?" Brenda choked, swallowed, and repeated. "Did you get the rabbits out? Are Elizabeth and her babies all right?"

"Mr. Downs opened all the cages. We'll have to hunt for them. They were scared, and heaven knows where they are now."

"How did it happen? What started it?" Brenda asked the question that had plagued Iris throughout the long hours.

"We don't know. The fire chief said it must have started in the loft and ignited the hay. That's the reason it spread so rapidly. The wiring was old, but we've always been careful not to overload the circuits."

The spectators drifted away until only the firemen were left. They sprayed the blackened ruins in shifts. Ruth and Alvin brought coffee and sandwiches and passed them out to the tired men. John stood among them. He'd found time to put on a sweatshirt. He seemed like a stranger to Iris now. She kept thoughts of what had happened between them from her mind and prayed that Brenda wouldn't hear the gossip. If she did, Iris hoped she'd be able to find the words to explain her actions.

The sun came up. For the first time Iris had a view of the fields behind the barn from the kitchen window. The blackened ruins stood out in bold relief. Wisps of smoke still curled up from deep in the bowels of the rubble. The fire trucks went back to town, and Alvin and Ruth departed. Only the fire chief's car remained. He and his assistant were writing on a pad and talking to John. The three men came toward the house, and Iris went out to meet them on the back step.

"It was overloaded wires, Miss Ouverson. There's no doubt about it. That old wiring is dangerous. The wire they put in that barn fifty years ago didn't carry much insulation."

"I knew the wiring was old. Brenda and I never used anything but a forty-watt bulb in the barn." Iris blinked back tears. She couldn't cry in front of these men!

"There was an extension run to the hog house," the chief said, scratching his head with the pencil. "I don't know exactly where it was plugged in."

"I plugged it into the socket that hung down nearest the south window," John said.

"Then that's what did it. I figure the fire started in the loft in the southwest corner."

"I had no idea . . ." John's eyes went from the fireman to Iris's frozen face.

She couldn't utter a word except a muted "thank you" to the fireman when he left.

"Iris . . ."

She stood absolutely still, while all the color drained from her face. Against the pallor, her eyes were dark with hurt.

"If I was responsible, I'm sorry."

She ignored the pleading look in his eyes, while tears welled up in hers. "If? . . " she choked on the word, then turned on her heel and left him.

Her hands gripped the edge of the kitchen sink. Pain knifed through her head and settled behind her eyes. She closed them and rocked back and forth in her misery. She was deep in the pit of despair. Then *his* hands were on her shoulders. She shrugged them off and stood there. Distress made her body wooden. He touched her again.

"Don't!"

"Look at me, for crissake! How do you think I feel?"

"I don't give a damn how you feel! Get away from me. Get out of this house!" A storm of words broke from her lips. "You think you know so much! Did you learn how to burn down my barn in those books? Didn't it occur to you to ask about running the extension? Or to wonder why I didn't burn a light in the hog house?" she added bitterly.

"No, it didn't occur to me. I wouldn't have had this happen for anything. Iris—"

She whirled. Her eyes blazed into his. "Your stupidity has erased forever a landmark that's stood for eighty years. Live with that while you're wondering whether or not to sell that livestock running loose out there because there's nothing to feed them. And what are you going to do for seed corn, Mr. Smart Alec? There isn't enough money in the farm account to buy more."

"What about insurance?"

"What about it? Do you think the policy will build another barn with hand-hewed oak beams? Ha! Maybe the insurance money will cover a prefabricated tin building half the size of our beautiful old barn." Rage and the blinding headache were making her sick to her stomach. "Get out your checkbook, Mr. Moneybags. You've won. It's all yours!"

She brushed past him and headed for the stairs. In her room the tight reins she had held on her facial muscles broke, and she crumpled. She threw herself on the bed and gave way to a flood of tears.

Iris woke to a thousand drums beating in her head. The pain was so intense she couldn't focus her eyes. Her stomach heaved. She staggered to the bathroom and leaned over the commode. Convulsions racked her, leaving her feeling as if her head was being squeezed in a vise. As soon as she could stand, she got the headache pills out of the medicine cabinet, took one with a sip of water, and immediately threw it up. She cried with frustration. Knowing it was useless to try again, she clutched the bottle in her hand and stumbled down the hall. She fell into bed and pulled the covers over her head. She didn't have the strength to lower the shades.

Sometime later she vaguely realized her head was being lifted and a glass was placed to her lips. She swallowed so she would be left alone, and sank again in a sea of pain. Sleep, stirring dreams. Pain and despair beyond tears. Blessed darkness. She floated in black clouds, helpless and lonely. She cried, but there were no tears.

When she awakened, her vision was blurred by pain and exhaustion. It was evening. She didn't know how she knew, but it was. Slowly memory returned, and the sounds recorded in her mind drummed in her ears. The roar of the fire, the siren, the whinnies of the frightened horses, the neighbors' voices. *I didn't know she was that kind of woman.* John was responsible for everything.

She didn't want to get up. Not now. And no more tears. Crying was a foolish waste of energy. She had to think. She turned her head carefully and looked at the ceiling. Pain still throbbed behind her eyes, but she wasn't nauseated. A glass of water and the prescription bottle sat on the night-stand. She took one of the tablets and drank the full glass of water. Nothing seemed important. She lay back and folded her arms over the top of her head. She closed her eyes and drifted to sleep again.

When she opened them, John stood beside the bed look-ing down at her. For a long moment they stared at each other. Smoky gray eyes stared solemnly up at him. The ache in her chest left no room for any feeling for him.

"How do you feel?"

"All right." A kind of brittle calm possessed her.

"Can I get you something? More water?"

"No. You can get out of my room, out of my house."

She rolled her head toward the wall so she wouldn't have to look at him.

"I realize you're depressed over losing the buildings," he said quietly. "But you could've lost more. The house, the machinery."

She turned her head slowly and looked at him with new eyes. He wore a chambray shirt tucked into his jeans, the sleeves rolled up to his elbows. Typical farmer clothing. Somehow they didn't go with the professionally styled haircut and the expensive gold watch strapped to his wrist. He reminded her of a man selling seed corn in a television commercial—a man dressed for the part he was playing, but obviously, so obviously, not of the soil.

Suddenly everything swung into focus. "I'll be downstairs shortly, and we can discuss the sale." Her eyes burned up at him resentfully.

"What sale?"

"Don't play games with me, Mr. Lang. I may have had a blinding headache. but I know perfectly well what I said. You've won! I'll sell our share of the farm to you. But I don't intend to discuss it in the bedroom."

"Then what happened here in this bedroom last night meant nothing?"

She could tell he was angry, but his voice remained calm. "Right. You're stupid if you thought differently."

Rage flashed in his eyes, darkened his face, and hardened the lines of his mouth. "You're the one who's stupid if you can't forgive a human error."

"Some error! You burned down my barn, destroyed what my family and I have worked for all our lives, and you want to chalk it up to a little human error?" She snorted in disgust and raised up in bed so suddenly the pain behind her eyes rocked her. "I should have sold out to you when you first came here. Now I don't suppose you're willing to offer the same price."

"I'm not offering *any* price," he said through clenched teeth.

"I can force you!"

"How? You'll have to put up the money to buy my share before you can force me to buy yours."

Angrily Iris threw back the covers and put her feet on the floor. She still had on her jeans and sweat shirt. "You're lower than I thought!"

"I can get lower!"

"You did. Last night!"

He moved so fast she had no time to move away from him. His hands gripped her shoulders. "Damn you!" he muttered.

"Get your hands off me," she hissed.

He dropped his hands and moved away. "There's an old Chinese proverb that says, 'If you are patient in one moment of anger, you will escape a hundred days of sorrow.' I advise you to remember that."

"You know what you can do with your Chinese proverb."

"I know what I'd like to do to you—shake some sense into that stubborn head of yours!"

"Then you'd better think again!" She stood stock-still, waiting for the dizziness to pass. She didn't care that her hair hung in strings, having come free from the ribbon she'd tied at the nape of her neck, or that her face was swollen. "Brenda and I will move out. *You* can run the farm and send us our share, or the profit, or whatever as I've done for you these past years."

"You and Brenda are staying right here." His voice was deadly calm. "You won't disrupt that girl's life because of your damned stubbornness." His hands on her shoulders gripped her cruelly, and he crushed her to him. "I'm mighty tempted to slap you!"

She believed him and was frightened, but determined not to show it. "And add abuse to your list of little human errors?"

"When I get my hands on you, abuse is the last thing I'm thinking of," he grated out.

She pushed at his chest. "Let me go! I don't want you to touch me ever again. I hate it!"

"You didn't hate it last night."

Shame and anger seared through her. How could he be so vile as to remind her? Instinctively, she felt he was about to kiss her, and desperately and recklessly she tried to defend herself with words. They fell from her lips in a torrent of blatant lies, out of place, wrong, uncharacteristic of her.

"Can you blame me for taking advantage of your expertise? I knew you were an experienced lover, and who better to take my virginity? I've been embarrassed because of it. Many times I'd have gone to bed with someone I cared about, but I didn't want him to know. You served my purpose very well!"

"You're a liar!" he snarled. His hands encircled her upper arms, and her eyes darkened as his fingers hardened like steel bands about her. His face was like a stone statue, hard and bitter. Iris was sure he was going to hit her. Instead his hands slipped up around her throat and his mouth came down on hers savagely, relentlessly, prying her lips apart, grinding his teeth against her mouth. His thumbs beneath her chin held her head immobile. She moaned, and struggled.

He pushed her against the edge of the bed. She fell, and he followed her down. Winded, they lay there breathing hard. His dark red hair shut out everything, and his mouth burned, delved, bruised her now, forcing her to lay still. His hands moved over her, tunneled under the sweat shirt, his fingers finding the high, warm swell of her breasts.

He lifted his head, and she gasped for breath. Her heart hammered so hard that her ears were ringing. She couldn't think. She couldn't speak. He stared at the white skin laid bare by the bunched-up sweat shirt. No bra covered her rounded breasts. He saw for the first time the rosy nipples he had caressed last night. His eyes flickered to her face, and she shook her head in silent protest.

"Be my Iris of last night, darling," he whispered. She heard the words as if mouthed by some distant mythical person. Desperately she fought down the desire to give up, surrender to the yearning building inside her.

"Nooo . . ."

"You know what happened between us was something like . . . like a miracle. To hold you like this—" His strange, thickened voice broke off; his mouth pressed against her throat, then slid up to close over her mouth. He kissed her gently now. Her mouth trembled. The searching movement of his lips parted hers, and he began a sensuous exploration of the inside of her mouth with his tongue.

The coaxing movement of his mouth awakened a strange, melting heat inside her. One of his hands moved back and forth across her breast in a soft, possessive caress. Loving the feel of the new calluses on his palm, she reacted automatically; her nipple became erect and sent messages throughout her body. Wetness sprang between her thighs. The weight of him felt so good! It took every ounce of her self-control to keep from wrapping her arms about him and flying away with him into the sensuous world where there was only his hard male strength to cling to.

"You see how it is with us." He breathed into her mouth, and his body moved urgently against hers.

Abruptly, she went cold, as though he had lifted her out of the depths of sexual chaos. "No," she said tightly. "Get off me!" She twisted out from under him, and he released her.

He sat on the edge of the bed, breathing hard, and watched her pull the sweat shirt down over her naked breasts, grab the headache pills, and head for the door. She turned.

"You've totally disrupted my life and you've destroyed the way of life I've built for Brenda. Don't you think you've done enough?" She saw him flinch as though she had struck him.

As she turned, he said quickly, "I'll admit I may have jarred you out of your humdrum existence, but I've taken nothing from Brenda. And that isn't all—I'm not going to allow you to take anything from her, either."

"I can't believe you'd attempt to control our lives! You're a stranger to us, and I despise everything about you!"

His bright blue eyes mocked her. "You're a liar, Iris," he drawled softly. "Not a word of what you've said is true, and you know it. You're hurt and miserable. I can understand that. But mouthing lies about how you hate me is juvenile, don't you think? We both know it isn't true, don't we?"

She wanted so badly to hit him that her fists curled into tight balls. Only self-respect kept her from hurling the curses that bubbled up within her. She walked down the hall, into the bathroom, and childishly slammed the door. The sound sent vibrations of pain shooting through her head.

"Why don't you slam the door, Iris?" John called from the other side.

Damn him! She looked at the door for a moment, then opened it and gave it another slam. She could hear his light laughter as he walked down the hall.

CHAPTER EIGHT

HER CALM VOICE and placid expression masking the wrenching ache that tore at her heart, Iris managed to get through the days following the fire. Every morning she went to the fields as soon as Brenda was on the school bus. She carried with her a sandwich and a thermos of milk, and she wore her old straw hat. Driving the big green tractor, she circled the fields, pulling the disc, not knowing or caring if anything would be planted there other than a seed crop to hold the soil.

John had told her once again he would not buy her out. If it had not been for Brenda she would have offered the farm to the bank at below market value, but she couldn't do that to her sister. She hadn't approached Brenda about moving to town either, wanting to give her time to recover from one shock before adding another.

The morning the man from the farm store brought the seed corn, Iris was pushed into making a decision on a matter that had floated around in her mind since the fire.

"Mr. Lang paid for it, Miss Ouverson," the man said, and scratched his head in puzzlement.

"I see." She turned and walked to the house.

Iris spent the remainder of the morning sorting through papers in the big rolltop desk in the dining room. Years of old farm reports had been dumped there, as well as personal papers. Everything pertinent to the farm operation, including the farm-account checkbook, was put in a cardboard box. She cleaned out every scrap of paper from the desk before getting out the furniture polish. She'd never seen the desk cleaned out before. It was a comforting task to polish the wood and to clean the brass drawer pulls. When she finished she carefully rolled the top down and left the house.

When she returned to the house in the evening a man with a bulldozer was pushing the debris that had been the machine shed and the garage into a heap. Another man was scooping it up with a loader and dumping it in a truck. Iris left the tractor at the edge of the field and walked to the house.

"I've filled all the water tanks." Brenda had been rather quiet since the fire.

"That's good. I thought we'd stick a couple of frozen dinners in the oven tonight. How does that strike you?"

"We had pot pies last night." Brenda's voice held a whine that irritated Iris, but she tried not to let it show.

"Okay. How about Welsh rarebit? You like that."

"No cheese."

Glory! Where had she heard that before? Then she remembered, and said quickly, "Then back to TV dinners."

"Are you going to fix a snack for them?" Brenda jerked her head toward the yard. "John said they'd work till they've got a place clear for a pole building. The men are coming tomorrow to put it up."

"Oh, really? That's news to me." Resentment rose in waves. "He seems to have things under control. I'm sure that includes a snack for the men."

"Oh, Iris," Brenda wailed.

"I'll get our meal started. I want you to take a box over to Mr. Lang." Iris brought the carton in from the dining room and set it on the kitchen table.

"What'll I say?"

"Nothing. He'll know what it is."

It was done. The management of the farm was in the hands of someone outside the family for the first time in its history. Iris forced her trembling legs to move around the kitchen. She prayed the lead weight in the pit of her stomach would dissolve.

Brenda came in. Iris didn't want to ask, but she did. "What did he say?"

Brenda lifted her shoulders. "Thanks." She slumped in a chair. "What's the matter with you, Iris? You've been a drag ever since the fire. Are you still mad at John? You are, aren't you?"

"Mr. Lang isn't exactly the love of my life." Heavens! Why on earth did she put it that way? A quick glance told her that the remark meant nothing to her sister. "He burned down our barn, honey. He needed only to ask either of us and we'd have told him the reason there was no light in the hog house."

"He didn't mean to."

"I'm sure he didn't, but he did. Now he can manage what's left any way he wants. I've had the responsibility for five years. Let him worry about it for a while." Iris tried to keep the bitterness out of her voice. "I've been meaning to bring something up for days. Do you remember when we talked about moving to town? Would you like to do that this summer? I'm almost sure I can get a teaching job in Central. I hear they'll need an art teacher next year."

"Move? Leave Sugar and Candy?" Misery and shock were etched in Brenda's young face.

"Alvin will board Sugar and Candy. You can come out every Saturday. In another year and a half you'll be driving the car." Please understand, honey, she pleaded silently.

"What about Buck and Boots? And Elizabeth?"

"We couldn't keep Elizabeth in an apartment, but there'd be no problem if we rented a small house." Iris opened the refrigerator. She didn't want to look at Brenda's stricken face. "I was thinking I'd sell Buck and Boots. They're getting old, and I don't ride them very much." She set her lips to keep them from trembling. "Mr. Jenson from the auction company is coming out tomorrow. There's going to be a big horse auction next Friday night." Her voice held a plea for understanding.

Iris didn't want to tell her sister that their insurance wouldn't cover the losses due to the fire and that the farm account was in the red. They would need money to live on until she got a job. They couldn't expect anything from the farm until the crops—if there were crops—were sold in the fall. She was seriously thinking about selling Grandpa's desk and a few other valuables in order to tide them over. But she couldn't have told her sister any of those things, even if she had wanted to, because Brenda burst into tears and hid her face in her folded arms.

"You don't like John! That's why you want to move

away from here." She raised her head to glare at her sister.

"For heaven's sake!" Brenda had been experimenting with mascara! It was streaking down her face. The crazy thought shot through Iris's mind before she spoke. "It's a matter of economics, Brenda," she said patiently, and tried to sniff her own tears away.

"No, it isn't! John bought the seed corn and he's putting up the pole building. He said he'd loan the farm account what it needed."

"When did he say all this?"

"He talks to me lots of times. He'd talk to you, too, if you'd only—"

"Damnation! He'll own our half of the farm, too, before we know it. He isn't doing this out of the goodness of his heart!" Bitterness edged her tone and lined her face.

"Well, I'm not going!"

"Brenda!" Iris looked at the younger girl with amazement. For the first time in her life her little sister had defied her. "This is hard enough without having to fight you, too," she said dejectedly.

"I don't understand why you're so mean to John." Brenda stood up, her eyes flooded with tears. "If you hate him so much, what was he doing here the night the barn burned?"

It seemed to Iris that her heart fell down through her stomach to her toes. "What do you mean?"

"He was in the house at three o'clock in the morning. Everyone knows that. Iris . . ." Brenda threw her arms around her sister's waist and buried her face in her shoulder. "What do we care what anyone else thinks? If you went to bed with John, it's all right with me."

"Oh, Brenda!" If her sister had suddenly sprouted horns, Iris couldn't have been more shocked. For a long moment she couldn't move, couldn't speak. She could feel her mouth hanging slack and her knees trembling. How could she preach to Brenda about morality when she . . . "Have you been embarrassed by the talk?" she asked quietly.

"No. Some of the kids think it's neat." Her face was streaked with tears and mascara, her lashes spikey. She looked very young. "John will marry you, if you ask him."

"I wouldn't think of such a thing!" Iris's hands gripped her sister's shoulders. "And you put that thought out of your mind. We'll manage. We always have."

"Let's stay here, Iris. Pl-eee-ze!"

"I can't make any promises, honey. You'll just have to trust me to do what I think is best for us. C'mon. Let's eat. Tell me about your day. Have you finished your math tests?"

Iris had never felt so defeated. How could things have gone so wrong in such a short span of time?

The man from the auction barn drove up the lane the next morning just as the school bus arrived. Iris cursed his timing and hoped Brenda didn't realize who he was. Her sister had said scarcely a word to her this morning and had only grunted a reply when she called out, "Have a good day."

Iris sighed and pulled her floppy straw hat down on her

head. She wanted to reach Mr. Jenson before he joined the crew unloading the material for the pole building.

She was too late. He was standing beside John when she went out the door. Damn! Adding to her irritation, John walked with him to the back steps, where she stood,

"'Morning, Mr. Jenson. Thank you for coming on such short notice."

"I want to talk to you for a moment, Iris," John said. "Will you excuse us for a moment, Mr. Jenson?"

Iris didn't look at John, but she knew from the sound of his clipped voice that he was angry.

"Sure. I'll just amble over and talk to the boys. T'was a shame about the fire. Miss Ouverson. It don't look like the same place without the barn."

"It doesn't seem like the same place, either," she said woodenly.

"What's he doing here?" John demanded as soon as the man was out of hearing distance.

"I'm not selling anything that belongs to you, if that's what you're worrying about," she snapped.

"You're not selling anything to him, period. I'm not stupid. He's a horse buyer, isn't he?"

"If you're not stupid, it's the first I've heard about it. Kindly tend to your own business."

"You are my business, you stubborn little fool!" he said tightly. His lips seemed to spit out the words. He stood with his hands in his pockets and glared at her. Abruptly he turned on his heel. "C'mon. I want to know where you think we should put the· building. It'll be ten feet longer and five feet deeper than the old one." He moved away as if she were going with him. She didn't move. He stopped and spun around. "Damn you! Do you want those men to go back to town with more gossip?"

"I couldn't care less what they take back to town. I'm no more than a whore in their eyes as it is! Put your damn building wherever you want. Preferably—"

"Shut up! I'll not stand for guttersnipe talk from you! All right? I'll put the building where I think it should be, which is twenty feet back from where the old shed stood. I don't want to hear you bitching about it later. Understand?"

"I understand more than you think, Mr. Lang. I'll do my share of the work, but when the crops are in, it's all yours. Got it?" She spat out the words in the same tone he'd used. Her head was raised so she could see him from beneath the brim of the floppy hat. Their eyes battled.

"You don't have as much horse sense in that beautiful head of yours as a . . . flea. You could learn a few things from your sister, you muleheaded little—" He seemed to catch himself just in time, and bit off the words. "I'm warning you, Iris." His finger came up under her nose, his voice more deadly because it was scarcely more than a whisper. "Don't try to take that girl away from here because you've got a hate on for me. This is her home, her security. I'll fight you every step of the way if you try it."

"You'll have to, because it'll be 'damn the torpedos and full speed ahead' when I decide what's right for us!"

"And you'll get blown right out of the water, little tug." A grin started in his eyes and spread to the rest of his face.

Iris snapped her teeth together in frustration, gave him a look that would have wilted a corn stalk, and headed for the pasture where the horses were kept. She knew she was being rude to Mr. Jenson by not calling out to him, but she was having enough trouble with the knot in her stomach and needed a few minutes alone.

Every encounter with John left her more shaken than the one before. Iris hoped the walk to the pasture would give her time to get her emotions under control. It did help. Buck and Boots came to meet her. She snapped the lead ropes to their halters, and they followed along behind her. Buck nudged her shoulder affectionately, and she had to swallow repeatedly the lumps that came up in her throat.

The horse buyer was waiting at the water tank. His experienced eyes flashed over Buck and on to Boots. He moved his hands over the black coat and gently pulled out tufts of hair.

"Shedding his winter coat," he murmured as if talking to himself. He ran his hand down the front leg and picked up the foot. "Hooves are in good shape." Boots stood obediently while the man looked in his mouth. "Nine or ten?"

"Eight. He was born here on the place."

"Ain't he the one that'll stand on the box like the Indian in the picture? *End of the Trail*, or something like that?"

"Yes, he'll do that. I've taught him several tricks."

She picked up a little stick and tapped the horse on the front legs. "Kneel down, Boots. C'mon, kneel down so I can get on." The horse tossed his head, then bent his front legs and settled heavily to the ground. Iris flung her leg over his back, and he got to his feet. "Good boy." She patted his neck. "I used to ride him while standing on his rump, but I haven't done that for a long time."

"We won't have no trouble gettin' a good price for him

if you'll go in the ring and show him off." He took his hat off and waved it. "Ain't neither one of 'em spooky."

"They've been handled a lot," Iris said lamely, and slid off Boots's back.

"I don't know about the other'n. He's got to be twenty if he's a day."

"He's eighteen. My dad bought him for me when he was about a year old. His mother had been killed by lightning."

"I don't know," he repeated, and ran his hands down the hind legs. Buck didn't like the touch, and laid his ears back. "Stiff in the hind quarters. I spotted that when he came in. Well, we can get somethin' for him. He's gentle. Someone may want him for a kid. Tell you what. Brush 'em up good. Get as much of that winter hair off as you can. You could even shine 'em up a little with some oil. We'll sell 'em. Ain't no doubt 'bout that." He screwed his hat down on his head. "I gotta be making tracks. Got more calls to make."

"Thank you."

"If ya ain't got no way to haul 'em, I can send the truck out and take the charge out of the sale price."

"All right. Friday morning?"

"Friday, before noon."

Iris managed to hold back the tears until the man was behind the trees and out of sight. Then she turned and put her arms around the neck of the big buckskin horse that had been hers since she was fourteen. Sobs shook her slender frame.

"'I'm sorry, Buck. I'm sorry!" Her voice was a pathetic croak. She buried her face in his dusty mane and cried as she hadn't done since she was a child.

Buck tossed his head and then stood perfectly still. Events flashed before Iris's eyes one after the other. Buck following her around the farm, more like a puppy than a horse; astride his back, racing through the fields with her thin legs clamped to his heaving sides, because she seldom took the time to put on a saddle; Buck standing quietly with his feet tangled in the barbed wire and her lying at his feet. Any other horse would have become frantic and kicked her. She would have been seriously injured or killed. She remembered now how proud she was to ride him in the Fourth of July parade, and one year had led the parade carrying the flag.

"Oh, Buck! Will you ever forgive me? What will become of you and Boots? Will some thoughtless kid run you until you're so stiff you can't walk? Will you be homesick for the pasture you've always known?" Tears streamed down her face like summer rain, and racking sobs shook her shoulders.

The horse bobbed his head and made a blowing sound with his lips, as if he understood.

Iris was so steeped in her misery that at first she didn't feel the hand on her back. When she did, she looked over her shoulder into John's face. Although her eyes were clouded with tears she could see that his were, too.

"Iris . . . sweetheart . . . don't—" He blinked rapidly. "I'm not going to let you do this." His voice quivered. It didn't sound like his voice at all. His hand moved over her back in a comforting circular motion. Just for an instant she almost yielded to the temptation to throw herself in his arms.

It was impossible that those tears stood on his thick, stubby lashes. No, it wasn't. He was feeling sorry for her!

Pity! It was more demoralizing than if he had been angry with her. She broke and ran as if the devil himself were after her.

"Iris . . ." His call floated after her, but she didn't stop until she reached the house. She caught her breath and sped up the steps to the bathroom and yanked the headache pills out of the cabinet.

After she gulped down a couple of tablets, she bathed her face and sat down on the edge of the tub. It took several minutes for her to realize that it would be easier to get herself back together if she were out in the field, where there was nothing but the tractor noise to disturb her thoughts.

She crammed the floppy hat down on her head. Then her long legs took the stairs two at a time. She sped through the dining room. In the kitchen she ran up against a wall of solid flesh and muscle. John had stepped from the side of the door to block her way. He had to fasten his hands to her shoulders to keep her from falling.

"You're getting another headache. That's two in a week."

"It isn't *your* head," she said belligerently.

"Don't go to the field today. We're not that far behind with the work. I've got young Jerry coming to help on the weekend."

She shrugged his hands from her shoulders. "Good for you. I hope you can afford it," she said sarcastically.

"I'm going to pay his father by overhauling one of his tractor engines after the planting season."

"Good for you," she repeated, and moved to go around him, then stopped. "Didn't you learn in the Navy you're supposed to knock before entering private quarters?"

"Attack is the best defense, huh? It won't work, Iris." He moved quickly for a large man. His body blocked the doorway. "I told Jenson the horses were not for sale."

Iris gaped at him. Her mouth opened, then snapped shut. "They're not your horses!"

"If you don't want them, I'll pay you for them. What do you want?"

"Five hundred dollars each," she shouted. The price was ridiculous, and she expected to see astonishment on his face.

"Sold!"

"No!"

"The horses are not leaving this farm." He spaced each word to give them all emphasis. "You can be as stubborn and as bullheaded as you want, Iris. But I'm telling you— those horses are not leaving this farm!" He was angry, very angry, so angry that a dull red covered his face and he clenched and unclenched his hands in an effort to keep them off her. "Buck has been here all his life. I remember seeing you ride him when you were no older than Brenda. He knows every foot of that pasture. He'd die of a broken heart if he were taken to a strange place. Do you want to see him pulling a trash wagon? Or ground up for dog meat? I'd rather take my rifle out there and shoot him!"

"You wouldn't be so cruel!"

"It would be a kindness compared to what could happen to him." Under heavy, slanting brows his gaze pinned her. "What's the matter with you, for God's sake? You're making Brenda's life miserable, my life a living hell, and you're not happy with yourself. Is it because I was caught in your house when the fire broke out and the old gossips are having a field day? We can fix that. We can get married and everyone will think you're wonderful again."

His bitter, shocking words rocked her. Blood drained from her face, and her heartbeat slowed to a dull thud.

"That's very kind of you." She spoke softly. Her bitter gaze seemed glued to his face, while the tip of her tongue came out and moistened her lips. "Thank you very much, but I must decline your generous offer to save my reputation."

"Good. I don't want you pushed into marrying me for any reason except the right one."

"And that is?" Her throat was so tight the words were difficult to get out.

"Love. I'll spell it out for you. L-O-V-E. I'll marry you if you love me and want to live with me, here, for the rest of your life. And because you want to share my dreams, my problems, raise my children, be my companion when we are old." His eyes raked over her and then rested on her trembling lips.

"Is that all?" she asked politely.

"No. I want you to want me every night of my life as you did the other night. I want you to give yourself to me, laugh, play, let the real Iris break through that cocoon you've built around yourself. You're as beautiful as a butterfly, but you act like an angry hornet!"

"I thank you again for the compliments. Now, as for an answer to your proposal, if it was one—it'll be a cold day in hell when I meet those qualifications. So, if you'll stand aside, I've work to do."

"Not yet. Isn't it customary to feed workers if they're here at mealtime?"

"Yes, it is. What do you plan to feed yours? I must

warn you, men doing hard work have large appetites."
She did her best to return his gaze coolly.

"You're not going to cooperate." The statement was
soft, menacing.

"Absolutely not! Take them to a restaurant. That
should put a sizeable dent in your pocketbook." She tried
to slip through the door.

"Hold it!" The words were as sharp as a pistol shot and
frightened her into pausing. He was beside her in an instant, and his hands closed around her upper arms. She
winced at the tightness with which he held her.

"There's a limit to how far you can push me, Iris."

"There's a limit to how far you can push me, too. I've
given you control of everything. You're the big *honcho*
now. But I won't be your hired hand."

He yanked her to him, lowered his head, and kissed
her bitterly, then pressed more hard, unloving kisses on
her mouth that took her breath from her. She struggled
without success and finally surrendered to his superior
strength. At last he lifted his head. His arms held her so
tightly she thought she would faint and her blood
pounded in her temples.

"I want you in my life. I want you in my bed. And . . .
hell! I want you, period!" He grabbed her hips and pulled
her even tighter against the aching hardness that throbbed
between them. "You've done that to me. You do it almost
every time I'm with you. I'm as horny as a stallion!
Dammit, I'll put up with it for a while. Then, you obsti-
nate little cuss, you'll get yours!"

"Don't you threaten me, you . . . you woodpecker!"

He raked his scorching eyes over each feature of her

face, then he laughed, a deep masculine laugh. "Iris, give up. You won't be able to hold out against me."

Her straw hat had fallen off during the attempt to avoid his kiss. She stood quietly, refusing to humiliate herself further by struggling. He held her tightly to him with an arm across her lower back while his other hand grasped the thick blond braid and brought it over her shoulder. He brushed his face with the bushy end. His eyes were full of laughter. He slid the stubby end of the braid back and forth across his lips while his eyes held hers. Then, playfully, he tickled her nose with it. She tossed her head but refused to speak.

"It's almost as much fun to tease you as it is to make love to you." He tugged on the braid, pulling her face closer, and kissed her on the nose. Pride kept her rigid. "C'mon, honey. Melt just a little and kiss me back."

Fighting the temptation to yield to the persuasive voice and gentle, coaxing lips, Iris squeezed her eyelids tightly together and tried desperately not to think about how warm and comforting it was to be held by John. She was concentrating so hard that his hand moved down her back, his long fingers delved beneath the elasticized back of her jeans and her thin panties, slid over and cupped the fullness of her rounded naked bottom. before she came out of her trance.

"What the—? Get your sneaky hand out of there!" she demanded. She pushed on his chest with all her strength. The arm across her shoulders tightened, the fingers in her jeans pinched her bottom. She let out an incredulous gasp. "Stop that!"

"Not until you kiss me." Laughter lines crinkled the

corners of his eyes, and his lips were spread in a wide grin.

Helpless against his strength, Iris considered kicking him, biting him, but decided capitulation was her only recourse. Hating herself for doing it, she kissed him lightly on the lips. then moved her face as far back as his hold on her would allow.

"Un-uh! Won't do. Put your arms around my neck and kiss me like I know you can." His voice was intimate, stirring little waves of response along her spine. His fingers caressed her flesh and traced gently down the valley between her buttocks.

Her arms moved up and around his neck, and she placed her lips on his. She heard the low triumphant sound that came from his throat. acknowledging her defeat, but she didn't care. When he lifted his lips to demand that she open her mouth, she obeyed without hesitation. With erotic symbolism, his tongue rubbed against her smooth, even teeth, and the hand in her jeans caressed her bottom. Iris felt a sudden rip in the fabric of her resentment that had so tenuously protected her from John. Swamped by mounting desire, it became impossible to remain passive. Every cell in her body surged to life, blocking out everything except the torch of his mouth that inflamed her.

A sharp rap on the door behind her brought Iris slowly out of the haze and into the present. Her mind was foggy. John raised his mouth, and she glanced over her shoulder to the woman standing on the other side of the screened door, her face a mask of shocked disapproval.

"Hello," John said, as if it were the most normal thing in the world to greet a visitor while holding her to him with one hand, the other out of sight in her jeans. "Honey, we have company." Without haste he removed his hand and tucked her shirt back into the waistband.

Stunned into silence, Iris could only stare at the visitor. Seemingly undaunted, John stepped to the door and opened it. "Come in. I'm John Lang."

Bristling with indignation, the woman swept by him and came into the kitchen. Iris felt as if she were a puppet being jerked into speaking by the pull of a string.

"Agnes Kratz," she said lamely by way of introduction.

"Stanley's mother?" John asked pleasantly, and held out his hand. Reluctantly the woman put hers into it. "You'll have to excuse me, Mrs. Kratz. I just came in to tell Iris we'll be having guests for lunch." His smile was truly charming. "There'll be three counting me, honey," he said to Iris. He lifted his hand in a gesture of farewell and went out the door.

CHAPTER NINE

"I NEVER, FOR one minute, believed the talk going around about you and *that* man." Uninvited, Agnes sank down onto a kitchen chair as if what she'd witnessed had taken the strength out of her sturdy body.

I bet! Iris thought, and felt the hairs on her scalp leap to alert, warning her to hold onto her temper. "You should have believed it, Agnes. It's true."

"Iris! Don't be crude, dear. I've known you long enough to know you're putting up a brave front." She smoothed the cloth on the table with a patronizing gesture. "Oh, Iris, Iris, Iris. Your daddy would turn over in his grave if he could see the state this farm is in."

"Do you *really* think so, Agnes?"

"Yes, I do. And what's more, we've got to do something about *that* man."

Iris stood with her hands on her hips, looking at Agnes. She noted her greasy, graying hair, her pallid complexion, her narrowed eyes, her pursed lips, the righteous shake of her head.

"What do you suggest, Agnes? Poison? Shotgun? Steel trap?"

"Dear, we can pray for the Lord to deliver you out of his clutches."

Iris blinked slowly and tried not to smile. "Do you mind if we peel potatoes while we're doing it? I've hungry men to feed at noon."

"Not at all. Let me do that while you do something else. Busy hands, you know, makes talking easier."

Iris brought a sack of potatoes, a pan, and a peeler and plunked them down on the table, wishing she had the nerve to hook the chair out from under her visitor's fat bottom when she lifted and turned it to face the table. Instead she took vengeance on the round steak she took from the refrigerator and pounded it vigorously with the meat tenderizer. She floured it and put it in the electric skillet, only half listening to the drone of Agnes's voice.

"Surely you know that, dear."

"Know what?"

"Oh, I'm sorry. You couldn't hear me over the pounding. I said, he isn't good enough for a sweet girl like you."

"Who?" She knew who! Damned old busybody wasn't going to give up until she'd said everything she came to say.

"Old Mrs. Lang's grandson. You know his father didn't amount to anything. I can't imagine why your daddy sold to them. Me and Stanley would've been glad to buy in. Well, all is not lost, dear. This farm can be divided. Me and Stanley was looking at the plat book. The drainage ditch runs right down through the middle."

"You and Stanley have given this a lot of thought,

haven't you?" Iris said pleasantly, proud of her self-control, though she was seething.

"Yes, dear. Is this enough potatoes? Now, if you're going to mash them you'll need a few more. I suggest you leave them in large pieces so they won't cook away."

"That will be fine. Thank you." Iris grabbed up the pan and dumped the peeled potatoes in the sink.

Agnes sighed. "It's so nice to be working with another woman. I've always thought of you as my own, ever since you were a little girl."

"Excuse me. I've got to get a couple of pies out of the freezer on the porch." Iris wanted to laugh and she wanted to scream, but most of all she wanted to run John Lang's body through the hay baler for getting her into this bizarre situation.

"You can't imagine what it does to me, seeing that trailer in your grove, knowing that you and that sweet child are here alone, at the mercy of that man. He's too worldly for a woman like you." Agnes continued when Iris returned.

Iris slid the pies in the oven and closed the door with a bang. "And what kind of woman am I, Agnes?" she asked loudly, indignantly, responding without thinking.

"Why . . . a good woman! Whatever did you imagine I meant? You've got a college education, you're a good worker. You shouldn't waste yourself on a no-good. You owe it to yourself and your sister to stay with your own kind."

"Like you and Stanley?" Oh, God, forgive me, Iris prayed silently, but I hate Agnes so much I may be sick!

"Yes, like me and Stanley. We both love you, and we'd take that orphan child and raise her like our own."

Iris checked a gasp. "Big of you," she muttered.

"God loves even a sinful woman, dear. You need only to confess your sins."

"Let's leave the Lord out of this, Agnes," Iris said flatly. "Did Stanley send you over here to propose to me?" Her patience was wearing thin, and she was tired of playing the game. She wondered what in the world she could say that would shock the pants off this woman.

"He wants you badly." Agnes lowered her voice. "Always has."

"He wants the farm," Iris said bluntly, and reached for a stack of plates. "I've only got half a farm, with no barn or other buildings."

"You've got the land, dear. With Stanley's machinery it would—" Agnes broke off and fidgeted with the buttons on her smock.

And, suddenly, just the "shocker" she wanted came to mind. "It's too late," Iris said, mock sadness coloring her voice. "I couldn't expect you and Stanley to take me in and take care of me in my condition. And there's my sister, and later . . . No. All three of us can't move in on you. It's too much to ask." She heard Agnes gasping while she calmly counted out the pieces of silverware and laid them carefully on the stacked plates.

"You mean you're preg-preg-nant?"

"Agnes, do you mind if I move your purse so I can put a clean cloth on the table?" She shot a quick glance at the shocked, reddened face when she handed her the heavy bag. That's a good bit of juicy news for you to carry to the neighbors, she thought viciously. They'll love it. They already think this is the biggest little whorehouse in Iowa! Bitchiness prodded her to add a little more oil to the fire.

"I appreciate your understanding, Agnes. You can be sure that I'll let everyone know that my dearest friend hasn't condemned me for my . . . ah . . . transgression. And that she'll stand by me."

Agnes shifted from one foot to the other. "Oh, dear! It's almost noon. I must be going. Stanley brought some baby chicks home. You know how I love baby chicks. I've got to see about them."

Iris smiled sweetly. "I understand. I'm sorry you have to rush off. Come back any time, Agnes."

As soon as Agnes was out the door, Iris giggled, suddenly feeling better. Phew, she'd really done it this time. She didn't give a damn now, but later she knew she might be sick. She listened to the car shoot off down the drive and decided she didn't need a headache pill after all.

A little later she did.

It wore on her nerves that she had been coerced into preparing the meal. Dammit! She should be outside. The day was beautiful, the air fresh and sweet-smelling. Her resentment grew. She wondered if she would ever know a carefree, happy day again, and if the time would ever come when she didn't have the feeling the world was cockeyed.

She lifted the lid on the skillet and sniffed the delicious aroma coming from the simmering steak. She heard soft footsteps and knew that John had come into the kitchen. She dropped the lid onto the pan with a clatter, swiveled to the sink, and began to break the lettuce into bite-sized chunks. Iris felt his chest press against her back, and bent at the waist to push him away from her. She knew instantly it was the wrong thing to do.

"Mmmm . . . I like that." His voice was barely a

whisper in her ear. He moved closer, and his thighs rubbed against the back of her legs and hips. His arms came around her, and his hands cupped her breasts. "No bra. I like that, too!"

"Get away from me, you . . . you wart!" With all her strength she jabbed her elbow back against his midsection. His quick expulsion of breath told her the blow had landed.

"I'll get you for that," he murmured, and moved away as the back door opened.

"Something smells mighty good."

"Hello, Mr. Olson, Mr. Volk. You can clean up in the washroom. Go through the door on your right."

Iris dished up the meal, all the time aware that John's eyes were on her. She skirted around him on her trips to the table, fuming at the looks he gave her.

"Everything is ready except the salad," she said to the men when they returned from the washroom. "I've got to add the tomatoes. Go ahead and start."

"Need any help, honey?" John smiled tauntingly, knowing the endearment irritated her.

"No. But thank you for your offer, Mr. Lang." She swore she was going to kill him the minute they were alone!

Iris washed and quartered some tomatoes and placed the wedges on the beds of lettuce in individual salad bowls. A movement on the edge of the sink caught her eyes. A small green worm humped its back as it traveled along. How did you miss being washed down the drain? she asked it silently. She delivered two bowls of salad and returned for the others. The little worm was still there.

A bright little red devil with a pitchfork in its hand

danced before her eyes, causing her lips to tilt at the corners. *Oh, yes! I will!* With the tip of a knife she scooped up the little worm, lifted a lettuce leaf, and dropped it in the salad bowl. And with an enormous amount of satisfaction she set the bowl beside John's plate.

The lunch conversation drifted easily into shop talk as the men discussed the merits of the different types of sheds they had erected. John carried the burden of the conversation very handily. His intelligent blue eyes honed in on each man as he spoke, making him feel as if he were drinking in his each and every word. He asked questions, recognizing their superior knowledge of their craft, and skillfully drew them out, doing more listening than talking.

They were flattered, Iris realized as she listened. *They'll leave here thinking he's the greatest thing since sliced bread!*

She watched as he stabbed his fork into his salad and lifted it to his mouth. Suddenly it occurred to her that the worm might crawl out of the bowl and inch its way across the table. *Heaven forbid that that should happen!*

The jangle of the telephone made her start visibly.

"Are you nervous today, honey?" John favored her with a grin. His hand found her knee beneath the table.

Iris ground her teeth. "Excuse me," she said tightly. She turned her back to the table when she answered the telephone.

"Hi, Iris. Mike Dalburg. How ya doin'?"

"Fine, Mike. You?"

"Doin' good. Say, would you like to go over to Brisson to the Buddy Holly Music Festival Saturday night? There'll be a couple of bands playing his music. Even some of the musicians who played in his band will be there."

"Who's going, Mike?"

"There'll be a party from the school. Donaldson and his wife will be there. They're back together, you know."

"I'm glad to hear it."

"Well . . . wha'd'ya say?"

The silence at the table behind her goaded her to reply, "It sounds like fun, Mike. What time?"

"How about eight o'clock?" he asked on a lilting note.

"Eight o'clock is fine. See you then. 'Bye."

Iris hung up the phone and swiveled. In her peripheral vision she saw John's face turned toward her. She couldn't have kept her eyes from going to his if her life had depended on it. Her mouth went dry as their eyes locked. The censorious look he leveled at her was ripe with anger. In spite of the steeliness of his gaze she allowed hers to look slightly amused, and sat down at the table once again.

"Who was on the phone?" he asked bluntly.

"A friend of mine, the Science teacher at the high school." She cursed him silently—*Oh, damn you, damn you! I'd never have said I'd go out with that Lothario if it hadn't of been for you!* Aloud she asked brightly, "Is everyone ready for pie?"

Iris stood up and began to remove the plates. Mr. Olson set his salad bowl on his plate and handed it to her. John did the same. She didn't dare look in the bowl immediately, but she did peek into it on the way to the sink. There wasn't even a piece of a lettuce leaf for a worm to hide under. Ah-ha, she thought happily.

It was hard to keep the smirk off her face when she returned to the table. She picked up the bowl with her own half-eaten salad—and sucked in her breath sharply. Humping its small body along the edge of a tomato wedge was the little green worm. Clenching her jaws together and forcing her lids to shutter her eyes, she turned from the table, only to be halted by John's softly spoken words.

"Sit down and eat your salad. We can wait for the pie."

Her eyes flew to his face. She felt the red coming up in hers and fought it down with all the self-control she could command on such short notice. His pointed smile told her that he *knew!*

Iris dished up the pie and served it, but she didn't return to the table. The conversation switched to the grain embargo, and the room was awash with voices. She seriously considered leaving the kitchen—going out to the field, to her bedroom, or locking herself in the bathroom. Instead she filled the sink with soapy water and began the cleanup.

The men continued to chat about the weather, crops, farm subsidies. As her morale deteriorated further, Iris began to think anew of escape. However, before she could formulate a plan, it was too late. Chairs were being pushed away from the table. The men joshed about being so full they needed a nap before they could go back to work. Individually they thanked her for the meal and left. It was too much to hope John would go with them . . . and he didn't.

"It was a good meal." He flashed her a devastating grin as he leaned against the counter. "Especially the salad."

"Thank you," she said with a formal politeness that didn't quite come off.

"You do everything well." He moved a step closer. "But . . . you're sneaky."

"Aren't we all?"

"Sweetheart, I've picked cockroaches out of a sandwich in Manila, ants out of pudding in Africa, grasshoppers out of stew in Brazil. It was no chore at all to spot that worm in my salad."

"Interesting. You can tell me your heartrending experiences another time."

"At first I thought it was an accident, but your face gave you away. You'd make a lousy poker player." A step, a turn, and he was behind her. Arms on each side of her, his body pinned her to the counter. Her head came up with a jerk. He was laughing softly. She could feel it vibrate in his chest, pressed to her back. The sound increased, then rumbled out of him until it was a deep, honest belly laugh he couldn't seem to control.

Iris stiffened her body and tried to lift her arms to push him away, but his had locked around her, and she was helpless.

"That's two things you've got to pay for," he whispered. "One for the jab in the gut before lunch and one for the worm." He nuzzled the back of her neck under her braid. The tip of his tongue explored the velvet-smooth skin behind her ear. "I always collect," he threatened softly. His hands cupped her breasts, his thumbs stroked her nipples.

Iris seethed in righteous anger, knowing she was in a classic no-win situation. Nevertheless, she had to try.

"Get your hands off me, you woodpecker, or I'll scream!"

"Oh, sweetheart! Life with you will never be dull!" He

was laughing again. "You're a lot of things, but boring isn't one of them." With a quick kiss on the side of her face he walked away, still chuckling.

Completely unnerved, her heart pounding with a mixture of frustration and desire, she heard the door slam and Arthur bark a joyous greeting. She directed her anger toward the dog.

"You worthless hound. You don't have a drop of loyal blood in your body!"

It was dusk when Iris drove the tractor to the edge of the field and parked it. She sat for a long moment, her arms folded over the wheel, and looked at the new profile of the homestead. The pole building, with its yawning open front, was finished, and John was stacking the leftover building materials. Begrudgingly, she admitted he had placed it in a more desirable location than the old shed had been. Not that she'd ever tell him so, she fumed silently, and climbed down off the machine. She walked quickly toward the house, vowing she wouldn't stop even if he did call out to her.

Iris had spent the afternoon deep in thought, trying to put her priorities in order. The one thing that was uppermost in her mind was Brenda's welfare. The next few years would be important, formative years in her sister's life. She must have the security of a stable home. This would help her through the tempestuous time of change from child to womanhood. Iris had come to the conclusion that she couldn't jeopardize the things Brenda needed because she was so deeply unhappy herself. They would stay here in the farmhouse, but as soon as the crops were in she was going to make finding a job her number-two priority.

Arthur ran to meet her when she came into the kitchen. He stiffened his legs and slid across the tile floor, crashing into a chair. After he righted himself, he barked a greeting.

"Oh, Arthur," Iris said tiredly. "You are absolutely the hairiest dog in the world. Brenda!"

"Hi. I've got supper ready." Brenda was in a good mood. She had smiles all over her face.

"Honey, you haven't brushed Arthur. Hair is coming off him in patches. If we had a spinning wheel we could go into the dog-yarn business."

"I'll brush him tomorrow. I promise." Brenda launched herself at her sister like a missile. "John said you're not going to sell Buck and Boots. He said there was money in the bank for us to draw on until the crops were sold." She wrapped her arms around Iris's waist and tried to lift her off the floor. "When I saw the sale-barn truck drive in this morning I almost got off the bus. I worried all day! I love you, Iris, sister, jailer, and slave driver. When I get out of school I'm going to work and take care of you. 'Course . . . you could marry John, and I wouldn't have to." She ended on a hopeful note.

"I love you, too, honey." Iris hugged her, ignoring the last remark. "I don't know what I'd do without you. I want you to have the very best education we can get for you, which means, exuberant miss, you've got to keep those grades up so we can apply for a scholarship."

"I will, Iris. I'd do anything for you."

"Oh? . . ." Iris drew back and grinned at her. "How about cleaning the bathroom after supper?"

"Bathroom? Aw, Iris . . . I've got homework"

Iris laughed aloud for the first time that day. Brenda had a way of putting things on an even keel.

Brenda lay on the bed with a pained look on her face. "What'er'ya goin' out with o' Dalburg for? All he wants is sex!"

The look Iris gave her was a mixture of frustration and surprise. "How do you know that, Miss Know-it-all?"

"He's always hugging up to ol' lady Hanley when he thinks no one's looking. Ardith saw him put his hand on her bottom."

"Ardith's good at stretching things. You told me that yourself." Iris tch-tch'ed at her sister and began flipping through the hangers in her closet. "What do you think of this?" She pulled out a fuchsia-red dress. She liked the color, but not the neckline, a shallow vee in both front and back.

"It's too bright. You'd look like a streetwalker." Brenda watched her sister slap the hook back on the rod with more force than necessary. "I'm not blind, you know. I watch *Vice Squad*, and all that."

"I'm not blind, either, sweetie. Get your feet off my bedspread." Iris was looking at a terra cotta cotton dress with a high neck and full sleeves.

"I like that."

Iris hung it back. "What are you trying to do? Sabotage my date?"

"You're going to need all the help you can get," Brenda advised. "You said when you went out with him before he had more hands than a centipede had legs."

"Maybe you're right." Iris took the dress out again and hung it on the hook on the door. She wasn't looking forward to the date. She'd had a set-to with Brenda, who'd wanted to stay at home alone. Her argument was that John would be nearby. It was finally settled when Iris called Jane Watts and asked if Brenda could spend the night. It was a trade-off. Stacy had spent several weekends at the farm while Jane accompanied her husband on business trips.

Iris lay back in the tub of warm suds and hoped the evening would go fast. She'd castigated herself time and again for agreeing to go. Brenda was more right about Mike than she realized. And Iris wasn't looking forward to his suggestive remarks and his dirty jokes.

Dreamily, she wondered how it would feel to be dressing to go out with a man you really cared about. Strange, she thought. I've been to bed with John, but I haven't been out to dinner with him, or to a show. It was still hard for her to believe the intimacy they'd shared. Now it seemed to her it was something she had dreamed, a very pleasant, wonderful dream—seeking male hands caressing her. Hard, warm naked flesh against hers, husky whispers, followed by seeking lips . . .

CHAPTER TEN

IRIS WAS GLAD Mike Dalburg had a talent for small talk even though his remarks were almost always preceded by the words *I, I'm,* or *I've.* It made the thirty-mile drive to Brisson endurable, if not enjoyable. All she had to do was add an occasional "oh, really" or "how nice." It was enough to keep him going. He had made his move as soon as Brenda got out of the car in front of her friend's house. Mike had put his hand on her thigh to keep her from moving over. He was the kind of man who would have loved to have the reputation of a superstud. Iris had firmly removed his hand, slid across the seat, and huddled next to the door.

It was all John's fault that she was out with this aging Don Juan. No, she had to admit, it wasn't anyone's fault but her own. She'd been so rattled by John that she'd actually thought she was getting back at him by accepting this date with Mike.

Mike parked the car and turned in the seat to smile at her. His perfectly capped teeth looked as if they could be used in a commercial. *Drop a tablet in a glass of water, folks, and soak your teeth until the water clears.* He was combing more hair forward now to cover his receding hairline. She wondered what he used on his moustache to make it so startlingly black. Was it hair dye, eyebrow pencil, or mascara? She hid a giggle behind a cough, then smiled at him. It wasn't his fault that for the rest of her life she would compare every man she met with a tall, broad-shouldered, blue-eyed, redheaded woodpecker, who could hypnotize her with his wide, cheek-slashing grin.

Nostalgia gripped Iris when they entered the dim ballroom. Couples were dancing to *Peggy Sue.* It brought back memories of other times she had been here, hundreds of years ago, it seemed, before responsibility for her sister and the farm had sapped her youth. She let Mike guide her to a crescent-shaped booth where Jim Donaldson and his wife, recently reunited, were sitting.

"Hello, Carol, Jim." She slid into the booth and accepted their warm smiles of welcome.

"I hope this booth is large enough. Several more couples from the school are joining us." Jim seemed happy, years younger.

Mike got the waiter's attention. "What'll you have, pretty lady?"

Iris seldom drank. but she felt the need of something to help her get through the evening. "Rum and coke, please."

Their drinks arrived, followed closely by Syble Brinkman, the music teacher, and her husband. They immediately engaged Jim and Carol in conversation, leaving Iris to suffer Mike's whispered flattery. When he suggested they dance she accepted with relief.

There were a lot of things about Mike she didn't like, but his dancing wasn't one of them. He was good. He moved around the floor like a professional, being careful to allow Iris time to get warmed up before he tried a series of difficult steps. He wanted to look good, so his partner must look good. And Mike concentrated so hard on his dancing that he had no time for insincere flattery or roaming hands. They danced to several numbers, and when they left the floor they went by the bar so Mike could get another drink.

The two couples were still in the booth, and the talk centered around whether or not the school superintendent was going to retire. Iris sat quietly and listened to the music. There wasn't anything she could have added to the conversation if she had wanted to.

The lights in the ballroom dimmed even more, and the band swung into a medley of old favorites—*That'll Be The Day, Donna, Chantilly Lace*. It was almost as if she'd been transported back into the days of saddle shoes and full skirts over layers of net cancan slips.

"Hello, everyone."

The lilting voice jarred Iris back to the present. She looked up and sucked in her breath, dismayed to see a beaming Louise Hanley at the end of the booth. Behind her, dwarfing her, was John. He looked hard at Iris. There was most definitely a storm warning in the blue depths of his eyes. She was startled. What did it mean? Was he angry to find her included in the party? Tough! Her lips curled upward, and she gave him the benefit of her best haughty expression.

Introductions were made all around. The talk resumed,

with Louise taking the lead, laughing and gesturing, clearly delighted to be with John.

This had to be the most miserable night of Iris's life, she thought wretchedly. Would it ever end? Mike's hand covered hers, where it lay on the table, and she asked, "Why are we wasting this good music?"

Pleased, Mike smiled smugly and asked Louise and John to excuse them. John stood. Louise, blatantly eager for John's attention, hung on his arm, looking up at him adoringly. Iris threw her a disgusted look before her eyes slid to John's. She felt a quick flash of embarrassment. He'd read her thoughts. She saw just a flicker of an eyelid. Had he winked at her?

"C'mon, small stuff," he said in a low drawl to Louise, "we may as well dance, too, as long as we're on our feet."

"I haven't finished my drink." Louise pouted and melted against him. The top of her head came even with his shoulder.

Iris moved with Mike onto the dance floor. She couldn't keep her eyes from following the other couple. They look like Mutt and Jeff from the funny papers, she thought irritably. She hoped John would step all over her size 3A shoes and Louise would throw up on his XL sport coat.

Mike pulled her tightly against him, and she followed his lead. "My favorite music, my favorite girl." He held her away from him so he could see her face. There was scarcely an inch difference in their heights. "So it isn't true after all?"

"Is that why you asked me out?" Her smoky eyes blazed into his. She made no pretense of not knowing what he referred to.

He laughed softly and whirled her around. "You know better than that. I've always had a *thing* for you."

"I know. The same *thing* you've had for every other woman in town," she said coolly.

"I love it when you're like this!" His hand slipped down to her hip.

"Regardless of what you've heard, Mike, I've no more intention of sleeping with you now than I did when you took me out before. So move your hand off my rear or I'll slap you!"

"Hey, baby. Don't get so steamed up." His hand slid back to her waist, and they danced in silence.

Now and then, Iris caught a glimpse of a dark red head and broad shoulders. Louise was snuggled against his chest. She didn't want to think the ragging pain that knifed her heart was jealousy. She'd always felt jealousy was a wasted emotion. But there it was, eating at her, and there was nothing she could do but endure it.

The music stopped. Mike seemed subdued. They passed the bar, and he bought another drink. Iris hadn't realized he was such a heavy drinker. He was holding it well, she thought, but if he had any more she knew who would be driving home. As they neared the booth, Mike's arm went across her shoulders. She let it remain there only because she saw John watching them.

Louise was seated. John was paying the waiter. He'd ordered more drinks, including another for Mike. Iris shook her head, feeling sick, when she saw Mike gulp the drink.

"Might as well dance with my partner," John said casually, and grabbed her hand. "Excuse us, folks."

"But, John, your drink will get warm." Louise used

her girlish voice, but her eyes were hard when they rested on Iris.

"Mike can drink it. I'll get another when we come back."

Iris started to protest, but he hooked her close to his side and she went along, knowing perfectly well he was capable of creating a scene. *Might as well dance with my partner!* The words almost scalded her. Heat seemed to drain from her trembling body down to her toes, leaving her cold, wooden.

Shielding her with his large frame from the stares of those in the booth, his arms encircled her and pulled her so close to him that the buttons on his coat hurt her breast. When he began to move it was impossible not to follow his lead. He lifted his arm, pushing hers up. It went around his shoulders. Her hand came to rest at the base of his neck, her fingers curled into the thick hair at his collar.

"Aw . . . this is more like it." His murmur was a moist tickling in her ear. "I hate dancing with short women."

"You should have thought of that before you asked her out." Cool words came out of a hot, tight throat.

"I had no choice," he whispered, his chin worrying her cheekbone.

"Oh? I suppose someone was standing over you with a whip," she snapped.

"You forced me to ask her out. It's your fault. What made you accept a date with that dandy? Did you do it to spite me?"

"Don't flatter yourself," she said, much too fast. "And he isn't a dandy."

"Damn near it. A drunk. too, if I'm not mistaken."

He chuckled when she refused to argue. "Are you still mad because Stanley's mother caught us with my hands in your pants?"

"Don't be crude." She tried to draw away from him, but his arms tightened. He laughed, and she could feel it all up and down her body. "I suppose you think it's funny that my reputation is in shreds," she managed to say coolly.

"I may be forced to make an honest woman out of you yet." His fingers moved up her back and around to stroke the side of her breast. "Now, don't sputter. Be quiet. I want to enjoy this. It'll be over all too soon." He pressed his lips to her ear, and she felt a small tug when he pulled at her earring with his lips. "Mmmm . . . sexy woman. You smell so good."

His feather-light kisses along the sensitive skin in front of her ear were sending the familiar butterfly wings to her stomach. "Don't do that! People are looking. We're not exactly an inconspicuous couple, you know."

"I know. You're the most beautiful woman here. I like you in this soft stuff." His hand moved the material of her dress caressingly over her back. "A movie star doesn't hold a candle to you, Farmer Brown." He chuckled again. She knew he could feel the pounding of her heart. "You're wearing a bra tonight. Good."

What did he mean by that? Iris didn't want to wonder about the *whys* or *wherefores*. She gave herself up to his tight embrace and simply enjoyed it. Her heart throbbed in her throat, and she couldn't move her cheek from his. Her eyes were half closed and filled with a look of intense longing. For the briefest moment she forgot anyone else existed except the two of them. She nestled her cheek closer against his and moved her arm further around his neck.

"Mmmm . . . you're very soft and sweet tonight, my wild Iris rose," he whispered.

"With that blatherin' tongue 'tis sure you've kissed the Blarney stone, me boy," she whispered back.

His laugh was low and private and sensuous. He lowered his head slightly and blew down her neck. "That isn't what I want to do, but it'll have to do for now."

Iris floated in a golden haze, aware only of the lean, strong body pressed to hers, the warm hands holding her, the intimate touch of their moving thighs. He moved his face, and she tilted her head slightly to look at him. Emotion was there. But what emotion? Was it love? Caring? Whatever it was, it had the power to stop her breath. His arms tightened convulsively when her lashes fluttered down. Wordlessly he pressed his cheek to hers again, and she surrendered all control to him. They glided around the room to the strains of a slow waltz. Iris felt enchanted.

John brought them to a halt when the music stopped, and he took a step back from her, letting his hands rest on her hips. He looked at her for a long moment and then lifted a hand to finger-comb the hair back from her temple.

"I like your hair done up like that. You look cool and confident like a princess." A slow smile lit his face. "I'm sure Old MacDonald didn't have anything like you down on his farm."

"I'll bet he didn't have a sailor, either," she said softly. There was a slight tremor when she spoke, but her smoky eyes held his unwaveringly.

"I can believe that." His laugh was deep, and people turned to look at them.

His hand rested on her waist as they walked back to the booth. It didn't go unnoticed by Louise, who sat alone with Mike. She stood so Iris could move in beside him.

"Thanks for bringing him back," she said brightly, as if Iris had led John to her on a leash.

"He's all yours." She wished her voice had been stronger.

"I know." Louise glanced at her over her shoulder, then looked up into John's face. "Shall we dance? I think Mike wants to be alone with his date."

Iris would have loved to wring her neck.

"Sure." John stood stock still for a moment, but Iris refused to look up at him. "Don't go away, you two," he said, and with his hand on Louise's back urged her toward the dance floor.

"Why didn't you come with *him*?" Mike's words were slurred, and Iris heard a warning bell ring in her ears.

"He didn't ask me," she snapped.

"He's playing you and little twitchy-fanny against each other. Smart of him."

Mike was drunk, very drunk. An angry flush heated Iris's cheeks. "I think we'd better go."

"Why? Because *he* won't be coming back for a while? He won't, you know. *She'll* see to it."

"You're disgusting!" Iris moved along the smooth seat and stood. Her haughty expression intimidated him enough that he got to his feet and lurched after her when she headed toward the door.

Iris threaded her way between the tables and booths, not knowing or caring if he was following. At the entrance she turned and waited for him. He had bumped into a couple and was trying to apologize. He gestured toward Iris, and they turned to look at her. She found her temper rising.

"Give me the keys, Mike."

"Nooooo one's driving my car but me."

"Give me the keys. Or as soon as you get in the car I'll call the police and have you arrested for drunk driving. You're in no condition to get behind the wheel." She looked at him steadily.

"You're a . . . bitch. That's what you . . . are. I should'a stuck with li'l ol' twitchy-fanny."

"Iris—" She heard John's voice before she looked over her shoulder and saw him. His long legs were eating up the distance between them. Louise was doing her best to keep up. "You're not leaving with him!"

She stared at him, observing almost impersonally the muscles that bunched along his jaw. "I don't care to stand here and make a spectacle of myself arguing. I'm leaving, either with or without him. But I'll drive him home if he'll give me the car keys."

"I'll take you home."

"I came with him, and I'll leave with him, if possible." Her temper was rising again. Louise clinging to John's arm reminded her of a monkey clinging to a vine.

"Give her the keys," he said to Mike in the commanding voice he must have used on young recruits. When Mike hesitated, he said, "Give them to her or I'll throw you down and take them."

"Aw-right. Ya don't have to get . . . nasty." He dug into his pocket and brought the keys out dangling from one finger, grinning foolishly.

John snatched the keys from his hand and handed them to Iris. "I'll follow you back to town. Take him home and I'll pick you up."

"John!" Louise protested. "They'll be all right. Let's not go yet. The place is just beginning to liven up."

"Stay, by all means, and enjoy yourselves. Don't cut your evening short because of Mike and me." Iris turned and went through the double doors.

Relieved to be out in the cool night air, she walked quickly to the car and slid behind the wheel. Mike got in on the passenger side and slammed the door.

"You sure turned out to be a . . . dud," he muttered.

Iris almost smiled at his childish pushing. He wanted to quarrel with her, but she remained silent and drove the car out of the parking lot and onto the highway. Headlights flashed in the rearview mirror. At the first stop sign she glanced in the side mirror and saw John's station wagon behind them. She didn't know whether she was glad he cared enough to follow her to see that she got safely back to town or whether she was irritated that he thought she was unable to handle things herself.

Mike slumped down in the seat. Phew! The smell of his breath was enough to make her sick. She rolled down the window so the cold wind could fan her face. She drove automatically, trying not to think of Louise snuggled up to John's side in the car behind.

By the time she pulled the car to the curb and parked it in front of Mike's apartment building, he was snoring. She would have left him sitting there, but John opened the door and, after a brief, disgusted glance, hauled him out and stood him up beside the car.

"Which apartment is his?"

"How should I know? Ask Louise." The snippy remark slipped out, and she instantly regretted it. She put the car keys in Mike's coat pocket.

"We can't leave him out here. Go open the door."

Iris couldn't tell whether John was angry or not. She could see Louise sitting in the middle of the seat, watching, gloating. John stooped, let Mike fall over his shoulder, and hoisted him up. Iris opened the glass-paned door of the apartment building, and John angled his body and Mike's through. He stopped and scanned the names over the mailboxes.

"Wait for me here," he barked at her.

Iris stood beside the door, hating to have to go out to the car and be driven home like some errant teenager whose date had gone sour. She watched John carry Mike up the stairs. He seemed to do it so effortlessly—the same way he'd carried her. Stop it, Iris! Don't think about that night. Better straighten yourself out, my girl, before you go out to face Miss "twitchy-fanny." She stifled a giggle. Where had Mike picked up such a phrase?

When John came back down the stairs, she was once more on the defensive, and when he took her arm to walk her to the car, she firmly removed it from his grasp.

There was plenty of room for her on the seat without crowding the door. Louise sat snugly against John. Even her knees were tucked beneath his long thigh.

"What in the world did you do to Mike, Iris? I've never seen him like that."

"I didn't do anything to him," she said with exaggerated patience. "He drank like he was going to be hung within the hour."

"He likes you a lot, and was looking forward to this

date. He's really a nice guy. He said the two of you had great times together."

Iris was well aware Louise was trying to convince John that there was a relationship between her and Mike. "I've only had one other date with him, Louise. Believe me, it wasn't all that great."

Louise lapsed into silence. Iris had expected her to pant and purr all the way to the farm. Suddenly, she was aware of the reason for the silence. John was taking her home. When they turned down the darkened street, Iris could almost feel the hostility radiate from Louise, who took her hand from his leg. Iris almost felt sorry for her . . . almost, but not quite.

John got out of the car and held the door open for Louise to slide under the wheel. She didn't answer when Iris said, "Good night."

Okay, so she'd made another enemy. Iris sank down in the seat and wondered for the hundredth time about the kick in the teeth fate had given her at this time in her life. She kept her face turned firmly away from Louise's door.

John was chuckling that deep, amused chuckle that so irritated her, when he got into the car.

"What's so funny?"

"Louise. She's mad as a hornet." John drove away from the curb, and his left hand groped for her. "Come over beside me. We've finally got rid of those two." His hand found her arm, and she had no choice but to move to the middle of the seat.

"She has a right to be mad. You should've taken me home first. She was your date."

"Only because I couldn't have you. This could have been avoided if you'd have mentioned you wanted to go to the dance. As it is, I had to scramble around to find a date when . . ."

"When you wormed it out of Brenda."

"Yeah. She's a fun kid. I haven't been around a girl her age before." His hand reached down to caress her knee. "Do you want something to eat? We can stop at the restaurant on the highway."

"No," she said quickly. Then she modified it. "No, but thanks." She grasped his wrist and gently but firmly removed his hand from her knee. Not because she didn't enjoy his touch, but because she was trembling and didn't want him to know it. She was tired, sick at heart. The emotional strain of the last few weeks as well as hard work had sapped her strength, and it wouldn't take much to push her over the brink.

What seemed like endless minutes later John pulled the station wagon into the carport and turned off the lights. Iris reached for the door handle and pressed it, but it was locked. He turned in the seat to look at her.

"You're working too hard."

Surprised by his words, she turned and found him closer to her. She tried for lightness in her voice. "No harder than you have. All farmers put in long hours during the planting season."

"The season is over. I want you to spend more time at the house." It was the last thing she had expected him to say, and his voice held a tenderness that was her undoing.

"I have to put in the garden." She turned her head away and tried the door handle again. She took a deep, steadying breath. "Thanks for the ride."

John reached out to cradle the nape of her neck and pull her toward him. Iris felt the strength drain out of her.

"Don't. Please . . . don't," she said feebly. Control left her, and mortification set in when she burst into tears. "I'm . . . I'm . . . sorry!" She was crying in great, ragged gulps, and tried to put her hands over her face, but her arms were pinned to her sides as his arms went around her.

"Darling, what's the matter?" His voice was husky, pleading. "Are you sick? Is it one of your headaches? Don't cry. I can't stand to see you like this." His words were interspersed with quick, light kisses on her wet face. "Tell me. Tell me what's wrong. Have I goaded you too far?"

"It isn't your fault." She struggled to gain control. "I haven't managed my life very well. I can see that now. I'm naive, self-centered where the farm and Brenda are concerned. I've let them become my whole life. I've tried to be the captain of my own soul and behave well whatever happens, but I've made a mess of it."

He cuddled her in his arms, and his lips moved over her face, avoiding her mouth so she could talk. "I've blamed you for everything, when the truth is 1 don't know how much longer I could have gone on alone. I know you didn't mean to burn down the barn. . . . And you'll probably do a better job with the books than I could have done. 1 don't like myself anymore."

"Shhh . . . I thought you felt guilty about being with me . . . that night."

"No. I wanted you to make love to me." What I really wanted was for you to love me, she cried silently.

"You've been lonely, sweetheart. You've had so much responsibility, and I came along with my trailer and really threw a spanner in the works here at the farm." He tried to kiss the wetness from her eyes. "I pushed too hard, sweetheart, when I really wanted to grow on you gradually. I'm told that's the basis for a lasting relationship. I made a wave and hit it head on, because I was so glad I'd found you. I care about you, darling. I care very much." He folded her closer to him and lifted her arm to encircle his neck. "I want to build my life around you and Brenda. I was hoping you'd come to care for me." He buried his face in her hair. "I hadn't planned to tell you this until I thought there was a chance for me."

"John . . ." she whispered shakily. She was unable to believe what he was saying.

"We can make it work. darling," he told her huskily.

Iris smiled through her tears. "Are you saying that you . . . care for me?"

"I'm saying I love you." His voice shook, and his arms held her so tight the air exploded from her lungs.

When his mouth closed over hers, Iris quit smiling, but inside her, laughter spread out. The kiss was long and sweet, and conveyed a message too poignant for mere words. It was slow and deep and warmed her, joining both their mouths in sweet excitement. She could feel the steady beat of his heart and the quickening of her own.

"I love you, love you, love you!" He said it against her mouth, her ear, her nose.

"And I love you," she cried happily. She had to touch him, was frantic to touch him. Her hand found its way to his waist and the belted trousers, then lower to the straining zipper.

She felt the breath expelled harshly from his lungs, and could almost feel the blood surge through his body. She moved her hand from the outline of his tumescence.

"I'm sorry," she gasped when his mouth left hers.

"Sorry? I don't want to hear that word for the next . . . forty years!"

Before the wildfire of emotion could sweep them into another burning kiss, Iris drew back until the tip of her nose rested against his and said in a sexy stage whisper, "Your place or mine?"

Happiness bubbled up, and laughter broke from their lips and gleamed in their eyes.

CHAPTER ELEVEN

IT WAS ONE of those rare nights when bodies spoke silently, ignited, and burned on for hours. It was almost dawn when he whispered to her, "Go to sleep, darling. I want to hold you in my arms while we sleep."

Almost immediately, Iris fell into a deep, satisfying slumber, but she was still subconsciously aware of the warm male body pressed spoon fashion to her own, the heavy weight of the arm across her body, and the hand that cupped her breast. It was a wonderful way to sleep. It was even more wonderful to wake in her lover's arms.

Something tugged on her earlobe. She shook her head, but the pull persisted. Then warm air was blown into her ear. She turned her head, and her nose collided with another nose, and lips nipped at hers. She was lying on her back, John on his side watching her. Her legs were looped over muscular thighs that were drawn up tightly to her bottom. A large hand spanned her stomach, and fingers dipped and squeezed.

"'Mornin'," he whispered just before his mouth covered hers.

" 'Mornin'," she whispered the instant she was able. "What time is it?"

"Time to make love again." His hand moved up to her breast and his palm circled slowly.

"The chores . . ."

"All done. Farmer Brown was up while Mrs. Brown was sleeping. He wanted this waking time with his lady."

"I wonder why." She circled his neck with her arms and rubbed his nose with hers.

"Want me to jog your memory?"

"Uh-huh."

He gently spread the thighs looped over his and she felt a prodding against the part of her that throbbed with heat and moisture.

She gasped. "You're indecent!"

"Yeah. But wait till I get the mirror put on the ceiling," he threatened huskily, and covered her mouth with his before she could protest. They kissed deeply, as lovers long familiar with each other. "You taste soooo good. You're sweet, sexy, and I'm smitten. I've been all over the world and I found this in Iowa. Unbelievable!" He muttered all those words as if talking to himself.

Later her yawn turned into a smile, and she stretched out on the comfortable bed. He peeled down the sheet and stooped to kiss her breast. "Wanton woman," he said intensely, and gave her a lecherous smile. "Get out of bed and fix my breakfast."

She laughed joyously. "Like this?"

"If you're going to fry bacon—no. If you're going to poach eggs—yes." He pulled on her nipple with his lips. "On second thought, I'll have my breakfast right here."

"Don't start anything you can't finish, sailor," she said

with the confidence of a secure lover. She laughed with pure happiness. She would never have dreamed she would say such a thing.

"Is that a challenge?" he growled.

"No, no!" His hand found her ribs and raked them playfully. They rolled on the bed, wrestled, tangled in the bedclothes.

"Then. heave-ho, me beauty!" He tossed her out of bed and swiftly sprang up when she landed on her feet. He caught her close to him. They stood in an ardent embrace, naked bodies straining together from knees to lips. "Look." He turned her slightly so she could see them in the full-length mirror that covered the closet door. "Don't we fit well together?" His voice was low, husky, and she could feel his desire stirring against her softness.

"You're right . . . for once," she teased, and wound her arms around him and her hair about his neck.

Breakfast was forgotten.

They showered together in the minute stall after John pinned her hair on the top of her head and found a plastic sack to cover it. They stood under the warm spray, kissing, touching, laughing, until the hot water was used up and they couldn't stand the cold water that came directly from the deep well. Then, wrapped in one of John's bathrobes, Iris ran across the yard to the farmhouse when John, from a lookout on his porch, gave the all-clear signal.

Jane Watts called later to say Brenda had gone to early church services with her family, and they were taking her along to dinner with them. She would be home by one o'clock. It would be a long time before Iris forgot that time. Not because it was the time when Brenda came home—she arrived a few minutes earlier—but because of what happened afterwards.

Brenda came bouncing into the house saying she wanted to change into jeans so she could ride Sugar. Iris smiled happily, knowing how pleased her sister would be when she heard the news. She and John had agreed to tell her together.

In a happy daze, Iris was only mildly curious when the long white convertible with a woman behind the wheel drove up the farm lane and stopped at the door. Thinking she was lost and seeking directions, Iris went to the back door and onto the step. The woman sat looking at her, her arm resting on the top of the door. Her hair was even lighter than Iris's, and was held back with a pale blue silk scarf that matched the sweater she wore. Iris, in her jeans and knit shirt, her thick braid hanging down her back, her face free of makeup, felt unattractive, even hickish, in comparison.

Something about the woman and the quiet way she watched her approach slowed her feet and caused a heavy plop of fear to drop on her heart. Suddenly she knew who she was, and panic squeezed her throat.

"Hello, Iris." The woman raised thin-plucked brows. "You never change. But I must say the old place has a new look. I see you've had a fire. Too bad it didn't take that ancient wreck of a house.

"What are you doing here?"

"I'll give you three guesses. You were always rather dense and dull, Iris. I see you haven't grown out of it, although . . . Good heavens! You must be past thirty. You were just a couple of years younger than I was when I married your father. Why wasn't I notified when he died?"

"There was no reason to notify you. You're not a member of our family." All the old hatred and resentment of this woman boiled up in Iris.

"I've learned that the custody of my daughter was transferred to you. I want to see her. I want to spend some time with her. I want us to get to know each other."

I want . . . I want. She was still the same. More beautiful, more confident, but still selfish and demanding. Protective instincts rose in Iris. She wouldn't allow this woman to spoil Brenda's life. She had John to stand beside her now. She no longer had to face this alone.

"I-r-is! Where's Candy's halter? It was here on the porch yesterday."

When Brenda stuck her head out the door, Monica got out of the car. She was tall, extremely thin, and dressed in expensively cut white slacks and slender-heeled shoes. A large diamond glittered on her finger when she fluttered her hand in Brenda's direction. Brenda came out and stood on the step, curious, and puzzled more by her sister's rigid, defensive stance than by the beautiful woman.

"Brenda, dear. Do you remember me? You're almost as tall as I am. Oh, for heaven's sake! I can't believe it." She laughed a tinkling, careful laugh. Brenda's brows drew together, and she glanced at Iris. "I'm Monica, your mother." Monica laughed again. "I've had my hair lightened; maybe that's why you don't recognize me."

"She was only seven when she saw you last," Iris snapped.

Monica put her arms around the tall, silent girl and hugged her. "My baby has grown up to be a beauty."

Brenda seemed to be stunned into silence. Her eyes appealed to her sister for help. "Iris? . . ."

"Brenda, baby. I know you're surprised to see me again. I would've called, but I wanted to make sure you'd be here when I got here." She smiled prettily after darting a pointed glance at Iris, and fingered the ends of the hair that fell to Brenda's shoulders. "Come sit in the car and talk with me. I've come all the way from California to see you."

Iris moved rapidly to the screened door and flung it open. "You can talk to her in the house, if she wants to talk to you."

Brenda looked from one to the other, then turned and walked back inside. Monica followed, then Iris.

In the living room Brenda sank down on the couch, and Monica sat beside her. Iris stood hesitantly in the doorway.

"I'd like to spend some time with my daughter . . . alone," Monica said.

"That's up to Brenda," Iris responded icily.

Arthur came bounding into the room and ran to Brenda, his tail wagging so hard and so fast in his pleasure that his hind legs almost left the floor. John followed him at a much slower pace. Iris fastened her eyes on his face and failed to see the look that came over Monica's when she saw him. Iris did, however, hear her gasp, and turned to see her getting to her feet, her face wreathed in smiles.

"Johnny? Johnny Lang! Darling . . . what in the world are you doing here?"

John stopped, and his eyes narrowed. He put his hand to his lower lip and pulled on it. "I don't think—"

"Sure you do. Monica. Monica Ouverson. Oh, my God! It was at least thirteen or fourteen years ago. You were here on leave from the Navy. Visiting someone? Was that it? We had a gorgeous time for a couple of weeks; then in San Diego—"

"I remember," John said slowly. "But I never connected you with this Ouverson family. The area is full of Ouversons."

By this time Monica had wrapped her arms around his neck and was kissing him. When Iris recovered from shock she was sure she was living out a nightmare. Her heart screamed for her not to listen to the logic that pounded in her mind. *John was the serviceman Monica had run away with!* The cold lump that was Iris's heart beat slowly. Icy fingers ran along her jaw, and she clenched her teeth to keep' her face from crumpling.

"Do you live here, Johnny?" Monica seemed to have forgotten there was anyone else in the room.

"Not with us. He lives in the trailer on his half of the farm." The words tumbled like chips of ice from Iris's stiff lips.

"You live here on the farm?" Monica's tinkling laugh added more fuel to the rage that was beginning to smolder in Iris.

"What's so funny about that?" John asked quietly.

"Nothing, darling. I just can't imagine you, of all people, living *here*."

"Get out!" The words burst from Iris. "I don't have to stand here and listen to your derogatory references to my home!"

"Darling . . ." Monica purred, ignoring Iris's outburst and looking up into John's face. "I'm sorry if I've ruffled Iris's feathers. I want to spend some time with my daughter. I'd like her to meet my husband. We've come all the way from California just so he can meet her. Iris has some insane notion that I'm a monster, or something."

John looked over her head to Iris. She gazed steadily back at him, her eyes wide and hostile. "That's up to Iris and Brenda." He moved out of the reach of Monica's clinging hands, "Brenda?" His voice seemed to jar the girl and she got to her feet. "Do you want to spend some time with your mother?"

"Who in the hell do you think you are?" Iris shouted. "Stay out of this!" Tight bands of tension were beginning to squeeze her head.

"Calm down, Iris. Brenda is old enough to make the decision for herself. She should spend a few hours with Monica if she wants to. The choice should be hers."

"Damn you! I don't need advice from . . . *you*!"

"Iris . . . don't." Tears stood in Brenda's eyes.

"Do you want to go?" Iris demanded.

"I . . . don't know."

John moved over and put his arm across Iris's shoulders. Iris moved out from under it and across the room to her sister. "Don't let him pressure you into going if you don't want to go," Iris said desperately.

"Oh, for heaven's sake! You'd think I wanted to take her on a trip around the world instead of just down the highway to the motel. My God! I'm her mother! I won't let any harm come to her."

"Some mother," Iris sneered.

"Iris, don't make it hard for Brenda." John was beside her. "Let her go. Let her use the common sense we both know she has." When Iris didn't look at him, or speak, he turned to Monica. "What motel and what name are you using?"

"My husband's name. Randolph. He's well known in real estate on the West Coast. Here's his card." She dug into her shoulder bag and handed him a business card.

"What are you going to do, Brenda?"

"Do you think I should go, John?"

Iris felt as if the earth were slipping out from under her. Suddenly John's wishes were more important to Brenda than hers.

"If you want to, kid," he was saying. "Someday you may want to know about the woman who birthed you. Giving birth to you and being a mother to you are two different things. If you remember, we've discussed that before."

"I think I'll go. If Iris . . "

Iris clamped her lips together and willed the tears to stay behind her eyes. She nodded and tried to smile into the young girl's pleading eyes, silently saying, I'm here and I love you.

Brenda followed Monica through the dining room and kitchen to the door. Iris stood as if frozen. John watched her for an instant, then strode through the rooms and out the door. Iris saw him talking to Monica while Brenda went around the car to get in on the other side.

The breakfast Iris had eaten so happily suddenly turned on her. Her stomach churned, and the pain on the top of her head knifed down between her eyes. Abruptly she was in a black, swirling mist. She stumbled to the stairs. Escape. Damn him! Damn the whole rotten world! Damn this pain in her head! In the bathroom she gulped down several pills with a sip of water and carried pills and water to her room.

Betrayed. Iris sank down on the bed and pulled the pillow over her head. An iron band was trying to crush her skull. Pain. She'd had more headaches since she'd met John Lang than she'd had during the last ten years. Headaches and heartaches. Peaks and valleys. Love and despair. Fate had really kicked her in the teeth this time. The man she loved had been her stepmother's lover.

She wept.

"Iris . . . sweetheart?"

She'd known he would come. There was no way she could have prevented it, so she hadn't tried. "Get out!" Her muffled voice came from beneath the pillow. "Get out of my room, my house, my life and . . ." my heart, she added silently.

"Did you take your pills?"

"Yes, I took the pills! Get the hell out of here! I don't need or want your sympathy."

"Don't worry about Brenda. Seeing Monica could be the best thing for her at this time in her life. She'll—"

Iris threw off the pillow and sat up. Her head was being split by the pain and her eyes were seeing colors running together.

"You . . . bastard! How dare you stand there and tell me, so piously, what's best for my sister?" Tears streamed from her eyes and glued wisps of hair to her cheeks. "You're the man her mother went away with! She left my father and a tiny baby for . . . you! Stay away from Brenda. Stay away from me. I've been ten times a fool, but no more! I finally see you for what you are! Ohhh . . ." She retched. It came without warning, spewed out of her mouth, down the side of the bed, and onto the floor. It was the final humiliation.

Iris fell back on the bed and pulled the pillow over her

head once again. From the depths of her weariness, she heard the bedroom door close. Once again she was alone in the private sanctuary of her room, safe from watching, critical eyes. She curled herself into a tight ball and surrendered to the overwhelming sense of loss that sent burning tears streaming down her face once again.

Later, exhausted, she slept.

She woke from a nightmare of a dream where she was wandering in a vast open plain looking for Brenda. Her sister was leaning over her.

"Are you okay?"

"Sure. I was having a dream."

"You called me. I've been sitting over there waiting for you to wake up. How's your head?"

"I don't know yet. I'm afraid to move it. Oh . . . watch it, honey. I threw up. It must be a mess."

"It's okay. John cleaned it up before I got back."

"Oh, God, no!" Iris groaned.

Brenda came around to sit on the bed. "Did my going with her cause the headache?"

"No. It was a combination of things. What time is it?"

"Almost eight o'clock. You slept a long time." Brenda climbed farther up on the bed and crossed her legs Indian fashion. "Are you hungry? Can I get you something?"

"A cup of tea sounds good, but I'll get it later."

"Can I tell you about . . . it?" Brenda questioned hesitantly. "I'm glad I went. But I could tell you didn't want me to go."

"Tell me only if you want to, honey. No, I didn't want you to go. I was afraid you'd be impressed with her glamour. And maybe I was just jealous. I don't know."

"That's funny, Iris. No one in the world could ever take your place. You and I are family."

Iris choked back tears. "Thanks for saying that, useless nuisance." She tried to bring some lightness to her voice, and failed miserably.

"I've been wondering about her. She's very beautiful. I can't imagine why she ever married our dad." Brenda's brows puckered into a frown. "Why'd she do it?"

Iris searched for words. "She must have thought she loved him. Her family was poor and Dad was lonely. He bought her pretty clothes and she was happy for a while."

"I'm glad you're not like her. She's pretty, but she gushes and she's not very smart or she wouldn't have married Mr. Randolph. I didn't like him. He's got fat hands."

Iris tried not to smile. "Is that the only reason you didn't like him?"

"No. He wheezes when he talks, and he smokes smelly cigars. I don't think he could bend over and tie his shoes," she said with distaste. "She fusses over him like he was a king or somethin'. Yuk! He wasn't even as tall as she was! On the way back she kept telling me how rich he was, and showed me her diamond. They've got a swimming pool . . ." Brenda's voice trailed off.

Iris held her breath for a long moment and waited.

"I'm glad I went with her, Iris. Now I don't have to wonder what she's like." Brenda lay down on the bed beside her and cuddled up to her as she had done when she was small. "Do you think I'll be like her?" she asked in a scared whisper. "I don't want to be like her!"

"Oh, honey!" Iris hugged her. Relief flooded her heart. "You'll be whatever you want to be. You won't be like me or Monica. You'll be you."

"But I've got her blood."

"Not only hers, but our dad's. Don't worry about it. You're sensible, beautiful, healthy, and smart! What more do you want, obnoxious brat?" she asked teasingly, and batted the tears from her eyes.

"I'll never, never leave you, Iris." Brenda's arm tightened and she hugged her desperately.

"Sure, you will. Do you think I want you hanging around here when you're fifty and I'm sixty-eight? You'll meet some nice man and fall head over tailgate in love with him. You'll build a home together and have babies . . . to bring back home."

"Iris. John told me not to talk to you about this, but—"

"Then, don't." The words came out sharper than she had intended, and she was afraid she had broken the fragile thread of communication between them.

"I want to tell you," she said stubbornly. "John didn't know Monica was married. He didn't know she was going to follow him back to San Diego."

"I don't want to hear about it, Brenda. That's his business and hers."

"I wished you liked him more. He likes you. I can tell. We've had some good talks together. He talks to me as if he thinks what I have to say is important. I've never known anyone like him."

"That's nice," Iris said aloud, then added silently, You haven't known many men, punkin'. He's had twenty years' training in winning young minds over to his way of thinking. Quietly, she said, "I won't tell you not to be friends with him, but leave me out of it. I can never be friends with John Lang."

—Or his lover, her heart cried silently.

CHAPTER TWELVE

"ABSOLUTELY NOT! YOU'RE making me angry, Brenda. You cannot ask him to eat with us tonight, or any night!"

"But Iris—"

"Don't argue." Iris yanked off her straw hat and wiped her forehead on the sleeve of her shirt. "I'm sorry, honey. I'm tired. I've got to get the rest of the garden in before . . . Arthur! Get him out of here, Brenda. He's digging up the cucumber seeds!"

"Oh, awright. C'mon, Arthur, or I'll tie you up."

Since Monica's visit Iris had worked like a demon in order to keep her sanity. School was out. Brenda did most of the household chores, leaving Iris free to work in the vegetable garden. The girl had been strangely subdued since the meeting with her mother. She hadn't mentioned her since the first night, which added to Iris's unease. That, and the fact that she was spending a lot of time with John.

Iris started the tiller as soon as Brenda left with the dog, Her arms ached from holding onto the heavy machine that chewed the soil, but that was nothing compared to the pain in her heart. She would get over it, she assured herself. It would take longer, since she had to see him every day, hear his voice, know he was near.

John had made an attempt to talk to her the day after Monica's visit, and she had stopped him cold.

"I may have to tolerate you here on the farm, Mr. Lang, but I don't have to tolerate your meddling in my private life. Butt out!"

He'd pushed his billed cap to the back of his head and glared at her. "You stubbom little jackass! You think everything is either black or white, and there are no shades of gray at all. You love me, dammit! You told me so a hundred times that night! You enjoyed our lovemaking as much as I did." Iris's face had flamed at that. "We could build a good life here together if it weren't for your damned stubborn pride. I'll tell you this once again, for the last time. I didn't know Monica was married to your father. I didn't know she had a child. I didn't ask her to follow me to California. You can believe whatever you want to believe. I've made my last move. Now it's up to you."

"It'll be a cold day in hell before I come to you for any reason at all!"

"We'll see about that," he said with a snarl, and walked away from her.

Now they were at loggerheads, and Brenda was torn between them.

Iris knelt to separate the spindly tomato plants. She was so deep in thought that she was startled when Brenda hunkered down beside her.

"John took Arthur with him, so I didn't have to tie him up. He took the pickup over to Alvin's to get some feed.

He says we'll have to put up another building soon. He says it's too much to ask Alvin to store stuff for us. John says he's going to have a talk with you about making the farm a corporation. I'd be an officer, too." Brenda was smiling broadly. "Won't that be funny? Me, Brenda Ouverson, chairman of the board."

"I doubt you'd be chairman, honey. *He'd*, more than likely, reserve that position for himself."

Her sarcasm was lost on her sister. "Oh, that's okay. I just wish . . . you liked him more." The phrase was becoming a familiar one.

"We can't all like the same things, or the same people, can we?" Iris tried to be patient. "Will you pour some water from the bucket in the holes I dug along the fence?"

Brenda got up. "John says he'll run a water pipe along the top of the ground so you won't have to drag that heavy hose all the way out here to water the garden, if you want him to."

"Brenda, please don't say, 'John says,' another time today. Do that for me, will you, honey?" Her words sobered her sister, and Iris felt a stab of guilt.

"You're like a cow with a sore tail," Brenda muttered.

"So? Well, this *cow* has work to do." Iris pretended to be absorbed in the planting so her sister wouldn't see the tears in her eyes.

"*He* asked me to ride into town with him after lunch," Brenda said stubbornly. "I don't suppose you want me to go with *him*."

"Go if you want to." Her voice was strained, her throat constricted with the jealousy she could not dismiss from her mind. She tried to hide it with a rebuke. "How many times have I told you not to take a negative attitude when you want something?"

"Cripes! I never know what kind of attitude to take with you anymore. You're always so cross."

"I'm sorry," Iris murmured, and plunged her hands down into the soft mud surrounding the plant.

Brenda and John didn't return from town until dinner time. Iris was standing at the kitchen sink, looking out over the yard, when the pickup came up the drive. Arthur was riding proudly in the truck bed amid sacks of feed. Brenda jumped from the truck the instant it stopped, and made for the house. John caught the back of her T-shirt and stopped her.

"Oh, no, you don't. The deal was that you'd help unload. So get to it. Take the bridles and the small stuff to the shed while I unload the feed."

Their voices and laughter drifted into the kitchen. With aching despair Iris walked slowly into the living room and turned on the television set to watch the evening news. There had been a mud slide in California, a flood in Mississippi, and a tornado in Oklahoma. The whole world seemed to reflect her mood. She turned off the set and waited in the quiet for her sister to come in.

The next afternoon Iris straightened her aching back and wondered why she had enlarged the garden. She and Brenda would never use all the fruits of her efforts. Two dozen tomato plants? And then squash, green peppers, peas, beans and even eggplant. Oh, lordy! What would she do with six bushels of beets? She took off her gloves and dug her hand into her jeans pocket for a tissue. While wiping her brow she walked to the strawberry bed. In another week, she mused, she'd be crawling between the rows picking berries.

"Iris! I-r-is!" Brenda's scream jerked her out of her musings. "*Iris!*" The frantic note in her voice caused Iris's heart to stop, then speed ahead in alarm. Sugar was coming up the lane from the field at full gallop, with Brenda clinging to her back. The colt ran behind trying to keep up. "John . . . John . . . John . . ." she gasped, and then wailed, "Ohhh . . ."

Iris grabbed the bridle to hold the excited horse still. "Calm down! Tell me!"

"He fell off the tractor and there's . . . there's blood!" she screeched.

"Oh, God, no! Call an ambulance!" The full impact of her sister's words hit Iris like a blow between the eyes.

"Help him! It'll be too late!" she wailed. She held out her hand. Iris took it and leaped up behind her.

Sugar took off on the run. Iris had to reach around her sister and grab the horse's mane to keep from sliding off the rump. Her hand encountered something damp and red on Brenda's jeans. Blood! Oh, dear God, don't let this be happening! Please don't let him be hurt, be . . . dead. She was almost petrified with fear. Her knees were so weak she could barely clamp them to the heaving sides of the running horse.

At the far end of the field she could see the big green tractor with the six-row cultivator attached. Her eyes clung to the machine and searched the ground as they came closer. Unaware that her respiration was coming in short, labored gasps, his name pounded in her mind with every beat of her heart. John . . . John . . . John . . .

Brenda pulled the horse up so short the animal almost

reared. Iris slid off and stumbled to where John lay on the ground, his body against the sharp tines of the cultivator. Blood-red wetness covered his chest.

"Call an ambulance," she screamed at Brenda. "Tell them to hurry." She wasn't aware when her sister put her heels to the horse and raced away. Her chest contracted with pain. It was as if someone were cutting her with a hot knife. "John . . . darling, darling . . ."

She fell on her knees beside him and looked into his face. It was smeared with dirt, and a streak of dark red ran down his neck from the corner of his mouth.

"Please, please, be all right. Darling . . . be all right!" His shirt was soaked, and his arm lay beneath him. She slipped her hand beneath his head to turn his face toward her. His eyelashes fluttered and his lips twisted in pain. "Thank God you're alive! Sweetheart, darling, I know you can't hear me, but lie still. Brenda's gone to call the ambulance." I must stop the bleeding, she thought wildly. But with what?

She drew her hand from beneath his head. It was sticky and wet. Her breath almost left her. Quickly she unbuttoned her shirt and slipped out of it. She bent over him to unbutton his shirt, and the white cup of her bra dipped in the thick red ooze on his chest. Sobbing, she stuffed her wadded shirt into his.

"I've been such a stubborn fool, darling." Tears ran down her face. "I love you. Please don't die. Live, so I can tell you how much I love you and how much I want to marry you . . . live with you . . . have your babies . . ."

A groan came from deep in his throat. Iris held his face in her hands and bent to kiss his lips. Arthur nudged against her. "Get away," she said frantically. Arthur backed off a few steps and looked at her. She turned back to John and stroked his cheek with a feathery touch. "Hold on, darling . . . help is coming," she crooned.

Arthur jumped over John's legs to reach the other side. To her horror he began to lick John's neck.

"You beast! You contemptible beast! Get away from him or I'll kill you!" Iris shouted between sobs, and tried to hit him with her hat.

Arthur backed off, cocked his head to one side, and looked at her.

John muttered and moaned.

"What is it, darling? Just lie still."

He muttered again, and she bent her head so her ear was against his lips.

"Kiss . . . me . . ." The words were barely a whisper.

"Kiss you? Yes, darling." She placed her lips gently to the side of his mouth.

Arthur's thick body pushed against her. The beast was licking again! This time it was John's shirt. Iris hit at him again. John muttered, and she placed her face close to his so she could hear him.

"What is it, sweetheart?"

"I said, I accept." His voice boomed in her ear. She jerked her head back and found herself looking into bright, twinkling blue eyes.

"What . . . did you say?" Iris felt her mouth go slack.

"I said, I'll marry you. Tomorrow. Thanks for asking me." His arms snaked out, grabbed, and crushed her to him. He rolled over and pinned her to the ground before she could catch her breath.

Blood pounded in her ears, and her vision blurred red. She teetered between reality and unconsciousness. The mouth that ground into hers had the taste of . . . smelled like . . . *catsup!* A ringing from far, far away filled her ears. John lifted his mouth. His face was all she could see. It was smiling! Reality and rage washed over her like a thundershower.

"You . . ." she sputtered. "You . . ."

Using strength she didn't know she possessed she pushed him off her and scrambled to her feet. His hand shot out and grabbed her ankle. She kicked at him with her other foot, and his steel grip tightened around her leg. Her rump hit the soft ground, and her hand landed on her straw hat. It was the only weapon available. She began to flay him with it.

"Take that . . . and that . . . you beast, worm, slimy toad . . . you miserable redheaded woodpecker! You're despicable, rotten, evil! If I were a man I'd beat you to death!"

"If you were a man, sweetheart, I wouldn't be so wild to marry you. Brenda! Get that hat away from her before she puts my eyes out!"

Brenda came from the other side of the tractor. "What's the matter, Junior? Can't you handle her? I did my part."

"Get the hat, dammit, before she beats me to death." John was trying to dodge the blows. "Cripes! That catsup has run down into my pants. You overdid it, brat."

"What are ya complaining about? It worked."

"Arthur thought I was a hot dog."

"Next time we'll use barbecue sauce. He doesn't like it." Brenda snatched the battered, smeared hat from her sister's hand. "Why'd ya take your shirt off? You've got catsup all over your bra, Iris. Cripes! You look funny! You've got it in your hair, too."

"You two planned this . . . joke. I hope you got your money's worth," Iris said shakily, her voice beginning to break.

"Get lost, kid," John said gently. "You've done your part. Now it's all up to me."

"It's about time. I was thinkin' I'd have to propose for you." Brenda had a look of disgust on her young face. "C'mon, Arthur, 'n' stop drooling."

"I don't have to propose. She already asked me and I accepted." His smile was anxious as he moved closer to Iris. She looked as if she would burst into tears any minute.

"Holy purple pot roast!" Brenda's face broke into a beautiful smile, and she jumped up in the air and clicked her scuffed sneakers together. "I'm a better actress than I thought I was. Superneat! Double superneat!" She threw her arms around her sister and kissed her. "Yuk!" She backed off. "That catsup is messy. Maybe we should've used tomato juice." She ran to the horse. "C'mon. Let's leave the lovers alone. Whoopee!" she shouted, and turned the horse in a circle before she raced away.

As if all this were happening to someone else, Iris watched her sister. Her eyes swung back to John, and they looked at each other for a long moment. His fingers were hooked in the waistband of her jeans, and his leg was thrown over hers, as if he expected her to scramble to her feet and run. He smiled at her quietly.

"Hi," he said softly. "Did you know you're sitting in the middle of a plowed field without a shirt, and you've got catsup on your bra?"

"You . . . fight dirty."

"I know. But I was desperate. Brenda came up with the idea." She saw pleading in his eyes. He wasn't as sure of himself as he wanted her to believe.

"You scared the hell out of me."

"I'm sorry." The words didn't go with the idiotic smile on his face. "I was sure you loved me. We had to figure out a way to make you break out of your shell and admit it." She looked at him blankly. "Do you want your shirt back?" He pulled it out of the front of his. It was stained, but he managed to find a clean spot and wiped her face. He removed his own shirt and tried to wipe some of the catsup off his chest.

"I don't know if I'll be able to take you and Brenda together," she said in a broken voice. The sobs were very near.

"A desperate situation called for desperate action, sweetheart. Are we forgiven?" He pushed her back into the soft earth and saw the tears run from the corners of her eyes.

"You . . . crazy idiots! I could've had a heart attack. It would've served you right, too!"

"You're not getting another headache?" he asked anxiously, and leaned over her to rest on his forearms, his thumbs on her temples to wipe at the tears.

"I don't think so. I've had enough headaches the last few months to last a lifetime." She wanted to bury her face against his neck and cry with relief.

"I'll do my best not to give you any more headaches. I love you." His lips moved across her face, found her nose, then her lips. He kissed her gently and lovingly. "I've been waiting weeks for that. Hum . . . mm, you taste good. Like a French-fried potato." His blue eyes held hers. "Put your arms around me."

"We shouldn't . . ." she whispered as she obediently wound her arms about his neck.

"No one can see us but the birds, and they're only interested in other birds."

"You're crazy, but I love you."

Their lips moved together. "Sweetheart . . . love . . ." He whispered love words softly, and his mouth moved over her face to meet her lips again and again, hard and demanding at first, then tenderly as his tongue moved to part her lips and taste the sweetness of her mouth.

"Talk to me, babe. Tell me everything that's happened in your life, and I'll tell you about mine. Darling, about Monica—"

She placed her fingers over his lips. "No, I remember how she was. I know what you told me was true. I just didn't want to believe it at the time. The hurt was too new."

"After we're married, I want to adopt Brenda. I've given it a lot of thought. I want to be more than a brother-in-law. I really love that kid."

For a few minutes Iris was swamped with emotion. She managed a shaky smile when she saw the anxiety in his eyes.

"Are you sure?"

"Absolutely., I'd like a boy, too. Wanta make one?"

"Here? Now?" She laughed and squirmed against him. Her taut nipples in the wet bra raked across his chest.

"He'd be a unique kid. Kids at school would say, 'Hey, Sam. Where were you conceived?' He'd say, 'Out in the

cornfield one warm June day. My folks were stuck together with catsup at the time.' "

"Mister, you've lost a few bricks!" Laughter bubbled
from her lips and danced in her smoky eyes.

"I love to hear you laugh." His voice was abruptly
husky. "Promise me you'll laugh every day for the next
fifty years."

"Make it forty and it's a deal." Her eyes remained brilliant with laughter and love. His face was a mixture of astonishment and delight. He pinched her bottom.
"Yeoo . . ." She choked off the yelp of surprise and tickled his ribs.

They rolled in the dirt and laughed. Then he kissed her
long and hard while running his hands down her slender
form. The bra was pushed aside, and the jeans, which
kept his hands from her soft skin, were loosened. They
lay entwined, not making love, content to be there together. There was plenty of time.

John lifted his head, and his eyes held hers in mischie-
vous bondage. Her eyes shone up into his, and her mouth
couldn't keep from smiling. It was so very magical to be
held close, with his arms locked around her, her tired
body resting against his—their minds attuned.

"If the neighbors saw me lying in the dirt with you
they'd think I'd flipped out, for sure."

"Yeah. I can hear 'em. Strange things goin' on over at
the Ouverson place, they'd say. It should liven up the talk
at the feed store."

"At the Lang place," she corrected gently.

He smiled and kissed her nose. His eyes glittered happily, and his fingers worried her nipple, gently exciting
her. "I can't believe my luck, wanton woman. I love you

very much and in many ways I didn't know a man could love a woman. I fell in love right away and nearly cried when you hated me so much." The smile in his eyes and on his lips was real. His hand moved over her body in what seemed a reverent way.

Iris wound her arms around his neck and pressed closer to him. She knew she was loved and that she loved in return. He knew it, too. She could tell by the unfettered look of pleasure in his eyes when he gazed at her. This was home—the safest, most wonderful place in all the world. It would still be home if they were on a Pacific island or in an Alaskan igloo. This long, lean body pressed to hers was the torch that lighted her life.

Iris felt hot breath on her face and dreamily opened her eyes. Arthur's nose was inches away. His head was cocked to one side, and his tongue lolled.

"Arthur! You're drooling." Laughter rippled in John's voice. He rolled her over him and away from the dog. He kissed her face and nibbled on her neck, biting softly and sucking gently. "Do you like that, sweetheart?"

"Uh-huh."

"Can't you be a little bit more enthusiastic?" he asked with a growl.

"Well . . ." Her eyes glinted down at him as she pondered the question. "They're better kisses than I'd get from Arthur."

Her peals of laughter were cut off abruptly.

BOOK TWO

AMBER-EYED MAN

To Mary Bruza
—because she is my sister
and I love her.

CHAPTER ONE

A SOFT BREEZE caressed Meredith Moore as she gazed from the bedroom window out into the velvet dark of the Mexican night. Carrying with it exotic sounds and scents, it coolly bathed her face and gently lifted her pale, shoulder-length blonde hair. She drew in her breath at the sight of the white fuscia and gardenia blossoms, glowing in the light of hanging lanterns, a border for the cobbled courtyard below. In the center, she could just make out a graceful mountain silhouetted against the darkening sky. As tired as she was from her journey, she could have looked out onto that scene forever, so different was it from everything she'd ever known. With an effort, she turned to finish unpacking the last of her suitcases.

Here again beauty greeted her. Softly lit by a pink-shaded lamp beside the bed, the room boasted deep rose bedcovers, matched by the drapes at the windows. When she moved toward the white dresser, painted with intricate gold designs on its curved front, her shoes sank deep into the soft white carpet. She soon found that the splendor of the bedroom was more than equaled by that of the attached bath. Eager to soak away the grime and fatigue of the long day, Meredith entered the turquoise and white room, and gasped with pleasure at the sight of the enormous tub, the glass-enclosed shower, the plush, fluffy bath towels hanging on gold bars and the bowls of tangy smelling salts and potpourri lining the marble top of the vanity.

After turning on the gleaming brass taps, Meredith scattered a cloud of bath crystals into the steaming cascade of water. As the haunting, seductive fragrance enveloped her, she settled gracefully into the tub, a smile on her generous lips. Perfect, she thought, just what the doctor ordered. Her immediate cares slipped away, and for the moment she could concentrate on relaxing—and could forget what had brought her to the secluded Mexican villa of Ward Sanderson, a man she did not even know.

The warm water of the bath lulled her, and Meredith forced herself to leave its comfort while she still had the energy to do so. She patted herself dry with a lamb-soft towel and returned to her room, her bare toes luxuriating in the rich carpet. Her hair, now a little damp, framed a heart-shaped face delicately and faintly sprinkled with freckles. An appealing face, with its straight nose, wide, generous mouth, and startlingly blue eyes, it seemed even more so now that her skin glowed like pale honey.

Lifting her hair with both hands, she piled it on top of her head and studied her reflection in the mirror. She didn't look one day older than twenty-five, though recently she'd felt at least one hundred. Meredith did notice, though, that wearing her hair up emphasized her slenderness and made her look younger. Abruptly she let the golden locks fall and turned to the bed to pick up her skirt and blouse.

Suddenly she leaped backward with a gasp. Something

had pinched her bare toes, though her alarm came more from surprise than pain. But she was quickly put at ease when she looked down. Instead of the curling back of a venomous scorpion, a yellow-ribboned braid of dark hair peeked out from under the rose bedspread. She knew it could belong to none other than Maggie Sanderson, and she determined to wreak playful revenge on her host's four-year-old daughter.

Quickly, quietly, she walked to the other side of the bed, then in a flash dived under it, reaching for the small wiggling figure. Despite her stealth and speed, however, Maggie escaped her grasp, and scrambled out to run screeching through the bathroom and into the bedroom beyond.

Meredith ran after her, her robe flapping around her bare legs. She arrived in the room in time to see two small feet disappear under the bed. She fell down on her knees and then flat on her stomach as she wiggled into the narrow space after the laughing, shrieking child. Grabbing the small sturdy body, she tickled her ribs and the child laughed even more, turning from side to side in an attempt to get away.

"So this is the monster that attacked my toe." Meredith nipped a small arm with her teeth. "I'll teach you, monster, to go around attacking people."

"No . . . No! I'm Princess Leia!" the child shouted between giggles.

"Oh, yeah? Well, I'm King Kong!"

The playful scene was soon shattered, however, when a voice boomed out, "What in the name of common sense is going on here?"

Meredith heard the deep voice before she saw the two shiny, black shoes planted firmly beside the bed. The child grew still at once, then a delighted, impish smile lit up her pixie face.

"Daddy!" In a flash she was out from under the bed.

Meredith could see the small, sandled feet beside the two large, black shoes. If ever in her life she wished the floor would open up and swallow her, this was the time. But, of course, no such miracle happened, and she attempted to climb out from under the bed with as much dignity as the circumstances allowed. She stood with her back to the man until she was sure the robe covered her, then turned her head up to look into the richest pools of amber she'd ever seen. She barely managed to stifle a gasp of surprise, but was unable to tear her eyes away from those brooding tawny depths, which despite her sudden appearance, bespoke a quality other than surprise. Was it hurt, Meredith wondered?

Yet while his eyes were soft, his voice was harsh as it broke the silence. "Who the devil are you?"

Meredith was frozen with shock. Her mouth opened and trembled. "Meredith Moore."

"Oh for God's sake!" he said in English before a torrent of Spanish curses fell from his lips. Stunned, Meredith watched his strange, light, tawny-colored eyes sweep over her. "Oh for God's sake!" he said again. "Jim didn't say. . . . I assumed you would be . . . well, to be frank, closer to retirement age!"

She licked her dry lips. "I have a ways to go, I'm afraid."

"I can see that!" He expelled a heavy breath, then lowered his gaze to Maggie, who had wrapped her arms tightly around his legs. He fondled the child's dark head before he returned his chilling gaze to Meredith, whose thin shoulders seem to brace themselves defensively. His eyes narrowed. "You're not at all what I expected," he said cruelly.

She took a quivering breath, despising the tears that sprang to her eyes.

"Daddy." Maggie shook his leg to get his attention. "I pinched her toe." Suppressing a giggle, she added, "She chased me."

His grim mouth relaxed as he looked down at the small face, but he seemed to grow tense as he turned his attention back to Meredith.

Though she had been desperate for a place to stay, Meredith had her pride. "I'm sorry I'm not what you expected," she said, trying not to lose herself in those eyes. "I'll leave at once." Bold words! She didn't know where she would go, but pride forced her to say them.

He didn't respond immediately, but allowed his gaze to flicker over her, the tawny eyes narrowed to mere slits. Then he gave a brusque gesture.

"We won't discuss it now. Be in the library in fifteen minutes."

For a long moment she didn't move. A play of emotions flashed through her—despair, doubt, and then resignation. She stared steadily at the man before turning toward her room, pride in every line of her slender figure and in the tilt of her poised head.

"Just a minute." His voice cut into the silence.

She stopped instantly. She turned, her face composed, but she knew her eyes shone unnaturally bright with tears between the fringe of her dark, gold-tipped lashes.

"Have you had dinner?" His voice was impersonal, crisp, and cool.

"No, I haven't." Her voice was equally cool.

Never removing his eyes from her, he nodded his head slightly and said, "Fifteen minutes."

"Certainly," she responded coldly. She managed to hold her head high as she left, but the more she walked, the more difficult it became to keep from sobbing out loud. As soon as she was far enough away from him, her pace quickened, and she ended up running into her room, already a haven, and flinging herself onto the comforting softness of the bed. Here she could sob until there was nothing left inside her.

She cursed her fate. Coming here had seemed like such a good idea! After having met the formidable Ward Sanderson, however, she wasn't sure. If only she hadn't seen Laura Jameson take her baby from the hospital that night, her life could have continued on its comfortable, safe way.

Though outwardly dramatic, the incident had at first seemed far from earth-shattering. Young and unmarried, Laura Jameson had been forced to give up her infant daughter for adoption. Yet she had wanted just a little time alone with her Jenny, and had seen nothing wrong with "borrowing" the child for a few hours. Meredith was touched by Laura's action, but became outraged when she learned that her own eyewitness testimony at an upcoming hearing could mean that the young woman might be forbidden from ever seeing her child again. Meredith could not help but remember her own childhood, a succession of drab holidays and forlorn birthdays, sometimes forgotten altogether by the foster family she happened to be with.

"How cruel!" Meredith had exclaimed to Jim Sanderson when the two commiserated about the turn of events over coffee a few days afterward. As the social worker on the case, Jim had been responsible for placing the infant with a young couple, the Thomases. Years ago, he had done the same for Meredith, bringing her from the orphanage to her first foster home, and ever since he had been a kindly uncle to her.

Jim nodded in agreement. "And the pity of it is," he said, "that I know Laura meant no harm by what she did. She just wanted to say goodbye. If only Bob Thomas had some time to cool off," he added glumly, "I'm convinced he'd change his mind about getting the court order." The two stared dismally into their coffee.

But only a few moments later, his eyes lit up. "Wait a minute!" he said. "I have a fabulous idea." He suggested that Meredith leave town for a few weeks so that she couldn't appear at the hearing. "My cousin Cullen lives in a magnificent home—an estate, really—in Guadalajara. I believe his brother Ward is there right now, along with his little child Maggie. I'm sure they wouldn't mind having a guest—especially for a good cause." Jim described his plan, his eyes dancing with pleasure and benevolent mischief.

"And I bet Ward would really welcome your company. I think you could be a big influence on Maggie—that feminine touch, you know."

"Why?" asked Meredith. "Has his marriage suffered the fate of so many nowadays? How did he get custody of the child?"

"As a matter of fact, he's never been married—the child was his younger sister's—Cullen's twin—but she was killed in the accident that paralyzed Cullen. Ward, of course, took the girl in as his own, and she's always been treated as his little girl. I'd be surprised if he hasn't spoiled her to death."

Meredith's blue eyes had widened in horror at hearing the tragedy that had struck the Sanderson family. How true it was, she mused, that even fantastic wealth could not shield anyone from pain. "I'm so glad Maggie had someone to take her in. . . ." Her voice trailed off as she remembered how lonely her own childhood had been.

Jim put his hand on hers. "Well just think how much better it'll be for both her and Cullen to have you around. And how much it will help Laura Jameson."

Yet what had seemed like the perfect solution then seemed to be just a very bad mistake right now. If only she hadn't been so impulsive, Meredith thought as she dragged her exhausted body from the bed. In the bathroom mirror, her now puffy blue eyes stared dully back at her.

"No!" she said aloud, pulling herself up to her full height. She splashed her face with cool water, then patted it softly with one of the luxurious towels. "You will *not* let that man destroy you. You've worked too hard to be where you are."

As she applied her make-up, she fought to forget Paul, charming Paul—so handsome he was almost beautiful, and so subtly elegant and smooth that it took Meredith almost four years to realize that under the glossy surface there was absolutely nothing. She would never again allow a man, and especially not a handsome man, to do what Paul had done to her self-esteem. If this Ward Sanderson thought he could bully her, he had another think coming. After all, he was just a man. . . . Even though, for a time back in Maggie's room, she knew she could lose herself for all time in those tawny eyes.

CHAPTER TWO

WHEN MEREDITH EMERGED from her room fifteen minutes later, a young maid was waiting for her in the hall.

"O, Señorita," she exclaimed as she put out a hand to touch Meredith's rich turquoise blouse, *"Es muy bella!"* She then remembered her position, and quickly drew back her hand. Meredith could tell by the look in her velvet black eyes that the young woman feared a reprimand.

"Gracias," she replied quickly, employing almost all of her Spanish vocabulary. She smiled at the woman, and made a gesture toward a stunning silver and turquoise barrette in her raven hair. *"Muy bella,* also," she said, and they joined in laughter at Meredith's mixing the two languages.

Heartened by the success of the exchange, Meredith scoured her memory for just a little more of her high-school Spanish. *"Mi nombre . . .* Meredith," she said slowly.

The other woman laughed, and pointed a dainty hand toward herself. "Elena," she responded. Then, with a shy smile, she led Meredith downstairs to the lower corridor and indicated another door some distance along the hall.

"Biblioteca, Señorita Meredith," she said. "Li-bra-ree," she translated with a smile.

Meredith nodded, returned a very well pronounced, *"gracias,"* and continued down the hall to the room in which the man she had begun to think of as her tormen-tor waited. She pictured him pacing, lionlike, ready to de-vour her after one quick scrutiny with those tawny, jungle eyes. Then she caught herself up. Come on, Meredith, she scolded herself, if you keep thinking like that, you'll be back in the same boat you were in with Paul. Picking up her pace, she strode with determination toward what she now considered her "moment of truth."

Yet when she got close to the library, she hesitated. The door was slightly ajar, and her host was talking on the telephone. Unfortunately—or perhaps it was fortu-nate, she thought ruefully, since she now knew exactly where she stood—the connection was not a good one, and Ward Sanderson's deep voice boomed even more loudly than it would have normally.

"No, I'm not angry, Jim," he was saying, "but dammit, you should have told me a little more about her. You said a woman who'd been working at the Mayo Clinic. I as-sumed she was older. How the hell was I to know she looked like a college kid? Different? Ha! I'll bet she's dif-ferent! How do you know?" During the silence, Meredith fumed. "I'll be the first to admit that Cullen needs young people around, but his mother will make things difficult once she hears about this. Norma's so damn afraid some girl will come along and catch Cullen's fancy that she can't keep her head on straight. Thank God she's away on another one of her cruises at the moment. Dammit, Jim! I know it's not a healthy situation, but what the hell can I do about it? Cullen's a grown man. He may not be able to walk, but there's nothing wrong with his head. This girl . . . doesn't she have any family you can send her to?" Silence. "Yes, I know that. I didn't say she was an opportunist because she was raised in foster homes. I said you should have . . ."

The awkwardness of the situation made Meredith clench her teeth. Fighting a strange tight feeling in her throat, she took a deep breath to build up courage before she faced the ordeal she knew was coming. The man stopped speaking, and she heard the click of the receiver being replaced. She waited a moment longer, then knocked on the door. When his command to enter came, it was with reluctance that she pushed open the door and entered the book-lined room.

He was standing in the shadows at the far end, his dark head outlined against the light draperies. He didn't bother to move as she closed the door.

"Sit down, Miss Moore." It was an uncompromising order.

Meredith remained standing. Her eyes never left the figure standing in the shadows. She heard a swift intake of breath and realized it was her own.

Ward Sanderson surveyed her with unconcealed impatience. "Please . . . sit down."

Deciding her legs were not all that reliable at the moment, she sought a small, straight-backed chair. She seated herself, then faced him.

He walked to the large, leather-covered desk in the middle of the room, and seated himself on the corner, all the while keeping his gaze fixed on her. Despite her determination to handle the interview coolly, she colored under his intent scrutiny, and felt as she once had when called to the principal's office in school for sticking her bubble gum in the hair of a girl who had taunted her about being a welfare child.

Suddenly Meredith realized that he was waiting for her to speak first. She straightened her back stubbornly and decided to say nothing, but her eyes seemed to be drawn to his, and he held them with a probing stare before moving from her face to her hair, then down the full length of her body. Although his glance was cool, almost clinical, Meredith's body responded to his scrutiny with an almost sensual shudder. She was furious. The conceited prig! Who in the world did he think he was to subject her to such treatment? What did he know about her kind of life? He'd never had to eat cornbread and milk for supper or put cardboard in his shoes to keep his feet out of the snow!

When he spoke his voice was softer than she expected. "How old are you?"

"Twenty-five." She was so angry she could hardly speak.

"Twenty-five," he repeated, meditatively. He leaned back and took a slim cigar from a box on the desk and with his eyes still on her he lit it with a silver lighter before he spoke again. "You look about . . . eighteen."

Meredith's lips tightened. "My problem, not yours." She said the words tensely.

A smile almost reached the tawny eyes. Unexpectedly he leaned forward and the smell of the expensive Havana cigar smoke invaded her nostrils.

"You're not what I expected. Jim said you were a technician working in Rochester, Minnesota at the Mayo Clinic. He neglected to mention that you were young and attractive so I assumed you were older. After all, that's quite a responsible job you have, and the Mayo Clinic—"

Meredith did not let him continue. "Well, I'm a responsible person," she said calmly, though she was furious inside. "I'm sorry Jim misled you. Naturally I won't impose on your hospitality." She couldn't keep the words from coming, but bit back and swallowed her desire to tell him what she thought of him.

He drew deeply on the cigar, his dark brows drawn closely together. She glanced at him from beneath her lashes and his expression seemed to be more serious than angry. He continued smoking without taking his eyes from her face and she felt herself becoming unnerved by his stare. She racked her brain for something to say. Damn, why didn't he say something? Abruptly she stood up, but her knees felt weak from hunger and the strain of the trip, and she held tightly to the back of the chair.

His lips barely moved, but she heard his words distinctly. "Sit down."

She did, wishing desperately she could leave this man's presence before she made some undignified outburst, just to relieve the tension. She sat on the edge of the chair, silent, a mingling of inquiry and rebellion on her face. The thought flashed through her mind that this was the kind of man Paul would like to be—rich, powerful, confident. But the shallow Paul would never make it! Sanderson would ooze confidence if he stood ragged and barefoot.

He continued to look at her. The tawny, wide-spaced, clear eyes were the color of a young lion. They were fascinating eyes, unwavering, and, as she had the first time she met him, Meredith sensed an undercurrent of pain just below their amber surface. Deep crinkly grooves marked the corners, put there when the eyes had squinted against the sun. There were other lines, too, that experience, tiredness, or bitterness had made.

But before she could speculate further, he stood suddenly, picked up some papers from the desk, and took them to a file cabinet at the end of the room. For the first time Meredith noticed he limped slightly when he walked. She also remarked upon the breadth of his shoulders and the narrowness of his hips in the dark business suit. He was, she was forced to admit, an impressive man, tall, lithe, with a head of crisp, springy brown hair, that blended well with his tanned skin.

She dreaded the moment when he would turn and look at her. This man had caused her confidence to come tumbling down. The golden glow of the few carefree minutes she had spent with his little girl diminished and died beneath the onslaught of his rebuff. She wished, desperately, that she could think of something cutting to say, to fling his hospitality in his face and leave!

He came toward her, but just walked past her to the door. With his hand on the knob he said, "Let's have dinner."

Meredith wasn't sure she had heard right. She got unsteadily to her feet and smoothed her skirt with shaky hands.

"Come on." He opened the door and stepped aside for her to pass through. Then he escorted her down the corridor and into a small room where a fire burned in a stone fireplace. A table was set for two and beside it stood a cart with gleaming dishes of food. He lifted the lid from a large tureen and a delicious aroma made her feel even hungrier than she had just moments before. Meredith stood inside the door. "Sit here." He held a chair out for her. His movements were easy and flowing despite his limp.

He placed a large bowl of soup in front of her, then served himself and sat down across from her. Meredith was almost afraid to lift her trembling hands to the bright silverware. More than anything in the world she wished to keep this man from knowing how crushed she was, how miserable she felt, how his attitude brought back memories of years spent, unwanted, in foster homes. Not for anything would she reveal her true feelings or anything at all about herself to this stony-hearted man who was, as far as she could tell, as compassionless and self-centered as Paul.

He buttered a large, hard roll and placed it on a dish beside her plate.

"These are called *bolillos* and are delicious with soup."

Meredith glanced at him quickly. Damn him! Why was he acting now as if she were a guest? He was eating and she was relieved his eyes were on the food and not on her. She began to eat, pleased that it was easier than she thought it would be. She had been sure she would be unable to swallow. Her tension eased and she had finished half the soup when he spoke again.

"While we're eating I'll tell you about Maggie."

His words were a shock, causing her to halt the spoon

in midair. She said nothing, nor did she look at him, and he continued.

"Maggie has spent the last few weeks here with my brother. In a few more weeks I'm taking her home where she'll start public school. I don't suppose you know that I actually live in Tulsa, although of course I do spend a lot of time here looking after the family plant in Guadalajara. At any rate, because Maggie was born in the fall, she'd normally have to wait another year to go to school, but I was told she'd be taken if she could pass an exam. It's difficult to believe that there can be entrance requirements for kindergarten, but that's what they tell me, and I'm not at all certain Maggie will qualify. The school prepared a list of the things she should know and when Jim called and said you needed a place to lose yourself for a while, I assumed you would be willing to take on that chore."

"And now that you have seen that I'm not middle-aged and fat, you don't think I'll be able to handle it." It was a petulant thing for her to say and she knew it. The twinkle in his eyes told her he knew it too.

"Maggie has had a procession of people looking after her. Despite all that, she's a well-adjusted little girl. What she really needs is children to play with. It's important for her to get into school now."

Meredith continued to spoon the soup into her mouth. He seemed to be determined to make conversation. "Jim said you took your training at Tulsa Memorial, but were in Rochester for the last few years. Did you like the work?"

She ignored his question, preferring to pose one of her own. "Now that you've seen the opportunist who was raised in foster homes at government expense, what do you think?" After speaking the words, Meredith carefully placed her spoon beside her plate and her eyes fastened on his face. When she looked at him she saw a glimmer of admiration cross his face, and his lips twitched slightly. He raised his brows.

"I eavesdropped," she said matter-of-factly.

He chose to ignore her confession. "Are you a good x-ray technician?" he asked again.

"I'm a very good technician." Her eyes held his. "I was top in my class or I wouldn't have received an offer to work at the Mayo Clinic."

"Have you had any experience with paralytics?" He had stopped eating and was looking at her intently.

"Only when they were brought to my department for x-rays."

"Do you know about my brother?"

"Jim told me he lost the use of his legs—and you said he was smothered by his mother."

He smiled. It seemed to her that a curtain had been raised. "You don't miss much, do you?"

"I can't afford to. I'm all I've got."

Meredith wondered how long her courage would last. She had had the pleasure of telling him she knew of his small-minded suspicions of her, and she had let him know she wasn't frightened of him. At least a little of her pride had been salvaged.

He removed the empty soup bowls and replaced them with a plate containing a small steak. Meredith shook her head, knowing she couldn't possibly eat the meat. He resumed eating before he spoke. "Eat what you can. You look as if the wind could blow you away."

She felt a stab of resentment and her heart pounded in response to her anger. Who was he to tell her what she should or should not do? She could look after herself, thank you very much.

Seeing the anger in her face, he grinned, his even white teeth a contrast to his tanned cheeks. The effect was at once devilish and attractive, and reminded Meredith of her image of him, a voracious lion, ready to devour whatever—or whomever—he chose. He finished his steak without saying anything else. Meredith managed to swallow only a few bites.

Yet the butterscotch custard, warm and laced with heavy cream, was another matter. When she first tasted it, her eyes widened in appreciation. She caught Ward looking at her and deliberately refused to look away.

"It's called flan and is Carmen's specialty. Do you like it?"

"Very much," she murmured.

They finished the meal in silence, and when Ward rang a bell, Elena came and piled the dishes onto a serving cart and rolled it to the door. He spoke to her in Spanish. She flashed a quick smile in Meredith's direction, then nodded to Ward before going out of the room.

Meredith felt uncomfortable. She didn't know if she was dismissed, and would be damned before asking if the master of the house had finished with her. He, however, seemed totally at ease, and why not? He was in charge. He stood and moved to a table for a cigar. Meredith rose, too, intending to leave the room, but was stopped by a wave of his hand. He motioned her to a deep, brown leather chair and she knew her ordeal was not yet over.

Elena returned with a tray and placed it on a table beside her chair.

"I thought you might enjoy our Spanish chocolate."

Looking far more composed than she felt, she accepted the cup he handed her and murmured her thanks. He poured a cup for himself and, sitting down, surprised her by saying, "Tell me about yourself."

Meredith had no intention of being taken in by a few kind words.

"You know all there is to know, Mr. Sanderson," she replied with a shake of her head. "Jim thought we could avoid unnecessary suffering if I didn't testify at a court hearing back in Minnesota about a child-snatching, or rather child-borrowing, incident I witnessed. Naturally I could have disappeared somewhere in the States, but Jim was insistent that I come here. He said you could use someone to help take care of Maggie. Apparently he was wrong. If I could trouble you for transportation into Guadalajara tomorrow, I'll check into a hotel."

As soon as she'd said the bold words, she chastised herself. Damn! Her pride made her so reckless. What would she do if she couldn't use any of her credit cards here? But she didn't allow any of the apprehension she was feeling to show in her face, and she looked at him with wide, clear eyes.

"Are you always so confident?" he asked.

"No, not always," she answered honestly.

"I know what happened to you in the hospital. Jim filled me in on that. He finds your sympathy for the young mother admirable. You're lucky to have him for a friend, you know. But I want to know more about you. Your plans. Your ambitions."

She was silent for as long as it took her to fight down the angry words that leaped to her lips. What nerve! He sat there like the master inquisitor! Somehow she managed to swallow an angry retort. She must be prudent. In a foreign country with little money and no transportation, she simply wasn't in any position to take offense to his prying. But—dammit—she didn't have to bare her soul to him either. Resentment of his attitude showed in the look she gave him.

"Mr. Sanderson." Her voice was wooden with control. "I fail to see how you can possibly be interested in my personal ambitions. You seem to think I came here under false pretenses, but let me assure you I did not come here to ingratiate myself with you or your brother. I am not seeking a rich husband. That you find me unsuitable to be in your home is your privilege, but to pry into my personal life is not."

Inside her breast her heart was thudding like a sledgehammer at her own temerity. It was unreal that she could have spoken these words to this man. She was a guest in his home. An unwanted one, but a guest nevertheless. She closed her eyes for only a second and when she opened them he was still sitting there, his head resting against the back of the chair, his eyes locked onto hers. He looked deep, as if he were looking into her past, her present, and her future. His face was expressionless and his words when they came shocked her, for she had expected a cruel retaliation to her brashness.

"Does anyone call you Merry?" His voice was almost lazy as if he were talking to himself.

Surprised by the question, Meredith shook her head. "Then I shall," he said softly. He sat up and flexed his shoulder muscles wearily. "It's been a long day. Go to bed, Meredith Moore. In the morning I'll dig out that list of requirements for Maggie."

Meredith's lips parted in dismay. "You want me to stay?"

He got to his feet and stood looking down at her, a somewhat puzzled expression on his leathery face. "Yes, Merry. I want you to stay."

She made an attempt to stand, then sank back down, a pulse throbbing noticeably in her throat. Color had seeped from her face and she felt light-hearted. Was he deliberately trying to confuse her? She pushed back a tendril of pale gold hair and stared at him.

A smile creased his cheeks, crinkled the corners of the tawny eyes and took away some of the strain from his tired face. He reached down a hand and pulled her to her feet. As he looked at her his incredible eyes softened and suddenly they seemed to envelop her in a warm snare of tender amusement. His hand came up and stroked her cheek. It was a large hand, strong but surprisingly gentle. Even his voice was deep and gentle as he chided her.

"Don't try to figure me out, Merry mía."

He turned her toward the door and in her confused state she was scarcely aware she was being conducted to the foot of the steps leading to the upper balcony. On the first step she turned, her face level with his, a curiously guarded look on her face.

He was standing very quietly, his eyes probing hers with a startling intensity. She hesitated, then started up the steps. Once she reached the top she looked back, but the hall was empty, and the last few minutes she'd spent with him seemed like a dream.

CHAPTER THREE

THE NEXT MORNING Meredith was up, dressed, and standing beside the window when the sun made its first appearance. She had spent a restless night, her thoughts preoccupied by the people she had just met. Neither Paul, the clinic, nor Laura Jameson had entered her mind. Ward Sanderson was another story. He had floated in and out of her dreams all night long. She wasn't sure why, but even now it made her faintly uncomfortable to think about him.

She looked down into the courtyard where the sun was brilliant on the blue mosaic tiles that surrounded the fountain. Made of lapis lazuli and patterned as intricately as a Persian carpet, the tiles were laid the width of the courtyard. In the shady oasis of a poinsettia tree was an inviting bench. The peaceful scene should have given her pleasure, but it didn't. Whatever was wrong with her, she asked herself impatiently as she moved restlessly from the window.

On impulse she threw on a lavender sundress and left her room. As she walked slowly down the carpeted stairs through the quiet house, it occurred to her that the dwelling boasted so many wings and courtyards that a large number of people could live there without intruding on one another. Still, was it large enough for her to avoid Ward Sanderson? She doubted it.

On reaching the courtyard, she was pleased to find that the sunlight was already warm. She faced the sun for a moment, her chin uplifted, eyes closed, and the palms of her hands extended. The warmth was delicious and seemed to penetrate deep inside, melting her worries away. Now, faint sounds of a child's voice came to her. She crossed the courtyard, and moved toward the back of the house. It seemed a long distance to Meredith until she realized the walkways branched off and came together, dividing plots of the garden. She rounded a corner and could see the glimmer of water in a swimming pool. She heard splashing and Maggie's excited voice.

"Don't let them see you, Merry."

Somehow Meredith wasn't startled by her host's voice. Ward stood in the shade of a flowering shrub. Wearing bathing trunks, he was rubbing his head with a large bath towel.

"Why not?" She surprised herself because the words came more easily than she expected.

"Cullen is teaching Maggie to swim. He'll be embarrassed if you see him getting out of the pool."

"Of course. I understand." Meredith nodded. She would be considered one of his peers. In the hospital, many young disabled men were reluctant to let young nurses assist them.

As if it were the most natural thing in the world, he

took her hand. "Let's go back and give Cullen time to get out of the pool."

She was almost breathless. Why was his hand so rough and hard? Rich men were supposed to have soft, smooth hands. She had to walk quite close to him on the narrow path and she noticed his limp was more pronounced when he walked on the rough cobblestones. He was taller than she remembered. She had been able to look straight into Paul's eyes when they faced each other, but she only came up to this man's chin.

They stopped beneath a latticed portal. A jungle of flowering vines and other leafy greenery hung from the ceiling. The perfume from the plants was faint and sweet. Ward released her hand and wrapped the large towel about his waist.

"Cullen is an excellent landscape engineer. He laid out these gardens and designed the fountain. Lately he's lost interest in everything except the plants in his rooms and his magic. I had to twist his arm to get him to teach Maggie to swim. I could have done it myself, but he and Maggie have a special relationship and I played on that."

"Doesn't his condition allow him to work?" Meredith looked up into tawny eyes and decided that she liked them—this morning, anyway. Last night they had been more ferocious.

"I suspect it has more to do with my stepmother. She's always been a possessive mother, and since the accident she's had an excuse to keep Cullen with her," Ward explained.

Suddenly Meredith felt annoyed at his cavalier attitude toward Cullen, just as she felt resentful at the strange hold he had begun to exert on her.

"Why do you allow it?" Her eyes challenged him.

"Allow what?" he countered brusquely.

Meredith was satisfied that he seemed annoyed by her bluntness. "Allow your stepmother to dominate your brother's life?"

"Why should I interfere? Cullen is a twenty-five-year-old man and if he doesn't have the backbone to tell his mother he can take care of himself, then he deserves to be henpecked!"

"You don't mean that," she replied calmly. "I can't believe you don't care enough about him to help him stand up to her."

He looked at her as if she had lost her mind. He stood quietly for a moment and when he spoke it was with puzzlement in his voice. "Do you always jump in with both feet?"

For an instant she was stumped for something to say, but she came up with a quick answer. "What have I got to lose?"

He laughed. She forgot herself and laughed with him. "Do you want to take a swim?"

"No." Her answer was too abrupt so she softened it. "No, thank you."

"Afraid you'll ruin your hairdo?"

"What hairdo? It's just that I don't have a suit."

"That can be fixed."

"I don't swim."

He walked away from her and said over his shoulder, "I'll tell Carmen you'll breakfast with Maggie and me."

She watched him move away and wondered about his leg. Her medical knowledge told her that his was not a recent scar. The operation must have taken place years before, probably when he was a teenager.

Not knowing what to do with herself, she went back to her room and applied a touch of lipstick, then ran a comb through her hair.

When she went downstairs, it was with Maggie's hand tucked firmly in her own. The little girl was a delight. She had come into Meredith's room, wet braids hanging over her shoulders and an impish grin on her face, with Carmen, the cook, right behind her scolding in broken English.

"Hair not dry, little . . . mule!"

Together they had unbraided Maggie's hair and sat her under the big drier in the bathroom. Afterward Meredith had brushed and rebraided it while Maggie kept up an endless chatter. The child lived in an almost imaginary world, talking about her dolls and stuffed animals as if they were living creatures. Meredith almost felt sorry for her. She did need other children to play with.

Breakfast on a shaded terrace was easier than Meredith had thought it would be. Maggie acted as a buffer between her and Ward. She watched him with his daughter. He didn't even remotely resemble the stern-faced man of last night; although more relaxed now, he was far from careless in his attitude toward the little girl. When she spoke he listened closely to what she was saying. And Maggie, Meredith was surprised to discover, took on a more mature personality when she was with him.

"How are the swimming lessons coming?" He had placed on her plate scrambled eggs from a covered tureen and was buttering a slice of toast.

"Unk said I paddle like a puppy." She giggled. "Unk

said I can't use the doughnut to keep me up any more. He said I wouldn't learn to swim."

"Your uncle is right. He knows a lot about swimming. He made the Olympic swimming team when he was in college."

Meredith drew in her breath at hearing this, and exchanged a quick glance with Ward. A condition like Cullen's was certainly hard enough for anyone to bear, but for a gifted athlete it would be doubly hard. Thankfully, Meredith noticed that Maggie continued talking, unaware of her reaction.

"I wish Unk would go home with us, Daddy. I asked him to, but he said no. He could swim with me."

"We won't be filling the pool for another couple of months, punkin. It's colder in Tulsa than it is here." He placed food on his own plate and poured coffee for Meredith and then for himself. "We're going to enroll you in school when we get home, so you'll be very busy." He again met Meredith's eyes, then spoke to Maggie. "Merry is going to teach you some things that will help when you start school."

Maggie looked at Meredith with eyes big and round with astonishment. "Are you Mary Mary quite contrary?"

Ward laughed. The amber eyes gleamed at Meredith. There was nothing too familiar in his eyes, so she smiled happily back at him.

"My name is Meredith, Maggie, but call me Merry if you want to."

"I want to," Maggie said simply, and filled her mouth.

"Chew with your mouth closed, Maggie. I don't think Merry wants to see all that food rolling around inside."

The child looked at Meredith for confirmation, her mouth still agape.

"It seems to me that I remember seeing Princess Leia eating with her mouth closed." Meredith directed this remark to Ward.

He nodded gravely.

Maggie's eyes moved from one to the other. Abruptly she closed her mouth. When she emptied it, she said breathlessly, "Did you see her on TV?"

"No, in the movie. Do they show American films here?"

Ward answered for her. "There's an American colony in Chapala. They bring in American movies occasionally."

"Can we go see a movie, Daddy?"

"We'll see, sweetheart. We'll have to check and find out what's playing."

They were still sitting in the sunlit courtyard when an immaculately dressed man appeared—dark-skinned, dark-haired, with bold black eyes. He was certainly one of the most handsome men Meredith had ever seen, very slim and not much taller than herself. Almost a Latin version of Paul, she thought. With some relief, she realized she was not at all susceptible to his showy good looks.

He stood before her, clicked his heels, then with a barely perceptible bow said, "My name is Luis Calderon. *Buenos dias, señoritas. Buenos dias*, Ward."

"Morning, Luis. Help yourself to coffee."

"*Gracias.*" He bent close to Maggie. "How are you this morning, my beautiful one?" His voice was an exaggerated whisper and Maggie giggled.

Ward glanced at his watch and asked drily, "What brought you out so early, Luis? As if I didn't know."

The bold black eyes smiled into Meredith's. She felt irritation tinged with embarrassment. He was giving her his complete attention, ignoring both Ward and Maggie while he gazed at her. Finally Ward spoke again.

"If you want to bedazzle Miss Moore with your Latin charm, Luis, do it some other time. I want to leave for the plant within the hour and I have things to do."

Luis looked stricken. "You have no romance in your heart. How can you look at such a beautiful woman and not feel *amor?*"

Meredith got to her feet silently and uncomfortably. Luis stood up quickly. Ward remained seated, a slightly irritated look on his face. Maggie's small hand found its way into Meredith's.

"Señorita." Luis's face took on a sad, dejected expression. "Perhaps you would be interested in joining me to see the surrounding countryside. Lake Chapala is very beautiful, you know."

Before Meredith could answer, Ward got to his feet. "Oh for God's sake, Luis! You've got the hunting instincts of a tomcat. She hasn't even been here twenty-four hours!"

Ward's curt words didn't seem to bother Luis in the least, but they did Meredith. She was quite capable of turning down her own invitations.

"Thank you, *Señor* Calderon. Perhaps some other time." Her smile was more friendly than she intended due to her annoyance with Ward.

Luis came around the table, seized her hand, and raised it to his lips. "I shall hold you to that . . . Meredith."

She tugged her hand from his, took Maggie's, and they

walked away. "Shall we call on your uncle, Maggie?" she suggested.

Maggie led her into the interior of the house and out onto a long, screened veranda. Meredith could see, now, that the house was built in the shape of an H, with a front and back courtyard. When they reached the end of the veranda, Maggie broke loose and darted into an arched opening.

"Unk! Unky!" she called.

Meredith followed her through the door and stopped. The room was huge, and plants of every kind and description were everywhere—on the floor, on low tables, hanging from stands, and lining the window ledges. They had obviously been arranged with care and the effect was lovely. Meredith felt as if she were stepping into a magical garden.

"Hi."

The wheelchair came silently across the tile floor. The slightly built man in it wore a mismatched jogging suit and a scraggly beard. Maggie sat on his lap, her small hand working the controls of the battery-driven chair.

"Hi." Meredith smiled warmly. "Excuse my open mouth. I'm awestruck by this wonderful place. I'm Meredith Moore." She held out her hand.

He hesitated a moment before touching it briefly. "Cullen Sanderson."

He looked younger than Meredith had expected. His hair was lighter and longer than his brother's, but they had the same tawny eyes and sharp features. Cullen was handsomer, Meredith thought, or would be if he didn't have such a dejected slump to his shoulders.

"Can we show Merry the orchids, Unk?" Maggie

squirmed around and looked into his face. "Please, can 1 show her my Margarieta?"

"I doubt if Miss Moore . . ."

"Orchids? Oh, but I would! I would love to see them. But we're not interrupting something, are we?"

"You're not interrupting anything."

Meredith followed the chair thinking he wasn't exactly enthusiastic about the visit, but she was determined not to allow that to dim her enjoyment at seeing his beautiful plants. Maggie looked back to see if Meredith was coming and almost ran the chair into a large fern. Cullen grabbed the controls.

"Watch where you're going, Maggie, or you'll upset us." He wasn't impatient or cross and Maggie giggled.

They went through a doorway and down a corridor. Meredith could feel the change in temperature. The air was damp and warm. When Cullen stopped the chair inside the door of a shaded, glass-enclosed room, Meredith moved past him. Along one side of the small room was a long bench with three slatted steps lined with pots of orchids. She was speechless. She had never seen anything so lovely. But that wasn't all. The other side of the room was a simulated jungle with tree trunks and vegetation growing from beds of moss and humus. Hundreds of orchids had attached themselves to the bark of the tree trunks and surfaces of rocks among the moss. The sight was stunning.

"They're beautiful! Absolutely beautiful!" She smiled into Cullen's eyes before he turned away.

Maggie slipped off his lap. "This one's mine, Merry." The plant was small and without a bloom. "I helped Unk divide it and next year I'll have a flower. I named it the Margarieta."

"Lovely! You'll have your very own corsage. I had one when I graduated from high school. My oldest and dearest friend sent it to me and I kept it in the refrigerator for days and days."

"Mine's going to be yellow," Maggie said proudly. "Unk said if we're careful the bloom will stay on for . . ." She looked at Cullen as if not sure of her information.

"About three months." He smiled fondly at the little girl.

"Do the blooms really last that long?" Meredith still found it hard to believe she was standing in a room full of growing orchids.

"They're not as delicate as you think. Like any other plant you grow, the requirements vary as to temperature, humidity, light, and moisture. These," he indicated the ones growing on the tree stumps and in the moss, "are the most common. They're called Cattleyas and are shipped by the thousands to the States because they are easily grown and the blooms last a long time." He wheeled his chair to the end of the room and turned a large water control faucet. A fine mist sprayed the growth. "They require a lot of water and plenty of ventilation."

Meredith moved to the door to allow the chair to pass.

Cullen reached down and plucked a large ivory bloom from one of the pots and handed it to her. Meredith's lips parted in speechless astonishment.

"Oh! Oh—you shouldn't have! It's beautiful. Perfectly lovely." She smiled into his upturned face and he didn't turn away. "Thank you. But," she protested, "I don't have a refrigerator to put it in."

He smiled this time with his eyes as well as his mouth, and she decided she liked him. He waited for Maggie to crawl back on his lap and they left the dampness of the orchid room.

"Would you like some coffee?" Cullen asked.

"I'd love some."

They passed quickly through the large room with all the plants and into a room cluttered with books, magazines, hi-fi equipment of every description, two television sets, a pool table, and so many other things that Meredith had a hard time taking it all in.

"It's rather mind boggling, isn't it?" Cullen remarked.

"Not exactly mind boggling, but very different from the rest of the house."

He helped Maggie off his lap. "It's a form of rebellion. Like letting your hair grow long. My mother hates it." Meredith wasn't sure if he was teasing. He moved his chair to a table, poured coffee, and passed it to Meredith. "What would you like, Maggie? How about a doughnut?" He opened a door beneath a long counter and brought out a plastic container filled with chocolate-covered doughnuts.

Maggie looked over the selection and picked the one with the most icing. Protesting "I really shouldn't" and "I don't need this," Meredith reached into the container when it was offered.

"You don't look as if you need to worry about your weight." Their eyes met, his amber and teasing, hers blue and shining.

"Not now, but there'll come a time when all this will catch up with me. While I was working at the hospital I walked a million miles a day and I could eat like a horse, but now . . . I don't get half enough exercise." Suddenly she realized what she'd just said. Was that a callous thing to say to a man tied to a wheelchair? Would he hate her for talking about walking when he couldn't? Their eyes met and she knew that he knew what she was thinking.

"You can swim in the pool."

"Can't swim. I've only been in a pool a couple of times."

"Unk'll learn you." Maggie licked the icing from her lips. "Won't you, Unk?"

"You mean teach, sweetheart," Cullen corrected her gently.

"I'd be hopeless," Meredith said quickly. "I'd sink like a rock. Besides I won't be here long enough for that." Then in order to change the subject, she said the first thing that came to her mind. "Your brother said that you're a landscape engineer. It must be very satisfying to create something as beautiful as the gardens here."

He shrugged. "It wasn't much of a challenge."

Maggie drew her arm across her mouth leaving a streak of chocolate. "Can I have another one, Unk. Please . . . ?"

Cullen surveyed her thoughtfully, a smile curving his lips. "Go ahead, but you've still got half a doughnut on your face."

Maggie jumped off the chair and went to him. He leaned over and she planted a wet, sticky kiss on his cheek.

"I love you, Unk."

"I love you too, sweetheart."

Meredith suddenly felt choked up, half on the point of tears. She had never before heard an open declaration of love between two people. It was so spontaneous, so sweet, so obviously sincere that she swallowed the lump in her throat and looked away.

"You'll miss Maggie when Ward takes her home."

She didn't know why she said that.

"Yes, I will." The resignation in his voice touched her. She looked at him directly. His thin face was curiously reminiscent of Ward's. He had the same quality of reserve, but there was a sadness in his face that was lacking in his brother's.

Maggie finished her second doughnut.

"Go find Antonio, honey. Your face is all yucky."

Maggie scrambled away and Meredith took the opportunity to ask: "Who is that fellow Calderon? I just met him at breakfast."

"Luis runs our plant in Guadalajara. I call him the dude, but I guess he's an okay sort of guy." Cullen grinned. He had loosened up considerably since they first met. "I bet he's tried to *enamor* you already."

Meredith laughed. It was easy to laugh with him. He was nice. "Practice makes perfect and I doubt if *Señor* Calderon misses an opportunity to practice. Kidding aside, I appreciate being here and hope I'm not too much of an inconvenience."

"Not at all. Ward explained what happened in the hospital and I'm glad you're here. It's been so darn long since I've talked to an American girl." He looked away from her and out over the cluttered room.

"May I come back and visit you again?" Meredith desperately wanted to fill the void and save him embarrassment. "I was a shock to your brother, you know, and to the housekeeper, too. I think they thought because I'm an

x-ray technician and unmarried I was a reject or something." She looked into his eyes with a conspiratorial
smile.

"Ward isn't easily shocked."

"Who says so?"

The voice came from behind Meredith and she knew
immediately who it belonged to. Embarrassment grew in
her when she remembered what she had said. But—hang
it all! It was true.

"Hi, Daddy." Maggie skipped into view. "We showed
Merry my Margarieta."

"Did you, now?" He pulled up a chair and sat down
beside Meredith. "Here's a list from the school." He
handed her a paper.

As soon as Meredith glanced at the list of five simple
requirements, she knew that Jim had asked his cousin to
create a task for her so she wouldn't feel awkward. She
kept her eyes on the paper until she could gather her
thoughts.

"May I see it?"

At his request, she passed the paper to Cullen. He
looked it over and said, "She knows her ABC's and her
colors, but she needs work on writing her name and tying
her shoes. Can you count to twenty, Maggie?"

"I don't know," the child said indifferently.

Ward pulled at her braid. "We'd better get to finding
out, pretty girl."

As Ward got to his feet, Meredith again noticed his
height and slimness, emphasized now by his dark business suit. He looked down and caught her eye. Despite
the glint of humor she saw there, there was something

else, something reserved, private, that hadn't been there this morning. His eyes went to the flower in her hand.

"I'll leave you with Cullen and Maggie, Merry. See you this evening." He moved away, then turned back. "I'll tell Carmen to have the dinner served in the dining room, Cullen, so Merry can wear her orchid." He went through the door without waiting for a comment from his brother.

"Can I have a flower and eat with you, too, Unky? Please . . ." Maggie used her most appealing voice.

"You won't be able to stay up that long, sweetheart. How about a flower for you to wear while we have lunch?"

"Can Merry eat with us?"

"Sure. If she wants to."

Meredith grinned. Now that Ward had left them, the wave of self-consciousness had left also.

"I'd like nothing better."

"You have a very expressive face," Cullen said after Maggie had skipped away. "You have what my Spanish friends would call speaking eyes."

Her eyebrows lifted with interest and she smiled mischievously. "Don't tell me you can read my mind."

"Not quite, but almost."

"Thanks for warning me. When I get ready to steal the silver I won't think about it." She liked him, really liked him. He was easy to be with. The crackling tension she felt with Ward was gone now. Everything was right out there in the open. Meredith was pleased to see that there was even laughter in his eyes.

"I didn't mean that and you know it."

"I know it, but what did you mean, for heaven's sake?"

"Ward. You don't have to be afraid of him. If the truth

were known, he's more scared of you than you are of him."

Her pulse gave an uncomfortable leap. "You're kidding!"

Cullen laughed at the amazement on her face. "No, I'm not kidding. It's a new experience for him to have a girl freeze up on him. Usually they fall all over him."

Meredith laughed nervously. "How do you know I didn't fall all over him . . . last night?"

"He told me. This morning. He said you were independent, stubborn to the extent that you would have foolishly left the *hacienda* because you took a dislike to him, and that you were stupidly proud."

Meredith sat very still and the grin left her face.

"I'm sorry," Cullen said quickly. "Have I embarrassed you? I guess I kind of got carried away. You see . . . it's been so long since I talked to a girl my own age."

There was such pain in his eyes when he spoke that it almost brought tears to her own. She reached out a hand to where his rested on the table and he turned his palm up to meet it.

"I'm not embarrassed, Cullen. It's a shock, I guess, to find out how you come across to other people. I've never thought of myself as being stubborn, or . . . stupidly proud. I have been foolish. Very foolish, in fact." There was a sad shadow lurking in his eyes. She caught only a glimpse of it and she came so near to telling him about Paul and her blind, foolish devotion to him that it almost frightened her. Their conversation was getting too serious. "Stupidly proud, am I? Well, your brother isn't the soul of diplomacy. There's something about the way he looks at me that gets my back up!"

Cullen laughed and released her hand. "He's a master at that. He's the only person alive who can make my mother back down. I feel kind of guilty at times because I don't help him with the business, but then again, since the accident I've at least kept my mother busy and off his back."

Maggie came in, trailed by a manservant. "Can I go tell Carmen we're gonna eat with you, Unk? Can I go pick my flower? Do I have to have a little one? Why can't I have a big one like Merry's?"

Cullen reached out an arm and drew the child to him. "Maggie, sometimes I don't think your mouth and your brain are connected. How can I answer all those questions at once?"

"I don't know."

"Now about the flower. You can have a little one. Antonio," he called. "Let Maggie pick a Cattleyas. Then," he said to Maggie, "you can go and tell Carmen that you and Merry are going to have lunch with me." He wheeled his chair around and called out to Antonio again. "Hurry back. If we're going to have company for lunch, we've got to clean up this place and make it worthy of our guests." With this remark he winked at Meredith, then turned to the task at hand.

CHAPTER FOUR

IT WAS NEARLY time for dinner and Meredith stood before the mirror, wondering for the hundredth time if the dress she had chosen was suitable. A blouson in butterscotch gold, its peasant top was gathered at a banded neckline. The full raglan sleeves were elasticized at the wrist as was the waist of the blouse. The material was soft polyester. The label inside the dress said, "machine washable–tumble dry." The only thing it had going for it, she thought wryly, was that it was soft and feminine and the color was right. She had no doubt the orchid she pinned to it would cost much more than the dress had.

That afternoon she had written a long letter to Maude Fiske, the social worker who had taken Meredith to the orphanage after her mother had been killed by a hit-and-run driver. All these years, as Meredith was shuttled from foster home to foster home, Maude had provided a sense of permanence and stability. She had been careful to keep a small box of personal belongings for Meredith and had visited her on Christmas and holidays. Along with Jim Sanderson, Maude was the closest thing to family that

Meredith had, and Meredith knew she would want to know about the unusual events that had brought her to this magnificent *hacienda* in Guadalajara, of all places. Before she sealed the letter, she asked Carmen for the address of the *hacienda* so Maude could write her.

"To your *familia?*" the housekeeper asked, indicating the letter.

"No. To a dear friend."

She asked Carmen if she had a family. The question opened the way for a full hour's visit. Meredith discovered the estate there at Chapala was a lettuce ranch that employed a large number of people all under the direction of Carmen's husband, Carlos. She and Carlos had three daughters; two were married and one was going to medical school in Guadalajara. The servants in the house were well-trained, but needed supervision. Carmen explained. The *Señora* Sanderson was reluctant to leave her home unless she, Carmen, came in to see that everything ran smoothly.

"I enjoy being here when *Señor* Ward is here. He is much a man." Her dark eyes flashed, then narrowed as she looked at Meredith's unresponsive expression. "No?"

"Oh, yes. He's very nice." How could she say, she thought, that he scared her to death?

"Ward give you a bad time, eh?" Carmen, her eyes warm with sympathy, spoke with the familiarity of a friend rather than an employee.

"No. He has a right to know about the people he takes into his home."

"Ward is not a hard man. He may appear to be so. He is a much important man. I've known him since he was a small boy."

Feeling a little guilty about discussing her host, Meredith listened while Carmen told her how Ward had taken over the running of the numerous family holdings when his father died. His grandfather on his mother's side, though an American, had adopted Spanish ways and was in some ways more Spanish in his thinking than the beautiful *señorita* he had married many years before. It was a great disappointment to them when their only daughter married an American and went to live in Tulsa. She had died young, when Ward was barely ten, and the youngster began spending vacations with his grandparents.

During those summer months the old man was harsh with the young boy and was determined to make him into the Spanish son he never had. As much as Ward loved his grandparents, he couldn't forget he was an American and was torn between two conflicting lifestyles. On the high plateau in the mountains south of Colima on the Rancho de Margarieta, named for his beloved wife, the old man bred bulls for the arenas in Guadalajara and Mexico City. It was here on the rancho that Ward, saving his grandfather's life when he was attacked by a dangerous bull, was himself gored, resulting in the injury that left his leg permanently damaged. After the old man died, Ward gave up breeding for the ring and turned the compound into a cattle ranch where sleek steers roamed on the undulating pampas grass. Now he divided his time between the Rancho de Margarieta, the lettuce ranch at Chapala, Tulsa, and the plant in Guadalajara.

"Ward is much loved by the people on the *ranchos*," Carmen said with twinkling eyes. "Much of the *señoritas, Americanas*, too. They all think they catch the rich husband." She laughed. "*Dona* Margarieta have different idea. She want him to marry with a Mexican girl and get a great-grandson before she die. Francisca Calderon, Luis's sister, is her favorite."

Meredith reflected on what Carmen had told her about Ward as she prepared for dinner. So his mother had died when he was old enough to miss her. She did understand him a little better, now, but pity him, she did not. She would be a fool to feel a moment's pity for such a self-assured person. Neither did she feel any pity for Cullen. She had seen many people with more severe handicaps doing much more with their lives.

Always having had to work, even as a young teenager, to help support herself, she simply couldn't feel much sympathy for someone who was content to sit in a chair and be waited on. She wondered what it would take to jar him out of his lethargy. Was it the fear that he would be unable to lead a normal sex life that had made practically a recluse out of him?

She caught herself up sharply. What was she thinking about? Maybe he wasn't interested in sex. Paul certainly hadn't been. During the three years of their relationship they had had sex exactly four times and, as far as she was concerned, the whole messy business was vastly over-rated. At first she had wondered if something was wrong with her that she failed to excite Paul beyond a few kisses. She remembered the time she had ached with the need for him to make love to her and dared to take the initiative, only to be told firmly he wasn't in the mood. She had been utterly devastated. Never again, she vowed, would she set herself up like that for rejection.

Meredith waited in her room until ten minutes before

nine, when dinner was to be served. Should she be on time? Should she leave her room now—or in five more minutes? What if Ward and Cullen dressed formally and what she was wearing was totally wrong? She stood beside the window and tapped her foot nervously on the thick carpet. And then, abruptly, she went to look in the full-length mirror. The dress was awful! Maybe if she did her hair up she would look less like a high-school girl ready for her first date. Quickly she brushed her hair up and secured it, pulled a few tendrils down at the nape, and looked at herself critically. That wasn't right, either! A soft knock interrupted her glaring at herself in sheer frustration.

She pulled open the door and there he was. Ward smiled at the surprise on her face.

"Why so surprised? I live here, too. Remember?" Just as they'd been that afternoon, his eyes were warmer, more friendly than last night. "I don't know how you managed to jar Cullen out of his rut, but he's waiting downstairs. He's even got himself all spiffed . . . up." The words died out as, all of a sudden, he was looking at her strangely. She wanted to go into the closet and hide.

"What's the matter?" she asked, forcing her tone to be light. "Have I got egg on my face?"

"It's your hair. You're not the suave, urbane type. It makes you look jaded, brittle, cynical." Was he teasing? He couldn't be flirting with her!

She tried to laugh. It wasn't much of a success. "Perhaps I am jaded, brittle, cynical."

He laughed and she decided again she liked his eyes. "No. You're refreshing, soft as a marshmallow, and . . ." He tilted his head and studied her. "And . . . whimsical."

"Whimsical?" Did he think she was a feather-brain?

"I should have added stubborn, argumentative, and late for dinner. Brush out your hair so we can go." He moved into the room. "Come on, Cullen's waiting."

She looked horrified. "Do you do this often?" What a rotten thought to pop into her head! She hoped he didn't.

"Ask women to take their hair down? Of course not. Sometimes I do it for them." He was grinning broadly. Could this be the same man who almost threw her out of the house last night?

"Stop that!" She was grinning broadly, now, too and stopped his hand as he reached to pluck away a pin. She had already made up her mind to take it down, but decided to resist a while longer.

"Well . . . ?"

"Okay. But if I look like a mess it'll be your fault."

"You couldn't look like a mess if you tried."

"You're totally . . . unpredictable."

"And you're wasting time."

She removed the pins and her hair cascaded to her shoulders in a golden wave. She turned to the mirror and carelessly ran the comb through it. He was behind her and she looked into the tawny, smiling eyes reflected in the mirror.

"I was right." The satisfied look on his face made her sorry she had given in so easily.

"Are you always right, Mr. Sanderson?"

"Not always, Miss Moore. I didn't think marsh-mallows could bite." There was mischief in the tawny eyes. Without thinking, she allowed him to take her hand.

"Hungry?"

"Starving," she admitted. And suddenly she was no

longer worried that she might hiccup at the table or use the wrong fork.

Ward didn't release her hand until they walked into the room where Cullen sat waiting. Quite different tonight, he had chosen to wear a white, pleated shirt opened at the neck, dark trousers, and dark leather oxfords. His hair had been trimmed and the beard shaved from his thin face, making him resemble, more than ever, his older brother. As they entered the room, Meredith was pleased to find herself in an old-fashioned study. An oil portrait hung above the fireplace, in a heavy gilt frame. The strong-featured man depicted was, despite his white hair and somber black suit, so like Ward and Cullen in features as to be startling.

Ward followed the direction of her glance. "Our father."

Meredith thought about remarking on the striking resemblance between the half-brothers, but decided they might think she was being too familiar.

She was surprised to hear them discussing what had been in her thoughts. "You look more like him than I do," Ward was saying. He turned to her. "Don't you agree that Cullen looks like our father, Merry?"

Ward was standing in front of her holding out a glass of sherry. As she took the glass, his warm fingers encountered her own. His eyes were as friendly as before and she dismissed the silly notion to act reserved. She looked at the two men, then to the portrait, and back at the two men.

"You both resemble him, but—he was much better-looking."

Ward looked at Cullen and toasted him with the last of his drink. "Just what we need, brother. A smartass!"

Cullen laughed in pure disbelief at his brother's words. Meredith laughed with him. They were playing, feeling each other out, she realized with pleasure. She hadn't been so relaxed or had so much fun . . . in a long, long time. She wasn't breathless or blushing any more. She loved being here, being accepted for herself.

Cullen made a joke about escorting Meredith to the dining room and she placed her hand on his shoulder and said, "Lead on, Macduff." The chair moved smoothly and she complained that she should have brought her track shoes.

They reached a long room illuminated by a crystal chandelier and diffused lighting from wide opaque panels in the ceiling. It was a pleasant mixture of old and new, the kind of room that created an instant illusion of warmth and welcome as well as luxurious living. The table was long and heavy, and the high-backed chairs would easily seat a dozen guests. There were three places set at one end. Cullen waited until Ward had seated Meredith before he moved his chair to the end of the table. She remembered the orchid and smiled into his eyes questioningly.

"Did I pin my flower in the right place?"

The eyes, lighter and more twinkling than she had seen before, smiled back at her. "No. It should be snuggled down in that gorgeous hair." He studied her seriously for a few seconds. "In that curve just under your left ear."

"Now you tell me. I don't have a bobby pin."

Ward got up and came toward her. "I'll fix it. I've got a paper clip in my pocket."

"You two are—nuts ! You don't go with these elegant surroundings at all." She felt foolish as he fumbled with her hair and stirred restlessly.

"Be still or it'll fall in the soup."

Meredith had to look at something so she looked at Cullen. He winked at her! What was he thinking? Was it that she was going to hop into bed with his big brother?

Ward took his place across from her and called out to Sophia, who was hovering in the background. "We're ready now, Sophia. Serve the soup."

This particular miracle of having dinner with two attractive men and feeling quite worthy of their attention made Meredith glow with animation. The ball of conversation was tossed from one to the other and when it was in her court she was as glib of tongue as she had ever been in her entire life. She didn't stop to weigh words or thoughts as she chatted easily. When the meal was over Ward tucked her hand in the crook of his arm and they followed Cullen to the library, where a fire blazed gently. The tray with the chocolate pot was on the table beside the chair.

"Chocolate? Whose idea was that? What's wrong with an after-dinner drink?" Cullen made a face at Ward as he said the words.

"I ordered it for Merry. Whipped cream to go in it, too."

"More cream!" Meredith exclaimed. "I'll be as big as a tank, and have high blood pressure, heart disease, diabetes, cirrhosis of the liver, atherosclerosis . . ."

"But—rounded, jolly, and soft as a marshmallow."

Meredith still couldn't believe these teasing words came from the man who last night, in this very room, had been so stern, so unyielding. A retort failed to come to her lips and she glanced at Cullen. A smile was playing around his mouth and she directed her remark to him.

"It isn't funny, Cullen. What red-blooded American girl wants to be referred to as a . . . marshmallow?"

He laughed. "You can be my marshmallow any day, Merry. A merry marshmallow!"

"Hush! You're making me self-conscious."

Ward had moved to the liquor cabinet and returned with a glass for himself and for Cullen.

"Drink your chocolate, Merry. We may persuade Cullen to play his guitar for us."

Later, in Cullen's room, she sat on the couch beside Ward and listened to the most beautiful music she had ever heard. Cullen's fingers danced over the strings and to Meredith it was like watching a ballet. She didn't know what she had expected, possibly a little diddling around with a ballad like "Greensleeves," but Cullen played magnificently. She didn't recognize the tunes but they were hauntingly sad in places, throbbingly passionate in others. She sat enthralled, not knowing when he finished one piece and started another. One song was so stirring that tears misted her eyes and she turned to see Ward looking at her. His hand came out and covered hers where it lay on the seat between them. She wasn't the least embarrassed for him to see she was moved by the sonata. She turned her eyes away feeling peaceful, content to let her hand remain beneath his.

The marvelous days continued, and she felt all the while as though she were suspended in time. The hours she spent with Cullen and Ward were both wonderful and strange for a woman who had never known family warmth before. The three of them acted as if they were very old and dear friends, visiting, teasing, playing cards or pool, listening to Cullen's music. She never allowed herself to think of Ward's life outside the *hacienda*. She didn't want to think of him as a wealthy man directing large corporations, but only as Cullen's brother and Maggie's father. And once, when he didn't return from Guadalajara, she and Cullen spent the evening together. That was pleasant, too.

"Do you use crutches, Cullen?" The words embarrassed her as soon as she said them.

He didn't answer for a long moment. "Sometimes. Why? Do you want to dance?"

"No, you jerk. I want to see how tall you are."

"I'm not as tall as Ward."

"Do you drive?"

"Yeah. Ward had a van fixed up for me. I don't use it much."

"Will you take me for a ride sometime? I don't want to leave Mexico without seeing something more than the inside of this *hacienda*, as beautiful as it is."

"Ward will take you. I'm sure you'd prefer it that way. If you're too bashful to ask, I'll tell him."

"You do and I'll punch you in the mouth!"

Both of them laughed, but suddenly his eyes grew serious. "I know what you're doing and I appreciate it, Merry. But believe me when I say I'm resigned to my life here. It's easier, a hell of a lot easier, being here than being out there trying to act . . . normal."

"Normal? What's normal?" She sat on the couch and

drew her legs up under her. "While I was working in the hospital, Cullen, I must have seen every abnormality there is. It never got to the point where it didn't bother me. I tried not to let it show, but one patient who was blind *and* paralyzed from the neck down detected a note of pity in my voice and said to me, 'Hey, sister. Don't feel sorry for me. I've got a good brain and I've got my voice, that's more than some people have.' You know, Cullen, he had the voice of an angel, a beautiful tenor voice that gave him and many others a great deal of pleasure. I'll never forget him."

"And the moral of the story is . . . there's always some-one worse off than you." Cullen picked up the guitar and began to sing. " 'Oh, Ru—by, don't take your love to town.' "

"Are you mad at me?"

"Kind of. But I'll get over it." He looked up and grinned. "You're as obvious as a tank."

She was relieved. "At least you can't accuse me of beating about the bush. You should be out there, living. You're very good-looking, you should be out there work-ing, meeting people, maybe falling in love and getting married, having kids. There's nothing to stop you." She waited for him to tell her to bug off, but he started strum-ming the guitar again. Presently he looked up. The sad-ness in his eyes affected her more than any words he could have uttered.

"I'd like that, too, Merry, but why dream about the im-possible?" His voice was very soft.

"You can't have children?" It was none of her business if he could have children or not, but for some reason she wanted to know. She already cared for this man like a brother. The hurt look on his face told her a great deal.

"Oh, I could have children all right, but for that you need a woman and what normal woman would look at me now?"

Meredith determined to carry the conversation through. "That's just not true, Cullen. You're feeling sorry for yourself again. Is there a girl you would like to marry?"

He heaved a deep sigh and absentmindedly strummed the guitar. After a brief pause he looked up at her again. "There was."

"Where is she? What happened?" They exchanged a long look and Meredith felt tears behind her eyes.

"I told her to get lost." He looked away and then back into her eyes with tears hovering in the corners. "Merry! Don't feel bad, sweetheart. Hey—like you said, there's a lot of guys worse off than me. I can live with it." He held out both hands. "See—look ma, no feet!"

"That's not funny, Cullen!"

"Yes, I know it, but what the hell! Better to laugh than cry."

She wanted to take him in her arms and hold him, soothe away the hurt. He was the brother she had never had, the child in the hospital who was frightened, but desperately trying not to cry. She had known him only a few weeks, but she knew he was kind, sweet, and gentle, and was coping the best he could after a cruel kick in the teeth. Why was it always the nice people of the world who got the shaft?

The following morning Meredith went boldly along the garden path to the swimming pool. Under the terry robe she wore a swimsuit borrowed from Carmen's daughter. Cullen and Maggie were in the pool. Sophia and Antonio stood patiently along the edge waiting to assist.

"Merry! Merry! Watch me. I can swim to Unk." Maggie, arms flaying the water, moved the few feet and threw her arms around Cullen's neck.

"Good girl. That's more than I can do." Now that she was here Meredith had cold feet about getting into the water.

"Well . . . come on in," Cullen called and splashed her with a spray of water.

"Will you give me a lesson?" She was stalling for time.

"Sure, but I'm expensive."

"Then forget it. I'll join the 'Y'."

The next hour spun past crazily. He leered unabashedly at the great deal of skin exposed when she dropped the robe, but the look was so open and so friendly that it only made her grin. A short while after she took the plunge, Sophia took Maggie out and Meredith and Cullen played like a couple of kids. He maneuvered in the water as easily as if he had the use of his legs. With his hand beneath her back he showed her how to float. One time he dove between her legs and sent her beneath the water. She came up sputtering, wiping the water from her face with her hands.

"Show-off," she accused when she could talk, then she exclaimed, "Oh, Cullen, this is fun!"

"For me, too."

"Tomorrow, same time? Same place?"

"It's a date."

She got out of the pool and wrapped herself in the robe. She didn't wait to see Antonio lift Cullen to his chair. It was too soon for that. Maybe tomorrow or the next day.

At lunch, which was usually served about three o'clock, Maggie and Meredith sat on the floor beside Cullen's chair and ate hot dogs roasted over a charcoal blaze Antonio had set in the fireplace. They sang crazy songs and laughed a lot.

Maggie planted a mustard and ketchup kiss on Meredith's cheek.

"I love you, Merry Merry. You won't go away, will you?" There was such hope and longing in her voice that Meredith thought a few seconds before she answered.

"Not right this minute, but someday. And I love you, too." If only she could record that little voice and keep it with her always.

"Not tomorrow?"

"Nope."

"The next day?"

"Nope. But one of these days I've got to go back to work. I work in a place where sick people go to get well."

"If I get sick, will you stay?"

"You're not going to get sick!" Meredith tickled her ribs and wrestled her down onto the floor.

"Don't, Merry! Don't . . . don't . . ." Between the giggles and screams Meredith heard the magic words. "Don't . . . pee pee . . ." She released her and sat back. "Don't you dare, you imp!"

Maggie laughed and darted away. "I fooled you!"

"You—little imp! That's not fair! You cheated!"

"This has got to be the noisiest place in Mexico." Ward came in, amusement spread all over his face.

"Daddy!" Maggie ran to him and he lifted her up and kissed her before he set her on her feet.

"Hi, punkin. Am I invited to the picnic?"

"There's none left. We ate it all."

Meredith got to her feet. She wasn't as relaxed with Ward as with Cullen. It was always the same for the first few minutes when she was with him.

"Never mind. I don't have time anyway. I'm going to see old *abuela*."

"Can I go see grandmother? Can me and Merry come with you?" Maggie's voice was coaxing and she wrapped her arms around his legs.

Meredith flushed because his eyes were on her.

"Not this time. Next time I'll take both of you. Hey—you're getting mustard on me, you . . . wiggle-wart!" He moved her away from him and wiped her face with what Meredith suspected was a very expensive handkerchief. "Off you go, now, so I can talk with Merry and Cullen for a minute." He watched her leave. "I'm going down to the *rancho* for a day or two, Cullen." Meredith started to move away. "Don't go, Merry, you're practically a member of the family." He smiled.

Meredith liked Ward better when he was smiling and was grateful to him for making her feel at home. She wanted to tell him and Cullen that she appreciated being a guest in their home and how much she had enjoyed the past few weeks, but she didn't wish to be gushy, or boring, so she stood quietly, her hands clasped in front of her.

"Merry's getting to be a pretty good pool player,

Ward." Cullen's voice broke the silence. "She'll be able to give you a good game by the time you get back."

"I won't be gone that long, brother." He looked teasingly at Meredith, his eyes going straight to the center of hers.

"Just be sure you come back," Cullen called after him. "Francisca just might get her hooks in you."

He turned his head and looked fully at Meredith. "That will never happen." He made the statement firmly and emphatically.

The look he gave Meredith caused a tingling to run through her to the very marrow of her bones. His look had been somber, and absorbed. There was purpose and intensity in his face. From nowhere the thought came to her that he wore his masculinity like armor. Though there was strength, muscle, purpose, and power in every line of him, she sensed an incredible softness inside, a center so tender that Ward would not expose it for fear of a mortal wound. The tawny eyes stared deep into her blue ones for an instant, and she wanted to reach out to this man, to comfort him. In that moment she knew that, all appearances to the contrary, he needed such comfort more than Cullen ever had.

CHAPTER FIVE

"MERRY, WAKE UP!" Meredith heard the voice vaguely through the veil of sleep. It had to be Maggie. Who else would run into her bedroom calling her by name? She wished her head would stop hurting so she could open her eyes. "Wake up, Merry!" As the voice called out again, the bed heaved and her stomach with it.

"Please, darling. Don't jump on the bed! Oh . . . my head! Move, honey. Hurry . . . I'm going . . ." She threw back the covers and got to her feet. She stood swaying while the room righted itself, then headed for the bathroom, conscious of another pain more severe than the one in her head. Each time she put her foot on the floor, pain shot through her. Tiny claws were tearing deep inside her stomach and she felt bathed in cold perspiration. She made it to the bathroom and, leaning over the commode, gave way to her nausea.

"Are you sick, Merry?" Maggie crowded in beside her.

Foolish question. Her insides were turning inside out.

"Yes, darling. Go play like a good girl. Okay?"

That sickening, spinning feeling was lessened

somewhat after she emptied the contents of her stomach and she sat down and peeled the band-aid from the place just above her ankle that was throbbing as if it had a life of its own.

Luis had come to dinner the night before and afterward she had walked with him in the garden and they had sat for a while on the veranda. It was while they were sitting there that she had felt the sharp sting and thought a gigantic mosquito had found her delicious. After saturating the wound with disinfectant, she had covered it with the plastic strip and forgotten about it. She looked at it now with disbelief. It was red and swollen. Something was obviously wrong! Definitely more than an ordinary mosquito bite, it needed more attention than she could give it. She stood and that sickening, spinning feeling came over her again. Any second she was going to fall flat on her face. She wished she hadn't sent Maggie away. Hot packs! That was what she needed to draw out the infection. She sat on the side of the tub and allowed the hot water to flow over her leg and foot until she had to throw up again.

She gained some temporary relief and made her way back to the bed. She tossed and turned, her mind uneasy about the bite on her leg. If Sophia would only come in, she would ask her to get Carmen. She would know what to do. Oh . . . She felt so strange—almost outside herself.

She slept. If Sophia came she didn't know it. She dozed fitfully. Her brain was clouded and her fevered head hot and dry. She woke to find herself shivering, her leg throbbing. The skin was tight and hot. She was lucid enough to realize she had to let someone know how sick she was, but she could barely raise her head from the pillow, much less make it to the door. Please, she moaned inwardly, somebody come! She couldn't remember a time when she felt so bad. She was almost too ill to care what happened to her. Feeling herself float away, she gripped her pillow tightly as the room swayed and dipped.

There was a knock on the door and a deep voice called to her. The words coming through the door were jumbled in a strange disorder. They didn't seem to mean anything. She put her hand to her forehead wishing the words made some sort of sense. Who would be calling her from so far away? Was it Paul? No! "I don't want you, Paul!" she managed to call out. She only wanted to sleep, but someone was coming toward her. She waited until he got nearer, just in case she knew him. It wasn't Paul. Paul was not so tall.

"Ward?" The word came out a mere whisper. She fastened her eyes on his face in mute appeal. "I'm . . . so sick."

He was there. Right there beside her, taking her hand in his. His voice was gentle, but urgent.

"What is it, Merry?"

"Don't touch me. I hurt so." Her eyes were bright with fever and her lips trembled when she spoke. Afraid he couldn't hear her, she clutched his hand. "I've got an infected mosquito bite on my leg, but there's got to be something more wrong with me than that." Big tears rolled out of the fevered eyes. "I'm sorry to be such a bother, but I need a doctor."

He turned back the covers to look at her leg. She gasped when he picked up her foot, sending waves of agony through her. Seeing the angry red lines running up toward her knee, Ward swore softly and gently eased her foot back to the bed and covered her.

"You have an infection all right, Merry. But don't worry—we'll get a doctor out to fix you up in no time." His face was near, yet curiously blurred. She closed her eyes with relief. Ward would take care of things. "Don't worry," he was saying. "Leave everything to me."

His gentle voice persisted in her mind. She didn't need to worry anymore. Ward had come and he said not to worry, that he would take care of things. She didn't bother to open her eyes when the tablets were placed in her mouth and she was raised so she could swallow them or when the cool cloth was placed on her head. Orders were being given in Ward's firm voice and she drifted away in a swirling mist, only to return as gentle hands slipped a clean, soft gown over her head.

"I'm sorry," she whispered. Speech was an effort. The thought seemed to travel a million miles from her brain to her lips, and finally when she voiced it, the words were so soft the man leaned over her with his ear to his lips to catch them.

"Just rest, Merry. The doctor will be here soon."

"Doctor? Yes . . . I need . . ." Her voice was weak and her breathing shallow.

"Don't talk. Just sleep until he gets here."

"Doctor? . . ." she murmured.

"Don't talk, Merry."

She wondered about being called Merry, but she was floating away again, light as a thistledown, floating right off the bed. She clung to the hand holding hers to keep herself from being swept away.

"It won't be long, now." Her hand was held tightly. She

wasn't alone! Please, don't go away, she begged silently. Don't leave me alone.

Vaguely she knew there were people in the room. She opened her eyes and tried to focus on the person bending over her, but the effort was too great and she closed them again. With listless disinterest she felt the pricks of the doctor's needle and heard the buzz of voice. Pain wrenched at her when her leg was moved. She cried out and heard someone curse.

"Don't hurt her for God's sake!"

The words faded and she was half lost in delirium. She didn't feel very much after that and when the voices had all gone away she slept deeply and dreamlessly, holding fast to the strong fingers interlaced with hers.

She woke once, her mouth dry and parched. Before she asked for a drink of water, an arm lifted her and a glass was placed to her lips. The water was cold and good. She was laid gently back on the pillow.

"Go back to sleep. You're going to be all right."

Her groping hand searched for the fingers she had clung to earlier. She slept. When next she woke Sophia was sitting in a chair beside the bed.

"Buenos dias, señorita." Her broad face expressed her concern.

"Is it morning?"

"Sí. Dos dias, señorita." She held up two fingers.

"Two mornings have gone by? It can't be!" She lifted her head from the pillow. It felt as if it weighed a thousand pounds. "I feel like I've been kicked in the head by a mule!"

"No," Sophia said seriously. "You very sick. Doctor say you drink." She placed a straw in Meredith's mouth and held it while she sucked up chilled juice. She was dry. She knew she needed the liquid after the high fever, but it was an effort to even draw it up through the tube. There wasn't a bone in her body that didn't ache and she was having difficulty keeping her eyes open.

"Thank you for sitting with me, Sophia."

"I tell *Señor* Ward you awake."

"No. Don't bother him."

"You no like *Señor* Ward?"

Meredith opened her shuttered eyes to see a puzzled frown on Sophia's face.

"Of course I like him. I just don't want to bother him."

"He say tell him when you wake, *señorita*," Sophia said stubbornly.

"All right. Tell him if you like." She was weary and wanted to go back to sleep. She closed her eyes, heard Sophia leave the room and close the door behind her.

Through waves of fatigue she came swimming back to a certain awareness. Her eyelids felt as if two weights were attached to each of them, but with effort she opened them and saw Ward standing beside the bed. From out in the never-never land her mind grasped one fact.

"You haven't shaved." It seemed perfectly all right for her to say that.

He sat down in a chair beside the bed. "Didn't you realize you'd been bitten by a poisonous insect, probably a spider or a scorpion?"

She knew it was not a rebuke, but weak tears filled her eyes. She tried to stop them, but she couldn't

"I thought it was a mosquito bite. It puffed up like a mosquito bite."

"It was more than a mere mosquito bite, Merry. The

doctor will be back this morning to give you another shot of penicillin." An experimental hand felt her forehead. "Your fever is down. Sophia will bring a pitcher of orange juice. Drink as much of it as you can."

"You got a bit more than you bargained for when you took me in, Ward. I'm sorry." Her lips trembled and tears ran down the sides of her face into her ears. She didn't know why she was crying. What was wrong with her! She was blubbering like a two year old.

"Yeah! You've been a real pain in the butt!" His face was very close and he was grinning at her. He picked up the edge of the sheet and wiped her cheeks. "You've been very sick, Merry. When you're better I'll tell you just how sick. Now go back to sleep and don't worry about a thing."

She couldn't have said anything if she wanted to. Instead, with uncharacteristic impulsiveness, she grabbed his hand and held it to her wet cheek for a short moment. Thank you. She didn't know if she said the words aloud or not, but she meant them with all her heart.

For the rest of the day she dozed intermittently. Every time she woke Sophia was there with the orange juice. The doctor came and she opened her heavy lids at the prick of his needle, then closed them and drifted into a heavy sleep.

When next she opened her eyes, the first thing she saw was a cluster of yellow roses. They stood in a vase on the table beside her bed. Everything was peaceful now. The bedroom lamps diffused a soft, warm glow and the curtains were pulled across the windows. She stirred in a soft warm nest and her body felt curiously light. Her eyes traveled around the room. She was alone. Sophia's voice drifted in from the slightly opened door, then Maggie's pleading one. A smile touched Meredith's lips because she knew Maggie was giving Sophia the full treatment.

"The *señorita* is sleeping." Sophia said firmly.

"Please, please, pretty please, Sophia. Just one look before I go to bed. I'll be quiet. I promise." The little voice was soft, wheedling.

"I'm not asleep," Meredith called.

Almost before she got the words out of her mouth the door opened and a small body hurled itself into the room.

"Merry, Merry. I've something to tell you! Guess what? Guess what?"

"Don't get on the bed," Sophia scolded.

"Have you been good for Sophia?"

Sophia looked at the ceiling in a gesture of impatience and a torrent of Spanish words fell from her mouth. Meredith had a perfect understanding of what she meant, although the words were strange. She smiled and hugged the child leaning over her.

"What's this big news that's making you so excited?"

"Daddy said someday I was going to have a mommy! One all my own that won't go away."

The smile stayed on Meredith's face but the sparkle faded from her eyes. "Hey—that's great! That is big news."

Maggie was so excited that she bounced onto the bed before Sophia could stop her, and the sudden jar of the bed caused pain to shoot up Meredith's leg and she winced in spite of herself.

"You hurt the *señorita!*" Sophia grabbed the wiggly child and started for the door. "It sleep time, little mule."

"Bye, Maggie. I'll see you in the morning."

The door closed and Meredith allowed her face to rid itself of the set smile it had been holding. For the tiniest moment she felt terribly disappointed. It was insane. She was glad for Maggie. It was only . . . well . . . she hadn't thought Ward was even thinking of getting married. Francisca! Whoever this Francisca was she had evidently got her hooks in, as Cullen had expressed it. What was it that Ward had said that last evening? He had said something like, '*That will never happen.*' He must have changed his mind.

A desperate feeling of loneliness possessed her, a loneliness that was her future. Turning on her side, she looked at the yellow roses. Lifting a hand, she gently stroked the fragrant petals. It didn't occur to her to wonder who placed them there, it just seemed they belonged . . . but she didn't. Her eyes roamed the room, taking in the beautiful furniture, the rich draperies and carpet, the outward manifestations of wealth. An abundance of love was the only wealth she craved, and if love were riches, she was most certainly a pauper.

The thought sickened her and she had no appetite for her dinner. She merely picked at the food and Sophia, coming back to collect the tray, looked at it disapprovingly.

"I did the best I could," Meredith said with a smile of apology, and Sophia carried the tray of scarcely touched food from the room.

When Ward came into the room, she knew by the look on his face that he had inspected the tray Sophia had returned to the kitchen. He came to the side of the bed and stood looking down at her. The weight Meredith had lost while sick gave her an ethereal fragility, and as the light tan she had acquired faded, her skin took on a translucent quality which made her eyes appear an even deeper, darker blue.

"Your tray was scarcely touched. Couldn't you have managed a little bit more?"

"Maybe later. It all seemed to stop here." She placed her fingers beneath her chin.

"The more you eat the sooner you'll get your strength back, *pequeña*." His eyes sought and held hers.

"Yes, doctor." The tawny eyes were having the most disturbing effect on her senses. The tip of her tongue moistened suddenly dry lips. "I wish you wouldn't call me names I don't understand." She hadn't meant to sound cross but it came out that way.

A faint smile touched his lips. "What do you think I called you?" His eyes lingered on her mouth as if fascinated by it.

The sound of the softly spoken words sent shivers along her spine and she had the strangest curling sensation in the pit of her stomach that was fear or apprehension, she couldn't be sure which. Making an effort to control the situation with humor, she gave a nervous little laugh.

"Dingbat?" She felt a small triumph at speaking the word so lightly.

He laughed now and pulled a chair up close to the bed and folded his long length into it. He studied her for a moment, then reached out one finger and slowly traced the soft outline of her mouth.

"The word I used was complimentary. You must learn to speak Spanish if you want to know everything I say. I can swear better in Spanish than in English."

"I remember." She smiled, and he did as well, also remembering.

"Maggie has missed you. Cullen, too."

"It's nice to be missed." She looked relaxed, but her brain was spinning. All sorts of wild thoughts were whirling around in her head. She wanted to say, "Are you going to marry Francisca?" Instead she said, "What bit me to make me so sick?"

"It could have been one of many things. Mexico is full of poisonous insects. The house and gardens are sprayed periodically and I can't understand where you picked one up. It could have been serious, Merry. Why didn't you let Carmen or Cullen know? They would have called the doctor immediately."

"I woke up so sick I could hardly make it to the bathroom to throw up. By the time I realized something serious was wrong with me, I couldn't get out of bed." At the remembered feeling of helplessness she wanted to cry. "Thank you for coming when you did."

Lying there small and still, with his eyes on her, her pulse began to hammer heavily. A strange sense of awareness of him sent a warm glow through her whole being. She looked at him with eyes unconsciously wide and appealing. For a moment neither one said anything and it was as if the two of them were frozen there in time, waiting for something to happen. She moistened her lips with the tip of her tongue again and did her best to meet his censorious gaze.

"You're so damn polite you make me sick!" It was just the right thing for him to say to break the tension and she grinned at him.

"I thought you'd never notice."

Ward began to pace around the room, stopping to move aside the curtains so he could gaze out the window. She again noticed that, for a man so tall and with an injured leg, he was extraordinarily light on his feet. Meredith felt panic grip her as she realized that he might marry soon and she would be out of his life forever. Cold sweat broke out on her forehead and her heart hammered in restless dismay. Her alarm was mirrored in her eyes and he turned abruptly and looked at her.

"Did I frighten you about the bugs and spiders?" He came to the bed and picked up her hand and held it in both of his. She pulled her hand away, grateful he couldn't read her mind. "I'll send Sophia in to help you get ready for a good night's sleep. Tomorrow or the next day, or when you are feeling up to it, we're going to have a good long talk about your past, Merry. And . . . your future."

He went to the door. With his hand on the knob he turned around. "I don't know if there *is* a Spanish word for dingbat." He waited to see her grin, then went through the door and closed it softly behind him.

CHAPTER SIX

MEREDITH SLEPT FITFULLY throughout the long night. Her mind refused to allow her to rest. Try as she might, she could not fully assimilate the words Ward had spoken to her. Her future. It could only mean some arrangements were being made for her to leave the *hacienda*. Words, thoughts, emotions, all whirled around in her mind. Morning came and she was tired, but her leg felt much better. She could move it without pain and she longed to get out of bed and get dressed.

After Sophia removed the breakfast tray, she admitted a visitor.

Luis came in almost staggering under the burden of an enormous basket of fruit. He placed it on the floor beside the bed, his dark, sensuous eyes filled with concern. He grabbed Meredith's hand and lifted it to his lips.

"*Niña! Mi poca niña*, what have they done to you?" His words were soft and caressing and she couldn't help but to laugh at his dramatic expression.

"It was a mean old spider that did it. I'm all right now."

"If there is anything I can do, you just have to ask me," he said with a flourish.

She smiled warmly and shook her head. He made a grimace and sat down.

"I detest independent women," he said with mock hauteur. "You must learn to be clinging, submissive."

She forced herself not to laugh. "How arrogant of you! Women are not submissive anymore."

"You think not, *mi poca Americana*? Spanish women are submissive and they love it."

"American women are not, Luis. They demand equality with men."

Luis lounged back in the chair. "I have pity for the American girl. All that freedom . . . and for what? She opens doors for herself, lights her own cigarettes, rides on motorcycles, and turns her bedroom into a public room. Poor American girl! Spanish girl is happy with a man who will curb her foolish ways, who will rule with a strong but gentle hand, cherish and revere . . . and master her."

"Do your Spanish women surrender without a struggle?" Meredith asked teasingly.

"No, *niña*. We enjoy our scuffles. They are like the chili pepper on the tortilla." He selected a plump peach from the fruit basket, produced a knife and proceeded to peel the fruit. "My sister, Francisca, is such a woman. She has been trained from birth to be wife, mother, and mistress to her husband. She lives with Ward's grandmother on the Rancho de Margarieta. It is Dona Margarieta's fondest wish that she and Ward marry."

Meredith watched the slender brown fingers, knowing his eyes were more on her than what they were doing. Instinctively she knew he was telling her this for a purpose. But why? He sliced off a portion of the peach and handed it to her, then served himself. They ate the fruit in silence. Luis was wiping the juice from her lips with his handkerchief when she raised her eyes to see Ward standing in the doorway. Unaccountably she felt color come up her neck and tint her pale cheeks.

Briefly she met his eyes and found their expression as much speculative as curious, one brow raised as if he were waiting for her to speak. She said nothing and he came slowly into the room.

"You seem improved this morning." He ignored Luis and stood at the foot of the bed.

"Yes. I'm getting up this morning." She flicked nervous eyes over him. Why did she suddenly feel as if he were the enemy?

"Rest in bed this morning. Maybe by late afternoon you can get up and sit in the chair." There was no *if* or *maybe* about it. He merely issued the order and her resentment grew. She should know when she was able to get up. She opened her mouth to say so, but he had turned to Luis.

"For the first time since we opened the plant we are behind in production. How come?"

The direct question caught Luis off guard. He returned his handkerchief to his pocket and got to his feet. There was a moment of silence, and Meredith's heart began to beat rapidly as she sensed the tension between the two men. An atmosphere charged with discord had pervaded the room.

"All the computer lines are right on schedule—we're

only behind in the electronic chess." Luis's voice was tight.

Ward persisted. "And why is that?"

"You know why, Ward." Was Luis going to lose his temper? Latins were notorious for that. "When you returned from Japan with the contract for the computer transistors, you knew it would put a strain on our production. The electronic chess game had to take second priority, as the other games were ready to be assembled." Meredith was surprised to note that, in talking business, Luis seemed to have lost much of his Spanish accent.

"It will be on the market for this Christmas season." There was a cold sting in every word Ward uttered.

"I do not think a lady's bedroom is the proper place for this discussion." Luis was angry. "Perhaps we can meet later."

"Then you will have to cancel your trip to the Rancho de Margarieta to talk strategy with your sister." There was a slight, cynical on Ward's lips.

"*Sí*," Luis said softly, politely. There was a tone of mock deference in his voice. When he spoke again it was to Meredith. His face was smiling, his dark eyes devouring her. He picked up her hand and brought it to his lips. "Don't fly away from me, little *paloma*. I'll be back when you are feeling fit again."

Ward stood watching, his face a mask of immobility. Somehow he reminded her of Paul, silent and critical. Paul had looked at her in just that way when she had displeased him. She didn't want to be reminded of Paul.

"*Adios*, little pigeon." Luis released her hand.

"Thank you for the fruit." Meredith called to him as he reached the door. "The basket is beautiful."

Luis smiled. He was his most charming self again. *"No estan bella como usted, querida."* He laughed softly as he left the room.

Desperate to break the ensuing silence, Meredith asked, "What did he say?"

"He said, not as beautiful as you, darling." Ward lifted one eyebrow. Then he was laughing. His face was transformed, his cheeks creased and small crinkles appeared around his eyes making him look years younger. She wanted to punch him.

"What's so funny?" She kept a lightness in her voice as if it didn't matter that he found her amusing, but it did.

"I was laughing at Luis. Sometimes I want to wring his neck, but I do admire the way he can turn on the charm when he wishes."

He was looking down at her with amusement and she wished fervently she had the nerve to slip the sheet up over her head so she didn't have to face that mocking stare. She glanced quickly at him and then away. She heard the soft tread of his footsteps as he crossed the deep piled carpet to the window. She hated to be lying in the bed while he was in the room. She looked at his back. He was as handsome and commanding from behind as he was from the front. Well . . . not quite. His eyes made all the difference. When they were unsmiling, his arrogance was unnerving.

The moment he turned and walked toward her she knew he had something on his mind. He came to the bed and sat on the edge of it. She forced herself to look into his face, although her heart was palpitating wildly. Her eyes were lost in his intent gaze and she hid her hands beneath the bedclothes so he couldn't see their trembling.

He stroked a strand of hair behind her ear, where his fingers lingered, their tips against her earlobe.

"Do you think you're in love with Paul Crowley?"

If he had said she had sprouted horns overnight she wouldn't have been more surprised.

"What . . . do you know about Paul?"

"You mentioned him when you were delirious. Are you in love with him?"

"No! But if I were, it wouldn't be any of your business!"

He smiled down at her, his teeth glimmering against his dark skin.

"I didn't think you were in love with him, but I wanted to hear you say it." He removed his hand from her ear. "Are you content with your life, Merry?"

"What do you mean?" she asked, mystified.

"Do you ever wish for a home, a family, and security?"

She was silent, her eyes stunned and wide. She didn't like this personal conversation. She didn't want to talk to him about her private dreams. The silence between them was deep while she hastily gathered her confused thoughts.

"I'm no different from anyone else. I suppose that's what most of us want."

"I'm an impatient and busy man, Merry. And I realize that sometimes I'm not a very kind one. But when I make up my mind about something I like to act as quickly as possible. I think it would be to your advantage and to mine if we were married. How does the idea strike you?"

She looked at him as if he had just dropped from outer space. He was looking calmly back at her as if what he said wasn't the most ridiculous thing in the world. Either he was out of his mind, she thought—or she was!

"It strikes me as insane. And I agree you are not a kind man to even suggest such a thing. You're not in love with me and I'm not in love with you." Yet as she spoke the words, she knew that, at least as far as her feelings were concerned, they weren't true.

"I know that. I wouldn't insult your intelligence by pretending that I was. I believe that people who marry on short acquaintance because they have fallen madly in love are taking a step into the unknown with possibly painful results. The smart approach, I think, is to grow into love with someone you respect. Someone with whom you share mutual attraction." He reached for her hand which had crept out from beneath the covers and held it in his large one. Leaning forward, he kissed her lightly on the mouth. "Did you find that unpleasant?"

"N—no." What was he doing?

"I found it very pleasant and I'm sure if I were lying there in bed beside you I could have done a much better job of it." His smiling eyes held her mesmerized.

She bit her lip, a hysterical desire to giggle suddenly overtaking her. "You're crazy. Do you know that? Just plain crazy!"

The smile left his eyes and he said rather impatiently, "Don't you want a home . . . children?"

"Of course I want a home. I wouldn't be normal if I didn't." The impatience in her voice matched his.

"And children?"

"Yes, but . . ."

"Your own?"

"Of course."

"Then you're going to need a man to accomplish that feat," he said drily.

She looked at him steadily. "I want love and a happy secure home before I bring a child into this world."

He looked at her and then away. "You're wishing for that old-fashioned relationship between one man and one woman, Merry. To be honest with you, I think that story-book, idealistic love is doomed to extinction. How, in this society, can anyone pledge his entire life and future to one person when it's impossible to tell what the next day will bring?"

She put out an unsteady hand. "How can you say that? I must try for a relationship that will endure. I have to have something to hold onto in this crazy world!" She held his glance for a moment then looked down.

"You can hold onto me. I don't repulse you. I can tell that much."

The cool assumption stung. She glared up at him. "You must know that marriage between two people from different lifestyles, who scarcely know each other, wouldn't work. I—I'm surprised you would even think of such a thing much less suggest it. It's ridiculous! How could you possibly be considering taking me into your family? You don't know anything about me."

"I know everything about you. I know you lived in eleven foster homes from the time you were five years old until you completed high school. I know the names of the families you lived with. I talked with one of your instructors who told me you are a girl with high principles and ideals. You were invited to take additional training in Rochester, Minnesota at the Mayo Clinic because you were second from the top of a class of one hundred and twenty. While in Rochester you were . . . friends with a man named Paul Crowley. He used you while he took his internship in the hospital where you were working. You helped to support his expensive tastes. When he got the opportunity to climb the social ladder, he took it and threw you over. You were unhappy, and when the child-snatching incident provided a good excuse for you to leave town, you jumped at it."

While he was talking Meredith wished she could die. The bastard! That he could pick up the telephone and lay bare every private aspect of her life caused her to hate him. The intense silence that followed seemed to press the breath out of her, drain all coherent thought from her mind until anger took over. Her lips felt stiff and it took every ounce of her control to keep her voice steady.

"That is the most malicious thing anyone has ever done to me in my whole life! How dare you pry into my background? You had no right!" Tears of embarrassment and humiliation ran down her cheeks. That her life had been held up to ridicule by this man was the most demoralizing blow she had received yet. She would leave this place as soon as possible!

"Get out of this room. Go! Get out! Give me the courtesy of allowing me to dress in private! I wouldn't spend another day in your house if I was dying. You've no right to drag my life out for ridicule!" She was crying and the sobs were shaking her voice.

"That was the last thing on my mind, Merry. I most certainly am not ridiculing your life. You have conducted yourself admirably. All I learned about you convinced me more than ever that I want you for my wife. I want no secrets between us. You must realize I couldn't ask you to become a member of my family without knowing as much about you as I could."

"What did you think I was, for God's sake? A call-girl?" The anger was leaving her and she just wanted to cry. How could he ever know the lonely and hard spots in her life? She had been respectable, dammit! Dull, but . . . respectable.

"Of course not. You're a beautiful, intelligent woman with good taste and charming manners. You're a good influence on Maggie and Cullen. I believe you will be an asset to my home, spend my money with good taste and in return I'm prepared to take care of you, be a faithful husband and an attentive father. That seems to me to be a sound basis for a happy and lasting marriage."

"You make it sound like you're buying a dependable car with good mileage. When I marry it will be for love."

"Love is a word that is tossed about quite a bit these days, but doesn't seem to mean much. Frankly, I'm not sure I know what love is."

"I can't believe you!" Meredith's words echoed back to her, seeming to emphasize her solitude. "Why? Why do you want to do . . . this?"

"That's a fair question. I want Maggie to have a mother. One that won't go away as she puts it. I want a home to come back to with more than a houseful of paid servants in it. I want companionship. I want a woman in my home to make love to and a son I can watch grow into a man."

"Then why don't you marry Luis's sister? He said it's what your grandmother wants."

He leaned toward her, giving her the full benefit of the anger in his eyes, but when he spoke it was calmly.

"I don't happen to like Francisca. As many hours as I will spend with my wife, I want one that I at least like."

"Am I to take that as a compliment?"

"That is the way I meant it."

A warmth ran over her skin, for he gave his words a sensual meaning. Her fingers tensed in his. As often on momentous occasions one notices and afterwards remembers irrelevant things, so Meredith's eyes fixed on the dark hair springing from the long open V of his shirt. She felt a curious kind of panic as if some proud wild creature was staring at her. It was a mad and fanciful image and she banished it. Her eyes fell helplessly to the hand holding hers, and the gold gleam of a watch at his wrist, from which dark hair sprang. The image returned and with it the fears and the loneliness. . . . She raised her eyes to his and thought about all that he was offering. She had only to accept him and she would be Maggie's mommy, the one that wouldn't go away. It would mean she would give up all her fanciful, sentimental notions of love and settle for a calculated union.

"I don't expect you to give me your answer right this minute, Merry. Think about it." Then abruptly he moved and gathered her into his arms. His mouth had found hers before she could turn her head. It was not merely a light kiss of affection. He kissed her as though she were a woman with whom he would share more intimate caresses. She felt his lips, his teeth, his tongue. She opened her lips to his as the intimacy of the kiss increased and felt a strange helplessness in her limbs, as if his sensuous mouth was absorbing her.

"We'll do all right together." His face was near, his eyes staring into hers. She was breathing fast and so was he. Her head was spinning. When he turned her face toward his, there was no triumph on his face or in his eyes, only concern . . . for her. She was unbearably aware of his closeness.

"Do you believe I can be tender? I have moments, Merry. I'm not always the bear." He whispered the words mockingly before the firm lips became silent and feathered light kisses along her brow, her temples, and down her jaw line to her throat and his arms curved and pressed her more closely to him. Ageless moments passed while her bones felt as if they were turning to water. Finally, when she thought she could not bear the longing an instant longer, his mouth took hers in a kiss that engaged her soul. His lips hardened, and her own parted under them, admitting him, submitting. She touched the tip of her tongue delicately against his mouth and felt him tremble. She wound her arms around his neck.

"We'll be good together, Merry. It's a start." The muttered words were barely coherent, thickly groaned in her ear as he kissed the bare warm curve of her neck, following it to her ear and back to the hollow in her shoulder, covering her skin with light, tantalizing kisses.

"I think you'd better go." The strangled voice sounded miles from her ears.

He cupped a hand behind her head and pressed hard fingers under the disarray of her hair and drew her flushed face into his shoulder.

"It was unfair of me to spring this on you now. I should have waited for you to get your strength back. Rest and I'll come back this evening." He stroked a strand of her hair behind her ear as he had done before and stood up. He seemed to be a mountain of a man standing over her. "Cullen would like to come up this afternoon if you feel up to it." He smiled. "He must want to see you. It's a real production getting his chair up the stairs."

"I'll feel up to it." She said it quickly. She wanted to see calm, earthy, sane Cullen.

"I'll tell him then."

He was gone. She was alone. She ran the tip of her tongue around the velvety innerside of her lips as his had done minutes before and her heart gave a disturbing throb. Oh, God! Why did she suddenly feel like she was in the ocean swimming against the tide?

CHAPTER SEVEN

WARD'S PARTING KISS left Meredith prey to a thousand conflicting emotions. At first she felt outrage that he would even suggest a marriage of convenience. Did he think she would sell herself for mere security? And yet, the burning memory of his embrace sent delicious tremors through her still feverish body. What was wrong with her? Ward didn't even believe in love—he'd been perfectly clear on that point. She didn't . . . she couldn't . . . love the man. And yet she found herself weighing the pain and disillusionment of the last few months, the loneliness she had known for most of her life, against the possibility of luxurious content as his wife. As she steadied herself in preparation for his evening visit, rehearsing a diplomatic refusal again and again, only a lingering doubt remained.

As Ward moved quickly across the large bedchamber, Meredith noticed an uncharacteristic agitation on his face, belying his confident stride. In a moment, he was beside her, larger than life, looking deep into her eyes.

"Well?"

The single word of inquiry exploded in Meredith's brain

and for a moment she could not speak. The well-rehearsed words died in her throat as a wave of longing, almost violent in its intensity, took their place. In a barely audible whisper, she heard herself telling Ward that she would be his wife.

"Now I would like to tell you about Maggie," he said quietly, his tone newly serious. "Contrary to what everyone outside the family thinks, she's not the daughter of my sister Connie."

Meredith drew in her breath. "But—"

He held up a broad hand, silencing her. "Let me finish. I know that Jim told you a bit about Cullen's accident, that our sister Connie was killed in it. But let me start from the beginning. You see, Connie went a little wild for a while and bolted during her college years. She went out to Arizona and joined a sort of traveling commune. They wandered about aimlessly, looking for God knows what. During Cullen's last year of college he went out to try and straighten her out and became involved with a friend of hers. It was this girl who later gave birth to Maggie. After the child was born, the girl died from an overdose of drugs. Connie brought the baby to me. She was sure the child is Cullen's. But before we three could have a family conference to discuss what to do, he was in the hospital and had all he could handle facing the fact that he would never walk again—and that Connie had been killed in the accident."

Meredith gasped. "Poor Cullen! How awful." She looked straight into Ward's eyes. Gravely, she shook her head. "But Cullen should know that Maggie could be his child. It might make all the difference."

"I mean for him to know, Merry, but he wasn't ready before, believe me. Now that he's starting to come out of his shell, I think he can handle the news. It'll be quite a shock, you know. Anyhow, I'm telling you now because in this short time I think I have come to know you very well. There may come a time when you'll have to give Maggie up and I don't want you to be hurt."

Was there warmth and concern for her in his voice? She saw in the deep, velvet look absorbing her that she had not been mistaken. But, she reminded herself sharply, he would naturally be concerned for her feelings, just as he was for Cullen's or Maggie's. Love and romance, however, were not part of the bargain.

"Yes," she said more sharply than she intended, "it will be easier giving her over to someone else if I know beforehand."

He took her chin between his thumb and forefinger and, tilted it, looked down into her eyes.

"You've got plenty of spunk, Merry. I know this situation is not of your choosing, but you're making the most of it, aren't you? You're still dreaming of a prince on a white charger who will sweep you away to his castle where there will be no more heartaches, no more problems. Life isn't like that, Merry *mía*, as you well know. If there were no heartaches, how would we know when we are happy?"

His words stayed with her for a long time after he left her.

Meredith sat beside Ward in the Mercedes, shocked that the past week had flown by almost as fast as the landscape was flying past now. Later today she and Ward would be married in a small church in San Antonio with only Jim Sanderson and his wife as witnesses. Meredith was glad that Ward had sent his cousin round-trip flight tickets the day after his incredible proposal. Having a kind, familiar face there would make the whole affair seem less fantastic.

If anything convinced her she was doing the right thing, it was Maggie. Because of her, life had taken on a new radiance for the child. Maggie was the leveler, the thing that helped Meredith keep things in proportion. They needed each other.

Ward stopped the car and pushed the button on the dashboard. The big iron gates swung open and she turned to watch them close after they had passed through. She looked eagerly at the countryside. It had been dark when she made the taxi trip from the airport and she hadn't realized the estate was so large. The bold landscape fascinated her. Nothing was blurred in this country. Everything was clear-cut and diamond bright, under a deep sky dotted with fluffy cotton-wool clouds.

"What will your grandmother say about . . . us?" It was a subject they hadn't discussed.

Ward answered her question openly and frankly. "I telephoned her this morning and told her. She is upset."

Suddenly the vibrant glow in the air vanished. Meredith felt slightly sick with apprehension. Her hands, clasped tightly in her lap, became clammy and she stared straight ahead, seeing nothing that actually existed. Seeing instead a blurred image of a faceless grandmother rejecting her.

"And Mrs. Sanderson, your stepmother, will she be upset, too?" She knew she was a glutton for punishment, but better to know now than later.

"Oh, yes," Ward turned to grin at her. "She'll rant and rave about my duty to the family and about whether or not your blood is sufficiently blue to mingle with that of the

Sandersons. But remember this, Merry. Her opinion or anyone else's means nothing to me. I am my own person. I make my own decisions. I please myself."

Meredith leaned back in the seat and drew in a deep breath. She tried to force her mind to pay attention to what was outside the car. They were approaching a ring of low, flat-topped hills.

She started when she heard Ward's voice. "What's worrying you?"

"I was just thinking that Luis wasn't very happy about our marriage either."

"Luis wanted to be my brother-in-law. He's a very mercenary fellow. He can't stand his sister, Francisca, anymore than I can, but with her married to me his own personal fortune would have been more secure."

"Are you always so frank?"

"Not always, but I will be with you. I said I wanted no secrets between us."

They talked off and on after that, but impersonally, about the land, the birds, the flowers. They were going into the downtown area to pick up some papers Ward wanted to mail while they were in the States. Meredith commented on the beautiful flowers growing in profusion in the parkway. She had always loved flowers.

"Guadalajara has one of the most ideal climates in the world," Ward explained. "The temperature hovers between fifty-eight and seventy-two degrees the year round. Many Americans retire here." He braked sharply as they rounded a curve and waited patiently for a horse-drawn cart to turn off the avenue. They continued in silence for a while and then he pointed out *Aqua Azul* Park and the *charro* ring. He explained that the bull riding contest was held here.

"The contest is equivalent to a rodeo in the States. The only difference is that a *charro* brings a bull to earth by the tail rather than by the horns. I'll take you to one some time. They are very colorful."

"Do they have the bullfights at the same time?" If that were the case she would have to find an excuse not to go. She didn't believe she could bear to see an animal tormented and slaughtered.

"No. The bullfights are held in the bullring. An altogether different sport."

"Do you go to the bullfights?"

"Never. I don't care for the sport."

In the heart of the downtown area he pulled the car to the curb so that she might see the giant cathedral.

"They began building this cathedral in 1571 and finished it forty-seven years later. It's a magnificent building. When you stop to think that it was built eighty years after Columbus discovered America and without modern technology . . . what an amazing achievement."

They paused in front of an office building and a uniformed doorman darted out with a briefcase. Ward spoke to him in Spanish and they moved once again out into the line of traffic.

Meredith didn't wonder that people wanted to retire to this beautiful setting. Her eyes wandered over the shaded plazas, green parks, glittering fountains, elegant statues, and the carefully tended flower plots which were ablaze with the deep orange of marigolds, the scarlet of zinnias, and the crimson petals of roses. It was a modern city with trolleybus and taxis, yet horse-drawn carts also seemed strangely at home on the busy streets crowded with small foreign cars all darting in and out of the traffic lanes. She marveled at how they wiggled into the smallest space with only inches to spare on either side. At every traffic light there was a blast of auto horns. Ward laughed at the expression on her face.

"It would be impossible for a Mexican to drive without a horn."

She grinned back at him, and wondered fleetingly when the beautiful coach she was riding in was going to turn back into a pumpkin.

A guard tipped his hat as they passed through a private gate at the airport. They drove some distance around long, low hangers to where a silver white plane waited. Ward drove the Mercedes up to within a short distance of the plane and stopped.

They went up the steps to the plane together, but when they reached the door he stood aside so she could enter. It was like walking into a sitting room. There was a long low couch, tables, lamps, occasional chairs, thick carpet, and even a beautifully framed landscape on the wall. She turned to Ward. Quite suddenly she was aware of nervousness, of uncertainty, of a number of nameless doubts.

"This is yours? We're going to fly in this? Alone?"

He met her tormented glance with puzzlement before he smiled. "Not alone. The pilot is going with us."

She didn't smile back. "Then you really do live like this." She said it half to herself with a little sinking feeling in the pit of her stomach. Good Lord! What was she doing here? How could this be real?

Ward saw the serious, scared look on her face and placed a reassuring arm across her shoulders. "Are you afraid of flying?" He searched her face.

Meredith was not fearful about the short flight, but she

was beginning to grasp the reality of Ward Sanderson's wealth. How would she bridge the gap from her world to his? She turned wide grave eyes to his face. How could she possibly stand beside this man as his wife? It would mean more than merely babysitting his child. She would have to direct servants, greet his guests, meet his business acquaintances. Her clothes, manners, all her actions would be scrutinized by his friends, his stepmother, the press. Oh God! She had forgotten about the press! Would they find out about the wedding? From what Jim had told her, everything the Sandersons did was news in Tulsa!

"Ward!" She looked at him now with a look that blended confusion and fear. "Let's talk about this. I'm not sure . . . I didn't think, didn't realize while we were at the *hacienda* that you were so . . . were so . . ." She didn't want to say the word "rich," but what other word could she say? "I didn't think about the kind of life you live. I should have thought this out more clearly. I don't usually let my judgment get so insanely out of hand. Surely you can understand now that you see me . . . here. I don't fit in! I've not been anywhere or done anything that would make me interesting to your friends. I've no experience, no . . . polish. I've never even given a . . . party!" Her voice caught on a sob.

"A party?" His arm tightened around her and his voice was sharp in her ear. "Who in the hell cares about a party? You're wrong about yourself, Merry. You'd be an asset to any man. You're you, Merry, and that's part of your charm. My life isn't as glamorous as you probably think it is. I have this plane because my work makes it necessary, not because I'm a jet-setter. And if you're worrying about managing my home"—his eyes glimmered—"wait until you've met Edna. She is the most infuriating, capable woman in the world. She runs the house like she was the master of a ship and spoils me terribly." He laughed. "I can't wait until she sees you."

"She won't like me any more than your stepmother and your grandmother."

"That's where you're wrong. She'll look down her nose, size you up, then take you under her wing and love you."

Meredith said nothing for a long moment, then turned tiredly and rested her forehead against his arm.

"If this doesn't work out, Ward, or if you meet someone, fall in love, and want to marry, this . . . arrangement doesn't have to last forever." Her voice was muffled and she felt stupidly close to tears.

"And if you should meet someone, you'll tell me? I'm hoping we'll be able to talk to each other about everything, Merry." He held her and swayed softly. In his arms, she felt safe.

Her answer was almost breathless. "I will. I promise I will."

Their eyes met. Hers were bright with tears, his gentle, questioning. It seemed both an end and a beginning for them. Reluctantly, she pulled away and sniffed.

"I don't cry all the time." She fumbled for a tissue.

"I'm glad to know that. I was beginning to think I'd have to order these things by the truckload." A handkerchief appeared in his hand and he wiped her eyes, his own bright with amusement. He urged her toward the back of the plane and into a small compartment. "We'll be taking off soon and there's something I want to show you." A number of boxes were stacked on the small bunk. Ward ignored them and slid open a door exposing a half dozen garments hanging on padded hangers. "Carmen selected some things. I . . ." The closed look on her face stopped him from saying anything else. He waited and her face relaxed and he smiled. "I knew you wouldn't have time to shop and every woman is entitled to a new dress to be married in, to put away in mothballs so she can drag it out twenty years later and see if she can squeeze into it. When we're airborne you can come in here and rummage around and select something."

Meredith looked down at the silk dress, her best, which Sophia had pressed for her. Now wasn't the time to allow pride to rear its head. Unconsciously she stroked a strand of hair behind her ear.

"Thank you."

Ward clamped his hands firmly to her shoulders and pulled her toward him. His kiss was quick and firm. He raised his head and grinned. His voice, when he spoke, was husky.

"I think that bears repeating."

His face came to hers and he kissed her longer and harder. The first time her lips had been compressed with surprise, but now they were soft and yielding. Her palms rested on his chest before they moved around to his back and she hugged him to her. He raised his head. They looked into each other's eyes and exchanged another smile. She was happy. God, she was happy! Back in the secret recess of her mind though, she knew it wouldn't last, couldn't last. It was too beautiful. When it ended she would adjust. . . . She always had. Voices forced her mind back to the present. The pilot was aboard and Ward was urging her gently back through the narrow doorway, to her future as his wife.

CHAPTER EIGHT

THE SUN SHONE warmly on Meredith's wedding day, its brilliance touching everything including the diamonds clipped to her ears and the magnificent pearl and diamond choker Ward fastened around her slender neck moments before they left the hotel room. She looked beautiful and stately as she approached the flower-decked altar in the large, almost empty church. Her trembling hand was clasped firmly in Ward's and he measured his steps to match hers as she walked in the new high-heeled pumps that matched perfectly with the soft gray cashmere suit that she wore. Ward was wearing a dark suit for the occasion with a small, violet orchid attached to his lapel. Meredith's bouquet was made of large violet orchids and Jim Sanderson's wife Ruth held a bouquet of beautiful yellow roses.

Ward had said he would take care of everything and he had. All Meredith had to do was choose her dress and sign her name to the marriage certificate. The ceremony itself was simple and the minister, an elderly man with wisps of gray hair combed over his almost bald pate, spoke his words solemnly.

"Dearly beloved, today we are gathered together in the sight of God and man to join this man and this woman."

It all seemed so unreal to Meredith, like Cinderella going to the ball. But this was no ball, she quickly reminded herself—it was her wedding day! This day she was joining her life to that of a rich, handsome, storybook prince charming. Would she wake up to find herself back in a foster home, with only a life filled with loneliness stretching out before her?

"Do you, Ward, take this woman to love . . . and to cherish . . . in sickness and in health . . . for richer, for poorer . . . till death you do part?"

Meredith's eyes went quickly to Ward's and found that he was looking down at her. His words, spoken firmly, echoed in the silent church.

"I do."

Meredith felt the impact of his words. *For richer, for poorer, till death do us part.* The circle of diamonds was being placed on her finger.

". . . I now pronounce you man and wife. What God has joined together, let no man . . ." The minister was smiling. "You may kiss your bride."

Ward bent down and brushed her cold lips with his, and took her hand and interlaced his fingers with hers. Suddenly, she was terrified thinking about the enormity of the step she had taken. How could Jim and his wife be smiling and Ward so calm? Oh, Jesus! She hoped when the time came for her legs to move they wouldn't fail her. They didn't.

The two couples moved out of the church and into the

bright sunlight. Here everything seemed so normal. Traffic moved, horns blared, and children raced by on the sidewalk. They got into the car waiting beside the curb.

"It was a beautiful wedding and you were a beautiful bride." Ruth Sanderson was almost tearful.

"Thank you." Meredith managed her stock answer for almost everything. Her lips trembled and her eyes felt misty. She longed for a tissue to wipe her nose, but since her hand was still clasped in Ward's, and her other hand clutched the bouquet, she allowed herself a small sniff. Ward looked at her strangely and she willed her eyes to stay dry and her nose not to run.

They arrived back at the hotel where they had met Jim and Ruth and where she had changed into her wedding clothes. The driver helped her from the car and then Ward's protective clasp took her to the private elevator that whisked them to their rooms. An elaborate buffet, including a bottle of champagne resting in a bucket of ice, awaited them.

The high heels of Meredith's beautiful pumps sank into the thick carpet. She felt more than ever like Cinderella. Ward had handled everything perfectly. They had driven from the airport to the parking ramp of this hotel, up the private elevator to the suite of rooms where Jim and Ruth waited. They had made the trip to the church and back without seeing anyone but the driver and the minister. Ward had shielded her from publicity as he had promised.

She stood beside the couch wishing desperately she didn't feel so nervous. If she felt shy, Ruth did not. She was plainly impressed with the elegance of the rooms.

"Isn't this room gorgeous, Jim?" She settled onto the

rose colored silk couch. "Could you just imagine our girls when they were little sitting here on Saturday morning with a bowl of cereal in their laps and their beady little eyes glued to the cartoons?"

Jim laughed. "And you running around in one of your faded flannel nightgowns?"

Their laughing eyes met and held. A blast of envy struck Meredith. Jim adored his wife.

"I want you to know, Jim Sanderson, that I may never leave this place. We've had a regular little second honeymoon ourselves." Ruth spoke to Jim, but her twinkling eyes were watching Ward and Meredith.

"You'll leave, love." Jim loosened his tie. "A team of mules couldn't keep you out of the car when I head for the airport." He said it dryly and winked openly at Meredith.

She liked them immensely, both of them, and longed to be like them, easy and relaxed. They were being themselves, honest, all agog at the splendor of this fabulous hotel. Her eyes went to Ward. He was watching her. Aware the tawny eyes were on her, she bit her lower lip, searching for something light and clever to say. Dammit! He knew how nervous she was.

"Tired, Merry?"

She met his eyes. "I guess so."

He gave her a sudden, gentle smile and the tawny eyes glowed warmly. He came toward her, lifted the bouquet from her hands, and placed it on the table. When he moved away from her to the cocktail cabinet, a chaotic rush started to whirl in her brain. She was married to this man, yet she hardly knew him. Though she felt that she was living a novel—rich man meets and marries poor girl and takes her to his mansion where she lives happily ever after—she now realized that her naive romantic ideals had allowed her to be fooled by Paul. All of a sudden she knew that most of her life she had floated around in a romantic mist, but now she had to face facts. She was in love with Ward! The words beat against her mind. It had taken a long time to recognize the signs that had been there for the noticing. The way her eyes seemed to be constantly drawn to him, the pleasure she felt when she looked at his tall erect body, the secure, protected feeling she had when she was with him.

She felt a sudden, delirious rush of joy. She had fallen completely, utterly in love with the man, the real man behind the figurehead that was Ward Sanderson. How could she bear knowing that he did not love her?

He came to her just at that moment and put the cold glass in her hand. The magic ended. She came back to reality with a jolt. She felt her cheek go paler. Evading his eyes, she took the glass and would have turned away, but his free hand caught hers. She looked up and met dark amusement in his eyes.

"Jim, you and Ruth come and drink a toast to my bride."

Meredith found it difficult to concentrate on what he was saying. Try as she would, she couldn't think of anything but the realization of what he meant to her. You're in deep water, Meredith, a voice inside her warned.

Time went fast. Then Ward moved discreetly into another room in the suite so Meredith could speak with her life-long friends. Jim and Ruth hugged her warmly goodbye. "I wouldn't have missed this for the whole world, Meredith. I suppose you know by now that I'm really a romantic at heart." There was an affectionate smile on Jim's face. "I think Ward got himself a super bride."

"I'm not sure I could have managed without you and Ruth here—it all happened so quickly. To think that if it weren't for you, Jim, I might never even have met Ward, no less married him . . ." Meredith shook her head in disbelief.

Jim's face grew somber. "So you do love him! I'm glad. Frankly, I was worried about that. More than anything, I want you to be happy. And Ward needs love almost as much as Cullen does."

"How is Cullen?" Ruth quickly interjected. "Have you been able to get close to him, find out what he's thinking? Is there anything you can tell me that I can take home to my sister?"

At Meredith's puzzled look, the older woman explained her remark. "My sister Becky has been in love with Cullen since they were sixteen. They became really close after the accident in spite of his mother's efforts to keep them apart. Then suddenly Cullen told her to get lost. It almost killed her. She has moped around for two years now doing nothing but work with her quarter horses and play her guitar. I wish there was someway they could get together. Is Cullen any better? Has he made an effort to do something with his life?"

"I've only known Cullen a few weeks, but Ward seems to think he's beginning to come out of his spell." For the first time in her life a feeling of belonging enveloped Meredith. She belonged to Ward, now, and Cullen and Maggie were family. "Cullen spends a lot of his time with his flowers and his music. He plays the most stirringly beautiful music I've ever heard. He seems to pour all the longing in his soul into it. Tell your sister he's lonely. If she loves him, she'll have to make the first move. Cullen feels he has nothing to offer a woman."

"I'll tell Becky what you said. She cares about him a great deal."

As the two of them moved closer to the door, Meredith said quickly, "I'll keep in touch. I appreciate your being with me today. I don't know how I can thank you."

"You already have. You've given us news of Cullen," Ruth said. The two women exchanged a hug and Ruth regretfully shrugged into her jacket. "Have a great time in Acapulco."

"We will."

Ruth hugged her again, and then she and Jim left. There was a tug at Meredith's heart as she walked slowly out of the room behind her. Ruth was a beautiful woman, beautiful inside where it mattered.

After a few suggestions from Jim on how to handle a wife and a playful exchange of banter, the door closed behind them. Ward reappeared.

There was silence.

"Well, Mrs. Sanderson?"

Meredith tried to remain calm. "Well, Mr. Sanderson?" The small laugh she tried refused to come convincingly. Her throat was tight with nervousness and she wasn't sure she could say anything more without betraying the fact to him. Soundlessly he had moved to put his hands on her shoulders and turn her to face him. Her heart gave a choking, little thump and she raised a tremulous gaze to his face.

"You were very beautiful today. No man could have been more proud of his bride than I was."

Her lashes dropped and her cheeks felt warm.

"Blushes, Merry? I do believe you're genuinely without vanity. What other virtues have I yet to discover in my wife? Patience? Modesty? Not meekness . . . I know that!" His brows came together, then raised in amusement. "I suspect you have unexpected depths, Merry, Merry, quite contrary. And before many weeks have passed I will have explored every single one of them."

She stood there, silently, watching him. He took her hand and led her to the bedroom door.

"I'm taking a shower. How about you?"

She nodded and went slowly into the bedroom.

"Which bath do you want? The pink? I'll take the brown. Don't use all the hot water."

Could he be nervous? Making small talk to cover up? His teasing words didn't go with the look on his face. She glanced at him in the mirror. He had taken off his coat and was in the act of removing his tie. His hands were steady, his expression guarded. He caught her eye in the mirror and she quickly averted her gaze and removed the clips from her ears and the necklace from her throat.

While she ran her bath and undressed, she wondered how many women Ward had slept with and how often he would expect to make love to her. Her sexual experiences with Paul had only left her feeling frustrated and used. She looked at her naked body, reflected from every angle by the mirrored walls of the bathroom, and the thought that it was no longer only hers, but Ward's as well, to touch and caress, sent a violent thrill through her. And he was hers. As if seized by a fever she brushed her teeth, tied her hair back and sank down in the tub to hide her nakedness.

She bathed, toweled herself until she was properly dry, and fought out a crazy mental dialogue with herself all the time. What did he expect from her? The thought of that big bed made her fingers and toes feel icy cold despite the steamy heat of the room. In the mirror her eyes were wide and darkly brilliant. The woman reflected there looked like a stranger.

She slipped the prim blue nightgown over her head. This was her wedding night and she was going to bed with her new husband in an old, five-dollar nightgown from the discount store. Abruptly she turned away and forced herself to be calm. She dabbed skin fragrance on wrist and temples and walked back into the bedroom.

Ward lay on the bed, his hands behind his head, a single sheet pulled up to his bare chest. He eyed her without moving. She sat down at the dressing table and picked up her hairbrush. While she was desperately thinking of something to say, he spoke her name, the one he had given her.

"Merry."

Her face was pale when she looked at him. She looked directly into his eyes and her mouth went dry. Her eyes flicked over him and hurried away. His bare shoulders had a silky bronze sheen to them and his chest was deeply tanned, but roughened by dark hair that grew down the center of it. A wild, sweet enchantment rippled through her veins and wordlessly she got up, went to him, and put her hand in his. He moved slightly and made room for her to sit beside him.

"Merry." When he said her name again it was a caress. He ran his hand up and down her arm. Finally he said, "I want you to want me, Merry. Anything else leaves me cold. I won't insist if you're not in the mood."

"No, Ward . . . it isn't that, I . . ." she whispered, her voice faint, her breathing ragged. "I'm willing to be a wife to you . . . in every sense of the word."

"Willing and wanting are two different words," he muttered in a hoarse, thickened voice. "If you need more time . . . "

Denial choked her throat. She almost wanted to cry. The knowledge that he wasn't trying to rush her into fulfilling an obligation brought its own welling of love, and tremulous joy came like a pain, so great it was, and her heart began to race. He watched her with eyes that were dark and anxious and through them she sensed the langorous restraint keeping a rein on his passion. No words would come so she reached out a hand and switched off the bedside lamp and slipped into the sheets beside him.

His arms were waiting for her and pulled her trembling body against his. They lay quietly for a long while, until her trembling ceased. Then he began to stroke her, his hands uncovering her body slowly, achingly, until she lay naked, soft and warm beside him. Carefully he turned her face to him and kissed her long and hard, his mouth taking savage possession of hers, parting her lips and invading it in a way she had never imagined any man would ever kiss her. His hands were moving everywhere, touching her hungrily from her thighs to her breast. While he was kissing her the compelling hands stroked her breasts, and her nipples hardened. His fondling fingers generated their own heat as her naked desire mounted and set her trembling again.

"Sweet Merry. Sweet marshmallow Merry." His voice

was thick, his lips touched the slope of her breasts, then down to tease the stiff nipples, caressing them delicately so that they hardened even more. His hand wandered down to the curve of her hip and stroked her thigh, his own thigh moving restlessly against her, his breathing faster and harder as he touched her.

He leaned over her, his breath warm and moist, his face a blur in the soft light. She wanted to caress him, to get to know his body as he was getting to know hers, and yet . . . the fear of rejection, of having him remove her hands from his body, nagged in her mind while she lay passively accepting his caresses. She could feel the tension building in him while her own body trembled and her lips longed to search for his.

"God!" he said bitterly, his hands gripping her shoulders. "Don't you feel anything?" He looked down into her face then buried his in the curve of her neck.

She felt her body tense, heard his intake of breath, and knew he was going to leave her. Her arms went round his neck, clinging. Her mouth touched his own so lightly it was like the brush of a lash on his skin. She breathed carefully, as though afraid she might frighten him away. Her hand came up and clasped his cheek, cupping it, holding it against her, and then the pressure changed. His lips hardened and her own parted under them, admitting him, submitting. She touched the tip of her tongue delicately against his mouth. They kissed hungrily, and explosive desire opened between them now.

"You want me . . . do you want me?" The muttered words were barely coherent, thickly groaned into her ear as he kissed the bare warm curve of her neck.

"Ward. Ward . . . I . . ." She didn't know what to say, afraid to put words to her fear.

He seemed to understand. With a swift look into her face he took her mouth again. He kissed her as openly and intimately as a man could kiss a woman. Her inhibitions left her and she arched against him, her hands moving over the smooth muscles of his back and down to the smoothness of his buttocks, aware of his tense excitement, listening to the heavy beat of his heart and aroused by the feelings she found in him. At least she was unafraid to let him know that she wanted him and when his husky voice groaned thickly in her ear she did not even try to decipher the muttered words. He might be merely a man who liked making love to women, and did not much care which one he took to bed, but it no longer mattered. She had never felt anything like the sensual enjoyment she was feeling now. Tonight she knew the excruciating drive to be satisfied. She moved against him, clutching at his back while he pressed into her. She wrenched upward and tensed, wanting to know and have every little bit of him. His weight pressed her slimness into the mattress, and her arms tightened about him as they rode out the storm.

When it was over he lay beside her and muttered, "Yes, yes," as if she had said something. Even in the dark she turned her eyes up to his in answer and he kissed her, slowly, sharing the moment of sweet tranquility with her. His arm left her and he reached to the wall above their heads and a softly fused light came on beneath the bed. He propped himself up on one elbow and looked at her. She sighed in contentment. In the soft cocoon of the bed her doubts and fears had dissolved, and her body drowsed, luxuriating in this new and wondrous sensation. He looked down at the pale luminous oval of her face framed in the tumbled hair that was soft and shining in his fingers.

"Your eyes have lights in the dark. Did you know that?"

She shook her head and raised a hand to his cheek. "Ward, I'm not very experienced." His hand stilled in the thick, vibrant hair. She felt a tension in him and hurried on. "I've done this only a very few times. Four in fact and I never . . . never really participated." Now that the words were out she only half wished them back.

He was still for a long moment before the hand in her hair moved to beneath her head.

"My God, what a bastard! That was why it took you so long to show any feeling. I thought that I might repulse you . . . somehow." He pulled her close and held her for a long time. He whispered softly in her ear as she ran her hands over his back. "My pleasure is greater when I give you pleasure. Did you enjoy it?"

"Yes! Oh, yes!" She framed his face with her hands and reached for his lips. This moment was hers; nothing or no one could ever take that from her.

He peeled down the sheet and stooped to kiss her breast. He did it so gently that her whole body cried out for him. She lay back among the pillows feeling happier than she ever had before and he loved her again, tenderly, unhurriedly, caressingly, stroking and entering her again and again. Her hands spent the night learning his body. They said little, but it was one of those rare nights when bodies spoke silently and ignited and burned on for hours. It was almost dawn when he whispered to her, "Go to sleep, Merry. The sweetest sleep in the world comes now."

She found that it did. She fell asleep almost immediately, falling into a deep, satisfying slumber, but all night she was subconsciously aware of the warm, male body pressed to her own, the heavy weight of the arm across her body and the hand that cupped her breast. It was a wonderful way to sleep. She woke in a wonderful way, too.

"Wake up, sleepy head. We leave on our honeymoon in twenty minutes." Ward was leaning over her, his tawny eyes sparkling and alive.

Her yawn stretched into a smile and she stretched out on the comfortable bed. It was extraordinary! Exposing her body to him was like the freedom . . . to fly. She smiled and slipped her arms about his neck and ran her hand down his back.

"Wanton woman," he said intensely and gave her a lecherous smile. "Come take a shower with me."

"You're indecent!" she protested as he pulled her from the bed and they hurried, laughingly, into the bathroom and into the stream of water that seemed to come at them from all sides.

"My hair! What'll I do about my hair?"

"Leave it on your head. I like it there."

She laughed joyously. She would never have dreamed she could be this happy or that he could be like this. He seemed a thousand years younger, boyish, devilish, but considerate and affectionate, too. He pushed the wet hair back from her face and pulled her to him. She tilted her face to meet his kiss and the shower ran full in her face until his head shielded her from the spray. Under the warm water they kissed. She felt his arms tighten around her and his body press against hers. Suddenly she was as hungry for him as he obviously was for her. The water rained down upon them and they couldn't seem to get enough of each other.

He moved his head to look down at her and the spray ran full in her face again.

"I'll drown!" She giggled and leaned her forehead against his chest.

He grasped her shoulders and turned her back to him. "We must remember not to do this when we're in a hurry." He said the words softly and slapped a wet wash-cloth in her hand and poured a flask of fragrant liquid soap down over her breast. "Wash up. The porter will be pounding on the door at any minute."

CHAPTER NINE

Two surprises awaited Meredith in Acapulco. The first came when Ward drove the rented car they picked up at the airport into the long, wide drive leading to the Acapulco Princess Hotel. The massive structure stood like a pyramid among a tropical garden of palm trees, bright flamed poinsettias growing the size of shrubs, golden marigolds in sculptured plots and a profusion of red, mauve, and pink blooms that lined the drive dividing it from the carefully manicured lawn. It was a scene she had seen many times on travel posters, but in person it was much more beautiful.

"Are we going to stay here?" The note of awe in Meredith's voice echoed her feelings.

Ward's tawny eyes warmed as he looked at her. "I thought you would enjoy coming here. Perhaps another time we'll try one of those little, private cottages clinging to the side of the hill up there."

Meredith's eyes followed his gesture and saw the pink cottages, each with its own private pool and surrounded by lush green, terraced into the side of a cliff.

"If you'd rather . . ."

Ward laughed. "Next time. I wanted you to see this place. It's one of the most beautiful hotels in the world. It was on the top floor that the multimillionaire Howard Hughes spent his last days."

"Poor man," she remarked and then laughed with Ward at the irony of her statement.

The awe was still with her when they entered the massive hall where live trees, shrubs, and hundreds of blooming rose bushes thrived in spite of being surrounded by tiers of hotel floors. The lobby was crowded with hotel guests and, as they passed, Meredith heard French, German and a Scandinavian language. With his hand firmly attached to her elbow, Ward propelled her to the desk and then to the elevator. She had little time to think, but she could not help but notice the way her husband commanded attention, demanding service in a quiet, firm manner then tipping without appearing flamboyant.

The second surprise came in the form of a telephone call from Jim just as they were preparing to go out to dinner. Meredith moved about the room restlessly while Ward talked. When he finished he came to her and dropped a light kiss on her nose.

"You can forget your worrying, Merry, Merry. Mr. Thomas decided to drop charges against Laura Jameson. You and Jim were right on target—once he had time to cool off, he took pity on the poor girl. There's even a good chance that she may pull her life together and get the child back. Anyhow, Jim says to tell you to enjoy your honeymoon."

Upon hearing the good news, Meredith felt a warm glow of satisfaction. For the first time in her life, things were going to turn out right! And when Ward sensed her mood and suggested, "Let's go celebrate—how would you like to see the Mexican boys dive from *La Quebrada* tonight?" Meredith agreed with a happy grin.

Later, standing beside Ward, his arm tucking her close to him, they watched a young diver. Perched on a torchlit spot high on the side of a cliff, he raised his arms, leaped out from the rock, and dove, like a graceful bird, into the narrow ribbon of water far below. Meredith turned her face into Ward's shoulder, sure the slim youth would be dashed against the rocks.

"Wait until you see him dive from the very top of the cliff. It's about a hundred and twenty feet down and they must wait until the water is at least twelve feet deep in the gorge. It's usually about eight feet in that area. It's split second timing that's important. I've seen them dive dozens of times and it always raises the hair on the back of my neck. But these boys make their living this way and they know what they're doing." Like a father with a frightened child he turned her around in his arms. "Watch this, now. He won't get hurt. I promise you."

Atop the rock the youth intently watched the surging green water rush into the chasm, and he timed his dive to the rhythm of the incoming tide. Meredith released a pent-up breath as the graceful body sprang out, two blazing torches held in his outstretched hands. She watched until the lithe, arrowlike body sliced into the green water, and then she turned her face once again to Ward's shoulder.

"Is he all right?"

"Sure. Look at him scramble out of the water. They know what they're doing. Their work is probably safer than driving a taxi down *Costera Miguel Aleman*." He looked down at her with warm, friendly eyes and she wanted to snuggle closer to him, but the show was over and people were turning away from the plate glass window that overlooked the chasm.

It was a honeymoon right out of a romantic novel. Although it only lasted four days and four wonderful, glorious nights, it was the kind of honeymoon that comes at the end of the story when love triumphs and the couple walk off into the sunset. These thoughts came to Meredith as she packed her suitcases. Ward had left the room reluctantly, saying he had a few things to attend to before they departed for the airport.

Meredith had learned a lot during the last few days about the man she had married. She found that he was as hungry for affection as she was, and any time she voluntarily put her hands on him he responded, whether it was while they were making love and she let her hand run over his chest or while they were walking on the beach and her hand sought his. At times she could hear his heart thudding powerfully against hers. At others, the warm light in his eyes and the smile on his face told her more than any words that he liked her to touch him. How different he was from Paul who had avoided any physical contact.

She also learned her husband could be possessive and almost cruel at times. It was as if he had two separate, quite distinct personalities in one body, the considerate, gentle man she loved—and the cruel, arrogant one who would whip with his tongue anyone who he thought was infringing on his privacy, or his property. That side of him had been demonstrated only that morning.

They had been sitting in the courtyard at a small table

under a huge umbrella. Meredith was writing a post card to Maude, passing along the good news about the Jamesons, when Ward was paged to take a telephone call.

"I won't be long. Will you be okay here or do you want to come with me?"

"I'll stay here and enjoy the sunshine; I just can't believe there's snow and ice in Minnesota." She held up her hand, and he squeezed it before walking away.

For several minutes she watched the crowds pass, then her eyes caught a scene unfolding farther along, at a table set under a palm. A young Latin man had attracted the attention of a middle-aged American woman. Meredith presumed she was one of the idle, rich women Ward had told her about, a hint of distaste in his voice. They came here seeking a diversion denied them in their own respectable home communities.

She leaned back in her chair and closed her eyes against the sun's fierce glare. When she opened them a tall, fair young man, with a smooth tan and direct, friendly eyes stood before her.

"Hi. I know it's an old line, but don't I know you?"

Meredith stared at him and after a moment came up with a smile. "No. I'm sure we haven't met."

"I swear I've seen you somewhere before. Was it . . . New York, Chicago, or San Francisco?" He laughed and moved to take the chair beside her. "A face like yours would be hard to forget." He was a handsome young man, dressed casually in expensive clothes. "I've covered the States. Was it the Riviera?"

Meredith had been guardedly polite, but the man's persistence began to annoy her. Was he one of those paid companions and lovers to deprived middle-aged women?

She was neither rich or middle-aged and she wished he would go about his business.

"I didn't invite you to sit down," she said coolly.

Undeterred, he looked knowingly into her eyes. "Did your husband send you off to vacation alone?"

Meredith felt his gaze slope down over her body and realized with sudden, cold clarity that he was mentally stripping her. Anger surged along with sudden embarrassment, but before she could express it a shadow fell across her face and she glanced up in heart pounding panic when she saw the look on Ward's face.

"Merry!" The word exploded from him, low and hissed.

"Mary." The young man got to his feet. "That's the name I was trying to remember. I knew I had met you somewhere."

"You've never met her anywhere! Come near her again and you won't have the equipment to ply your trade!"

"Look here . . ." A flush came up in the man's face. Meredith didn't know if it was anger or embarrassment.

"You look here, Lothario." Ward said the word with an unmistakable sneer. "If you're too goddamn lazy to make a living any way other than taking bored women to bed, that's your problem, but stay away from my wife!"

"Who the hell do you think you are?" The young man's voice rose with indignation.

Meredith looked around. They were attracting attention. She got to her feet and took Ward's arm.

"I'm her husband, that's who I am! And if you don't want to lose your teeth, you'll get the hell away from here!" Ward was flaming with fury by the time he finished. Meredith's hand insistently pulled at his arm and he moved away with her.

They didn't speak a word until they were in their room and Ward turned to her accusingly.

"I'm not gone ten minutes and you engage some gigolo in chit-chat."

She flushed angrily. "That's unfair! I didn't engage him. He thought he recognized me."

"How stupid can you be? He took one look at that desirable body of yours and he thought he had it made. Good looking and rich, what more could he want?" He said it jeeringly.

The coldness of his tone was unbearable and somewhere deep in her heart a small hope died a quiet death.

"If he thought that, he was in for a big surprise. I don't have two *pesos* to rub together!"

"With you, money would have been secondary. Bed was on his mind!"

"And you have a nasty mind!"

"Maybe, but what did you expect? Did you think I'd stand by and watch you react encouragingly to a pick-up?"

"I didn't encourage him!" Her eyes were sparking angrily at him.

He looked down at her, his tawny eyes dangerous. "You know damned well you did! He liked what he saw and you were flattered. Well, get this—you're married to me and I won't stand around watching you flirt with every Don Juan that comes along."

"If you thought there was any likelihood of that, why did you marry me?" Before he could answer the question, she rushed on. "All I did was be polite and you have me in bed with him!"

"If I really thought that I'd be breaking your neck by now." He said it softly and menacingly.

Their eyes met in a long, silent war. Her breath began to come fiercely and she desperately wanted to cry. Then he turned away and strode into the dressing room. She went into the bathroom, closed the door, and let tears slide down her cheeks.

Meredith managed to control her emotions. She faced the mirror squarely and with care, dreading the moment she would have to face him again. It came as soon as she opened the door. He was standing there.

"I was about to come in and see if you had floated down the drain. Ready for lunch? We've about time before we pack up to go." He smiled and the lazy charm of his glance took the edge off her nervousness.

"Sure. And I'd like a huge bowl of mixed fruit with that delicious green dressing." Their eyes held and she smiled. He looked at her closely then lowered his head and kissed each eyelid as if kissing the tears away. She knew that this was the nearest thing to an apology she would ever get, but, nevertheless, it was enough. His hand moved down her arm and grasped hers. She interlaced her fingers with his.

CHAPTER TEN

A LITTLE MORE than an hour after the plane left the Acapulco airport it landed on the Rancho Margarieta. A dust-covered jeep, driven by a Mexican in white, baggy pants, came out to meet them. He embraced Ward as if he were a relative and when Ward introduced Meredith, the man took off his straw hat and bowed low before striking Ward a blow with the hat and bursting into laughter followed by a stream of Spanish that set Ward to laughing, too.

When they reached the *hacienda*, the jeep stopped outside the walled courtyard and they walked through an arched gate. Brick-paved and dotted with trees, shrubs, tubs of flowering plants, and graceful fountains spewing cool water, it was like an oasis in the desert. The house had thick walls with arched doorways leading on to wide verandas. Hanging baskets of flowers were everywhere. Meredith hardly had time to take it all in before Ward urged her forward and into a wide tiled hallway where they were met by a very old woman in a long black dress.

Again Ward was hugged like a favorite son. He gently kissed the wrinkled cheek and introduced Meredith. Alert, bright eyes looked her over before a huge smile appeared. She embraced Meredith much the same as she had Ward. Meredith was both surprised and touched.

"Saldana has been with my grandmother for many years. They are about the same age." He explained this to Meredith, then spoke more slowly to the woman. "Is my grandmother well, Saldana?"

She made a gesture with her hands. "Ah . . . *sí*, sometimes. We are not young like you, my young stallion." Her eyes twinkled up at him and she smiled an almost toothless smile. "It is *siesta* time. Take your bride up to rest. I will tell your *abuela* that you have brought your new *esposa* to her. Do not be surprised if she is angry." The old woman laughed. "But not as angry as Francisca, no?"

Saldana's frankness caused questions to swirl through Meredith's mind. How was she going to face this hostile grandmother? Would she feel, once again, like the unwanted child thrust into a foster home? Pride surfaced. No, by damn! If the old lady didn't like her, tough!

Later while waiting in an unfamiliar room for him to come for her, some of her bravado faded. The room itself was intimidating, its tall, mirrored doors reflecting the monstrously large bed positioned between narrow windows. The bed had high lofted mattresses covered by a woven spread of coarse white cotton which emphasized the darkness of the Spanish bedroom furniture and the highly polished wood floor. The room would be fitting for a Spanish bride. Had Ward's mother been conceived on that large bed?

Just then Ward came into the room without knocking, and she welcomed his intrusion into her thoughts.

"Ready?" He looked her over, smiled, and reached out to tuck a strand of blond hair behind her ear.

She had dressed carefully in an apricot silk dress with a short jacket and flared skirt. She had applied a minimal amount of make-up and when she looked at her reflection thought she looked plain and washed-out compared to Mexican girls with their midnight black hair and white skin.

Trying to be flip to cover her nervousness, she flashed up at him what she hoped was a confident smile. "Ready for the lion's den," she replied.

"It won't be that bad." His eyes searched hers and there was such a tender look in them that her heart lurched crazily. "She's disappointed that I didn't marry a Mexican woman, but when she gets to know you it will be all right. She's really a softy where I'm concerned. You'll see."

"I hope so." She slipped her hand into his and her confidence came dribbling back.

But her uneasiness returned as they walked down the broad, carpeted steps. What thoughts were going through his head, she wondered? Had he seen Francisca? How was she going to bear up under the strain of living with him, knowing he only liked her, was more than satisfied with their sexual relationship, but didn't love her? At any time he might meet someone and fall in love! Would she be able to bow out gracefully? Would the decision she made to marry him demand more of her than she would be able to bear?

They came to high, double doors and Ward put his hand on the ornate knob. She looked up at him imploringly.

"Just be yourself. You look beautiful," he murmured.

They walked into a cool, quiet room. The ceiling was

high and fans with thin, wide blades whirled slowly and noiselessly, stirring the air. Heavy, high-backed velvet upholstered chairs, square tables, and a long, low couch decorated the room. At first Meredith thought the room was empty because the small lady in the dark dress sitting on the large chair blended with her surroundings.

With her hand firmly clasped in his Ward led her forward. He bent and kissed the old lady's cheek.

"Here she is, Grandmother. I told you she was beautiful." His voice was soft, almost reverent. There was a gentleness about him when he looked at this small, wrinkled woman.

Very dark, bright eyes looked steadily at Meredith and she looked steadily back. Instinct told her this woman would look with contempt on anyone who stood meekly, passively, under her stare. Her features were small beneath jet black hair threaded with silver. It was wonderfully thick hair, piled in soft swirls atop her proudly held head. Her hands were slender and well cared for and gripped the arms of the chair as if she were about to rise up. The silence dragged on as the two women looked at each other, and Meredith realized she was going to have to speak the first words. She pulled her hand from Ward's and held it out to the woman who sat so stoically.

"I'm glad to meet you, *señora*." It seemed to Meredith she held her hand out for ages before a hand came out to meet it. The clasp was firm but didn't linger.

"Sit down." She was still looking at Meredith and her words were more of a command than an invitation. Meredith walked back a few steps to an identical high-backed chair, but before she sat down the woman said to Ward, "Leave us." Her voice softened only a fraction when she spoke to her grandson. Meredith's eyes flew to Ward's. He came to her and slid his arm across her shoulders. His eyes told her he wouldn't go if she wanted him to stay. She moved out of his embrace.

"I think your grandmother and I should get to know one another on a woman-to-woman basis, darling. Do you mind?" She sat down in the heavy, straight chair, her feet just comfortably reaching the floor.

"Not if that's what you want, sweetheart." He bent over her and looked into her face before he dropped a kiss on her cool lips.

"I'll be fine." She mouthed the words to him while his face blocked his grandmother's view of her lips. His hand lingered on her shoulder and he squeezed it reassuringly before walking away.

A calmness had come over Meredith. She looked at a sliver of sunlight on the floor and heard the soft sound made by Ward's closing of the door. She looked into the cool, dark eyes and smiled. Lady, she thought, you would be surprised to know how many times I've sat in a hard, straight chair and faced a stranger who had the authority to dictate my life. Never again. I'll meet you on equal terms. Whether we shall be friends or not is up to you. She knew Ward's grandmother was waiting for her to say something, but decided to let her steer the conversation into whatever channel she chose. When she did speak it was to the point.

"I wanted my grandson to marry a Mexican." The words were firmly and calmly spoken.

"I know. Ward told me."

"He has roots in Mexico. Obligations here."

"I'm sure he does."

"American women do not strive for family unity. They are interested only in being liberated from what they consider dominance by their husbands or male counterparts." She spoke sharply, accusingly, and with scarcely an accent.

Meredith sat quietly realizing the *señora* expected her to debate her statement.

"I'm sure you have certain reasons for your opinions, *señora*. Some American women are so dedicated to getting equal rights for women that they seem to have forgotten that the core of every great nation is family solidarity. Each family unit must have a head, which doesn't necessarily mean a woman is any less equal than her husband. They only have separate functions within the family."

"Submissiveness is not an American trait."

"That is true. However, submissiveness means different things to different people. To me it means yielding to authority, and for this world to survive we must have authority. To others it may mean admitting to being inferior, being humble, meek, submitting oneself to dominance without any effort to control one's own destiny. The latter meaning does not apply to me, *señora*."

The *señora*'s face gave no inkling of what she was thinking. The dark eyes continued to look at her. She was a true aristocrat, Meredith decided.

"Do you love my grandson or did you marry him because he is rich?"

The question caught Meredith unaware and she sat for a moment before she spoke.

"*Señora,* I didn't know when I married Ward what it was like to be rich. I have never had money so how was I to make a comparison? I will tell you frankly that I married him because I yearned for someone of my own, a family. You see, I have no living relatives that I know of, and Ward's proposal was very tempting. Since the wedding I have come to love him very much. He is the man I dreamed about when I was a child—kind, loving, dependable, protective. The fact that he is rich just happens to be an added factor and can very well be more of a hindrance to my happiness than a benefit."

"I want him to be happy. He tells me he loves you. I'll have to accept you."

"Thank you, *señora*. I'll try not to be a disappointment to you. I want Ward to be happy, too. I hope that can be a basis for a friendship between us."

"We will have coffee." The old woman took a small, silver bell from her pocket. The musical sound was soft but must have reached the ears of the young girl who pushed a noiseless teacart into the room.

"This is Leticia, Saldana's great-granddaughter."

"*Hola.*" The girl kept her face turned away and Meredith barely heard her whispered reply.

"*Muchas gracias,* Leticia." As soon as the *señora* spoke the girl left the room, her face still averted. "There are times when perhaps there is too much submission."

Meredith looked up and thought she caught a twinkle in the old woman's eye.

When Ward returned, they were drinking coffee as Meredith discussed her work in the clinic. He came to her and reached for her hand. She looked up at him with all the love in her heart in her eyes, forgetting, momentarily, that his grandmother was watching. She got to her feet and he pulled her close to him. Snapping black eyes, undimmed by eighty-two years, watched intently as Ward's hand moved up and down her bare arm.

"I will send Leticia for you when the meal is ready," she said to Meredith, dismissing her briskly. "Stay, *nieto*, we have much to talk about."

Ward squeezed Meredith's hand then she went to the door.

"I am an old woman and have not long to wait for a grandson." The words reached Meredith as she left the room and her lips lifted into a grin.

She had quite liked the aristocratic old lady with the bright black eyes who had shown by her every word and look how much she idolized her grandson and wished for his happiness. The interview had gone much better than she had hoped, and there was a lightness to her step when she went up the stairs to the room she would share with Ward.

At the top of the stairs she came to an abrupt halt. A woman stood there glaring at her with the same snapping black eyes as Ward's grandmother. She was several inches shorter than Meredith and more rounded. Her black hair was parted in the center and drawn severely back into a coil at the nape of her neck. Large, loop earrings swung against her white skin as she tossed her head in an angry gesture. The red slash that was her mouth was set and her eyes spit venom. Meredith almost took a step backward, the woman's hatred was so obvious.

This must be Francisca, she realized, the woman who had nourished the hope of becoming Ward's bride. Meredith almost felt sorry for her. But pity left as soon as the woman spoke.

"You'll never be accepted. A nobody from nowhere!

He only married you because he was angry with *Tia* Margarieta for insisting he make our . . . relationship legal in the eyes of the church. Nothing will be changed between us." The words were said with such contempt that a chill crept over Meredith's skin.

"Really?" Anger warmed her.

"I have known Ward since childhood. I was groomed to take my place beside him as his wife." She waved her hands, her eyes fiery.

"Groomed since childhood?" Meredith looked her up and down insolently. "You mean even then no one thought you'd be able to find a husband on your own?"

She stepped around her and went into her room, closed the door, and leaned against it. She was breathless with anger but rather proud that her parting shot had rendered Francisca speechless. It had been a long time since she had traded catty remarks with another woman and the short exchange had left her with pounding temples.

She took deep breaths to calm herself and began to dress for dinner. Ward had told her that his grandmother liked the evening meal to be formal and had suggested she bring her blue chiffon gown.

By the time he came to the room she was calm. Less confident than she had been when she left his grandmother, but calm. She had taken pains with her appearance and knew she looked her best. Ward must have thought so, too. He looked her up and down and smiled.

"Grandmother is not quite so sure I made as disastrous a mistake as she first thought. You must have held your own with her." He took off his shirt and reached for a clean one.

"She's naturally concerned for your happiness. I can't fault her for that."

"You must have convinced her you have my best interests at heart." He grinned at her while his fingers worked at the buttons on his shirt.

"I tried."

She caught the sparkle in his eyes. Happiness engulfed her like a tidal wave and washed Francisca's words from her mind. She was actually beginning to think of herself as his wife, his love. Careful, she cautioned. This was all so new and heady she must not forget that he once ridiculed the "old-fashioned" relationship between one man and one woman.

"Don't let Francisca get under your skin." He was coming toward her with the box containing the diamond earrings and necklace she had worn at the wedding. "She has a boutique in Guadalajara and one in Tulsa and isn't really so bad when you get to know her. She's a damn good businesswoman, and you might as well get used to her."

Meredith went slightly numb on hearing this news, but managed a faint smile. Ward put the necklace around her throat and she lifted her hair so he could fasten the clasp. She took the earrings from his hand and clipped them to her ears.

"Grandmother wore these at her wedding. I want her to see you wearing them."

"Ward, no!" Meredith stood on legs that trembled. "She might resent—"

"No, she won't. She knows we're married. The diamonds were to go to my bride." His mouth curved at one corner. "As far as grandmother is concerned we are married forever. She doesn't believe in divorce."

"I feel as though we're deceiving her." The words came slowly.

"Why?" He raised his brows and somehow his features reminded her of the aristocratic features of his grandmother.

"You know . . . when we talked, we agreed that we might not . . . stay together always." She hated herself for stammering.

His voice was uncompromising, unfriendly. "As a matter of fact, I don't believe in divorce."

Meredith had gone white. "But, you said that . . ."

"Are you sorry already, Merry?"

"About what?" She was dumbfounded. Why were they quarreling?

"About marrying me?" He was looking at her as he had the night she arrived at the *hacienda*. He seemed to believe that she was deceiving him in some way.

"No!"

Now was not the time to tell him that she was frightened of the responsibility of being his wife, frightened that she was making herself open to heartache because he didn't believe in permanent love between a man and a woman. And terrified that he was having an affair with Francisca. She couldn't tell him any of those things.

I still don't know him, she whispered soundlessly to herself when he turned away from her to go into the adjoining bathroom. How could one love a man yet not know him? And yet it seemed she had known his tall form, the sound of his voice, and the way he moved, forever.

She was standing beside the window looking down into the courtyard when he came back into the room. She heard him rummaging about in his suitcase, then felt his presence beside her.

"It'll take me forever—can you put these in for me?" He held out gold cuff links. All traces of irritation were gone from his face. He looked darkly handsome in slim-fitting dark pants and a contrasting white jacket, and suddenly she wished to go into his arms, to be held hard against his heart and feel the warm smooth skin of his lean jawline under her fingertips. But she could not make the first move, the fear of rejection was too great. Instead she smiled up at him and with fumbling fingers attached the cuff links.

When she was finished, he framed her face with his hands and the lionlike eyes that looked down into hers held an emotion she was almost sure was tenderness.

"I'd kiss you, but I'd smear your lipstick." How quickly he could change his mood.

"It might be worth it." She forced herself to answer lightly.

He leaned toward her and kissed her very lightly on the nose.

"It's getting to be a habit," he said with her face still in his hands.

"What is?"

"Wanting to kiss you." He said it lightly, jokingly, and it was hard to keep from communicating all the love she wanted to give him. She covered her confusion with a light laugh and twisted away from him.

They entered the dining room with her hand tucked firmly in the crook of his arm. They paused and he bent to whisper in her ear. "Eat a lot. Grandma thinks you're too skinny to have babies."

"You're kidding!" Her eyes shone like bright stars until she saw the malice in Francisca's.

The woman was standing beside the *señora's* chair in a long, flowing dress of red velvet. Its close-fitting bodice had a wide, deep V-neckline that molded her breasts and revealed the pearly whiteness of her neck and shoulders. Her hair was drawn back sleekly and secured to the back of her head. A high, handsome comb, studded with spangles, rose majestically above her head. It was a wholly Spanish look, complete with a long, black, lace handkerchief dangling from her wrist.

All Meredith could think of was how badly she had wanted a red velvet dress when she was a child. She remembered it vividly. She wanted red velvet, longed for red velvet, had asked the Santa Claus at the welfare children's Christmas party for such a dress. She could feel her disappointment, even now, when on Christmas morning she had opened her package to find a pair of green corduroy slacks and a print shirt.

Ward's arm slid around her, possessively, and he urged her toward the two women. "Darling, I want you to meet Francisca Calderon, a relation of mine."

Meredith forced her stiff lips to smile and nodded to the woman.

"Francisca, my wife, Meredith."

The red lips barely moved. *"Señora."* There was no mistaking the hostility in her eyes.

Ward bent to kiss his grandmother's cheek and on impulse Meredith did the same. The old lady looked long and hard at her before she smiled. "The necklace becomes you. Did Ward tell you I wore it on my wedding day?"

"Yes, he did, *señora*. And I was proud to wear it on mine."

Ward helped his grandmother to her feet and handed her a silver-handled cane. Meredith was surprised when she stood to see how small she was. She had never considered herself tall, but she towered over these two women as much as Ward towered over her.

The rectangular table had been laid for four in intimate proximity at one end of the polished wood. The setting breathed of quiet elegance, from the candles to the vivid poinsettia blooms floating in a delicate glass bowl. The *señora* moved to the left of the table with Francisca beside her. Ward seated his grandmother and politely held out the chair for Francisca before coming around to seat Meredith. He sat at the head of the table as if he were the master of this large estate.

It was not as difficult a meal to get through as Meredith had anticipated. Ward made sure she was included in the conversation and as time went on and Francisca remained silent it became easier.

The meal was superbly cooked and served and ended with a delicious creme caramel dessert. Openly admitting to having a sweet tooth, Meredith devoured every spoonful, much to Saldana's delight.

The *señora* left them as soon as the meal was finished. Ward walked her to her room with Saldana trotting along behind. Meredith, not wanting to remain alone with Francisca, walked out into the large entrance hall. She hesitated for only a moment before she went up the stairs.

She glanced at her watch after she closed the door to the bedroom. Perhaps she shouldn't have disappeared after Ward and his grandmother left them. Francisca might think she was avoiding her. Well, in fact, she was, but not because she felt intimidated. She was confident she could hold her own with the fiery Mexican woman. It was just that conflict was upsetting to her and she wanted to keep that happy, peaceful glow that had been with her since her wedding night. In a few minutes she would return to the sitting room.

Her honeymoon was almost over. Tomorrow they would go back to the *hacienda* and perhaps by the end of the week to Tulsa. She had almost succeeded in banishing the doubt that she was incapable of filling the position demanded of Ward's wife. The last four days had been the most wonderful days of her life and anything that could happen to her in the future would pale in comparison.

She stood beside the window and looked down on the courtyard. It was dark, but lights from the room below cast a soft glow on the statue of the Madonna standing peacefully in the garden. Meredith was about to turn away when she heard Ward's voice. She looked for him, then realized he was on the veranda beneath the window.

"That's nonsense, Francisca." His voice was biting in the way it could be when he was out of patience.

"But why did you do it, Ward? Why did you marry that . . . ?"

"I don't have to justify my actions to you. I never gave you any reason to believe I'd marry you."

"But I have to know." The voice was soft and persistent. There was a pause during which Ward didn't say anything. "She's in love with you. You only have to look at her to know that!" The words were bitter. "Are you in love with her, *querido?*"

Meredith's face grew warm and she tilted her head toward the window, anxious to hear Ward's answer.

There was the briefest of hesitations, then, "That need not concern you. Our relationship has not changed, Francisca. Meredith will not interfere."

Meredith clutched her throat. She wanted to tear herself away from the window, away from the words that could spell ruin to her newly found happiness. But fear and hunger for the truth, no matter how destructive, kept her prisoner beside the window.

"I don't want *her* to know." Francisca had a sob in her voice.

"She won't know unless you or Luis tell her. I don't know what you're worrying about. I'll take care of you. You know that."

"I know that, *querido*. But I thought it would be as your wife. *Tia* Margarieta wanted—"

"Enough, Francisca! I'm not a boy to be commanded to wed." A soft shuddering sob by the woman below reflected Meredith's own feelings. "Go to bed, *prima mía*. Tomorrow you will go back to Guadalajara with us. I have a meeting at the plant and then you and I will go to the boutique. How's that?"

"I don't have much choice, do I?"

"No, you don't. It's up to you to adjust to this new situation."

"I hate her!" This was hissed with fiery venom.

Ward laughed. "Well, I don't."

"Tell me you don't love her?"

Softly and patiently Ward said, "Francisca, I don't think that need concern us . . ."

The words trailed away. They were moving into the house.

The word "us" echoed in Meredith's brain, causing her limbs to come trembling back to life. White-faced and sick at heart, she turned and went to the bathroom. There, the door locked behind her, safe from Ward's eyes if he should come to their room, she took great sobbing breaths while she fought for control. No longer a barely tolerated visitor in someone's house, for the first time in her life she had begun to feel that she was wanted, that she belonged. Was it all going to be taken from her so soon? she thought miserably. Or were her own fears of rejection making her jump to conclusions? Choking back the sobs, Meredith vowed that she would keep her suspicions to herself. A confrontation would only let Ward know how much she loved him, how utterly she was in his power. She couldn't do it—she had been hurt too many times before. The tears spilled out from her anguished eyes and her mouth worked convulsively. So much for no secrets between them, she thought bitterly. Very slowly control won and she opened tightly clenched hands and pressed them to the cold marble washbasin.

This was all her own damn fault! She had wanted so desperately to believe that he would come to love her as she loved him. Now she feared that he never intended to be a faithful husband. She stared at her white face in the mirror. You are a gullible, dumb . . . broad, Meredith Moore! Tell him to bug off, you don't need him. Her eyes filled again. What if she was wrong? Either way, she couldn't let him go.

She went back into the bedroom, took off the chiffon dress and flung it over a chair, removed the earrings and necklace, grabbed up a nightgown, and was back in the bathroom in a matter of seconds. With trembling hands she washed her face. Taking the wet cloth with her, she returned to the bedroom and climbed into the massive bed.

A minute later Ward came into the room. She was curled up on the far side of the bed, the wet cloth over her eyes.

"What's the matter, Merry?" He sat down beside her. "Do you have a headache?"

She nodded and gave a soft groan and wished with all her heart that was all that was the matter with her.

"Did it just come on?"

Again she nodded and pressed her hands to her temples. She wanted to scream *liar!* Instead she gritted her teeth and whispered almost inaudibly, "Let me sleep. I'll be all right in the morning."

"Sure. Go to sleep." His hand lingered on her upper bare arm. The bed swayed slightly when his weight was removed from it.

Meredith huddled, miserable, on the bed. She could hear him moving about and opened her eyes a crack. He was hanging her dress in the zippered bag they had used to bring it and her other things from the plane. He put the earrings and necklace back into their box and tucked it into her suitcase. When he began to remove his clothes she closed her eyes.

Ward got into the bed, moved close up against her back and put his arms around her. She felt his kiss on her shoulder before he settled back and was almost instantly asleep, his breathing coming gently against her neck. No longer needing the cloth to hide her swollen eyes, she removed it and let the tears slide down her cheeks. . . .

It was the muffled sound of Ward moving about the room, trying not to wake her while he dressed, that awakened her. For a few seconds she lay motionless, then memory returned, and with it, pain. She pretended sleep until he left the room, then threw back the covers and sat up. This morning she was firmly in control of her emotions, determined to play out the charade.

She managed to put on a good face when she said goodbye to the *señora*. The very nature of the occasion demanded it. If her voice stuck in her throat, it was due to the very real headache that last night's emotional upheaval had left with her.

Francisca was in better, if not exuberant, spirits as she stood in the foyer beside her cases. Ward had not mentioned the fact that she was going back to Guadalajara with them and Meredith had ignored her.

Meredith dreaded being with them in the close quarters of the plane, but it was easier than she expected. Ward spent most of the time in the cockpit talking with the pilot, leaving the two women to sit alone. Meredith felt no obligation to make small talk, and the silence pressed down upon her like a tangible thing. The monotonous drone of the engines soon lulled her into a feverish daydream where her fears were given free rein. What was she supposed to say to Francisca, her husband's mistress? That she could have him on weekends but he was hers on weekdays and holidays? Half asleep now, Meredith thought miserably that somehow she must find a way to end this charade, this mockery of a marriage, before she was irretrievably hurt.

CHAPTER ELEVEN

WHEN THEY ARRIVED at the *hacienda* in Chapala, they were greeted with the news that Norma Sanderson, Ward's stepmother, had returned. Ward reacted with a grimace, Francisca with a smile, and Meredith with the desire to retreat to her room as soon as possible. Ward foiled her escape by attaching his fingers firmly to her wrist.

"No use putting off the inevitable. All the best generals agree it's better to attack than to be attacked." She sensed his amusement and she grew more annoyed. He started off down the hall taking her with him.

Ward opened the door to the sitting room and walked in as if he knew his stepmother would be there, and she was. She sat in regal splendor behind a magnificent silver service as if she were posed for a photograph. She looked even more haughty and aristocratic than Meredith had expected, although younger and more beautiful. She was slender, and blond, and Meredith instinctively knew she was tall even though she remained seated and looked at her with cold, blue eyes. She had exceedingly lovely, almost wrinkle-free skin and held her head in the slightly tilted position that women use when they want the skin of their neck to appear firm. It was obvious she was aware of the marriage, disapproved, and had chosen to show her displeasure by refusing to greet them when they arrived, forcing them to come to her.

Her coldness and hostility didn't seem to bother Ward. "Hello, Norma. Back so soon? Wasn't there any royalty aboard the cruise ship? I thought you'd have caught an earl or a count by now and be ensconced in a castle playing queen over the peons."

"Don't be vulgar," she snapped.

He laughed. "Well, if you didn't find a mate, I did. This is my wife, Meredith." He placed an arm across Meredith's shoulders, and his hand caressed the side of her face possessively, his eyes full of sparkling enjoyment.

Meredith smiled pleasantly, but her thoughts were racing. She was only an instrument of his spite! Not only was he rebelling against his grandmother's wishes when he'd married her, but he'd done it to spite his stepmother, as well.

"Darling." He was smiling down into her eyes. "This is my sweet-tempered stepmother, Norma."

The woman didn't even glance at Meredith. Her eyes were focused on Ward with pure hatred.

"This," she tilted her head in Meredith's direction, "I would have suspected of you, Ward. But I did not expect you to take advantage of my absence to persuade Cullen to leave. If anything happens to him, it will be on your conscience and I'll never forgive you as long as I live."

Meredith gave a start at the news, but Ward coolly controlled his surprise.

"That's the best news I've heard in a long time. Where's he going?"

"Not going. Gone. It seems he received a telephone call from the girl, the one that hung around here for so long after the accident. She's the sister of that brassy woman Jim married. He packed that ridiculous van, took Antonio, and left without a word to anyone. It isn't like Cullen to be so thoughtless. You must have instigated his leaving. Heaven knows where he is. He hasn't called and I'm worried sick."

"Oh, I'm so glad!" The words burst from Meredith. "Not that you're worried, Mrs. Sanderson, but that Cullen and Becky will have a chance to be together and work out their problems. I know he loves her."

The eyes the woman turned on Meredith were filled with cold contempt. "You know nothing of the sort. Kindly keep out of this. This is family business."

"Hold it, Norma!" Ward's words were sharp. "Merry is my wife and I expect her to be treated like family."

"Family? You're a fine one to be talking about family."

"Yes, family. And I'm thinking you had better be remembering who is the head of this one. Speaking of family, where is Maggie?"

Meredith moved away from Ward's encircling arm. She began to grow hot and angry, tension like acid in her stomach. She had to get out of this room. The dissension here was straining her nerves to the breaking point.

"Sophia took Maggie to Carmen's," Norma said. "I couldn't bear the sight of her moping about the house."

Ward urged Meredith toward a chair and pressed her

down into it. "Pour the coffee, Norma. I could use some and so could Merry." While he was speaking the telephone rang, then stopped when it was answered in another part of the house.

He brought coffee to Meredith and was about to sit down with his own when one of the servants beckoned to him. He went to the doorway and they talked in low tones. He returned and set his cup on the table.

"Excuse me. I have a call."

"If it's Cullen, tell him I want to talk to him."

"It isn't Cullen."

Silence fell when Ward left the room. Norma turned contemptuous eyes on Meredith and left them there. The stare was meant to put her firmly in the category headed "inferior." The knowledge made Meredith coldly angry and she returned the stare with equal arrogance.

"You didn't lose much time, did you?"

Meredith refused to answer or change her expression. She had learned, long ago, that to say nothing was sometimes more effective than saying a lot.

"You had to have a better game plan than just getting him to bed. Ward's been to bed with scores of women."

Meredith saw with satisfaction that her psychology was working. Norma's cheeks were now tinged with color. She decided to wait a moment longer before speaking.

"One can't help but wonder how you managed."

"Wonder all you like." Meredith gave her a sly smile.

"The Sandersons are among the best-known and most respected families in the southwest. We are also wealthy, as I'm sure you knew when you came here. With wealth goes the responsibility to retain . . . certain values." Her eyes were bitingly sharp and Meredith had to admire her control. She was furiously angry. "I simply don't understand Ward besmirching himself and . . . all of us, in this manner."

"Shouldn't you be discussing this with him?" Meredith asked coolly.

Norma ignored the question and asked one of her own. "Who are you?" She spoke with a ponderous solemnity and Meredith was forced to swallow an almost hysterical giggle.

"I'm Meredith Moore. Meredith Sanderson, now," she corrected. "I'm twenty-five years old, I'm an x-ray technician, my parents are dead, and I've got all my own teeth." She showed them, her smile barbed. Norma gazed at her, her face set in hard, angry lines.

Ward came in and picked up his coffee. He remained standing. Meredith got to her feet, smiling pleasantly, proud she was able to do so when she really wanted to walk over and punch this priggish woman in the mouth. She would have to think of a special torture for Ward for what he had done to her, for using her to get at Norma.

"It was lovely meeting you, Mrs. Sanderson," she said with exaggerated sweetness. "If you'll excuse me, I'll go up and unpack." She stood for a moment looking from one to the other. Neither spoke or looked at her and she allowed her face to show all the scorn she was feeling for them. Ward looked up and she met his eyes. They stared at each other for a long moment, blue eyes contemptuous, tawny ones filled with anger.

Meredith walked away from them and out into the hallway where she paused to compose herself before making the long trek up the stairway. Norma's voice reached her easily.

"How could you do such a thing to us? Why did you marry a creature like that? She is ill-bred, has the manners of a barmaid, and is entirely out of our class. Your grandmother and I would have been happy to accept Francisca into the family. If not her, then some other girl from a good family. You did this to spite me, didn't you, Ward? You've never liked me from the day your father brought me home. You'd do anything to make me suffer. Even this!"

"Shut up, Normal" The shout echoed into the empty hall. "And as long as you've brought it up . . . no, I've never liked you from the moment my father brought you home. You cared nothing for him. You cared for his money and his position. You have never cared for anything in your life except yourself and Cullen, and your grasping hands have almost squeezed the life out of him. My responsibility to you, my dear stepmother, is to see that you are cared for in the style you've grown accustomed to and that is all. Kindly keep your nose out of my affairs!"

"You'll not drag Cullen down with you. I won't have it!"

Meredith fled up the stairs and into her room. The quarrel going on downstairs brought back memories of how she used to cringe under the bedcovers when her foster parents quarreled. How she hated conflict! She was glad she had the unpacking to occupy her mind, but it didn't last nearly long enough.

When her suitcases were stored in the back of the wardrobe, she picked up the ornate wooden box holding the earrings and necklace. She couldn't resist opening the box and looking at them. They were so beautiful, but not for her. She snapped the box shut and placed it on the stand beside the bed.

With nothing to do she paced the room, stood beside the window, and looked down on the courtyard. Her nerves were strung as tight as a bow-string. She would take a bath. Almost always she could relax in a warm bath.

Even then, her thoughts refused to lie still. She seemed to be pressed to make a decision and she finally came to forming a plan. She would not mention to Ward until they reached Tulsa that she now felt their marriage was a mistake and that she wished to terminate it. Somehow she couldn't bear to think of all the pleasure her decision would bring to Norma and Francisca. She didn't want to embarrass Ward, either. She had to admit he had placed his cards firmly on the table when he asked her to marry him. He had made it clear he didn't believe in that old-fashioned relationship between one man and one woman. But he had promised to be a faithful husband! It wasn't his fault she had fallen in love with him, she reasoned. She had been lulled into a mythical world during that wonderful honeymoon. The nights they had lain in each other's arms had been heavenly. Ward had thought so too. He had said so repeatedly.

Meredith knew, despite her surface bravado, that when she was under stress all her old insecurities came rising to the surface. Could they be blinding her now? If only she hadn't overheard that conversation with Francisca. Even now, the remembered words cut into her heart like a knife.

She was dressed and sitting beside the window when Ward came into the room. It had been several hours since she left him. Had he been with his stepmother or Francisca all this time? Meredith longed to throw herself into his arms, to confess her fears and suspicions, but he was looking at her like a stranger, his face turned to ice. He stood with his back to the door and spoke expressionlessly.

"There's someone downstairs to see you."

"To see me?" She thought he must be joking, but he wasn't smiling. "Cullen is back!" She got to her feet.

"Not Cullen. It's Crowley. Dr. Paul Crowley."

The nail file fluttered from her nervous fingers and for a moment she was speechless.

"Paul? Here? I can't believe it!"

"Well, it's true. And if you don't want him brainwashed, you'd better go on down. Norma took him in hand as soon as I left him." He was so quiet she didn't know if he was angry or indifferent. Coherent thoughts fled her mind. She was shocked into numbness.

"What does he want?" she asked through stiff lips.

"How in the hell do I know?" He shoved himself away from the door. "He called from the airport and Ramon called me to the phone. He said he had business with you."

"Was that the call you took while . . ."

"Yes."

"Why didn't you tell me he was coming instead of waiting until he arrived?" She was resentful and didn't care if he knew it. She glared at him and his face changed to weariness.

"I wanted time to think. Go on down and see what he wants." She went to the door, but his next words stopped her. "He came about a week late, didn't he?"

She turned to look at him, opened her mouth to say something, thought better of it, and went out the door. Her mind was spinning wildly. What in the world was Paul doing here? And how did he know where to find her? Then she remembered. Maude, of course. Paul had met Maude on one occasion and she was completely charmed by him as most women were. It was too bad, she thought angrily, that she hadn't filled Maude in on just what a conniver he was.

Norma's tinkling laughter and Paul's deeper tones guided her to the library. She stood in the doorway and watched them. Paul's head was bent attentively to Norma. He certainly was a beautiful man. His blond hair, thick and shining, was styled to cover the tops of his ears. A deep tan from the health club's sunlamps enhanced his features, which had the classic lines of a Greek god. When he smiled, deep dents appeared in his cheeks and his lips spread to reveal teeth worthy of a toothpaste commercial. He was tall, slender, and always dressed right for the occasion. She saw him now with new eyes. He was a beautiful doll. Nothing more. How could she have devoted four years of her life to this shallow, conceited man?

He saw her. "Meredith. How nice it is to see you again."

"Hello, Paul."

"I'll leave you to conduct your . . . business, doctor. My invitation for dinner and to spend the night stands if you should change your mind."

Paul took Norma's hand and raised it to his lips. "Thank you, gracious lady. As much as I would like to enjoy your hospitality, I have friends waiting for me in

Guadalajara and an important operation to perform tomorrow."

Meredith raised her eyes to the ceiling. Shades of Doctor Kildare! This was Paul at his best and, from the look on Norma's face, she was swallowing it hook, line, and sinker. He walked the beaming woman to the door and when she passed through it he closed it behind her and turned to face Meredith. The smile was gone, now, and in its place was, of all things, concern.

"Why did you run away, my darling? You knew the thing with Connie wouldn't last." He came to her and took her hand before she could step away from him. "You're not still angry with me? I've missed you! I didn't realize how much you meant to me until you left me."

Meredith jerked her hand from his and moved a few feet away from him.

"I'm not angry, Paul. I'm through with you. Finished."

"Darling, you can't be. We can't be finished after all we've been to each other." There was soft pleading in his voice and Meredith had the hysterical desire to laugh.

"Stop it! I know all your acts. I'm married now, but I'm sure you knew that when you came here."

"I did know that and I also know that you love me, as I love you."

"Love me? You don't love anyone but yourself, Paul." This time a chuckle escaped her.

He was quiet for a long moment. Then suddenly his hand darted out and seized her wrist, tightening until she gasped with pain and indignation.

"Don't laugh at me," he snapped.

"Let go." She tugged at her wrist.

"Stand still." Paul's face was petulant and vicious.

She raised angry eyes to his. All the loathing and contempt she felt for him was mirrored in her face. "Get out! Get out before I call my husband and have you thrown out!"

He threw her hand from him and turned his back to her. When he faced her again, his look was unruffled and arrogant.

"How did you ever get that cold fish to marry you?" No pretense, now. The charm had gone with her rejection of him.

"What do you want, Paul? Say it and go."

"I'll have to admit you're smarter than I gave you credit for." He spoke as if she hadn't said anything. "He married you and you should be able to get a hefty divorce settlement. Face it, darling. There will be a divorce. You don't have the polish to hack this sort of life. His mother as much as told me the family was devastated because of the marriage."

"His stepmother," she corrected firmly. "How did you find me?" She knew, but wanted him to say it.

"Maude Fiske. Who else? She also came through with the news you had married Tulsa's favorite son. Well, maybe not the favorite, but certainly one of the richest."

"Is that why you're here? You thought to go through me to get to Ward's money?" There was a sneering edge in her voice. "Did Connie let you down, or was it her father?"

"Forget Connie. And of course I came to get money. You owe me, you know. After all, I did contribute to our *joint* income. I want what you have in the savings account." His mouth twisted cruelly.

She was shocked almost speechless. This was the last

thing she would have expected of him. "You didn't save one cent of what I have in the savings account and you know it. That little amount of money would be a drop in the bucket to you."

"Every little bit helps, darling."

"You're not . . . serious!"

"Oh, but I am. I want it. I'm going to open a practice in Minneapolis."

"So? What does that have to do with me?"

"Stop hedging. I want the money. I need it."

She knew he was lying. The amount of money she had wouldn't buy reception-room furniture for any office he would open. He had to make her suffer in order to restore his hurt vanity and injured pride.

"And if I don't give it to you?" She met his eyes levelly.

"Then I shall accept Mrs. Sanderson's invitation to spend the week. And as a doctor and someone from your . . . past, I will feel it is my obligation to warn the family that you are a nymphomaniac and were discharged from the clinic for molesting the male patients." He looked into her shocked eyes and smiled. A part of his crushed ego was restored. "You know I can be very persuasive when I set my mind to it."

"Ward wouldn't believe you!"

"It doesn't matter if he were to believe me or not. His mother would. She would spread it among his friends. The people in Tulsa would believe it. You'd be black-balled! Ward Sanderson and his bride would be on every scandal sheet in the country. He'll wish he'd never set eyes on you."

"I never, in my wildest dreams, thought you were this vile, this corrupt."

"Now you know. But don't start with the 'after all I've done for you' routine. You were paid tenfold for what you did for me. I'm not stupid. You had a certain amount of prestige because I paid attention to you. Now are you going to get me the money or shall I join my hostess?"

Meredith was shaken, heartsick; not because of his words but because she had been such a gullible, blind fool. Suddenly tiredness welled up in her, enveloping her like a shroud. She felt as if her head were bursting. Hate and frustration joggled against despair.

"I'll get my purse and give you a check," she said wearily, hearing the defeat in her own voice.

She left him on trembling legs and during the long trek up the stairs prayed that Ward wouldn't be in the bedroom when she reached it. She couldn't face him, or anyone else, at this moment. He wasn't there and she grabbed up her purse and left the room in a matter of seconds.

Paul was standing pretty much as she had left him. She walked past him without looking at him and sat down at the desk. He came to look over her shoulder and took the checkbook from her hand and thumbed through it.

"The last time I looked at this you had considerably more on deposit. What did you do with it?"

"I spent it on airfare. Take it and get out. I hope I never have to see you again." From somewhere inside her hate and fury hardened her voice.

"You'll see me again. Never doubt that." He put the check in his pocket. His fingertips caressed the polished wood of the desk and his eyes lingered on the rich draperies and the priceless Persian carpet. "Tulsa is looking better to me all the time. I never did like the winters in Minneapolis."

"Get out of my life and stay out!" Meredith was screaming inside, but her voice was low, controlled.

Paul laughed. "Stay married to your sugar daddy for as long as you can, sweetie. I'll expect regular donations, to my . . . free-will clinic."

She clenched her fists and held them tightly to her sides to keep them from flying up and hitting him.

"You won't get another cent from me."

"Not you, darling. Your husband, Ward Sanderson. Play your cards right and he can make us both happy. Hang in there, now, and I'll see you soon."

He opened the door and stepped out into the hall. Meredith followed and her stricken eyes saw Ward coming toward them. Paul, charming once again, moved forward and held out his hand.

"It was nice meeting you, Sanderson. Thanks for lending me your wife. She's been very helpful . . . beyond my expectations, as a matter of fact. You've got yourself a real little jewel here. She's not only beautiful, but smart too."

Ward took the hand extended to him and nodded his head briefly, his eyes resting intently on Meredith's white face. "You're leaving." He said it bluntly.

"I must. A doctor's time isn't his own." He looked fondly at Meredith. "Goodbye, Meredith. I sincerely wish you all the happiness you deserve."

"Goodbye." She thought her face would crack when her lips moved. She didn't dare look at Ward. She kept her eyes focused on Paul, all the while despising herself for ever having thought he was a decent human being.

Paul went down the hall and Ward followed to see him out. Meredith stood clutching the door frame until they were out of sight, then with a moan of pain she ran up the stairs, wishing with all her heart she could turn back the clock and relive the last forty-eight hours. In a trancelike state she closed the door and rested against the paneling, too stricken to be aware of her surroundings. She took deep breaths and awareness came rushing back. Ward would want some answers. She had to think. She went to the bathroom and bathed her face with a wet cloth, retouched her make-up and returned to the bedroom to see Ward coming in the door, her purse in his hand.

"You left this on the desk."

"Thank you." She took the purse from him, placed it on the bureau, and picked up her hairbrush.

"Meredith!"

The voice was loud, harsh, and cut across the room like a whip. She jumped as if he had struck her. When she turned, she caught him looking at her in a way that shriveled her soul. It was a cold, angry, violent look, like the time he had accused her of flirting in Acapulco, only a hundred times worse. She stared at him silently.

"Were you so upset to see him go that you couldn't see him to the door?" His eyes trapped hers. Her heart beat so fast it seemed to fill her ears.

"I was glad to see him go. I never want to see him again."

"Don't lie. Your expression was transparent." He stood there, his feet spread apart, his arms across his chest, for what felt like an eon. She stared back with wide, sorrowful eyes. "I didn't like him," Ward said slowly. "He's a phoney if I ever saw one." There was something strange in his voice. Accusation? He came close to her and her eyes were level with his chin. He needs to shave again, she thought crazily.

"What do you want me to say? I didn't ask him to come here." Her heart was pounding. She tried to think empty thoughts. She didn't want him to read anything in them. She didn't want him to know how . . . frightened she was.

"What did he want, Merry?" There was gentleness in his tone, now, and she wanted to cry.

"He wanted information." She didn't look at him. She knew that he knew she was lying.

"And you carry that information around in your purse. I'm no fool! If you don't want to tell me, say so, but don't lie!" His words were measured.

Suddenly she was tired of it all. Exhausted. Tired of being pushed by Paul, by Norma, by Francisca, by . . . him! She felt as if someone had stuck a knife in her and was slowly twisting it.

"I don't want to tell you!" The words burst from her angrily.

An interminable silence filled the room. She knew that the fragile hope she had secretly nourished that perhaps he might give up Francisca and come to love her had just vanished.

"That's better. At least we're being honest." That couldn't be hurt in his voice. She glanced up to see a nerve pulsing beside his eye.

Wearily she turned from him. She wanted to go home. Home? Where was that? Her eyes filled with tears and overflowed down on her cheeks.

"Do you mind if I lie down for a while?"

"Go ahead. I won't stop you."

The door closed behind him and she was alone. It was a relief and a sickening misery in one. She could cry now. There was no one to see her. She lay down on the bed. The tears came in an overwhelming flood. They poured from her eyes, rolled down her cheeks, and seeped between her fingers that were pressed hard against her face. Presently she roused herself long enough to take off her and shoes and slip between the sheets. Her mind longed for rest and she sought the sweet oblivion of sleep.

She awakened during the night and lay staring into the darkness. She was alone. How strange, she mused, that after sleeping beside Ward for such a short time she could feel so alone without him beside her, without waking to find her head pillowed on his shoulder, his hand cupping her breast.

It had not taken him long to return to his old love, she thought bitterly, and tears once again began to slide down her cheeks. Throughout the night she tossed restlessly, wondering what would have happened to her if she had not left Minnesota. Would she have kept reliving the pain of Paul's rejection? No! She liked to think she had more sense than that.

She must have slept because when she woke there was something warm and soft beside her. Her eyes flew open and she stared into Maggie's pixie face.

"Hi."

"Did I wake you up?"

"Yes, but it's all right."

"Can I stay for a while?"

"Sure, if you want to."

Maggie moved nearer, slid an arm around her neck,

and snuggled into the curve of her body. Meredith hugged her tightly, seeking to comfort and be comforted.

They were lying like that when Sophia came looking for Maggie. "There you are, little mule. You no bother the *señora. Señor* Ward say let her sleep."

"She's no bother, Sophia. Do you think she and I could have our breakfast here in the room?"

"Ah . . . *sí.*" A smile appeared. "Get dressed, little mule. I bring breakfast."

"Sophia," Meredith called as she opened the door. "*Señor* Ward? Is he . . ."

"Guadalajara, *señora.* He take the *señorita* with him."

Thank God. Meredith wasn't sure if she had said the words aloud or not. She was relieved she wouldn't have to face Ward or Francisca for hours. Maybe not until evening. It would give her some time to get herself together.

She devoted the day to Maggie. They played games, rearranged the furniture in the dollhouse, dressed all the dolls, and read stories. Meredith read dozens of stories, mimicking voices when possible to keep the child amused.

In the middle of the afternoon, when Maggie's head had fallen against her shoulder, Meredith eased the child down on to the thick carpet and placed a pillow beneath her head. She no longer had an excuse to stay in the room, but was reluctant to leave it so she placed all the toys in their proper places and stacked the books back in the bookshelves.

Sophia came silently into the room. "*Señora.*" Her face was unsmiling for once. "Come to the telephone. *Señor* Cullen wish to speak to you."

Meredith's smile was real. "Cullen?"

"*Señora,*" Sophia's voice was urgent. "He no want to speak to his *madre.*"

"He wants to speak to me and not his mother?"

"Ramon say you come. Come to *Señor* Ward's telephone."

Meredith followed her down the hall into a large square room. It was a man's room, furnished with large pieces of heavy, dark furniture. There were no extra accessories. Everything was functional and necessary. The telephone was on a table beside the bed and the receiver was off the hook. Meredith picked it up.

"Hello. Cullen?"

"Merry, Merry, my marshmallow Merry. How are you?" He was happy. There was a joyous tremor in his voice.

"I'm fine." She wasn't, but she hoped she convinced him she was. "Where are you?"

"I'm with Becky. We're going to be married and I'm going to write music and she's going to raise horses and kids!"

"Cullen! How wonderful!"

"I got to thinking about you and big brother, marshmallow. You've done miracles with old sober-sides. And Becky, well, she decided to call me after Ruth got back from the wedding. I've been a stupid ass, Merry. I sat there feeling sorry for myself, thinking my life was over, and hell, the best part is yet to come."

"Give my love to Becky and tell her I think she's the luckiest girl in the world."

"Didn't you mean second luckiest, marshmallow?" Cullen laughed and waited, but she could think of nothing to say. "Ramon said Ward was at the plant. Tell him where I am, will you?"

He hadn't mentioned his mother and she felt she should tell him she was here. "Cullen? Your mother is here. She's terribly worried about you."

There was a short silence before he spoke. "Yes, I know. She wired she was coming. That's when I decided to split. Couldn't face up to it. I was going to wait until you and Ward came back because I hated to leave Maggie, but if I'd stayed there would have been a battle royal. Just say I'm a coward." He laughed. "How is the little monster?"

"She misses you. She loves you very much."

"I miss her. Do you suppose she could spend some time with me and Becky?" There was an anxious tone to his voice.

"I'm sure she can. Of course I can't speak for Ward, but I'm . . . sure she can." She repeated herself because of the sudden lump in her throat and it was something safe to say.

"Is everything okay, Merry?"

"Everything's fine, Cullen. We had a wonderful time in Acapulco. We stayed at that fabulous hotel where Howard Hughes stayed and we saw the divers dive off the cliffs. There were people there from all over the world. Flowers were everywhere. The water was warm and we found a spot on the beach that wasn't overloaded with people. And, oh yes . . . I met Ward's grandmother. She was naturally concerned about our marriage, but she was very gracious and I liked her." Oh, why don't I shut up, she thought desperately. "Cullen . . ."

"Did you meet Francisca, Merry?"

She drew in a deep breath. "Yes. Yes, I did. She came back here with us. I think she . . . went with Ward today."

"Damn!"

"It's all right, Cullen." She forced a laugh.

"If she and my mother make it rough for you, Merry, tell Ward. He'll set them straight."

Meredith wanted to say, "A lot you know, my lad." Instead she said, "It's okay, Cullen. We'll be going to Tulsa soon."

"Hang tough, marshmallow. You've got me and Ward on your side. Say . . . take down this number and have him call me."

Meredith copied the number and repeated it to him to make sure it was correct. Then after wishing him and Becky happiness she hung up and wrote a message to Ward beneath the number.

The afternoon rolled into evening. Meredith wished for Ward's return and dreaded it. She bathed, shampooed her hair, and put on her cream silk dress. Somehow she didn't want to wear the new clothes Ward had bought for her. She knew she would have to get over the feeling if they stayed here at the *hacienda* much longer. The things she had brought with her were beginning to look worn.

As time for the evening meal approached, her anxiety grew. Would she be expected to take the meal with Mrs. Sanderson if Ward and Francisca didn't return? She stood beside the window and watched car lights approach the *hacienda*. A cold stillness enveloped her as she watched. The car stopped and Luis and Francisca got out. Where was Ward? Was he going to stay at his apartment in town? At least he wasn't with Francisca, she thought with a certain malicious satisfaction.

Her legs were trembly and her heart was beating too fast. She realized this weakness was partly due to the fact she hadn't eaten anything since her light breakfast. If Ward didn't return, there would be no reason for her to go to the dining room.

Sophia brought her a tray and she ate hungrily. She felt some disgust with herself for being so cowardly. Next time, she promised the braver part of herself, next time she'd put on her best face and defy them, but not tonight.

She sat beside the window until almost midnight before she put on her gown and robe. With slow, tired movements she cleaned her face and brushed her teeth and returned to her vigil.

Once again automobile lights came up the drive. This time Ward got out of the car and stood for a moment in the courtyard. Meredith didn't know for sure if he looked toward the window, but she drew back and groped her way to the bed and lay there trembling.

CHAPTER TWELVE

TENSION LAID A grip on Meredith, making her oblivious to all but the fear that Ward would come to her room and expect to make love to her. She couldn't let him! She couldn't . . . now that she knew about Francisca. It was too much to expect of her. Even if she still loved him, she couldn't do it! Though she could be worrying for nothing, she reasoned with herself. He hadn't come to her last night. There was the possibility that he had already become weary of her and had begun the gradual easing out of their relationship.

Imprisoned in her thoughts, she scarcely heard the door open. The lights were switched on, blinding her momentarily. She sat up, clutching the bedclothes to her. Ward closed the door and came to stand in the middle of the room. He was wearing dark slacks and a white shirt. His tie was loosened and several buttons on his shirt were open, yet there was nothing relaxed about his attitude or his expression. His face was completely colorless and the small pulse beside his eye was throbbing in a way she had seen before when he was upset.

She half rose to get out of bed, but his eyes passed over her coldly and then away. She sank back down. "Cullen called. He wants you to call him. I left the number on the pad beside your telephone."

Silence.

He took a step toward her. His shoulders were slumped tiredly and his limp more pronounced than she had ever noticed before. Watching him, she marveled that a man who looked so weary and pale could grow even more so before her eyes. Now she was terrified and wasn't sure why. She drew in a deep, quivering breath.

"What is it, Ward?" When he didn't answer, fear burgeoned inside her and she dug her nails into her palms and tried to think what dreadful news could make him look like this. The silence went on and she couldn't stand it. "What is it? What's happened?"

He was close to the bed now, staring down at her as if he despised her. Why in the world was he acting like this?

"I waited up for you tonight," she said because she had to say something.

It seemed as if he hadn't even heard her. "Something very unpleasant has happened. The diamond earrings are missing." The words came out of the frozen mask that was his face. "Would you have any idea where they might be?"

"The . . . earrings?" The words hung in the air. "I . . . don't know." She looked at the table where she had placed the box when she took it from her suitcase the day before. It wasn't there. "Didn't you put them away? I don't have them."

"I *know* you don't have them. Until this afternoon Paul Crowley had them." His words were slow, measured.

"There's got to be some logical explanation." And he waited for Meredith's reply.

"What are you talking about? That's impossible!" Meredith felt as if she were falling into a bottomless pit. Ward would naturally be extremely upset over the stolen diamonds, but she could not fathom why he was staring at her coldly, his eyes angry and guarded. He remained silent, waiting for her to speak.

Suddenly it dawned on her—he suspected her! The realization crushed her like a living force. It was a nightmare, of course. This couldn't be happening to her. Did Ward actually expect her to defend herself? She crossed her arms over her chest and stared defiantly back at him.

Wearily, Ward put his hand in his pocket, drew it out and held it palm up. The earrings lay in his palm. From his other pocket he brought out a folded sheet of paper.

"Dr. Crowley apparently got cold feet. He returned the diamonds."

She shook her head numbly, too shocked to speak.

"They were delivered to my office this afternoon by special courier along with this letter. Read it for yourself." He tossed it down, but didn't move away.

Sitting on the side of the bed, her bare feet on the floor she unfolded the paper with trembling fingers, and began to read. "Dear Mr. Sanderson: No doubt you will be surprised to find enclosed your wedding gift to your bride. Had I realized the value of the earrings, I would not have accepted them when Meredith insisted that I take them to help finance the opening of my clinic. I am sure she has by now, informed you about our former relationship and that I came to your home to collect funds from our joint bank account. This is true. When she left Rochester, she took everything and, as I'm sure you can understand, I wanted what was mine. Meredith gave me a check for a very small portion of what was in the account. I wish her no harm, but in all honesty I cannot accept the earrings. I am returning them to you for safe keeping. I sincerely hope that your relationship with Meredith will not be concluded as mine was, with possessiveness and jealousy threatening my career. Dr. Paul Crowley."

The paper fluttered from Meredith's numb fingers and for a moment she was speechless, unable to believe that Paul would have concocted such a story. Then it came to her that he was capable of it, but . . .

"How did he get the earrings?" she whispered hoarsely. She stared up into Ward's face, willing reality to return and change that ashen mask to the smiling one she had known on her honeymoon. His face wavered and blurred.

"I was hoping you would tell me."

Ward's words beat against her eardrums, his cruel interrogation threatening her sanity. My God, he was as good as accusing her of the theft! She was engulfed in such horror and rage that she scarcely knew what she was saying.

"So you believe your wife is a thief?" she shouted.

"I never said that—I'm just asking for an explanation."

At his words, horror receded and in its place came a fierce anger that gave her strength. "How dare you ask me to defend myself," she hissed. "I never would have suspected you as you do me. No amount of evidence could have made me think you anything less than an honorable man. But that's because . . . because I love you. You wouldn't understand anything about that, of course."

"Calm down—no one has accused you of anything, but you're not exactly acting like an innocent party now, are you?"

Meredith paused for breath, watching him walk to the window where he stopped, his back to her. She marveled that she could have dared to dream that this cold, precise man would come to love her, to really love any woman. The absurdity of such a thing made her bitter and angry all over again.

"Your investigation into my past wasn't as complete as it should have been, Ward. You should have insisted on a more detailed report. You would have found out that during my fifth year at school I stole an eraser, was caught, and had my hands spanked with a ruler. That was the beginning of my criminal career. In junior high school I took a book from a girl's desk, but she missed it, found that I had it, and I had to give it back. Then I got into the big time. I was called to the principal's office because money was missing. Who would have taken it, except the kid who had no money? They were unable to prove that I stole the purse—because I hadn't. But that didn't stop them from talking—"

He swung around and looked at her. "Be quiet, damn you. No one knows about this but you, me, and Crowley. I want to keep it that way."

"You won't tell Francisca and your stepmother? You would deprive them the pleasure of seeing me disgraced?" She threw back the covers and stood up despite the trembling that had set in and threatened to cause her legs to collapse under her. "Oh, how stupid of me. It isn't me you're thinking about. You don't want them to know what a horrible blunder you made when you married me!

You married me to spite them, but the joke's on you!" Hysterical laughter burst from her.

He grasped her arms and shook her. "Shut up or I'll slap you."

"You don't slap thieves. You put them in jail. Or do they cut off their hands in Mexico?" Tears were streaming down her face, but she didn't know it.

Ward backed off, his arms held stiffly at his sides. "Stop this nonsense at once!" he barked. "What am I supposed to think? You refuse to tell me a thing about what's really going on between you and that Crowley." The pulse next to his eye was beating furiously.

Meredith returned to the bed and sat down. Her face crumbled, and tears filled her eyes.

"You're obviously in no shape to talk about anything now." Ward sounded disgusted. "Try to get some sleep and I'll see you in the morning."

Meredith couldn't have answered if she tried. Her eyes were screwed tightly shut, her body wracked by dry, silent sobs. When she managed to open her eyes, he was gone.

In all her life she had never felt such crushing anguish. She tried to hate him, but the hate wouldn't come. Sorrow, hurt, and regret came, but not hate. He was suffering, too. There had been sadness in his eyes.

Bitterly she recalled her conversation with Paul. What he had done was so out of character. He zealously guarded his reputation. It wasn't like him to consign something to paper that could be turned against him. How was he to know that Ward wouldn't prosecute? How did he get the earrings? What chance did she have of proving she didn't give the earrings to Paul if he said she did? It didn't really matter—she had known the marriage was doomed for days now. Anyway, she had no intention of allowing herself to be humiliated again in the morning. Her worst fantasy had turned into a living nightmare. She knew she had to get away and now.

Wearily she got up from the bed and began to collect her belongings, stuffing them haphazardly into her suitcase. She took only the things she had brought with her, leaving behind her wedding ring and the gifts and clothes Ward had given her on her honeymoon. She lovingly fingered the shell necklace before placing it on the bureau beside the hammered silver bracelet.

Her packing complete, she dressed in gray slacks and a white cowl-neck sweater. It was useless now to try and impress anyone with her one silk dress that Sophia had pressed so carefully the day she thought it would be her wedding dress.

She wandered for the last time around the beautiful room. She would miss it. And although she had never seen the house in Tulsa, she felt a sense of loss there, too. She would never see it now. Never swim in the pool with Maggie. Maggie! Oh, God, she had forgotten Maggie. The child would think she had deserted her. Her heart ached with the memory of her own desertion, of being left at the county home among strangers. But Maggie would be all right. She had Cullen and Ward.

Ward. It was strange that nothing could alter her feelings for him, not even the fact that he thought her a thief. Would she ever be able to push him back into a small corner of her heart and go on with her life? Would the shame and humiliation she felt at his unspoken accusation ever be dimmed? If he should suddenly open the door and walk in and tell her it was all a mistake, would she be able to forgive and forget? The answer eluded her. Of course it would never happen. Once Ward made up his mind he would not change it easily.

Meredith set her suitcase beside the door and looked at her watch. It was almost three A.M. She slung the strap of her purse over her shoulder and switched off the light. For several minutes she peered out the window. All was quiet. She would leave now. Nothing could induce her to wait until morning and have to walk out of this room past Francisca and Norma. She admitted it was cowardly to slink away, but Ward was convinced of her guilt, so what did it matter if she left the house like a thief in the night.

Without a sound she made her way down the stairs, across the foyer, and out into the courtyard. She was on her way down the drive and still no plan had formed in her mind. She wasn't afraid. What could anyone do to her that was worse than what already had been done? She welcomed the quiet darkness. The sneakers she wore ate up the distance to the first gate. She followed the fence until she found a gap she could squeeze through. She then made her way back to the drive, her feet carrying her on and on.

Later Meredith was to think a guardian angel had sat upon her shoulders. She reached the second gate, crawled through an opening, and followed the ribbon of paving toward Guadalajara. She was beginning to feel the weight of the suitcase when a high-powered car came roaring toward her, its lights making a path in the darkness, blinding her so that she stepped to the side of the road and waited for it to pass. A few yards behind her it screeched to a stop and backed up beside her. A young, girlish voice called to her. "Are you an American?"

"Yes, I am."

"What the devil are you doing out here?" This voice was young and male.

Meredith's mind searched frantically for something to say. "I ran out of gas and I've got to get to the airport."

A tall boy got out of the car. "Come on. We'll take you. Can't have one of our own running around out here this time of the morning. That blond hair stopped us. It would be sure to stop the next car that came along and you might be in trouble."

"Oh, but you were going in the other direction."

"Doesn't matter. Come on. When does your plane leave?" He took her suitcase from her hand and flung it behind the seat. Meredith got in beside the girl. The car lurched ahead, its tires protesting against the paving.

"1 really do appreciate this." The corners of Meredith's mouth turned up, obedient to her inner command.

"Where are you from?" The girl was young and pretty in a brittle way.

"Minnesota." Meredith was still holding the smile in place. "And you?"

"Chicago."

"Will your car be okay? It could be stripped by daylight." The young man leaned around the girl to look at Meredith and she wished he would keep his eyes on the road.

"I'll call my friends from the airport and they'll pick it up." She must congratulate herself on lying so magnificently, she thought. She couldn't be here doing these things. She must be insane.

At the airport the boy climbed out and maneuvered her suitcase out from behind the seat, and she took it from his hand.

"I don't know how to thank you. I'd really like to pay you something." She felt like her artificial smile must have set like a plaster cast.

"No. Glad to help out."

"Well, thanks. Thanks a lot. I'd better run. Bye." She walked briskly away.

Luck stayed with her. This was not a popular time of the day to begin a journey, and there was an empty seat on a flight to Brownsville, Texas. They accepted her credit card and she was on her way. Not until then did she allow herself to think about where she was going or what she would do when she got there. She couldn't think now—the hurt and humiliation were too raw.

CHAPTER THIRTEEN

IT WAS RAINING when Meredith arrived in Oklahoma City and the gray skies were in keeping with her mood. It had been a long, tiring trip from Brownsville on the Greyhound bus, but at least she'd had time to think, and there had been no need to use the plastic smile.

She had never been to this part of the country, but she felt drawn to it, maybe because it was near Tulsa—and Ward. For almost two days she wandered around the city looking for accommodations, but it was not until late the second evening that she found an efficiency apartment on Portland Avenue. It was a far cry from the last room she had occupied, but it was clean and cheap.

For the first few days she remained sequestered in her room, too miserable to do more than make a hasty trip to the supermarket down the street and prepare the simplest meal. But by the end of the week the knowledge that her funds were running low forced her out of her shell to face reality. People didn't die from broken hearts, she told herself. Besides, hers wasn't broken. It was mangled and badly bent, but it was still beating. She had no alternative but to go on living.

After breakfast she put on her sunglasses and walked briskly to the shopping center. April in Oklahoma City was warm, the air scented with budding shrubbery. Newly planted petunias, verbena, carnations, and nasturtiums rested in freshly dug beds. Moss rose lined the walks beneath the mimosa trees. None of this beauty lifted Meredith's spirits.

She had already passed the telephone booths when she decided to call Maude. She turned and retraced her steps. It had been a week since she had left Mexico and in that time she hadn't seen a familiar face or heard a familiar voice. It would be wonderful talking to Jim, too. He always knew how to comfort her. But he was too close to Ward and she didn't dare. She called the operator and paid for three minutes before she heard Maude's voice on the line.

"Hello, Maude?"

"Meredith! Where in the world are you?" Her voice sounded so good, so concerned that it was hard to keep back the tears.

"I've lots to tell you, Maude, but I've only paid for three minutes. I'll call you another time and fill you in. You'll think you're listening to one of your stories on TV." Meredith fought to control her voice. "How are you? I hope you haven't been worrying about me."

"I've been worried sick about you. Mr. Sanderson called and he wants me to call him if I hear from you."

"No!" She hoped the word hadn't sounded as sharp to Maude's ears as it had to her own. "Don't call him, Maude. Please. I don't want him to know anything about me."

There was a surprised pause on the other end of the line.

"I won't tell him if you don't want me to, Meredith. Where are you, child?"

"I'm afraid to tell you now." She shivered. "What did he say?"

"Only that he wanted to get in touch with you. He gave me a number to call if I hear from you."

"Our marriage didn't work out. If he calls again, tell him to have his lawyer prepare the divorce papers and to get in touch with you. I don't want to see him, and I don't want to know anything about him. Someday I'll tell you the whole story, Maude, but not now. Our three minutes are about up, but I'll call you again, soon. Don't worry about me, I'm fine. And Maude . . . I love you." A sob rose in her throat and she hung up the phone.

Too unstrung now to think of looking for a job, Meredith went back to the sanctuary of the apartment. Ward needn't worry, she thought bitterly. She wouldn't ask for a settlement. She wanted to be rid of him as much as he wished to be free of her. Even if he should discover proof of her innocence and want to apologize, it would make no difference. No apology would be able to make up for his earlier doubts. She was too bitter toward him to ever want to see his face again. Bitterness was the only emotion left in her. All others seemed to have been drained away.

Two days later she ventured out again. This time she walked past the row of telephone booths where she had called Maude. A few blocks farther down she passed several fast-food restaurants. Across the street was a small drive-in with a large sign—BILL'S BAR-B-QUE. In the window was a HELP WANTED sign.

Half an hour later Bill gave her the job and handed her the apron. She went to work. It was strictly a take-out order business. She made sandwiches from the meat Bill sliced and placed in the warming trays. The pay was a far cry from what she had received at the hospital, but it was sufficient and she didn't dare seek a job in her field right now because Ward might be trying to trace her. Later, when she'd earned enough money, she would head out to Oregon and take up her profession again. Oregon was beautiful, she knew, and she could start over again there. She walked the six blocks to Bill's and back each day. Some days she went to work as much as an hour early, and if business was good she stayed late to help. She kept every hour of her day occupied and defiantly kept her emotions buried. It was as if she were enclosed in a plastic bubble, aloof and suspended from human contact.

Each day for several weeks she walked past the telephone booths. Gradually the urge to call Maude returned. One evening she yielded to the temptation, called the operator, paid for ten minutes, and asked for Maude's number.

When she heard Maude's voice, she was so glad she had called that it took a while for her to find her own. "This is Meredith. How are you?"

"Land sakes! I could tan your hide. I've been worried sick about you."

"I told you not to worry. I'm fine. I've been busy. I have to walk several blocks to get to the phone and I've just neglected to call." She hated lying to Maude.

"Are you working in a clinic or a hospital? And where are you?"

Meredith answered by asking a question of her own. "Has . . . did you hear anything about the papers I'm to sign?"

"Noooo . . ." The word was drawn out and a suspicion came to Meredith's mind.

"Has Ward called again? Has he been there? Maude, don't believe anything he says about me. Please! You're my only friend and I couldn't bear it if you lost faith in me." The tremor in her voice angered her. Dammit! She'd better not bawl!

"What a thing to say! Nothing could make me lose faith in you. You're like my own child, Meredith. I couldn't love you more if you were my own flesh and blood."

"Thanks for saying that. You've been like a mother to me all these years. I just don't know what I'd do without you."

"Fiddlesticks! When are you coming to see me? You still haven't told me where you are."

"Do you mind if I don't tell you for a while? I'm well and working in a barbeque drive-in. The work is hard, but the food is good." She managed a laugh. "I'll call you again in about a week. If Ward should call, don't tell him anything about me other than that I'll sign whatever he wants me to, and he needn't worry about having to see me."

"Yes, I'll do that, if that's what you want. Don't wait so long to call again."

"I won't. Bye for now."

The next day was her day off. Meredith stayed in all day. She washed her hair, cleaned the room and the kitchenette, did her washing in the bathtub. For the first time in weeks she was able to think rationally. She was wasting her life grieving. She knew she would never love any man again, but that didn't mean she had to remain in a shadow for the rest of her life. One day, perhaps, she would come out into the sunshine and be able to not merely smile with her lips, but with her heart as well. She had always had the resiliency to spring back after she had encountered one of life's unfair blows. She had to make the effort.

The decision was easier to reach than to implement. She had spent so many evenings alone in the room that the habit had become too ingrained to be easily overcome. Like a swimmer taking the plunge into icy water, she decided to walk to the shopping center and see a movie. She threw her trench coat over her arm, because it looked like rain, and left the apartment before she changed her mind. She would see the early show and it would not be too late when she walked home again.

It was with a mixture of unease and increased loneliness that she walked into the darkened theater and found a seat. The movie began and she wished she hadn't come. A beautiful girl walked slowly across the screen to a man, immaculate in dinner jacket. Slowly he came toward her and kissed her mouth, his fingers trembling as he arranged the mink about her shoulders. The girl turned to face him and raised her lips and he gathered her to him and their kiss deepened.

It wasn't until the screen blurred that Meredith realized she was crying. With an angry shake of her head she dug into her pocket for a tissue, berating herself for being such a fool. She'd be glad when the dumb show was over! Next time she would check and see what was playing before she bought her ticket. For the price she paid, she should feel at least as good when she came out as when she went in, she told herself angrily.

It was raining when she came out of the theater. She stood beneath the marquee and put on her trench coat and waited with the other theater patrons for the downpour to slacken. A wind came biting around the corner and she dug her hands into her pockets. Dammit! Why had she chosen this night of all nights to spread her wings? The thought of the warm apartment and a cup of hot cocoa was enough incentive to make her take the first steps out into the rain.

She hurried across the street and gained shelter beneath the canopy that fronted a row of shops. She paused there and pulled the collar of her coat up around her ears. It was then that she saw a man coming across the street. He was walking fast and his limp reminded her of Ward. She turned away. She couldn't bear to look. She didn't want to see anyone or anything that reminded her of Ward.

She bent her head and darted out from beneath the shelter. She shivered and her steps increased. Oh, why hadn't she thought to bring a head-scarf? A gust of wind blew rain in her face, almost blinding her. Something hard grabbed her arm, spinning her around. Frightened, she looked up.

"No!" It couldn't be Ward's tawny eyes staring down at her out of a wet, bleak face! "No!" She said it again.

"Merry." When he spoke she realized he was real and not an apparition.

"Get away from me!" she screamed. "Get away!" Her voice was shrill with the terror that gave her strength to jerk away from him and put her feet into motion. She began to run as if her life depended on it.

CHAPTER FOURTEEN

SHE RAN IN manic flight along the darkened street, oblivious to the rain, oblivious to the fact that her coat was flying open and she was getting soaked. It didn't enter her mind to wonder how Ward had found her or why he was here. She just wanted to get behind the locked door of her room. She tore across the lawns and through gardens, her shoes leaden with mud.

"What can I do?" she cried out, but she cried into a silence that gave no answer.

She was stripped of everything but fear while groping for the security of a locked room. Her fear was intensified by the path of light that forged out of the darkness. A car was behind her! She darted behind her building and came around to the front and along the walk to her door. It was an eternity before her icy fingers could turn the lock. She slammed the door behind her and threw the dead-bolt in place. Her fingers slowly relaxed their hold on the bolt, and she leaned her head against the door. Her lungs felt as if they were about to burst and her heart thudded as though it had a life of its own. A sharp rap on the door caused her to jerk away from it. The rap came again.

"Let me in, Merry. I want to talk to you."

She held one hand to her aching chest, the other to her mouth while a thousand tiny hammers pounded in her head.

"Open the door, Merry." The voice was louder now, more urgent, and it was followed by several hard raps.

Go away, she screamed silently. If she had a phone she would call the police, she thought wildly.

Bang! He had kicked the door! Had he lost his mind? He'd woken the entire court.

"I'm not leaving until you open the door. I just want to talk to you. What's the matter with you, for God's sake? Open this goddamn door!" The pounding that followed jarred the wall.

"Let him in, lady, or I'll call the police." This was shouted from the apartment opposite hers.

Ward continued pounding on the door.

"Get the hell out of here, fella. Can't you understand she don't want ya?" The shout came from the other end of the court.

"I'm not leaving, Merry. Open the door or there's going to be a big ruckus out here."

All at once she realized the childishness of refusing to let him in. The neighbors might complain to the landlord and she would have to move. Let him in and get it over with, she reasoned with herself even while she was unbolting the door.

He stood there in the pouring rain, almost unrecognizable to her in his sodden condition. She stared, eyes large and frightened. He made no move to come in.

"I have a suitcase in the car. May I bring it in and change into dry clothes?"

She nodded numbly, turned her back on him, and went to the bathroom and began stripping off her own wet things.

When she came out, a kind of brittle calmness possessed her. Ward had turned on the lights and his shoes and dripping wet coat lay near the door. He was kneeling beside an open suitcase and stood with jeans and sweater in his hand. Meredith heard the door to the bathroom close as she opened the folding doors to the tiny kitchenette. She turned the burner on under the teakettle and set out two mugs.

In unconscious defiance she had slipped into old jeans and a faded checked shirt. She had toweled her hair and carelessly run the comb through it. Her face was free of make-up. She was pouring the water over the chocolate mix when Ward came up beside her.

"One of those for me? Good! I don't know when I've been so cold."

"I'll sign the papers, Ward. Let's get on with it. I don't want you here." She picked up the hot drink and went to the chair, leaving the couch for him.

He sat down and cupped his hands around the mug. The nerve beside his eye was jumping, but she didn't notice. She knew he was looking at her, but she refused to return his gaze.

"I don't blame you for being bitter, Merry."

"Don't you?"

"I know you didn't take the earrings. I was . . ."

"So? What else is new? I knew that!"

"I realize you must hate the sight of me, but at least

let me tell you what happened and give me a chance to apologize."

"If it will make you feel any better, I accept your apology. Now, if you don't mind, I'd like to bow out of your life and get on with mine."

She knew her biting words affected him. His lips tightened and his hand on the cup was shaking.

"That next morning I got to wondering why Crowley sent me a typed letter. His name was written clearly, too, which is also unusual for a doctor. I went up to Rochester. Needless to say, he was surprised to see me. He was as nervous as a cat on a hot tin roof. He thought I was there to get your check back, which I did, by the way."

He handed her the check. She looked at it and ripped it into several pieces and dropped them on the table.

"Now you know all my little secrets," she said with sardonic emphasis and he looked up sharply.

"Not all, Merry. I don't know what he was threatening you with, but he won't bother you again."

"God must be smiling on me once more."

"I gave Crowley every opportunity to mention returning the earrings. He didn't. If he had, he would have used the occasion to expound on his exemplary character. He's not much of a man." These were the first caustic words he had spoken.

He looked tired, haggard. There were deep creases on each side of his mouth. It hadn't been easy for him, either, Meredith thought, but she refused to soften toward him. He deserved to suffer for what he put her through.

"I don't need you to tell me that, either." Her curt response was openly hostile.

"I went back to Guadalajara and soon discovered who set you up as the thief."

"Francisca." She said it calmly and looked defiantly into his surprised eyes.

"How did you know?"

"She was the only one who hated me enough to do that to me. She was the one who would gain the most if I left . . ." Her voice cracked and she turned her face away.

"Sophia saw her leaving your room just after you had been there to get your purse. I confronted Francisca and she admitted she took them on an impulse after she heard you talking to Crowley through the double fireplace that connects the library and the sitting room. After she took them she didn't know what to do with them, but Luis did. The scheme was hatched up between them. With you out of the way I'd marry Francisca and their future would be secure. They know my grandmother will not last out the year and that I will want her to be happy."

Meredith's laugh was harsh and hollow. "It sounds more like a soap opera all the time. 'Mistress steals diamonds to frame wife of her lover.'"

His face turned a deep red and their eyes did battle.

"If you meant that to be funny, it isn't." His voice was full of impatience. "I have never been Francisca's lover and wouldn't be if she was the only woman on earth."

"No?" Her cheeks were suffused with color, her balled fist evidence of her anger.

He made an irritated gesture. "I don't understand you. I told you, when I asked you to marry me, that I would be faithful. And we promised we would be honest with each other."

Anger brought her to her feet. "All right. I'll be

honest. I want out of the marriage. And just to set the record straight, I overheard you talking to Francisca the night we spent with your grandmother. You said and I quote—'Meredith will not interfere with *us*, she has nothing to do with *us*, I'll always take care of you . . . nothing has changed between *us*.' Don't sit there and tell me I didn't hear that with my own ears."

His expression mirrored his astonishment. "You took that to mean she is my mistress?"

"I may be naïve, but I'm not stupid!" Her tone implied that he was. "I was going to ask for a divorce even before you practically accused me of being a thief."

He was quiet for so long that she looked at him and was surprised to see the shadow of pain in his eyes.

"On the strength of what you overheard?" he said in mild reproof.

"Exactly." She looped her hair behind her ears with trembling fingers and walked to the end of the room.

"Part of what you overheard is true," he said to her back. "I didn't think our marriage would change anything between Francisca and me. My responsibility to her is to see that she is taken care of financially. It's my duty." He went to the kitchenette, set his cup on the counter, and returned to the couch.

When Meredith turned to look at him, he was rubbing his thigh and flexing his leg. He looked up to see her watching him and held her eyes with his. Now he could see the ravages in her face, ravages no cosmetics could disguise. Her cheeks were hollow, her skin so pale it seemed to be transparent, and her blue eyes were bruised and sullen.

"Merry." He held out his hand. "Come and sit down and let me tell you about Francisca."

She walked past him and sat down in the chair.

"Francisca's mother was disinherited by my grandmother's father because she married beneath her class. It's a long story, but the gist of it is this. Francisca's mother died and her father married again, and Luis is the result of that marriage."

Meredith shifted uncomfortably. "It isn't necessary for you to tell me your family history."

"I know it isn't," he said evenly, "but I want to." After a pause he continued. "Francisca was only a little child when her mother died. All her life she's felt she's missed out on something because her connection to the family was so weak. For a long time her main goal in life has been to marry me. She saw security and status in being my wife. That's all there is to it. I don't love Francisca. I have never loved her. Often, I don't even like her. I helped her start a business, hoping she would get over her obsession. She's a good businesswoman. As for Luis, I have no blood ties to him, but I've employed him because he is very capable. Needless to say, Luis is no longer on my payroll."

They sat silently, but the tension was alive between them. Meredith's hand shook violently as she raised the cup to her lips and she prayed he wouldn't notice. She felt emotion begin to infiltrate the icy barrier with which she had protected herself. The bitterness she had felt for so long seemed to dissolve in one shuddering sigh, leaving only emptiness.

The lionlike eyes that could seem so fierce looked at her sadly. "I can't tell you how sorry I am for coming to you before I found out the truth. But even though I behaved badly, you should never have run away—you should have weathered the storm."

She stared at him with eyes dilated with pain.

"It's impossible for me to forget you doubted me. Regardless of what evidence anyone had given me about you, it wouldn't have shaken my faith. I'd never have believed you a thief." Her lower lip quivered.

"Perhaps not, but you did believe that I was unfaithful to you, and surely that's much worse. The truth is, Meredith, that you doubted me as much as I doubted you."

She realized that what he said was true. If she hadn't already believed that Ward didn't—couldn't—love her, she never would have left.

"When we're hurt and angry," Ward continued, "we all say things we don't mean. I was angry and I was hurt and disappointed. I thought you wanted Crowley. Most of all I was angry at myself for allowing my feelings to get so involved with a woman."

He stood up. She knew he was looking at the top of her head. "I want to be honest with you, Merry. I never believed I'd truly love someone. Any ideals I ever cherished were smashed at a very early age. All the women I met seemed the same. They wanted a man to desire them and they set out to provoke physical desire. Then their mercenary little heads took over." He stood there and seemed to be waiting for her to look up or say something. "When I met you I knew you were different." He said it softly and she felt his hand lightly touch her hair. "I knew you would be faithful to me, but even before we were married I wanted more. I wanted your love as well."

She looked up, now, at his unsmiling mouth and with all her heart she wanted to believe him. But conviction refused to come. She got up quickly. She had to move away from him so she could think. She went to the sink and rinsed her cup. When she turned he was beside her.

"I keep thinking about what you said that night. You said you would have believed me because you loved me."

"One will say most anything when one's desperate." She tried to laugh, but her eyes were frightened, like those of a trapped animal.

He grabbed her forearms and jerked her toward him. "I can't lose you!" His eyes glinted like amber agates and the strength of his fingers brought a bruising, physical pain. "We had the beginning of something good. Better than good—wonderful! Like the gold at the end of the rainbow."

Her voice choked on a cry and her face crumbled helplessly. Great tearing sobs shook her, and with a soft groan he pulled her against his chest.

"Don't cry, darling. Don't cry," he said against the top of her head. He held her close, waiting for the storm of tears to spend itself. "Hurry, darling," she heard him say. "Hurry and stop crying so I can kiss you." Firm fingers raised her chin and a soft handkerchief wiped her eyes and nose, then his lips were on hers.

She felt the warmth of his breath before she felt the heat of his mouth as it parted hers, his arms drawing her to him. Yielding, her arms went around him and he pulled her even closer.

"I love you," he whispered against her lips. "God, how I love you! I've been through hell these past few weeks. I could have killed Francisca and Luis!"

She was trembling and wildly flushed. A corner of her mind still couldn't believe he could love her. She put her hand on his chest and held herself away from him.

"Please . . . don't say something you don't mean. I couldn't bear it."

He looked at her with half-closed eyes, a passionate satisfaction on his face.

"Before God, I love you. I want you for the rest of my life. You *are* my life! I was so wrong about love, darling. It is real. It's both hurtful and wonderful!" Her heart turned over. She closed her eyes and leaned her forehead against his shoulder. "Put your arms around me, darling." There was an anguish in his voice that pierced her like a thorn. "Hold me. Tell me you love me. I need assurance, too."

"I do love you." Her arms went tight around him. "I thought I was going to die from it, I love you so much."

They stood locked together in the middle of the room. Their embrace was like finally coming home, like finding a safe harbor in a storm, truly like reaching the pot of gold at the end of the rainbow.

The rain continued all night. The wind came up and tortured the trees, and lightning flashed, making an eerie light in the darkened room. Ward and Meredith lay in the pull-down bed oblivious to everything but each other. They talked in snatches of whispers between kisses.

"Are you sure this thing won't fold up in the wall like they do in the movies?"

"I'm not sure of anything right now." She laughed happily.

"No? Not even one thing?"

"Well . . . it's still raining," she teased, hovering over him.

He crushed her down to him and rolled over, pinning her softness beneath him.

"I'm aching for you and you tease me!" He ran his hands down her slim body. He framed her chin with his hand. She felt the faint tremor in his fingers, felt the quickening of his breathing. "I couldn't bear to lose you again," he whispered hoarsely. "You make me come alive!"

"Please . . ." she whispered, and a hunger like an intense, physical pain pierced her. She clung to him desperately, her body young and alive.

"Sweetheart, my love . . ." He whispered love words softly and his mouth traveled over her face to meet her lips again and again, hard and demanding at first, then tenderly, as his tongue moved to part her lips and explore the sweetness of her mouth. Her fingers loved every part of him and she moved slowly and lovingly over him. It had been so long since she had held him, and even then it wasn't like this.

He seemed to read her thoughts. "Loving makes all the difference," he murmured.

Afterward they lay amid the rumpled sheets feeling weak and satisfied, engulfed by a warm, sweet lethargy. Her arms were around his neck, her limbs molded to his, and his tender caresses felt like the calm after a storm.

"How did you find me?" It was the first time she had thought about it.

His eyes shone like bright stars and his lips twitched.

"I don't know if I should tell you. You might turn me over to the police." He kissed her soundly. "I put a tracer on Maude's telephone. It's against the law, but I was desperate. I traced the booth where you made the call and found the drive-in where you worked. All I had to do was patrol the neighborhood until I found you. I saw you come out of the theater and got out of the car to come meet you. I didn't dream you would run from me. Don't do that again, my love—ever."

"Did Maude know you tapped her telephone?"

"No. She was as protective of you as a mother goose. She called me a dumb coot for letting you get away from me. Do you approve of people calling your husband a dumb coot?"

"Maude said that?" Laughter bubbled up.

"And more. She's fiercely devoted to you. I'm glad she's a she."

"You're nuts! Do you know that?"

He kissed her long and hard while running his hands down her slender form. In the middle of the bed they lay entwined, content to be there close together. Meredith wound her arms around her husband's neck and pressed herself closer to him. This was home. The safest, most wonderful place in all the world. This long, lean body pressed to hers was the torch that lighted her life.

"Are you going with me on my honeymoon?" he asked in a voice stripped of all seriousness.

"Sure, if Bill will give me a few days off."

"I might have to punch Bill in the nose."

"On second thought, maybe the barbecue industry can survive without me."

"It's going to have to, because I can't," he said huskily and began to make beautiful, tender love to her.

Want to know more about romances at
Grand Central Publishing and Forever?
Get the scoop online!

GRAND CENTRAL PUBLISHING'S
ROMANCE HOMEPAGE

Visit us at www.hachettebookgroupusa.com/romance
for all the latest news, reviews, and chapter excerpts!

NEW AND UPCOMING TITLES

Each month we feature our new titles
and reader favorites.

CONTESTS AND GIVEAWAYS

We give away galleys, autographed copies,
and all kinds of fun stuff.

AUTHOR INFO

You'll find bios, articles, and links to personal
websites for all your favorite authors—and
so much more!

THE BUZZ

Sign up for our monthly romance newsletter,
and be the first to read all about it!